ILLICIT LOVE

Mustering all her self-control, Elena pulled herself away from him. "So, you're asking me to come to Spain as your mistress?"

"Yes." He caught at her hands, but she evaded his touch.

"No. If I'm not good enough to marry, I'm not good enough to . . ."

"Elena, please, be not so hasty. Don't you realize this is all I can ever offer you?"

"I understand that compared to the largest bull ranch north of Toledo, I'm rather a paltry prize."

Anger blazed in his face. Seizing her, he welded her against his body. His mouth came down hard and demanding on hers. Though she fought against his kiss, she could not keep a part of her from rejoicing in it, enjoying even this fierce battle of wills as he forced her to yield to him.

Other books by Patricia Phillips:

FLAME OF LOVE
MORE PRECIOUS THAN GOLD
MARIE FLEUR
TOUCH ME WITH FIRE
CAPTIVE FLAME
JENNY
ANISE
LOVE'S DEFIANT PRISONER
MY SOUL WITH THINE
ROYAL CAPTIVE

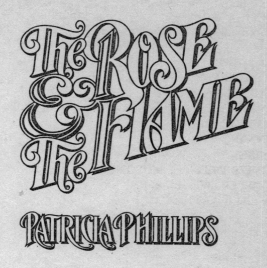

THE ROSE & THE FLAME

PATRICIA PHILLIPS

LEISURE BOOKS ◼ NEW YORK CITY

A LEISURE BOOK

August 1989

Published by

Dorchester Publishing Co., Inc.
276 Fifth Avenue
New York, NY 10001

Copyright © 1989 by Patricia Phillips

All rights reserved. No part of this book may be reproduced or transmitted in any form or by any electronic or mechanical means, including photocopying, recording, or by any information storage and retrieval system, without the written permission of the Publisher, except where permitted by law.

The name "Leisure Books" and the stylized "LB" with design are trademarks of Dorchester Publishing Co., Inc.

Printed in the United States of America.

Chapter One

The summer dawn was heavy with the scent of dew-wet roses. Elena breathed deeply of the perfumed air as she pushed a wayward raven curl beneath her jeweled hairnet. Her dark-lashed tawny eyes shone with excitement as she listened to the hunt assembling at the stables.

After her marriage this afternoon, Locke Hall, with its surrounding acres of wooded parkland, would become her home. The unpleasant prospect sent a chill through her veins. Elena glanced back at the steep-gabled half-timbered manor house where rows of mullioned windows caught fire in the rising sun. She would be a virtual prisoner, no longer free to do as she pleased. Tossing her head in false bravado, she turned her back on the house and headed for the stables.

Elena held her head proudly—some said arrogantly—her chin jutting with determination. As she crossed Locke Hall's velvet lawns, the morning sun caressed her high cheekbones and soft red lips. Hers was an intriguing beauty: lustrous black waving hair, skin softly golden as a ripe peach, flaring nostrils betraying the old Arabic strain come down to her through her Spanish blood. Yet her large luminous eyes—in some moods

1

green, in others yellow—were her most striking feature. Men rhapsodized about Mistress Elena's eyes, desirous of earning a glance of approval from those half wild tawny pools. In a country of light-skinned, light-haired women, her darkly sensual beauty never failed to turn heads.

Elena owed her unusual beauty to her Spanish mother. She had inherited no visible legacy from Thomas Watkins, the Welshman who married Aña Muñoz, lady-in-waiting to Katherine of Aragon. This exotic blend of Welsh and Aragonese blood gave Elena a fierce pride and forged a temper quick to rouse and slow to appease.

When Elena was ten, both her parents died of the sweating sickness. And her 20-year-old half brother, Will, became head of the Watkins household. Elena's mouth hardened at the memory. Her marriage to Locke Hall's young heir marked the culmination of years of Will's scheming to make them important landowners.

The laughing wedding guests hailed her as she entered the stable yard.

"Elena, my love."

Her spine stiffened as she heard the whining voice of her husband-to-be. Slowly Elena turned, the skirts of her glowing velvet habit rippling like a sapphire pool across the cobbles.

Randle stood before her, his slack mouth revealing prominent, uneven teeth. On his light blond hair was a scarlet cap with a waving blue feather. His knobby wristbones projected noticeably from under the frilled cuffs of his dun velvet doublet.

"Greetings, Randle," Elena replied stiffly, curtsying in response to his courteous bow.

Randle stood over a head taller than she, a fact Elena found surprising in a boy barely turned seventeen. Habitually hunching his shoulders in an effort to minimize his height, Randle's poor posture succeeded only in exaggerating his sunken chest. Chronic ill health imparted a greenish pallor to his soft face. Even the gaze that rested on her close-fitting bodice was dull and lackluster, yet when he eagerly grasped her arm, his grip was unexpectedly strong.

"I wish the hunt were done—then we'd enjoy far pleasanter sport," he whispered, his bawdy tone and accompanying leer at odds with his boyish face.

This unexpected change in Randle's behavior was disturbing. She had always dismissed him as a spoiled, overgrown child. Today all trace of boyishness had flown. Quickly she stepped back, not anxious to encourage more lascivious thoughts.

Blue-liveried grooms hurried about the stableyard, leading forth the guests' mounts, while stable boys attempted to keep the stamping, snorting beasts in check. This early morning hunt had been arranged for the amusement of the wedding guests, though some preferred to lie abed, planning to join the others later for the ceremony in the family chapel. Much feasting and dancing would follow the wedding. When the revelling was done, the guests would bed the bride and groom in uproarious Tudor fashion.

When Elena contemplated the drunken guests' ribald advice, her stomach churned. What followed the crude bedding ceremony might be even harder to endure. Elena chilled at the thought of Randle's lovemaking. She was not cold by nature, for a handsome man's appreciative smile never failed to set her pulse racing. Like most girls, she had daydreamed about a brave, handsome man who would do battle to win her love.

"Come, ride beside me," Randle urged, his high voice cracking. This painful reminder of lingering adolescence both annoyed and embarrassed him. Today he had wanted to impress Elena by appearing manly and mature.

"Yes, it will be expected," Elena agreed as she assessed her future groom. To her great disappointment the quickened heartbeats, the building excitement she longed to experience, failed to materialize. Though young, by no stretch of the imagination could Randle be described as virile. There was a delicate, girlish quality about his narrow shoulders and slender neck. Were he not habitually scowling, his long face might have been described as pleasing.

Elena allowed Randle to assist her into the saddle. They took their place at the head of the riders, leading the cavalcade down Locke Hall's broad, beech-lined drive.

Before them spread the fertile Lichborne Valley, lushly clad in summer green. Miles of rolling down-land dotted with stands of thick trees and isolated dwellings soon disappeared as they approached thick woods. Their jingling reins, laughing voices and clopping hooves startled flocks of birds and sent them twittering for cover.

The July day promised to be hot. Sunshine was always considered a good omen for a wedding. So far, this summer of 1554 had been wet. Torrential rains had nearly drowned Queen Mary's young Spanish groom on his journey to Winchester. It was said the Spaniard found no favor with this most typical of English welcomes, for he despised the wet, chill climate, longing instead for the hot sun of his native land.

Tensely, Elena gripped the reins, forcing her thoughts from the Queen's recent marriage to her own imminent fate. Her brother had not been able to rest until she was wed, afraid the sickly groom would die before they tied the knot.

She had lived nine years at Windland Farm with Will and her Welsh sister-in-law, Ronwen. It made Elena sad to think she had spent her last night beneath Windland's creaking eaves.

The riders crossed the gorse-dotted heath, trampling purple mallow, pink orchids and golden vetch beneath their horses' hooves. They entered the silent woods where the light was a mysterious murky green. Occasional shafts of sunshine penetrated the trees.

The scent of deer was strong around them. Horses whickered nervously, and the pack of hounds grew increasingly restless as the lead dog bayed, straining at the leash. Then came the signal they awaited—three shrill notes on the hunting horn. Excited dogs yelped as their handlers released them, and neighing horses skittered restlessly, eager to begin the chase.

They were off! The finely dressed riders made a brightly colored stream beneath the trees. Ducking to avoid low hanging branches, they thundered along the broad chase through Lichborne Forest. A great antlered deer was glimpsed through the trees, the baying hounds in hot pursuit.

Elena wasted no more thought on her unwelcome marriage, focusing her attention on the chase. The hunters plunged into a clearing where startled peasants leaped aside to let them pass. Randle showed off for his bride, maneuvering his leggy roan to the forefront of the pack, where he struggled to keep pace with the leading riders.

Several men rode beside Elena, urging her to greater speed. Their laughing glances conveyed their mingled appreciation of her beauty and their admiration of her skillful riding. She easily maintained her place, ducking, swerving, proving her ability to keep her seat as the terrain grew rough and the path narrow. Groups of riders began to fall back, Randle amongst them. His face was crimson, and he was having difficulty catching his breath between bouts of coughing. Knowing what was expected of her, Elena reluctantly abandoned her position in the lead, dropping back until she rode beside her groom.

"Are you well enough to go on?" she shouted, trying to calm her excited mount.

"Of course," Randle cried. How much he had longed to excel, to beat the leading riders. Now she would think him a baby. Yet perhaps there was still something by which he could redeem himself and convince her he was not just a silly boy.

Hungrily licking his lips, Randle contemplated that forbidden deed. "Come, let's be off," he shouted, "they're leaving us behind." Mustering all his strength for this new challenge, he bolted forward.

Elena rode after him. They flew beneath the trees, the sounds of the hunt growing fainter, the call of the hunting horns far off. Randle kept a breakneck pace, clearing all obstacles in his path. Elena glanced about in alarm, this stretch of the woodland unfamiliar to her.

"Aren't we riding too far west?" she shouted, spurring ahead to match his pace.

Randle still rode like one demented, twin spots of color blazing in his pale cheeks. "No, I know this country well," he shouted back before doubling over in a fit of coughing.

"Stop, you'll injure yourself."

Elena frowned as Randle took a particularly difficult jump over a gate and an adjoining stone wall. She followed, handling her mount well. Artan cleared the obstacle with ease, sailing gracefully into the pasture. Now she could not even hear the hunt.

"Randle, stop, you're only making a fool of yourself,"

she shouted. She knew he heard because he started to draw rein before reconsidering and urging his mount on. "If you're trying to impress me with your bravery, 'tis a miserable failure," she yelled, drawing abreast of him. "You're too foolhardy for your own good."

Ah, now she had goaded him to reply. He slowed his pace, muttering unintelligibly. Glaring at her, his mouth surly, he shouted indignantly, "Wenches always swoon over brave men."

"Aye, but not over fool boys who needlessly risk their necks," she snapped. "Would you be carried into the chapel on a stretcher?"

Her taunt wounded him. They were at the fringe of the woods, where drooping branches nearly obscured the trail. Angrily Randle grabbed for Elena's reins, but she neatly sidestepped him.

"Enough foolishness. Let's catch up to the others."

"No. There's but one I intend to catch."

To Elena's amazement Randle was out of the saddle and seizing her reins. He wrapped his arms around her hips as he tried to drag her from her horse. They struggled, the startled horse making Randle's task more difficult as it shifted and tossed its head. Shouting in anger, Elena slapped Randle's face. He exerted even more force in his desperate struggle to unseat her.

"You're mine, Elena. I'll show you I'm not some puny boy. . . . I'm a grown man!"

"Have done, you silly fool! What are you about?" she cried, finally lashing at him with her crop.

Randle bellowed in pain and fury, leaping back to nurse his crimson cheek where an angry welt made a livid splotch on the skin.

"Damn you," he screeched, "I'm no pot boy to be so insulted."

"If you behave like a pot boy, that's how I'll treat

you.''

Uttering this final defiant retort, Elena turned her horse about and headed for the trees.

Beside himself with rage, Randle stared blindly after her, tears blurring his vision. Then, wrenching about, he scrambled into the saddle, determined to catch her.

Elena ducked the bending branches as she sped beneath the trees, exhilarated by the wild ride. Now she understood why Randle had tried to draw her away from the others. It took little imagination to guess what he intended had he successfully pulled her from her horse. The idea infuriated her. He needed to be taught a lesson. Unfortunately she was not familiar with this part of the woods or she could have led him a merry chase.

To her surprise, she rounded a stand of birch saplings and saw Randle's flame red cap through the trees. He saw her at the same time and yelled for her to stop.

Swiftly changing direction, Elena plunged down a narrow trail that took her racing downhill through tangled grass and wildflowers. The woods thinned, and cornfields were visible through the sparse trees. Picking up speed, Elena galloped into the open.

Randle also emerged from the trees, shouting again for her to stop before he doubled over, coughing from the exertion of his attempt to head her off. Elena galloped around a barn and headed in the opposite direction.

A few minutes later she was hidden by the trees. Thinking she had finally given him the slip, Elena slackened her pace until once more she heard the thud of approaching hooves. There he was again, crimson faced with excitement at having spotted his quarry.

Muttering fiercely beneath her breath, Elena chose a narrow trail virtually hidden by low hanging branches.

Randle would soon be whacked from the saddle, for he was not as adept as she at dodging obstacles. It would serve him right to be unhorsed, she thought gleefully. She could not believe he had planned to seduce her! This unexpected display of spirit prompted a total review of her former opinion of him. He had some backbone after all. Spirited herself, Elena abhorred the idea of marrying a mealymouthed pap who danced without question to his mother's tune.

The path turned abruptly uphill, and her gelding scrambled valiantly up the shifting terrain, loosening showers of earth and crumbling rock beneath his hooves. A tumbledown cottage lay ahead, and Elena plunged through a gap in the masonry and out through the other side and on into the trees.

Then came Randle, skidding and sliding as he tried to maneuver his galloping roan around the side of the derelict building. Recklessly he set his mount at a wide eglantine-swathed hedge, the horse's hooves clipping pink blossoms as he barely cleared the jump. Ill prepared for the unexpected downhill slope, the animal lost its footing and stumbled before righting itself. But the horse's recovery came too late. With a scream of fright, Randle sailed through the air.

Elena heard his cry, swiftly followed by a splash. Then all was quiet. Stubbornly she rode ahead a few more paces before finally drawing rein. It was deathly quiet in the heart of the wood. Could her groom be dead? Joy swiftly filled her, but was soon replaced by a guilt so sharp that it spurred her to action. Elena retraced her steps, walking her mount through a break in the rose hedge. The land sloped downhill to a water-filled hollow where Randle's riderless horse stood cropping weeds. A dark shape lay partially submerged in the stagnant pool. Praying, for what she was not sure,

Elena quickened Artan's pace.

"Randle," she called, her voice echoing through the trees. The eerie sound made her shiver.

Dismounting, Elena attempted to walk over the shifting ground. The mud sucked at her blue kid buskins and left small bubbling pools in her wake. Randle's finery was smeared with mud. His eyes were tightly shut; the lids appeared transparent, and it seemed that the blue of his eyes showed through.

Elena tried to pull him from the water, but his sodden clothing made him surprisingly heavy. Though she repeatedly urged him to wake and assist her, Randle was deaf to her entreaties. Silly fool, he deserved to be thrown, she thought to herself, muttering as she tried again to drag him from the water. His breathing sounded curiously labored. After a moment's consideration, she decided it was not a death rattle, merely the sound made by congested lungs.

The sun's warmth failed to penetrate this secluded copse, and Elena shivered in the dank chill rising from the boggy ground. Panting with exertion, she again tried to pull Randle from the water. So skeletal was his build, she was amazed by his unexpected weight.

She pondered whether she could fasten Artan's reins beneath Randle's armpits, and have the horse pull her unhappy groom-to-be from the mud. Then from the trees she heard the welcome jingle of a harness.

"Whoever you are, please help me," Elena shouted, her voice sounding small and defenseless in the vast wood.

A huge black horse burst from the undergrowth on the far side of the copse.

"Oh, thank heaven," Elena gasped. A member of their party must have heeded her cry for help.

The big horse and rider floundered down the slope

toward her, slipping on the loamy ground before finally sinking hock-deep in the ooze as the man reined in. He swung lightly from the saddle, landing on a partially submerged rock.

Now that she saw him up close, Elena discovered this man was far too richly dressed for the hunt.

"Oh, sir, thank heaven you rode by. He's too heavy for me to pull from the water." To her annoyance, her voice wavered as if she were close to tears.

"Have no fear, mistress. I'll soon have him out. Is he hurt?"

"He's unconscious, but the cold water might have shocked him. . . . He's very delicate."

Three more riders clad in homespun emerged from the trees, their attire suggesting they were the nobleman's servants. Two of the men dismounted to assist their master; the third went to capture Randle's wandering horse.

The nobleman lifted Randle's face out of the mire. Then he supported him against his knee while he cleansed his face with a kerchief. Placing his arms around Randle's thin chest, the man locked his grip and heaved. With a sickening squelch, Randle was pried from the bog. The servants carried the bedraggled lad to a patch of dry bracken and leaves. Randle was filthy and sodden, but very much alive.

From their saddlebags the nobleman's servants took blankets and soon had Randle swathed in warm wool. Randle's rescuer pressed a leather bottle to his lips, forcing some spiced wine into his mouth. After much sputtering and coughing, the color flooded back into Randle's cheeks.

Elena crouched beside the stranger. "You're lucky to be alive, Randle," she said, and another pang of guilt smote her for her first wild hope that he had died.

When Randle struggled to sit, the man gently pushed him back.

"I've naught but a few bruises," Randle protested in humiliation, finding his shame complete. To have been unhorsed in front of Elena was bad enough, but to have been rescued from that stinking hole by a stranger was the ultimate disgrace.

"Do you think he will be all right?"

"He's wet and damnably cold, yet there don't seem to be any broken bones," his rescuer replied after quickly running his hands over Randle's limbs.

When Elena finally looked the nobleman full in the face, she felt as if the ground had been pulled from under her. So intense was the sensation that she gasped, momentarily disoriented as he held her gaze. The irises of his large, light blue eyes were rimmed in black. And the open appraisal she saw there excited her beyond belief. How handsome he was! The acknowledgment sent a delicious thrill through her body. His nearness, and the shared intimacy as their gazes held, robbed her of breath.

"Your brother's none the worse for his fall, mistress, though you'd best teach him not to be so foolhardy in the future."

Now the man bent over Randle, lifting his muddy hair as he finished his examination. He nodded with satisfaction when he found no wound.

"Brother," Elena repeated numbly. Oh, would that it were so! Finally gathering her wits, Elena smiled back at the man as they stood to face each other.

"And you, mistress, are you hurt?" he asked in concern. "Your clothing's wet."

"Only because I tried to pull him from the water. Thank you again for coming to our rescue."

"Consider it my pleasure. Let us hope that, with

God's grace, the lad suffers no ill effects from his ducking. Let me introduce myself—Luis de los Santos, at your service.''

The Spanish name rolled off his tongue so quickly, she barely grasped it. Now the man doffed his plumed hat and bent over her outstretched hand. Elena stared down at his thick waving hair gleaming with golden highlights even in this murky wood. Suddenly she was seized with longing to plunge her hand into that lustrous mass, to slip her fingers over the smooth brown skin beneath his pearl-encrusted collar and caress him in the way of lovers. . . .

Gasping as if she expected him to read her mind, Elena felt her hand fly to her mouth. Blood mounted in her cheeks, bringing a pretty flush to her face.

"I . . . I am Elena. And this is Randle . . . Locke," she managed as she finally found her tongue.

"How fortunate I am to have found such beauty in a quiet English forest," he said gallantly, brushing her hand with his warm mouth.

Though the touch was feather-light, Elena shuddered as her blood coursed hotly along her arm.

"You are a Spaniard," she blurted rather foolishly, unable to think of anything else to say. The sensation his nearness caused was most pleasant, yet at the same time highly debilitating. Her wits seemed to have flown.

"From Castille. I'm in the service of your lady queen's husband."

"Philip! You came here with him?" Elena gasped, overawed to discover she spoke to a genuine courtier.

"Yes. I'm the guest of Lord Settle—perhaps you're acquainted with his lordship."

Elena shook her head. Lord Settle was far too grand to be an acquaintance of hers. But seeing that this Spanish gentleman assumed she, too, was of high degree, she did not want to spoil his illusion.

"Dispense with the chat—I'm likely to catch my death of cold," complained Randle from his blanket, his teeth chattering.

"Of course, how neglectful of me," said the Spaniard. He uttered a reluctant sigh as his gaze shifted from Elena's pretty face to the hapless Randle.

Luis de los Santos gave his servants an order in Spanish. As a child, Elena had been familiar with the language, for her mother had spoken it to her. Now she doubted she could speak one word of Spanish, though she was surprised to find she still understood it.

The servants carried Randle, still wrapped in blankets, to his horse. A stout fellow mounted behind him and held the youth in the saddle.

When the Spaniard stepped aside to issue a further order to his servants, Elena jabbed Randle's side through the layer of blankets. "Surely you've got the grace to thank him," she snapped, annoyed that so far he had displayed nothing but peevishness.

Randle scowled at the Spaniard whose back was toward them. "I don't bow and scrape to foreigners."

"You can at least show him as much courtesy as he's shown you."

Shamed, Randle bowed his head.

"Mistress, allow me to assist you to your horse."

Elena's heart began a frenzied beat as she felt Luis de los Santos's hands on her waist. His action surprised her; she had expected him to kneel in the manner of a groom, offering his hands for her to mount. Instead, he grasped her about the waist, lifting her and settling her in the saddle almost before she realized what was happening. She fancied his hands lingered on her waist as she became highly aware of their heat penetrating her damp velvet habit. When he finally removed his hands, she felt bereft, for she had enjoyed his touch immensely. An unexpected tingling in her breasts warned her that her blood craved an even more intimate caress. Elena flushed, and quickly looked away from the Spaniard's arresting, disturbing eyes, convinced he could read her mind.

"Do you live nearby?" he asked, interrupting her reverie, and forcing her to raise her head.

Elena swallowed, her mind still in a confused whirl. "At Locke Hall. It's several miles from here."

"Allow me to escort you and your brother home. Are you with the hunting party we passed earlier?"

"Yes. We became separated and got lost."

"I'll send a man to tell them about your brother's accident. Tomas's English should be adequate." He motioned to a short, dark-haired man and told him to deliver the message.

Elena sighed happily. This wood had become an enchanted place. When the handsome stranger looked at her and their gazes locked, they might have been the only two people in the world. His servants, and more importantly, the peevish Randle, seemed to miraculously dissolve into thin air.

"Now, mistress, pray lead the way, for I'm unfamiliar with this land."

Randle moved alongside her as the Spaniard spoke with his men.

"You still haven't thanked him," Elena admonished, her face stormy.

"Nor have you told him I'm not your brother," Randle countered sullenly. "You've been far too busy making sheep's eyes at him. He's the typical oily Spanish don who deliberately sets a maid's juices running."

"Randle!" Elena snapped, finding Randle's crude

description offensive. ''Besides, he looks as English as you,'' she countered as she pulled ahead, her cheeks hot.

Had her feelings been that apparent? Had she smiled too often and too sweetly at Luis de los Santos, so that even dull Randle had correctly interpreted her feelings for him? Setting her juices running indeed! That was the language of the scullery. Yet, she reluctantly conceded, it was probably an apt description for this strange pulsing in her blood and the expectant tingle in her flesh.

The riders pulled into the open, and Elena pointed to the east where a road wound through the trees. Her surging blood and thundering heartbeat, coupled with that hot, quickening sensation when their gazes locked, all betrayed her desire for a more passionate involvement with the handsome Spaniard. When she looked deep in his eyes, she saw something exciting and forbidden beckoning to her, yet warning her that she proceeded at her own peril.

''Thank you for rescuing us, sir,'' Randle said unexpectedly.

His reluctant, somewhat disgruntled apology took Elena by surprise. When she glanced at him, Randle's challenging expression seemed to say ''now it's your turn'' as he looked pointedly toward the Spaniard.

Elena knew that if she did not tell Luis de los Santos their true relationship, Randle would; yet she was loath to reveal the unpleasant truth. Once again, she turned to admire the slim, broad-shouldered stranger clad in a rich bronze velvet doublet slashed to reveal cream-colored silk. The doublet's high collar was embroidered in seed pearls, as were the narrow panels decorating each sleeve. Around his neck swung a large gold medallion on a heavy chain of alternating gold links and pearls. Tall black boots of the finest leather fitted his strong legs like a glove, his muscles rippling the supple surface whenever he moved. The boots were of an unfamiliar design and came midway up the thigh, revealing little of his black hose. His cloak, pearl-embroidered gloves and the band of the feathered hat perched atop his thick gold hair were black also, in perfect contrast to his fair coloring. With his golden hair and blue eyes, Luis de los Santos could have come from Lichborne.

Like many of her countrymen, Elena thought all Spaniards were swarthy skinned with black hair and eyes. The English had been most surprised to discover their Queen's husband was as fair and light skinned as they. Perhaps Luis de los Santos looked very like his king, Elena mused, glancing sideways at him. They said Philip of Spain was handsome, yet surely he could not be as handsome as this man. Intently studying his profile, she noticed his long nose was hooked slightly, giving his expression a predatory look. Heavy brown brows and thick dark lashes framed his arresting eyes. A shiver went over her as her gaze shifted to his sensual lips beneath the slim mustache, which curved about his firm chin to form a small pointed beard. No, she was convinced King Philip could never be as handsome as . . .

"Luis de los Santos."

"Yes?"

Elena gasped and her hand flew to her mouth. She had not intended to speak his name aloud. Flushing, she laughed self-consciously. "I was practicing saying your name. My mother was Spanish, too . . . from Aragon."

Randle still glowered at her, the reminder of her omission virtually bursting from his lips.

"I want to thank you again for rescuing Randle,"

Elena began, forcing herself to break the man's disturbing gaze.

"It was nothing. I only wish I'd ridden by sooner, then you'd have been spared the distress of trying to revive your brother."

"He . . . he's not my . . . brother," she stammered, each word dragged from her. Damn Randle, how pleased he looked! He was fully aware of the effort this disclosure cost her.

"Oh!" The Spaniard's brows raised quizzically. "Naturally I thought—"

"Randle is my bridegroom. Today is our wedding day."

Her words hung like lead on the fragrant summer air. Elena could see the Spaniard was surprised by the news. And, she liked to think, extremely disappointed. Had he thought to pay her court? Would he, if she were free? Quickly she dismissed those foolish thoughts. She was far from free, lacking only a religious ceremony to bind her forever to Randle Locke. How she wished this handsome stranger could be her groom!

"Will you honor us with your presence at our wedding?" she blurted. Her courteous suggestion was a spur-of-the-moment brainstorm; by it she bought a little more of this arresting man's presence. She assumed he was too well mannered to refuse her invitation; though he hesitated, glancing at his servants before turning back to her. "He must be our guest, mustn't he, Randle? It's the least we can do to show our gratitude."

Randle's scowl became even darker. "Yes, sir, you must be our guest. I won't take no for an answer."

"Thank you both. It will be my pleasure to join you in your celebration. I'll send a servant to tell my host I'll be delayed." His gaze rested briefly on Elena's face as he studied her flushed cheeks and dark-lashed tawny eyes. A ragged sigh escaped his lips. "You'll make a breathtaking bride. Your groom's the luckiest man in England."

Chapter Two

The small chapel at Locke Hall was filled to overflowing with finely dressed guests. The noon sun shone through the stained glass window behind the altar. Faded blue velvet cushions and tall vases of lilies were all that softened the austere interior of the family chapel. The brightly colored medieval floor tiles were discreetly hidden beneath a carpet of chamomile-sprinkled rushes.

Eager to curry favor with the late boy king's protector, Edward Seymour, the Locke family had reformed their former Papist chapel. Unsure how the winds blew in this new era, they had yet to restore their chapel with an eye to endearing themselves to Catholic Mary Tudor. That move would come after Elena received her court appointment.

Elena's stomach lurched at the thought. She stood stiffly before the altar, pretending to listen to the local parish church's white-robed choirboys. Last year her brother had petitioned the Queen to grant her a court position in payment for their family's past loyalties to the Tudors. Lady Locke had been much taken with the heady prospect of having a daughter-in-law at court. Elena wondered at the enormity of her mother-in-law's wrath if a court appointment never materialized.

The choirboys ended their song on a pure, silvery note that filled the stone chapel. A hush fell over the assembly as Father Tom stepped forward and Randle and Elena knelt in unison on the embroidered cushions at the communion rail.

The young groom wore white satin trimmed in silver lace and pearls, the unwise color choice making him appear more delicate than he actually was.

Elena's long-waisted, full-skirted gown of ivory velvet and heavy Venetian lace had a long train that spead across the steps and into the aisle between the pews. The ivory velvet oversleeves were slashed to reveal gold satin, which was puffed through the fabric to resemble two glorious honeycombs. The gown's square neck was softened by a border of embroidered lace, and a wire-stiffened lace collar framed her face. Elena wore a pearl-edged gold satin French hood well back on her head so that her thick, and oftentimes unruly, black curls were visible above her smooth brow. Her long hair hung unbound down her back in the customary style of virgins. Around her slender neck was a single drop pearl set on a fine gold chain—a wedding gift from her brother.

Will, anxious to impress their neighbors, had not skimped on Elena's wedding finery. Though the lavish gown set off her dark beauty to perfection, Elena was not fond of the garment. Attired in this sumptuous fabric, she felt like a holy icon as she stood before the altar, the embodiment of the Locke and Watkins families' hopes for future glory.

Randle's mumbled responses were barely audible, while her own clear voice echoed through the high-arched chapel. Incense wafted about them in a nose-tickling cloud and Elena caught her breath, fighting the urge to sneeze. At last they turned from the altar, the

ceremony over. Now she was Randle's wife in the sight
of both man and God.

Her sister-in-law, Ronwen, handed Elena her bridal
spray of waxy lilies bound with ivory ribbons and gold
lace. Tears streamed down her apple cheeks, and her
smile was of purest love.

Elena smiled softly in reply, clasping Ronwen's
reddened hand, rough from years of working in the
dairy. Then the bridal pair moved sedately down the
aisle while the sweet-voiced choirboys sang a hymn of
joy.

Halfway down the aisle, Elena felt compelled to look
to her right. The handsome Spaniard was watching her.
He smiled, nodding slightly in greeting. Elena's heart
lurched and she felt slightly dizzy as a rush of emotion
sped through her veins. He had such a strange effect
on her! There was joy and excitement in abundance,
yet her pleasure always seemed tinged with fear, as if
there were something forbidden about the indulgence.
Which, in truth, she supposed there was. As a new bride
her attraction to the handsome stranger was unseemly.

The chapel door opened wide, and the July sun
exploded in a golden blaze. Elena narrowed her eyes
against its brightness, while, beside her, Randle gasped
at the painful contact with his weak, watery eyes.

They crossed the flagged courtyard to the candle-lit
banquet hall. As Elena walked dutifully beside her new
husband, she was highly aware of Luis de los Santos's
presence in the press of people crossing the courtyard.
Though she steeled herself not to turn about, she could
still feel his gaze.

Lady Locke met them at the door, resplendent in a
lavish square-necked gown of scarlet taffeta over white
brocade.

Will and Ronwen stood beside her to greet the bridal

pair. Will wore his best doublet of chestnut velvet
lavishly embroidered in gold, a small ruff projecting
above the doublet's high neckband. Because he was bull-
necked, Will was obliged to hold his head haughtily
erect or suffer the indignity of having the fabric in his
mouth.

"Welcome, daughter," said Lady Locke stiffly as
she enfolded Elena against her bony chest. Her gaunt
face was highly powdered and rouged, as were her thin
lips, in a futile attempt to restore lost youth. Gray eyes
anxious, she quickly turned her attention to Randle,
searching his flushed face. On the pretext of caressing
him, Lady Locke felt his brow for fever.

"Mother," Randle hissed between his teeth, not taken
in by the ruse, "let me be. I'm a married man now."

Though his admonition was low, those close at hand
heard it and snickered.

The wedding guests filed noisily inside the gloomy
manor house, which was filled with the mingled aromas
of highly spiced dishes, wine, ale, beeswax and heady
flower perfume. A carved screen over fifteen feet high,
which normally divided the medieval Great Hall, had
been moved aside. Trestle tables covered in fringed red
brocade cloths and arrayed with pewter and wooden
utensils were arranged around the dark oak-panelled
walls, leaving the central space open for dancing.

Elena already felt oppressed by Locke Hall as the cold
unrelenting gaze of Magdalen Locke held her captive.
Deliberately turning her back on the unwanted scrutiny,
she beckoned to Ronwen to walk beside her. Will, who
was never very attentive to his wife, could be heard
holding forth about his grand plans for Elena's future
at court.

"Thank God it's over," Elena whispered, squeezing
Ronwen's hand.

Ronwen slipped her plump arm about Elena's shoulder.

"You were the loveliest bride ever, *Cariad*. You made me cry, so lovely you were."

"Oh, Ronwen, you flatter me too much," Elena protested, swallowing hard. "I'm going to miss you . . . and Windland. I might even miss Will."

Ronwen laughed. "That's stretching it, love. You two usually go at it hammer and tongs."

Ronwen glanced toward her husband and sighed. Long ago she had learned to expect little from Will. She had fulfilled her purpose by bringing him Windland Farm and its surrounding lands. Besides, she was forty-five—no longer young. It was not for her to expect kisses and pretty words.

Standing aside, Ronwen allowed Elena to mount the shallow steps leading to the main table where she would share the place of honor with her groom. Elena glanced wistfully after Ronwen's broad figure, wishing she could have sat beside her. Ronwen's old-fashioned white coif was soon lost in the press of guests, and Elena could no longer see her familiar periwinkle silk gown. Will's generosity had fallen short of lavishing new finery on his wife. The omission incensed her.

When Will came to escort her to her place, Elena could not contain her annoyance.

"Why didn't you dress poor Ronwen half so fine?" she demanded, looking pointedly at the rings on his fingers and the gold chain about his neck.

Will paused, genuinely taken back by her question.

"Ron's happy in what she's wearing. Curb your tongue. No one suspects what a waspish little bitch you can be. . . . And thank the Lord for that!"

"If it wasn't for you, I wouldn't be here today."

"That's right. And you should thank your maker that

at least one member of the family is ambitious.''

Will pulled out her chair and thrust her none too gently onto the seat. Placing a polite kiss on his sister's hot cheek, he stepped back.

Randle soon took his place beside her. Their laughing guests were being seated at the tables by liveried servants. Lady Locke sat beside Randle, and the Lockes' friends and relatives quickly filled the remaining seats at the main table. To Elena's humiliation, her own family was forced to sit at a lower table.

A place had been hastily prepared for their unexpected foreign guest. The local gentry eyed the richly dressed stranger warily. Had he not rescued the senseless young groom from almost certain death, he would never have been invited to the wedding. The man spoke their language and his manners were courteous; yet, even had he greeted them each on bended knee, they would still distrust him because he was Spanish. Granted, Mary Tudor chose to take a Spaniard to her bed, but that did not mean they must take one to their bosoms.

Aware of the strained atmosphere, Elena wondered if she had been ill advised to invite Luis de los Santos to her wedding. He intercepted her wistful gaze, and a smile of pleasure lit his handsome face. Elena gasped in surprise at the warm glow that filled her body. His smile seemed to say it did not matter if none but she bid him welcome. Elena drew a shaky breath and reached for her goblet, which a servant had filled with malmsey. Perhaps this banquet would not be so terrible after all, she thought, stealing another glance at the Spaniard. He no longer looked at her, but it did not matter. The pleasure of his special smile was hers forever.

At a signal from Lady Locke, the musicians in the minstrels' gallery struck a chord to signal the official start of the wedding feast. Two maidens clad in silver and gold led a garlanded lad inside the room. Their appearance was greeted by a round of applause, and with the constant refilling of the wine cups, the atmosphere inside the hall grew livelier.

The maidens sang the chorus, the lad the verse, of an old English song in praise of brides. Whistles and laughter greeted the ending of the piece.

Four servants appeared carrying a great platter containing the highly decorative Warner, a gilded masterpiece designed to alert the guests to the start of the banquet proper. The sugar, plaster and pasteboard extravaganza was in the form of a glittering pink sugar castle afloat on a sugar syrup moat. Much applause greeted the lavish creation as it was borne ceremoniously about the hall.

After greeting the bride and groom with a suggestive couplet, the household steward opened the castle walls to reveal the tableau within. The newly married couple were depicted in various stages of marital bliss. First came the courtship, the lad kneeling before the simpering lass. Next the couple embraced beneath a sugar-frosted quilt in a marchpane bed. Roars of laughter greeted the third scene. Here the lass, her belly grotesquely swollen, was alone in the room, clutching her body and grimacing in pain.

Elena flushed at the crude humor, trying to shut out the guests' bawdy comments, while Randle snickered self-consciously.

A procession of servants now entered the room, each carrying an elaborate dish for the first course. Great glistening shields of brawn, a whole stuffed kid bathed in saffron sauce, stewed rabbits floating in red wine, dishes of lampreys, a silver tureen of oysters in bastard gravy, steaming pottage of greens, custards and molded jellies of diverse shapes and colors. As if this were not enough, there followed gooseberry flummeries, dishes of ripe strawberries mounded with cream, platters of gilded marchpane figures and slices of rolled Lech Lombarde served in sweetened red wine syrup.

Ale, Gascon wine, malmsey and sack were brought inside the hall by the gallon. The choicest dishes went first to the main table before being passed around. Pewter and wooden trenchers served the lesser diners, while the guests of distinction supped off silver platters. Daggers were used to spear the meat, and the guests supped gravy from their own spoons, which they had brought to the feast so as not to go unfed.

Elena ate sparingly. A molded swan of boiled almonds, rice and cream, colored pink with sandalwood and scented with rosewater, was the centerpiece for the second course. She found the smooth pink mixture soothing to her throat, which went dry each time she thought about the ordeal that was soon to follow.

Numerous toasts were raised to the bridal pair, and some of the guests were becoming boisterous and tipsy. Randle kept sneezing, irritated by the highly spiced food. To Elena's disgust, he blew his nose loudly on the tablecloth.

For the benefit of those few who had still not heard the tale, a colorful account of the young groom's misfortune in the morning hunt was given. All eyes shifted from Randle to his rescuer as Luis de los Santos rose to take a bow. A toast was drunk in his honor; then he proposed a toast of his own. Forsaking the fine Gascon wine, he endeared himself to the assembly by toasting the bridal pair's health in good English ale. Cheers broke out as he quaffed the contents of his cup. Everyone had heard tell how Philip's grandees despised England's national drink, yet here was this fellow imbibing with the best of them. And were it not for this Spaniard, that numskull Randle would likely be floating face up and this would have been a wake instead of a wedding.

The singing girls returned to offer a song in praise of the brave deed, begging the Spaniard to dance with them. To the audience's delight, one bold wench stole a kiss from the handsome hero.

Now the minstrels struck up chords for dancing, and a general scramble to the center of the room took place. Those who preferred to feast were left lolling drunkenly at their tables.

Elena felt light-headed as she took to the floor. Randle declined to partner her, sulking instead over his wine cup. The honor was passed to an elderly relative whose tortured breathing soon forced him to abandon the dance, wheezing too much to continue. This signalled that Elena was now available to any partner. The men thrust forward, eager to claim a dance with the lovely bride, and after the first set there was an outcry for her to honor the hero of the day.

Her heart racing, Elena waited, anxious in case Luis de los Santos declined to dance with her. She need not have fretted, for he came eagerly to her side and bowed politely over her hand. The musicians, who had paused to allow the dancers to regroup, began the music again.

"You're a very good dancer," Elena said breathlessly as the Spaniard whisked her through the coranto, a running dance in triple time.

"It is you who inspired me, Elena," he whispered, laughing as he bent low to her face.

His casual use of her name pleased her. The touch of his warm hands and the flattery in his smile made her head spin with excitement. All too soon the coranto was over and other men clamored eagerly around her.

A gay galliard was requested, and she hoped the Spaniard would partner her again. But this time Randle came forward, tired of the handsome stranger being the center of attention. Laughter and applause greeted his appearance on the floor. The lively galliard was almost too much for him, and he barely contained a fit of coughing until the final bar.

Randle dabbed his nose and eyes, sneezing repeatedly.

"You're certainly enjoying yourself," he remarked peevishly, scowling at Elena's flushed cheeks and sparkling eyes.

"Why shouldn't I enjoy myself? It's my wedding day."

He ignored her rejoinder, being too busy glowering at the Spaniard who had received the guests' enthusiastic acceptance. Women clamored to partner him.

"God's toenails," Randle swore, "that scurvy Spaniard's after all the wenches. Likely he'll infest the whole county with the Spanish pox. Bastard—I'm the one who should be the center of attention. It's my wedding day. Anyone would think he was the groom."

While the musicians tuned their instruments for the next set of dances, Randle leaped to his feet, holding up his hand for silence. At first he was ignored; then someone noticed the lad trying to speak and shushed the others. The squealing notes from the gallery died away. His confidence buoyed by several cups of malmsey, Randle found it unexpectedly easy to assume his place as host.

"Ladies and gentlemen, thank you for coming to our wedding. It has been a memorable day. And now, with due respect, I, as the groom, would make it a memorable night."

His next words were drowned by a great gale of

laughter. Applause echoed through the room. Brows raised, for no one had expected such wit from the young milksop.

"My bride and I are weary of feasting and dancing—"

"And would fain be weary from bedding down, eh, lad?" bellowed a hearty male voice. The man was laughingly shushed by his fellows.

Randle grinned slyly as he reached for Elena's icy hand.

"We bid you good night. Enough of dancing and feasting. . . ."

The scraping of benches, the thumping of many feet and the general din of a half-drunken assembly drowned out whatever else he had intended to say. The guests stood to raise their goblets, and many swaying revellers found themselves grateful for the support of the table. A red-bearded man took it upon himself to act as spokesman.

"As our young groom has said, enough feasting and dancing. We've finally come to our real purpose—the bedding. So, my friends, let us, in a manner of speaking, get to the meat of the issue."

A gale of crude laughter greeted his announcement.

Smiling reassuringly at Elena, Ronwen pushed her way through the finely dressed ladies so she might prepare the bride for bed. Aware that it was her right— wasn't she the only mother the girl had known these past years?—she did not allow the grand Lady Locke to intimidate her.

Roars of laughter filled the hall as someone shouted a rude couplet, and the general clanking of ale cups suggested the men would stay to enjoy a few more tipples before ceremoniously bringing young Randle to his lovely bride. Sweetness and romance had little place at a Tudor wedding. Raw jest and drunken good humor were the order of the day.

Elena's knees shook as she walked from the hall. The bawdy wit passing back and forth between the men only added to her discomfort. Without Ronwen's support the ordeal would have been unbearable. Laughing maid-servants lit their way, and grotesque shadows made by the flickering candles flitted over the low ceilings and panelled walls as the small group traversed the final corridor and stopped before the nuptial chamber. Here the maids sprinkled herbs on the threshold while they chanted an ancient rhyme.

"Come forth, Elena. Be fruitful." Magdalen Locke held wide the door. "And happy," she added as a decided afterthought.

Elena smiled stiffly, knowing full well her mother-in-law was little concerned for her happiness. Elena was merely a vessel to carry the precious Locke heir.

"Thank you, Lady Locke. May the Almighty bless our union."

A murmur of approval met Elena's pious wish. Some of the ladies followed the bride and her relatives inside the oak-panelled chamber.

A great carved bed with gold fringed green hangings dominated the room. Muted blue and red tapestries softened the dark panelled walls. Narrow mullioned windows, bright with the glow from the fire, were left with the curtains pulled aside. The room's only other furnishings were a padded bench and the trunk holding Elena's clothes. The rushes were sweetened with rose petals.

"Don't be afraid, *Cariad*," Ronwen whispered, kissing Elena's cheek as she sat solemnly before the hearth.

"I'm trying not to be."

"I've had two husbands and managed to survive."

Elena smiled, knowing the assurance was kindly given. Ronwen brushed Elena's black hair and helped her undress. At last she was ready, and her shift was slipped over her head. Her skin had been rubbed with musk, her long hair perfumed with rosewater and brushed until the curling black mass gleamed like ebony in the firelight.

Elena was uncomfortably aware that her nipples showed through her shift where the fullness of her bosom lifted the bodice in a most provocative fashion. She suspected the firelight shining through the thin lawn would also reveal the shapeliness of her thighs and buttocks.

Chanting a Welsh rhyme, Ronwen turned back the heaped bedcovers and removed the bed warmer. She sprinkled the sheets with holy water. After blessing herself, she beckoned the giggling maids, who curtsied to the bride and took her hand to lead her up the steps and into the bed.

Other women pressed forward now to wish Elena luck, happiness and fruitfulness, strewing flower petals and crushed herbs on the sheets to promote fertility. Elena sank thankfully into the deep feather mattress, seeking the warmth where the pan of coals had rested.

Thumping steps and drunken laughter announced the groom's arrival. Elena swallowed nervously, clasping her hands so tight the knuckles whitened. Ronwen kissed her cheek reassuringly before plumping the feather pillows and rearranging Elena's hair.

The door burst open and the finely dressed groom was thrust inside the room.

Elena huddled miserably inside the covers. When she pulled the blankets to her chin to hide her exposure, Lady Locke thrust them down, reminding her it was not proper for a bride to huddle as if she were afraid. Besides, Magdalen Locke was eager to show the bride's voluptuousness to her guests, pleased with the prize she had secured for Randle.

Smiling indulgently, Lady Locke took her son from his aged grand uncle, who, as the eldest male relative, had the privilege of escorting him. In more primitive times it had been customary for bride and groom to be naked, but in this enlightened age, Lady Locke deemed that a little modesty would not come amiss. Many curious ladies craned forward, eager to learn if the girlish Randle were indeed a man. Just before his final garment was removed and a fine lawn nightshirt slipped over his head, his mother moved forward to successfully block their view.

The atmosphere grew heavy with the mingled odors of sweat, heavy perfume and ale-tainted breath. A rousing song heralded the end of the ceremony.

Aware of the men's lecherous stares, Elena placed her hair strategically over the bodice of her shift. All those crudely worded tips on how Randle should conduct this first coupling had filled her with shame. Tears pricked her eyes, and she longed to flee the room.

Elena grew aware of an intense gaze fixed on her. Glancing up, she saw Luis de los Santos standing in the shadows beside the windows. When their eyes met, he gave her a reassuring smile. Shyly, she returned his smile, glad of his understanding. So full of self-pity had she been this past hour that she had pushed all thought of the attractive Spaniard to the back of her mind. Now she wondered what he would think if he knew she longed to substitute him for her groom. The thought that he might have read her mind made her flush. She looked down at her hands, then nervously patted her hair, the unconscious movement making the black cloak slide from her shoulders.

When next Elena stole a glance at Luis, she found his gaze resting on her bodice where her breasts were now visible through the thin material. In her foolish naiveté, Elena had thought his admiration a romantic tribute far removed from earthly lust. Now she realized how silly she had been. Before he left, elbowing his way through the throng, he paused beside the bed. His eyes glowed with admiration and his sensual mouth curved as he mouthed something to her in Spanish. Then he was gone.

Elena was shaken by the emotion that passed between them. Despite the fact she had not understood what he said, excitement coursed through her veins. Her imagination could supply a multitude of choices. How she longed to follow him instead of continuing this charade with Randle.

Randle! The reminder jolted her back to the present. Glancing to her right, she saw him standing there, blushing self-consciously at all the well-meant advice.

The laughing men seized the bedcovers and flung them aside while someone held a brace of candles aloft to illuminate the scene. The bright light revealed Elena's thin shift molded delectably to her curves. Men grew lecherous at the glimpse of her softly rounded hips and thighs, slim ankles and dainty feet. Randle was thrust in bed beside her, with a final exhortation to make everyone proud of him.

Forming a line, the men stumbled from the room, singing a drunken ditty as they went, belching, hiccuping and laughing when the words eluded them. After offering Elena some whispered last-minute advice, their women followed. Now only Ronwen, Magdalen Locke and Randle's valet remained.

"Good night, *Cariad*. Be brave," Ronwen whispered

in parting, giving Elena a final kiss.

"Randle, remember your father's dream—many sons to carry on his name," were Lady Locke's parting words before she kissed her son's hot brow.

The door closed and they were almost alone. "God's toenails, I thought they'd never leave. You may go also, Barton," Randle ordered imperiously, waving his hand at the valet who still hovered in the shadows. "I'm old enough to find my way out of my nightshirt. And be sure the pot's within reach. You know how I hate searching for it. Good night."

The valet bowed, seeming reluctant to leave. He eyed Elena hungrily as he said, "Good night to you, my lady. Please to remember what I told you, my lord." Then he left.

After the uproar made by their tipsy guests, the sudden quiet was shocking. Elena fought increasing waves of nausea. Fortunately, her wedding night had never been shrouded in much romantic illusion; had it been, Randle's undue concern about the chamber pot would have dampened the romance.

"Are you ready?"

Elena gulped in surprise, hardly expecting Randle to put matters so bluntly. The gleam in his eyes and his flushed cheeks were an unpleasant reminder of the morning's attempted seduction. So far she had not chastised him for his abominable behavior.

"Had you got me out of the saddle, you intended to rape me, didn't you?"

Perversely, her outrage pleased him. Randle had supposed that after the humiliating accident all had been lost. "Of course," he replied airily, "and I'd have succeeded too, if such damned ill fortune hadn't struck."

"Then you deserved to be thrown."

"There's no need to be peevish."

They eyed each other with mounting dislike.

Suddenly, Randle lunged at her, taking Elena as much by surprise as he had done this morning. She cried out in alarm, trying to defend herself as he quickly covered her with his lank body, exhibiting unexpected strength. Breathing hard, Randle pressed her into the mattress, his lips hot and wet. She thrashed her head this way and that, trying to escape his wine-drenched mouth. His body burned with fever, and she, too, felt consumed with heat, yet this was no searing passion—rather a terrible, suffocating sensation she was unable to escape.

Fighting to imprison her beneath him, Randle brutally attacked her mouth, bruising her lips as their teeth clashed. As he struggled to rip open her shift, he touched her soft pink nipple. Curiously, he pinched the pliant flesh, using such force that Elena yelped in pain.

To her disgust, Elena felt the increasing pressure of Randle's rousing manhood against her thighs. While Randle struggled to keep her shift above her knees, he uttered a string of hoarse obscenities in her ear. Elena winced at the force he was using in a desperate effort to penetrate her, but she fiercely resisted.

Then, almost as quickly as it had begun, the assault was over. She could hardly believe her good fortune as Randle fell back on his own side of the bed, whimpering and clutching his manhood. In the dim light Elena saw blood on the sheet. It could not be from her maidenhead, for Randle's ineffectual performance had not deflowered her.

"Damn you, Elena, you've torn me," Randle accused between sobs as, still whimpering, he took a candle to examine his injury.

Elena was aware of her heart thudding so hard that her body seemed to shudder. Anger and disgust swirled through her stomach. "Me!" she gasped at last. "You're the one who attacked me."

"If you'd opened to me as you should, this wouldn't have happened. Now see what you've done."

She purposely looked away from the puffy, torn skin he indignantly displayed, having no desire to view his nakedness.

"I'm bleeding! *You're* the one who's supposed to bleed." Blubbering in self-pity, Randle dabbed his torn flesh on the sheet, wincing at the painful contact.

Furious that his wife dared refuse to look at him, he finally seized Elena's chin and twisted her face about, forcing her to inspect the damage she had inflicted. Though she did not know what it was called, Elena saw the skin had torn when he tried to force himself inside her.

"It's your own fault. You shouldn't have gone at me like some wild animal."

"It hurts," Randle whined piteously, tears sliding down his hot face.

"Well, you hurt me. Now you know what it feels like."

"Cruel wench, have you no heart?" he whispered, sniffling and rubbing his eyes with the back of his hand. "I can't send for Barton, or he'll know I've failed. We must get a babe! Come, Elena, let us try again."

She knew he was right, for she had also been drilled about the vital need for an heir. Once she became pregnant, perhaps she might be left in peace. It was a comforting thought. Elena was relieved to find Randle no more developed than a ten-year-old boy. Terrible visions of being torn asunder had made her less than eager for lovemaking, her fears aroused by other women's frightening tales of men as big as stallions.

Stoicly, Elena endured Randle's unwelcome caresses,

forcing her thoughts from the present. At the first hint of pain he backed away, the hurt shrinking his manhood.

"We aren't doing it right—that's what's wrong," he finally snapped as he pulled away from Elena.

"Attacking me like a field hand can't be the way. That's why you're bleeding."

"Barton showed me how to do it."

A cold chill went over Elena. "What do you mean, showed you?"

"With a girl from the village. And that's the way they did it."

Elena swallowed. "You watched them do . . . that?"

Sullen, Randle nodded, still nursing his throbbing wound. "I had to find out what to do somewhere— Mother never let me watch the animals. Barton said I could do the girl, too, but I . . . I didn't want to. She stank of cow dung and her hair was dirty."

The chill deepened. Elena drew slightly away from him, fighting a rising wave of nausea as she pictured the scene. "Did Barton attack the girl like you attacked me?"

"That's how you're supposed to do it."

"No, Randle, first you make love to a woman. You should be gentle," Elena explained softly. She was convinced she was right, though instinct alone guided her, for she knew less than he about the subject. "Men woo women with kisses and sweet words."

"I don't know any sweet words."

After a few minutes of sullen silence, he turned back to her and made an effort to follow her suggestion. Elena braced herself as he explored her maidenhead with an inquisitive finger. But even this approach was doomed to failure.

"I can't do it," Randle sobbed in frustration. Each fresh assault strained his wound further until he wept at the slightest touch. All the terrible failures of this day crystalized in his inability to complete the act that would prove his masculinity beyond doubt. If he could not enter her, there would be no child; he knew that much. And until there was a child in Elena's belly, he would have no peace from his mother.

It was true he had treated her badly, acting alternately spoiled and loutish. Yet Elena felt a stirring of pity for him. Randle had never had a life of his own, with Lady Locke always there to direct his every move. She was surprised Lady Locke had not insisted on remaining to instruct him on his wedding night. The outrageous idea amused her.

"What are you smiling about?" he demanded pettishly, his mouth turned down.

"I was wondering why your mother didn't stay to guide you."

Randle gave a rather sheepish smile. "It wasn't from lack of hinting. I thought you'd be shamed to have her here."

Elena suspected he would have been shamed also, but she allowed him a vestige of manly pride. "Don't worry, there'll be other nights."

Far from soothing, Randle found her reminder alarming. "No," he gasped, "it must be tonight. She'll ask. I know she will."

"Then we'll lie and say all went well."

"She'll know it's a lie. She always knows."

"Randle, don't be such a . . ." Elena stopped short of calling him fool. "Trust me. She'll never learn the truth from me."

Eyes wide with surprise, he stared at her. "You mean you won't tell her?"

"What goes on in this room is none of her business."

"She'll make it so."

"Then I'll unmake it."

"But you're still virgin."

"Surely she won't have me examined."

Randle smiled wanly. "She might."

"Look there's no reason to doubt our story." Inspired, Elena pointed to the sheet where smears of blood from Randle's injury had stained the linen. "Everyone will think it's mine."

"She'll know we lied when you aren't with child."

"This won't last forever. Put some salve on your . . . wound."

Damn them all! It wasn't his fault, Randle thought angrily. He wasn't to blame for this. Had he had a father or older brother to instruct him, even a close friend, he would not have had to seek information from a servant.

With a sigh of exasperation as fresh tears began to trickle down his cheeks, Elena slid from the bed. On the mantle stood the decanter of rose water used to perfume her hair. Perhaps it had some healing properties.

"Here, bathe your . . . it . . . in this," she suggested uncomfortably.

Though he did not say so, Randle was grateful for her understanding. Maybe Elena could be his friend. He had never had a friend. Previously he had thought of women merely as playthings, yet it was possible she could be a source of pleasure and comfort to him. The lechery he had contemplated when he admired her from afar might still be possible at some later date. He lay back awaiting her ministrations.

Having no desire to touch him, Elena thrust the decanter in his hand and gave him the cloth the women had used to sponge her body. Then she went to the hearth, leaving him to attend to himself.

He alternately cursed and sobbed as he bathed his wound. Elena did not know whether to laugh or cry. A great wave of self-pity swept over her as she rested her head against the cool mantel, trying not to listen to his blubbers of pain. God, how much she wanted to be loved and cherished. What a cruel twist of fate that she, whose body was ripe for passion, whose heart ached for love, had been given Randle Locke as husband. How different tonight might have been had Luis de los Santos been her groom. Wistfully she tried to imagine that encounter. Would he lavish tender kisses on her while caressing her shapely body . . . ?

"Elena."

Her pleasant imagery shattered, she turned to face her husband. His nightshirt fell modestly to his ankles, and there was only a blood stain to remind them of his shame.

"You've been most kind to me, Elena."

"I'm nothing if not kind, Randle," she said, feeling far older than her 19 years. "Come, let's try to sleep."

As Elena plumped the pillows, Randle smiled at her with affection. Elena would act as his second mother, he decided with relief. Perhaps he would not need to be manly and strong. He hoped not, for the burden of proving himself had taken the last ounce of his strength. He was so tired. All he wanted to do was sleep.

While Elena blew out the candles, he asked, "You promise not to tell Mother, don't you, Elena?"

"Yes, I promise. Your secret's safe."

He squeezed her hand in gratitude. When Elena turned on her side, he moved closer and slid his arm about her waist. Though she wanted to push him away, to send him back to his side of the bed, she steeled herself to endure this small, unwelcome embrace. While they lay waiting for sleep, the bed shuddered several times, and she suspected Randle wept again in self-pity.

For a long time Elena lay staring into the darkness as the long summer twilight finally went to its death beyond the wood. A new moon had risen in the midnight blue sky. Night lay silent upon the land. After the warm day this room felt unexpectedly chill, the atmosphere as clammy as the touch of her own skin. Even her hair was damp with sweat after that unwelcome battle to preserve her maidenhead. And for what? Once Randle's puny flesh healed sufficiently for a fresh assault, she must eventually submit. When his mother pressed him for news of her pregnancy, or when Barton discovered his failure, Randle would be driven to assert himself. But until her boy husband was goaded into proving his masculinity, she had won a reprieve. And for that small favor she was immensely grateful.

Tears trickled from under Elena's closed lids, running into her hair, her ears, falling slowly on the pillow. For the rest of her life she was tied to this overgrown child who had more need of a mother than a wife.

Finally Elena became drowsy. In this half-waking, half-dreaming state, she pictured Luis de los Santos paying her court. And she smiled with pleasure in the darkness.

Then, in the harsh gray dawn Elena woke and knew the dream for what it was. Birdsong blended with Randle's snores. He moved, flinging his arm across the pillow. As she watched, his thumb found its way to his mouth and he began to suck contentedly.

The sight of her husband's infantile habit merely rubbed salt in the wounds. Soon she would have to face Lady Locke's cross-examination about her wedding night. She was determined to pretend all had gone well, the lie as much for herself as to protect her husband's pride. Intense dislike for Randle's mother made Elena almost relish the deception. As she lay formulating her story, the sun climbed higher, spattering the panelling with gold. In the distance, cocks crowed and the parish clock struck five.

Chapter Three

"To the bride and groom, long may they live in happiness and prosperity."

The hearty toast echoed around the oak-panelled room as the departing guests raised a cup of wine. Arms linked, bride and groom smiled stiffly, thanking their guests for their good wishes. When Elena tried to escape to the window seat, Randle pinched her and gripped her arm so tightly that she was forced to stay beside him.

"My friends, we'll drink another bumper together in less than a twelvemonth to celebrate my grandson's christening," promised Lady Locke as she escorted her guests to the door.

"What a surprise, Randle, I didn't know we were soon to be parents," Elena mocked as she wrenched herself from his grasp.

She went to sit on the blue velvet cushioned window seat, rubbing her forearm where Randle's spiteful pinch was darkening to a bruise. The beautiful garden spread before her, sloping lawns filling the old moat. To her left was the intricately designed rose garden; beds of lupins, wallflowers, snapdragons and gillyflowers made a brilliant splash of color against the grass. The abundance in this peaceful garden seemed a mockery of the emptiness of her life.

Turning to Randle, Elena snapped, "As God is my witness, pinch me again, you little bastard, and all shall know the truth."

"Shut up," he ordered, glancing toward the door. "You promised."

"And 'tis a promise I've kept, though God knows it's hard when I hear you boasting about your prowess. How could you shame me so?"

"It was expected."

"By whom? Yon drunken louts who would eagerly spread the tale to every pothouse in the land?"

"Enough, Elena—Mother's coming."

A scowling Lady Locke swept inside the room. "You could have been more gracious, wench. One would think you fresh from a nunnery by your vinegar sour expression. All's meant in good humor. Fortunately dear Randle saved the day."

"I'm sorry if my attitude offended. I did not think it fitting to discuss our bed habits in public, madam."

"Randle has naught to be ashamed of, have you, precious?" cooed Lady Locke, smiling at her son. "Tell me, Elena, have you felt any sign of a babe?"

" 'Tis hardly time. We've only been wed a fortnight."

"Of course, eagerness overwhelms my sense."

It was an observation with which Elena heartily agreed. She turned back to the sunlit gardens. Those two weeks seemed like months. Such a pother of constant bickering, questioning, whining—between the mother and son, they'd turn her into a shrew before the month was out.

Randle's fever alternately blazed and waned. His nose and eyes streamed. Most nights he spent coughing and complaining until Elena longed to strangle him so she at least might have some peace. The blue circles under her eyes, which their departing guests had slyly suggested came from endless lovemaking, were the result of sleepless nights.

" 'Tis time for your nap, precious."

Randle pulled a face at his mother's sugary suggestion.

"I'm not tired, Mother. Elena thought we might ride—"

"Nonsense! You're far too ill. I'll hear no more of it. Being a groom's an arduous task. You must renew your strength."

Elena seethed as Randle obediently turned tail and headed for the stair. His mother's suggestive chuckle only added to her anger. "Randle has a cold, madam. His current lethargy has naught to do with me."

Eyes snapping, Lady Locke seized her wrist, her bony fingers gouging deep. "Enough, you ungrateful chit! Randle took you to wife—a nobody . . . daughter of some Welsh upstart and a foreign maid—"

"My mother was a Spanish noblewoman in the service of Queen Katherine," Elena corrected icily, not deigning to struggle.

"And my son is heir to this estate. He's brought you much with this marriage. Surely to ask for civility in return is a small request. Now go upstairs and make yourself available to him. There must be a child soon. You can see he's unwell—we can't afford to let time slip by."

Elena's mouth opened in protest before she reconsidered her folly and clamped it shut.

In the dimly lit reception room her mother-in-law's eyes glittered malevolently. "Randle's delicate health kept him from . . . developing like other youths. He may need some encouragement. Though, God knows, you look whorish enough to rouse any man.''

How Elena longed to shout out that had she been the greatest whore in Christendom her talent would have been wasted on Randle; yet, mindful of their deception, she merely swallowed her anger and forced a meek smile.

''Lady Locke, you wound me with your words. Dost call me whore?''

Hardly expecting so sweet a rebuke, Lady Locke mumbled uncomfortably, ''Nay—forgive me, Elena, I know you're chaste. 'Twas my clumsy attempt to call you desireable—the very reason I chose you for my lad.''

''And the fact I'd soon serve Her Majesty.''

The two women faced each other, all pretense flown. Lady Locke seethed inwardly to admit she had met her match.

''Just get a babe, Elena, and you'll earn my respect. I crave a grandchild far more than all the court appointments in the land.''

The sincerity of Lady Locke's words briefly disarmed her. Much against her will, Elena felt a smattering of pity for her mother-in-law.

''I'm a healthy vessel. The seeding is up to your son, Madam,'' Elena said as she turned and walked from the room.

Elena stiffly mounted the stair, lips compressed to keep back the truth. If Randle did not overcome his difficulty, there would be no hope for a child. But she said nothing. Silence was her ally.

''What did Mother say to you?'' Randle wanted to know when she walked inside the bedchamber and slammed the door.

''The usual reminder to make sure you get me with child.''

"Oh." Randle looked downcast. "Shall we . . . do it?"

Elena pulled off her white pearl-trimmed headdress and gave him a withering look. "The problem's yours. And so is that decision."

"I thought you were going to be my friend," Randle whined, his eyes filling with tears. "You're hateful, calling me a little bastard. I'm your lord and master. How dare you speak so to me?"

Her head snapped up and she tossed back her black hair, which tumbled about her shoulders in a glorious curling mass. "Never will you be my master. And, from the looks of it, neither will you be my lord."

"Spoken like a true bitch," he cried, his voice wobbling.

She had not meant to wound him so severely. As his head bowed and tears trickled down his nose, she felt remorse. Oh, dear God, why had she turned so shrewish of late?

"You're right, I was cruel. Forgive me. Mayhap it's too many sly pinches and pokes, too many accusations, which make me so disagreeable. Mary, Mother of God, will it always be like this?"

"Like what?"

"I feel as if I'm married to your mother. You agreed we were going to ride. Why didn't you insist on it instead of buckling under to her demands? If you want to become a man, you could start by defying her."

Randle stared speechless at her, his tears dry.

"She always knows what's best for me. Still . . ." He gazed wistfully at the summer afternoon beckoning beyond the open casement. "I don't think a ride would have hurt me."

"Then say so. Hurry, get out of your bedrobe."

He made no move to leave the bed, appearing very

small beneath the mountain of covers. He wheezed just then, and despite his furred bedrobe, Randle began to shiver.

"Maybe tomorrow. Yes, we'll go tomorrow."

"Tomorrow never comes. I'll go by myself. Dear God, I can't endure another afternoon twiddling my thumbs whilst you snore and cough and whine. Or mayhap I should go downstairs for a delightful exchange of barbs with your sainted mother."

Randle gaped at her, shocked by her outburst. She cursed and raged at him like a stranger—his Elena, the gentle woman he had expected to mother him while she satisfied his bodily craving. Gradually a smug smile replaced his shock. "I'd forgotten—you can't go alone. It's forbidden."

"What?"

"Those are Mother's orders. The servants will enforce them."

Elena swung about, her cherry red damask skirts swishing against the wainscot. "We'll see about that! Look through the window. You can watch me gallop over the fields."

She marched from the room, for once too hot with emotion to notice the dank chill of the upper reaches of the old house. She sped down the broad carved stairs and across the courtyard until she stood in the stable yard. A groom appeared, and she could hardly believe her ears when he repeated what Randle had said. She was even forbidden to enter the stables to see her horse. When she tried to force her way past the man, he apologized for the need to restrain her, but was determined to obey Lady Locke's command.

When next Elena entered the bedchamber, she trembled with rage; her face was flushed and she panted from the exertion of running up three flights of stairs.

One glance at her mutinous face told Randle he had been right. "See, didn't I tell you?"

She stood in the doorway, fighting tears. Riding had been her final solace. If Randle remained too spineless to defy his mother, or became too ill to ride, she would be imprisoned in this house. Poor Artan must be pining in the stables, wondering why his mistress had forsaken him. She was even forbidden to groom her horse for fear she would sneak off for a wanton ride about the estate.

"Damn your mother and her rules!" Elena exploded, smashing her fist in her palm.

Color heightened her cheeks, and her flashing tawny eyes and the black mane cascading over her shoulders added greatly to her allure. Randle stared at her, suddenly overcome with desire. In Elena's absence he had examined his injury and found the pain lessened. Perhaps he would surprise her by becoming her lord, for she was a woman in need of mastering.

"Come here," he commanded, making his voice deep.

So different did he sound, Elena's head snapped up.

"To the bed," he continued, pushing aside his bedrobe to reveal his mounting readiness.

Her stomach heaved at the sight. Memories of that abortive wedding night, of the ineffectual performances she had since endured, came rushing back. Yet she knew they must continue this parody of lovemaking if they were to get a child. If Randle could perform just one time, there was hope for that miracle.

She took a reluctant step toward the bed. When she came closer, he grabbed her arm and swung her toward him. With his mouth buried greedily in the hollow between her breasts, he groped beneath her skirts. Impatient, he ordered her to lie on the bed and pull up her petticoats. Like a sleepwalker, she obeyed, longing to strike him. Panting with excitement, Randle fell on her, forcing her into the mattress. Sweat from his hot face dampened her brow as he probed and forced— then came the usual squeals of pain before he fell back in defeat.

Much later, while Randle dozed, Elena knelt before the open window. Somewhere beyond these confining walls life continued. Maybe not today, but soon, she would gallop Artan over the countryside and the consequences be damned. She felt so low in spirit that she even found herself longing for Will's promised visit on his birthday six weeks hence. Will, for whom she bore so little affection, with whom she quarreled more often than she conversed . . . Elena smiled wryly. Perhaps even quarreling with her half brother was preferable to the monotony of being confined with her boy husband and his doting mother.

Far from improving, the situation inside Locke Hall grew steadily worse as the weeks passed. Though Lady Locke was still desperate for a grandchild, Randle's failing health frightened her. Bitter, she blamed Elena for his decline.

"Madam, it will be my greatest pleasure to take a chamber of my own," Elena announced angrily when she had endured enough. "That way your son will be assured of his rest."

Eyes flashing, the two women glared at each other. Finally, her lips clamped in a grim line, Lady Locke agreed.

"Very well, Elena, I'll have the adjoining chamber made ready."

It was almost more than Elena could do to hide her joy. She did not care what the adjoining chamber looked like. All that mattered was that it had a bed she need not share.

The following day Elena oversaw the outfitting of her new chamber at the southwest corner of the house. Windows on both sides presented a panoramic view of the garden and surrounding countryside. There was little here to remind her of Randle and his doting mother. The soft crimson velvet bedcurtains, the lambswool rug beside the bed and the carved cedarwood chest were of her own choosing.

Unfortunately, Randle's racking cough penetrated thick walls, until at times Elena buried her head under a pillow to shut out the sound. During the day she tried to humor her ailing husband, whose childish whines were now interspersed with tantrums. He screamed and drummed his heels at the slightest provocation, trying her patience to the limit.

One beautiful summer afternoon in early August, life inside Locke Hall took a decisive turn. The days had become a boring routine of meals, needlework, lessons in household management, lectures on behavior and tedious hours spent trying to entertain her bedridden husband. On this golden day, the deadly monotony was broken by the arrival of a wise woman who brought a cure guaranteed to banish Randle's ills.

Looking like a beggar woman in soiled clothes, her stringy gray hair matted beneath a linsey hood, the famed wise woman did not inspire confidence. Yet Lady Locke was far too desperate to be particular. She admitted Mad Meg, promising her much gold if she could halt the deadly course of Randle's illness.

When Meg saw Elena standing in the shadows, she stopped and peered closely at her. "Well, my treasure, you're too pretty by far for yon lad with his rotting lungs. Life, hot blood, excitement—that's what you crave."

Elena drew back from the old crone's reaching claw. "Are you a witch?" she asked, longing to flee, yet mesmerized by the compelling stare of those beady eyes.

"Some say so. Is young Randle Locke bewitched then?"

"I don't think so. He's always been sickly."

The old woman moved with surprising agility, her odorous garments wafting a mingled aroma of dirt, mildew and lavender. Elena was trapped against the wall.

"They say Locke men never make old bones. Perhaps you've heard that before."

The old woman took a handful of Elena's hair. Sniffing the perfumed blackness, she nodded in satisfaction. "Lucky you, girlie. Soon you'll get your heart's desire. But not inside these walls." When Elena tried to pull free, Meg admonished, "Nay, don't fear me. I'm no enemy of yours."

Elena was relieved when Meg finally lost interest in her and went inside Randle's chamber. She puzzled over Meg's prediction that her heart's desire was soon to be granted. Even she was not positive what actually constituted her heart's desire. Freedom, definitely—and the need to love and be loved.

"Elena, come inside and close the door," snapped Lady Locke. "Don't stand gaping like the village idiot."

Banging the door behind her, Elena ignored her mother-in-law's sharp glance of disapproval. She had no desire to attend her husband in his stuffy, stench-filled sickroom.

"Come, sit by me, wife," commanded Randle, sniffling piteously into his kerchief, for the wise woman terrified him.

"Surely I'll just be in the way."

"You're my wife. Your place is at my side," Randle said, his voice quivering in fear as he saw the curved knives and steel bodkins in the wise woman's basket.

Elena perched uncomfortably on the edge of the bed, waiting while Meg ground herbs in a mortar and pestle. After adding liquid from a vial, she mixed in white powder and pronounced the physic ready.

"No—it smells vile!" Randle protested, gripping Elena's hands until the bones cracked. "Taste it first, Elena."

"I'm not the one who's ill."

"Taste it," he shrieked. "Make sure it's not poison."

"Randle, sweet, 'tis only to make you well," cajoled his mother. "Take just a little."

"No!" Randle clamped his lips, mutely shaking his head. He turned aside when his mother raised the spoon.

Wearying of the charade, Elena finally offered, "If I taste it first, then will you drink some?"

Randle shook his head stubbornly. Then he smashed the bowl to the rushes.

"Oh, Randle, now see what you've done," Elena cried in exasperation, trying to salvage what was left of the medicine.

The wise woman watched, her bright eyes missing nothing. "Come, young master, just a few spoonfuls," she wheedled in a high-pitched voice. "One for the lungs, and one for the stomach, one for the head, and one for the heart."

"No. Begone, you old witch! I'm lord here. I give the orders."

"Randle, enough of this foolishness. Take the medicine or you'll have a thrashing."

Randle and Elena gasped in unison at Lady Locke's angry declaration. She stood grim faced, holding the last of the medicine clenched in her hand.

"Mother . . . even you turn against me," Randle whimpered, his resistance collapsing. His lower lip quivered. He could hardly believe she had issued the ultimatum. "Ever since Elena came it's been 'Randle, do this, Randle, do that. Get me a grandson, Randle.' Don't you understand, Mother, I can scarce sleep an hour without coughing up my guts? How can you be so cruel?"

"Do what your mother says, Randle." Elena intervened, having tired of the whining. "It's for your own good."

"You shut up! You shan't tell me what to do. We were happy until you came, weren't we, Mother? I thought you were going to be nice to me—instead you're hateful. You always . . . ugh . . . ugh . . ."

As his mouth widened in a great wail, Lady Locke deftly pushed the spoon between his lips, then clamped her bony hand over his mouth to keep him from retching.

"Elena, go to your room. You make matters worse."

"That's much to my liking, madam. I shall stay there the rest of the day."

Elena swept from the chamber, not waiting for Lady Locke to say more. The wise woman glanced up and held her gaze, nodding in reassurance, a smile curving her withered brown cheeks.

"You shall have your heart's desire," repeated the voice in Elena's head. "No," she muttered aloud as she wrenched open the door. What a relief to escape from that hot room where a fire blazed despite the summer's warmth, where the odor of sickness and unemptied chamberpots, of acrid medicines and unwashed linens, all served as reminders of that hated part of her life.

Elena entered her own cool chamber filled with the

fragrance of roses and lavender borne indoors by the breeze wafting through the open casement. Feeling terribly weary of what life offered inside these walls, she sank to her knees before the ivory crucifix. Bowing her head, she began by offering thanks for the blessed sanctity of this room. "Oh, Holy Mother, how much longer must I endure this terrible imprisonment? How much longer must I . . ."

Elena raised her head, her mouth set in determination. She was no mealymouthed weakling beseeching the heavens for aid at every step. She had endured this situation far too long, meekly accepting her lot like some holy martyr. No more! It was high time she set about changing her fate.

Quickly she seized her buckram-framed headdress and cast it on the rushes. She pulled off her purple brocade gown, struggling with the voluminous skirts and intricate lacing. Her lawn petticoats and boned bodice followed, until she was clad only in her shift. How light, how good it felt to stand nearly naked with the soft sweet breeze fanning her flesh. The removal of her embroidered gown and headdress was symbolic, for with it she cast aside her duty to her husband and his mother. In her shift she had repossessed her own identity, becoming Elena instead of Randle Locke's glorified handmaiden. And Elena had reached the limits of her tolerance. Today she was going to ride!

Elena pulled on her sapphire velvet riding habit, fastening the hooks as best she could; then, taking her blue buskins out of the cedarwood chest, she worked the supple leather over her slim feet and legs. Now her crop. Elena did not bother with a hat, or even a net, allowing her hair to curl loosely about her shoulders in a further act of defiance.

The clatter of heavy feet in the corridor outside

Randle's room announced the arrival of several men-servants. Likely they were going to hold him down to be bled. Soon bloodcurdling shrieks, which seemed to rattle the very doors, proved her guess correct. Elena could hardly wait to be free of this house.

She hurried outside through a small side door beside the buttery. Laughing servants stood about the ale barrel, discussing their young master. She had no difficulty in slipping past them undetected.

The stable was deserted on this warm afternoon. Loud whickers of pleasure met her, and she wished the animals were not so eager to see her lest they betray her presence. It was useless to try to shush Artan, who threw back his head and tossed his mane, letting out great bellows of delight at the sight of his mistress.

Elena slid her arms lovingly around his great muscled neck, hugging the hot smooth body, trying not to weep as she felt the horse reciprocate with tremors of joy. Whispering soothingly, she saddled him and deftly fastened his bridle.

Just as she was unlatching the stall, a huge hand closed over hers. Elena cried out in shock, raising her eyes to encounter a tousled fair head above a ruddy face blotched with freckles. The hand trapping hers was like a haunch of bacon.

"You're not allowed out alone."

"Today I intend to ride."

Hodge grinned as his hand stole to her shoulder. Shaking off his unwelcome caress, Elena stood her ground. The fear that had gripped her at first was gone; anger and sheer desperation to be free of this stifling house now commanded her reaction. When their gazes met, she saw a flicker of admiration in the undergroom's hazel eyes.

"And what if I says you're not?"

"But you won't . . . will you?" She smiled in an unconsciously disarming manner that came as naturally to her as breathing. "Please, let me have just one ride."

Hodge caught his breath and his heart raced. When he spoke, his voice sounded strangled. "What will you give me for it, then?"

Instantly her smile was gone. "I'll give you nothing. You do it merely to please me."

At this preposterous suggestion he laughed derisively, his confidence returned. "Hows about a kiss, Milady Spain? Surely that's not too much to pay for an afternoon ride?"

Elena considered his unwelcome proposal. Hodge's huge shoulders, massive forearms and hamhocks of hands barred her way. Behind her, Artan quivered with excitement; she could feel the vibration through the leather as he impatiently waited for the word. Together they might push this impertinent stablehand aside and force their way outside . . .

"A kiss is too much to ask."

Hodge's face fell. Elena's stomach pitched and her visions of freedom began to evaporate. Forcefully overcoming her physical revulsion for the young groom, she suggested, "I might consider a kiss ifyou promise to let me ride on other days as well."

With furrowed brow, Hodge considered his probable punishments for disobeying his mistress, none of which outweighed the temptation being dangled before him. This exotic creature was about to grant him a kiss. Locally it was said the Spanish piece was bewitched, and in truth her tawny eyes probed his very soul.

"Awright."

Steeling hereslf against the taste and smell of him, Elena raised her head, keeping her crop between them in case the groom attempted to take more liberties—a

kiss was sacrifice enough. His sweating face glowed
crimson with excitement as he grasped her back, trying
not to crush her delicate bones. Elena tilted her finely
shaped head. His hot, wet mouth fastened over hers,
and she held her breath, fighting the urge to gag.

The kiss bestowed, she swiftly stepped away, bringing
up her crop when his heavy hand casually brushed her
breast. "Don't be insolent. A kiss was our bargain,"
she reminded sharply. "Now get out of my way."

Hodge stared at her resentfully before he finally
lumbered aside. When he pulled open the gate, Artan
surged from the stall, tossing his great head and
switching his tail.

Not wanting further contact with the groom, Elena
used the stone mounting block in the shadow of the
building. Artan obligingly stood alongside to assist his
mistress. Hodge had held out his hands to help her, but
she tapped them aside with her crop, her dark eyebrows
raised in silent warning. And, still somewhat in awe
of her, he hesitated to press his advantage. The reward
he had already received went far beyond his wildest
imagination. He never noticed how she frantically
scrubbed her lips to erase the taste of his mouth.

Elena kept to the shadows of the buildings, wishing
Artan's excitement were not so great, for his great
hooves rang like church bells on the cobbles. The warm
breeze abuzz with bees and noisy with birdsong made
her feel tinglingly alive. Glancing back several times
to make sure Hodge was keeping his word, she was
delighted to find the stableyard deserted.

Joy speeded her blood, and her hands trembled at the
longed-for feel of leather against her palms. Dear God,
how she had ached for freedom. Her pace quickened,
and the scented breeze rushed past her, stirring her hair
and flapping her skirt against the chestnut's flanks as

they sped across the meadows toward open country. Twelve miles to the west lay Windland Farm. She could hardly wait to surprise Ronwen with this unexpected visit.

Chapter Four

Elena could have wept when she reached Windland Farm to find both master and mistress gone to Appleton Market.

She had galloped these last five miles in high spirits, eager to see Ronwen, aching for the sight of a familiar face. Too much time inside gloomy Locke Hall must have dulled her senses. Had she half a brain, she would have remembered today was market day, she thought in disgust as she turned Artan about for the homeward journey. When she had lived at Windland, she had looked forward to the monthly outing, eager to buy new ribbons and lace, to gorge herself on sweetmeats and admire the goods on the trademen's stalls.

Elena wondered if she should ride to Appleton, but she soon dismissed the idea. By the time she arrived, much of the excitement would be over. Besides, if Ronwen and Will chose the alternate route home, she would still miss them. Defiantly, Elena tossed her head, blinking back the annoying prickle of tears. Too many hours spent in Randle's company was turning her into a sniveling fool.

Lush meadows sprinkled with buttercups and daisies surrounded the old timbered farmhouse. A herd of black and white cows grazed contentedly in the fields, and a kestrel circled high in the cloudless sky. Homesickness beset Elena, and quickening her pace, she resolutely turned her back on Windland Farm.

Myriad shades of gray, yellow and bronze rippled as the summer wind sighed through ripe barley, corn and wheat fields. Blood red poppies grew amongst the corn. Early August marked the old Celtic season of harvest. Like many of Welsh descent, Will still observed the time-honored tradition. These fields would soon be stripped bare.

For the next mile Elena rode beneath tall elms bordering the narrow, sunken road, their bluish green foliage reaching to the sky. At the crossroad, she chose the way through the woods, following broad Lichborne Chase. Elena's spirits rose as she cantered along the silent trail with nothing but the insistent coo of wood pigeons to disturb the peace. In the dim green light beneath these gnarled trees, it seemed like an enchanted world. And, glory of glories, that mysterious place was not inhabited by sick boys or their doting mothers.

Straightening her shoulders, Elena laughed aloud out of sheer pleasure at finally being free, her laughter echoing back through the trees. Today the wise woman had told her she would be granted her heart's desire. This surely must be it, for lately she had pined to ride through the countryside, released, if only for a little while, from the burden of her odious marriage.

She heard the distant clop of hooves, and felt a pang of resentment that another rider should disturb her blessed solitude. When she finally rounded the bend in the road, that resentment turned to joy. Hardly able to believe her eyes, she blinked, thinking she must have manufactured the image to match her daydreams. Less than a hundred yards ahead rode four men. She could not mistake the distinctive set of his square shoulders, the proud carriage of his golden head.

"Don Luis," she shouted, her breathing so uneven she could hardly get out the words. At first she thought he had not heard, then she saw him rein in and turn about.

"Mistress Locke! Surely you aren't riding alone!"

The shock in his voice momentarily checked her enthusiasm. Somehow she had imagined his delight would match her own. But, of course, she alone inhabited that secret world where nothing mattered beyond the fulfillment of one's heart's desire. Elena's pulse quickened as the phrase jogged her memory. Could the wise woman have known the deepest secret of her soul?

"Has your husband met with another accident?"

Gathering her wits, Elena flashed a radiant smile as she reined in beside him. Luis de los Santos was regarding her gravely, the searching gaze of his compelling blue eyes alternately chilling and exciting.

"No, there's no accident. I'm riding alone. What a surprise to find you here. I thought you'd have gone to London. They say your prince desires his countrymen about him at all times."

He grinned. "My prince desires much that he's not granted on these shores, mistress. But riding alone—is that wise?"

"Probably not, but it's very wonderful."

"Then I'll not intrude on your solitude," he said stiffly, apparently reading into her words a message she had not intended.

"Oh, no, I'd enjoy your company," Elena blurted. "I meant . . . Well, no matter what I meant."

The smile suffusing his handsome face had the power to melt her heart. Elena swallowed, trying to quell the unexpected shudders that attacked her like the ague.

"Then, Mistress Locke, this afternoon will be made joyful by your presence," he said gallantly. "Later, you must help me find a place to sup."

Swiftly she agreed, giving no consideration to the wisdom of her action. From that moment on, Lichborne Forest was transformed into a wondrous, magical world of murky green light, twittering birds and fern-fronded bowers.

They ambled side by side along a leafy offshoot of the main chase. Though at first Elena found herself somewhat tongue-tied in Don Luis de los Santos's magnificent presence and he had to carry the conversation, she soon let all her unhappiness spill forth. This was not what she had intended to tell him, yet once she began, she seemed powerless to stop. The unburdening of her resentment and growing disgust lightened her body and sent her heart soaring.

Luis listened patiently, quick to offer sympathy, or advice, if he considered it of value. They were both aware there was little he could do to alter her situation.

When her story was told, Elena drew a deep, shuddering breath, shaking off the burden of the past. "Thank you for hearing me out, Luis. Now I'm a new woman."

He smiled as he reached out to flick a damp leaf from her hair. "What a pity—I liked the old Elena far more than is wise."

His soft, husky words recalled the intimacy of their previous meeting, wherein he had admired her body through her thin shift and had made no effort to conceal his interest. Now, like a fool, she was riding beside him in this lonely spot. Her cheeks flushed as her returning senses warned her of the danger of her action. If they were seen together in this secluded area, the very worst construction would be put on their meeting.

"Loneliness had made me witless," she said uncomfortably, glancing about at the silent trees. "What if we are seen?"

"Who's to see us but birds and foxes? Please, Elena, don't waste what can be a beautiful afternoon worrying about convention."

His voice was so persuasive, his blue eyes so softly lambent, her unease evaporated. Of course he was right. There was no one here to see except his own servants.

Presently Luis suggested they should find a picnic spot. Elena hesitated, knowing as long as she stayed in the saddle little harm would come to her. Each time he looked into her eyes, her legs trembled and her heart raced. There could be no clearer warning of her susceptibility to his charms. Furthermore, he had never made a secret of the fact that he found her attractive. She was insane to contemplate sitting beside him in the seclusion of this magical green forest.

Then the warmth of his hand penetrated her sleeve as he drew her attention to a mossy stretch beside a stream, and her last shred of sanity evaporated.

"Don't you think that would be a good spot?"

"Oh, yes, perfect," she cried in delight. After all, a picnic was hardly a seduction. Yet some primitive sense warned her that today they could be one and the same.

They led their horses down to the meandering stream to drink. Crystal clear water tumbled over a rocky bed, bubbling its way downstream. A hundred yellow stars of wood pimpernel dotted the mossy bank, while behind them lush ferns and spikes of pink and white foxglove blended into a bramble thicket festooned with fragrant honeysuckle.

"It's so lovely here, so romantic—a magic place,"

she cried in pleasure. Suddenly aware of her unwise choice of words, Elena feigned great interest in the wildflowers at her feet.

"Surely that's the highest recommendation you could offer. Wild horses wouldn't persuade me to sup elsewhere."

Luis beckoned to his servants to bring blankets and a wicker picnic basket. This done, the servants retreated a discreet distance beyond the bramble thicket to eat their own meal.

Flaky, golden venison pasties, black currant tarts with clotted cream, brown bread, earthenware crocks of fresh churned butter, huge golden plums and a flask of cold cider constituted their picnic fare. After spreading the food invitingly on the blanket, Luis waited on her. Elena sat with her legs drawn up modestly beneath her sapphire habit. Gurgling water and the rhythmic purr of wood pigeons were all that disturbed the tranquility of this place.

At last Luis remarked, "You're very quiet. Have I said something to offend?"

"Oh, no." Quickly Elena turned toward him, a shiver of pleasure shooting through her as she looked at his smooth, tanned throat exposed by the unbuttoned collar of his purple doublet. Again today, he wore a dark shade to highlight his fairness, the deep purple looking black in the green half-light. "It's only that I feel rather ill at ease after baring all the secrets of my soul."

He smiled understandingly and offered her a black currant tart. "You mustn't. Unhappy secrets only fester when locked inside the heart. Perhaps your situation will improve in time."

"But most likely it will not. Luis, would you think me very wicked if I told you I sometimes wish Randle were dead?"

"No—merely honest. Most of us have obligations in this life that are not of our choosing."

When she raised her eyes questioningly to his, puzzled by his somewhat bitter statement, he deliberately avoided her gaze.

"It's sacrilege to waste such beauty on a foolish boy. If he finally succumbs to his ailment, pray God, next time you'll be allowed someone of your own choosing."

They finished their meal in silence. When they were done, Luis returned all but the flask of cider to the hamper. His servants promptly materialized from the shrubbery to remove the basket.

Elena picked handfuls of delicate wood pimpernels and made a chain of golden flowers. When he saw what she did, Luis laughed, joining her in making a golden garland to drape around her shoulders. Growing more ambitious, he fashioned sprays of sweet honeysuckle into a crown. The soft green twilight beneath the trees made his eyes appear dark when he knelt before her to place the fragrant wreath on her flowing black hair.

"Now you are queen of the forest, Elena," he whispered, a bemused expression crossing his handsome face. He drew back to admire his handiwork. "*Dios*, you are so lovely. If I didn't know you were mortal, I'd swear you were some enchanted woodland creature," he breathed almost to himself.

Admiration shone so clearly in his face that Elena shuddered with pleasure. How much she longed for his kiss! He was so close, she had merely to stretch out her hand, to smile invitingly. She became possessed by a powerful emotion, as if another woman had taken possession of her body. She sought his hand in the soft, velvety moss, tenatively at first, then growing bolder, and finally taking his long slender fingers in hers. Luis wore several heavy rings, the stones gleaming against his suntanned skin. She looked down at his strong hand. Merely imagining his caress made her shudder.

As she hoped he would, Luis quickly responded, grasping her hand in his own. Elena's pulses began to race.

"Queen of the forest—surely you flatter me far too much," she protested breathlessly, capturing his intense gaze.

His sensuous mouth curving in a slow smile, Luis swept his free hand tantalizingly across her cheek, the feather-light touch igniting sparks of fire. "There's not enough flattery in all the world for that, little Elena."

A multitude of forbidden thoughts passed between them. He moved imperceptibly until she became aware of the heat of his leg pressing against her thigh. All Elena's senses were heightened by his nearness. She drank in the hot fragrance of his body and felt his warm breath against her brow as he whispered, "Would that I could change places with that useless boy for just one day . . . one hour."

Elena smiled, unconsciously raising her face to receive his kiss. They were so close that she saw her own reflection in his light blue eyes. She was momentarily surprised by the thickness of his lashes before her thoughts were swept away by a tumult of sensation as his lips pressed tenderly against hers, hot, fragrant, arousing. Elena was barely aware of his arm against her back as he drew her to his shoulder.

"My beautiful Elena, if only you were mine," Luis murmured ardently against her hair.

"Dreams sometimes come true," she whispered as she nestled closer. Deliriously, she drank in the intoxicating masculine scent of her body, losing herself in the magic of his embrace. Dear God, she prayed fervently, may this wonder never end.

Suddenly, one of his servants appeared through the bushes. Luis gripped Elena's shoulder to prevent her from pulling away from him. Curtly ordering the man home, he said he would follow later.

The servant bowed and backed away.

Elena swallowed hard. Now an element of fear mingled with her delight. Though the command had been given in Spanish, she understood Luis had sent his servants away. There was no need for him to do that unless . . .

She stirred in his embrace, knowing if she did not make the effort now, all would be lost. "Luis, we mustn't stay here like this," she protested, her voice tight.

"Why? I find it most delightful."

"You know why."

The lazy smile that met her words set her heart racing. Yes, he knew—in fact things were progressing exactly as he intended. Her stomach pitched in a fresh surge of unease. She had to stop him now before it was too late. She was Randle's wife. Even her kisses were forbidden to this man.

"I love you, Elena."

His husky words were music to her ears. How she longed to slip her arms about his hard shoulders, to draw his body close to hers and feel the beating of his heart.

"You know there can be no love between us," she protested feebly, salving her conscience by at least making the effort.

"It's there already."

"Oh, no . . . Luis, please."

"Hush, *querida*, I know you want me to kiss you again."

She longed to refute those confident words, but her emotions swept away all protest, until suddenly she was

drowning in overwhelming passion. She longed to stay
forever in his arms, to be granted the privilege of kissing
his arousing mouth . . .

"If you truly want me to stop, I will," he offered
at length. "We can go back."

Tormenter! She smiled languidly as she touched his
hot smooth brow and traced her finger down his high-
bridged nose, over his mustache to those tantalizing lips
that lured her to the brink of damnation.

"Yes," she agreed, without making any move to
break his embrace. "We must go back."

"It's the right thing to do."

"Someone might come."

"Oh, Elena, love me, love me."

Again the husky urgency in his voice struck a re-
sponsive chord that led to all the secret places of her
body. Elena ached to love him and be loved by him.
That was the greatest desire of her heart. Gasping in
shock, she drew slightly away from him.

"This is what she meant!"

"What who meant?" he asked, slipping his hand
under her mane of hair to caress the sensitive nape of
her neck.

"A wisewoman told me I'd soon be given my heart's
desire."

At her words his mouth tensed, the light of desire
deepening in his blue eyes.

Fool! She had just unwittingly destroyed herself.
Elena swallowed uneasily, knowing she must move
from him before it was too late. Instead, she sought
again his hot firm mouth; his kisses only made her long
for more. Pressing close to him, the rhythmic thud of
his heart music to her ears, Elena traced the tip of her
tongue along the vee made by the neck of his unfastened
doublet, tasting his salty and fragrant flesh.

Luis swept the honeysuckle crown from her head. Burying his hands in her silken tresses, he drew her face to his. His passionate kisses burned over her closed lids, her nose, her cheeks; he pressed his hot mouth beneath her hair to the nape of her neck, then moved to the wildly beating pulses in her throat.

"Elena, you don't know how much I love you. Since first I set eyes on you, I knew we were meant for each other. I've never felt this way about a woman before."

His impassioned words both thrilled and frightened her. Only in her wildest dreams had she imagined him voicing such sentiments. And in that unreal world she could give herself to him without fear of the consequences. Reality, however, was a far harsher master.

"Luis, do you really love me?"

"Yes . . . yes, I swear it."

He devoured her mouth with burning kisses. Though he remained tender, a subtle change came over him, bringing a new urgency to his caresses. Instinct warned Elena she was minutes away from possession. Seized by a wave of panic, she struggled in his arms, forcing her mouth from his. The refusal that she had intended to make died on her lips as her treacherous tongue betrayed her.

"Oh, Luis, darling, how I've longed to hear you say that. Sometimes at night I dreamt we kissed . . . that you held me close. I also knew from the beginning . . . oh, sweetheart . . ."

Joyously, he silenced her faltering voice with his eager mouth. Rolling her to her back, he pressed her into the spongy moss, fitting every inch of his muscular frame against hers. Elena shuddered in delight at the pressure cutting into her soft flesh, straining to meet the throbbing emotion that pulsed hotly through his virile body.

Delicious shock overcame her when, through her sapphire velvet bodice, he captured her hardened nipple in his mouth. The burning sensation robbed her of breath. Just when she thought she could not endure another second of painful pleasure, his mouth moved upward. Their lips met in a rapturous kiss. Her eager response was as passionate as any man could wish. Instinctively, Elena arched her shapely body toward his, unconsciously tempting him to fondle the voluptuous swell of her breasts.

With a strangled gasp, Luis eagerly obeyed her unspoken command. Arrows of fire sped through her veins as his hands moved lovingly over her full breasts. Luis trembled with suppressed passion as he felt her flesh respond eagerly to his touch. Elena did not help him unfasten her habit, but he negotiated the hooks with ease. If she had found his initial caresses electrifying, the meeting of bare flesh made her nearly swoon with delight as he cupped her breasts lovingly in his tender hands.

The fire in his eyes quickly ignited her blood. Heightening passion throbbed through her veins as she gave into his desires. Though Elena had suspected Luis might try to seduce her, she had not anticipated her own joyous response to his advances. She had not thought herself capable of such heat.

They kissed deeply. He reached beneath her skirts to lovingly acquaint himself with her smooth, rounded thighs and the curving globes of her buttocks. Now his mouth captured her nipples in turn, drawing them out until tears of delight pricked her eyes. It was as if every nerve in her body was connected. Elena felt the heat from his body shoot between her legs until she burned with fierce longing.

"Let me take you, Elena. Say yes. Oh I need you so."

"Yes, yes," she whispered huskily against his tantalizing mouth, half delirious with passion. This wonderful sensation was like nothing she had ever experienced before, so beautiful and painful that she wanted to weep.

Luis pressed her hand against the swelling inside his velvet breeches. Elena gasped as she touched his pulsing brand. When she tried to draw back from the searing discovery, he would not let her, urging her instead to caress him. She was astonished that her touch gave him such delight. With shaking fingers, he quickly unlaced his clothing, spilling forth the hot, smooth wonder of his flesh. The unexpected intimacy of his action made Elena gasp in surprise. Tentatively, she explored the length and breadth of that fiery brand, marvelling at its strength and fullness. The sheer pulsing life of his fully aroused flesh leaping beneath her touch was magnificent, yet intimidating. Though she had no wish for Randle's memory to intrude on their lovemaking, Elena could not help comparing his pathetic manhood to Luis's throbbing virility.

Aware that she might be afraid of him, Luis stroked her neck, gently kissing her face as he assured her he would try to be gentle. Because she had not actually told him she was still virgin, Elena was further surprised to find he had already guessed.

Eyes gleaming with moisture, she gazed up at him with sheerest love, excited yet fearful of the outcome of their terrible passion. Every time she shook beneath his hands, Luis became even more aroused. Her body also craved fulfillment, seeking the unknown delight she had never found in her marriage bed. Desire, love, passion, all became the same beneath the expert touch of this handsome Spaniard.

Luis positioned her on the moss. This time there was no struggle to part her thighs, for they opened to him eagerly of their own accord. Yet when he finally thrust, gentle but insistent, Elena drew back from the demands of his hot flesh. Luis held her tight while he kissed her and tried to soothe her fears.

"No, *querida*, you mustn't be afraid. Let me love you as you've never dreamed love could be. There will be pleasure for you, too."

"Oh, Luis, darling, I love you and I want you to make love to me . . . but I'm afraid."

He continued to stroke and reassure her, lulling her fear with mounting pleasure. Gauging her response, he made that final thrust. Luis penetrated her in a burst of hot, sharp pain, which was gradually transformed into flooding heat as he slowly invaded the depth of the passion-sweet chamber between her legs.

Elena did not know whether to weep or gasp with delight, so overwhelmed was she by the sensations his questing body roused. Luis seemed so big, he threatened to split her asunder. Yet she discovered if she relaxed, allowing him to go deeper, the intense pleasure made her forget her pain. Sinking her hands in his thick gold hair, she shuddered repeatedly, not knowing what to expect next as he filled her body with fire. Elena gasped at the building pressure in her abdomen. Fiery, swirling delight seized her loins as the heated pleasure inside her expanded until she was afraid she could no longer contain it. Rhythmically Luis moved back and forth, still kissing, stroking, whispering endearments as he gently coaxed the utmost response from her virgin body.

Weeping in the depth of her emotion, Elena finally abandoned all conscious effort to control her pleasure, allowing herself to be swept away on a soaring tide of passion. Instinctively, Luis quickened his movements, almost as if he knew the exact point of her arousal. Finally he plunged to the hilt in the welcoming sheath of her body, swelling until he finally burst, hot and sweet, inside her.

Elena fought for breath as if she were drowning, unable to control the shuddering climax that possessed her. Fear of the unknown, delight over her wondrous discovery, bright lights and comforting velvet blackness followed in its wake.

Clinging to Luis, her tears stinging his lips, she shuddered and sobbed quietly in the devastating aftermath of their passion, before allowing herself to drift on a sea of contentment. For a long time she lay quietly in his arms, still impaled by the searing length of his flesh. When Luis finally withdrew, he did not abandon her, but held her close, whispering endearments and cherishing her in the lonely aftermath of surrender.

When Elena finally opened her tawny eyes, crystal teardrops quivering on her thick lashes, she whispered, "Oh, Luis, darling, why didn't you tell me making love was so devastating?"

He smiled, his clear blue eyes soft with love. Gently tracing her bruised mouth with his forefinger, he whispered, "I told you we were meant for each other."

"You did. And I never doubted your word."

They exchanged statisfied smiles, basking in the wonder of their mutual love. Finally, Luis started to move from her, but Elena seized him, her little hands biting into his fine purple doublet.

"Promise to love me forever."

"I promise, wherever I go, my heart will stay here with you," he vowed softly. Lifting the hair off her white brow, he placed a soft kiss there before allowing his tongue and passion-soft mouth to follow the curve of her cheek until his face rested in the fragrant hollow of her neck. "When can we meet again? My impatience will torment me—oh come, *querida*, be not so cruel. Name the day, the time."

She smiled, bemused by the urgency in his voice. Chill reality gradually invaded her satisfied body. Hateful pictures of a furious Lady Locke and a whining Randle stole some of her pleasure.

"Oh, Luis, darling, it might be days before I can get away to see you."

"How many days?"

"I don't know. Maybe next week—I'll try to slip away then."

"I'll send you word—or better yet, you send me word."

"No! I can't. The servants are loyal to my husband's family."

He frowned, sensing her unwanted withdrawal. "You say you have your own chamber—I'll throw pebbles at the window. Leave the catch open and I—"

"No! They keep watchdogs—you mustn't." Horrified by his bold suggestion, Elena visualized all manner of tragedy should Luis be discovered inside the grounds. "Perhaps it would be wisest for us to meet here."

He said nothing as he rearranged his clothing and refastened his points. Elena knew her suggestion had not pleased him. How she ached to call Luis her own. She grew weak with deepest love for him, yet society would consider love a poor excuse for behaving like a penny drab with this handsome Spaniard. The pulsing excitement she had known in Luis's arms in the magic twilight of Lichborne Forest must remain her secret.

Seeing his scowl, she drew him to her.

"Don't look so fierce. I swear I love you more passionately than any other woman could ever do. For now, Luis de los Santos, you must content yourself with that. In all honesty I can promise you no more."

Her sincere words finally coaxed a smile from him.

"You make me both the happiest and the saddest of men with the same breath. So be it, you temptress, you give me little choice but to abide by your rules. Each day I'll ride at the same hour. If you can steal away, we shall meet here. Pray God I won't have to wait long. Long distance love can quickly chill the blood."

In mock annoyance she swung at him, though his words caused her a quiver of alarm. Had it been his way of saying he would not wait forever?

Laughing, Luis seized her hands to cover with kisses. They finally found their way to the mossy ground where they lay in each other's arms, his eager mouth passionately seeking hers. For some time they stayed wrapped in bliss until the growing chill in the air reminded them both of the lateness of the hour.

After exchanging a final lingering kiss, they reluctantly broke their embrace.

"I must go back. It's so late, I might already have been missed."

"There'll be trouble if you're gone too long," he agreed, taking her hand to draw her to her feet.

Luis lifted Elena to the saddle, his hands lingering on her small waist. Had it been possible, he would have kept her with him, but the unpleasant reminder that she was another man's wife made him turn away.

Their return journey through the darkening forest, noisy with the twitter of homebound birds, made Elena sad. With every clop of the hooves, a little more of her magical world dissolved. And, though she fiercely fought against the idea, she could not help wondering if they would ever see each other again.

Luis and Elena parted on the main chase, clinging to each other while they exchanged kisses and soft words of love. Elena turned for a final glimpse of him, seeing only a blur through her tears.

Once she was clear of the forest, Elena quickened her pace, alarmed to find the long summer twilight far advanced. In the distance, cattle lowed and laggard birds noisily sought their nests. The sky was a milky turquoise, and a ghost moon rode high above the forest. Black and purple shadows stretched lengthening fingers over the lawns, shrouding Locke Hall in gray. Candlelight shining through the mullioned windows looked like giant fireflies in the gloom.

To her relief, the stable yard was deserted, and Elena returned Artan to his stall without being noticed. He should have been rubbed down after his gallop, yet she dared not linger. Picking her way through the gathering shadows, she reentered the house through the unlocked door off the buttery. The servants chattered in the kitchen, and the clang of pots and pans masked her steps as she raced upstairs.

Hardly able to believe her good fortune, Elena entered her chamber without being detected. The murmur of voices from the adjoining room revealed that Randle was still awake.

A few minutes later, when she answered a rap on her door, Elena's stomach pitched as she realized such luck had indeed been too good to be true. Lady Locke stood on the threshold, her long face tight with anger.

"Ah, so you're back. We've unfinished business to discuss."

Lady Locke marched into the room, banging the door behind her. The candle she carried shed an eerie light over Elena's face.

Though Elena's first inclination had been to pretend she knew not what business lay between them, one glance at her mother-in-law's stormy face told her such pretense was useless.

"I'm not your prisoner," she declared sharply.

"So, you're not even going to deny it!" Lady Locke was temporarily at a loss for words. She had been expecting vehement denials, to which she would have reacted by bringing forth that wretched Hodge. "You knew you were denied permission to ride and you disobeyed my orders," she spat, her jaw tense.

"My horse grows fat without exercise."

"The grooms can exercise the beast. Your place is beside Randle. I've forbidden you to venture abroad for very good reason. Where in God's name did you go, gallivanting about the countryside without attendants like a slattern?"

Calmly, Elena faced her mother-in-law, though her heart hammered uneasily, "I rode to Windland only to find my family had gone to market."

"That took seven hours?"

"I rode through the countryside as I was wont to do before my marriage. There was no harm in it. When I finally noticed how low the sun had sunk—"

"Damn you, wench, you'd best be telling the truth!" Lady Locke grasped Elena's wrist, fully aware she bruised the delicate skin. Her anger increased when she realized her daughter-in-law was too proud to flinch. There was no effective way to deal with such damnable pride. Yet the trait was not wholly without commendation. In fact, Elena's fierce pride earned her grudging admiration.

"If you doubt my word you can question my brother's servants."

"Nay, let it pass." Lady Locke released Elena's

wrist. "Never disobey me again, do you understand, wench? Randle's been calling for you this past hour."

Elena gulped. So Randle was to blame for her being caught. The discovery made her dislike him even more. "I don't know why—surely you serve his needs far better than I."

"Not all of them. Damn it, wench, he's sickly, but he's still a man. Go to him now."

With great reluctance, Elena followed her mother-in-law. The sickroom stank of vomit and the vile medicines with which her husband was being treated. Randle lay propped against his pillows, white faced, yet, to her surprise, he appeared unusually alert.

"Where have you been, wife?" he demanded squeakily, his voice cracking on the question.

Elena scowled. "I told you I'd find a way to ride."

Lady Locke discreetly slipped from the room, closing the door behind her. For once, Elena wished she had stayed.

"I needed you and you weren't here," Randle complained.

"You had the wisewoman, your mother and all the servants to attend you. What need had you of me?"

Smiling secretively, he beckoned her closer. "There's something I want to show you."

Elena took a couple of steps toward the bed. Only this morning they had bled him. Surely he was not strong enough to launch another abortive attack on her virginity—her heart lurched at the realization she was virgin no longer. "Aren't you too ill to contemplate . . . that?" she asked, not misinterpreting the leer that curved his mouth.

Randle threw aside the covers. "See!" he crowed triumphantly. "Soon we shall truly be man and wife."

Thick bandages smeared with yellow ointment

swathed his member. Elena glanced up in surprise. "I don't understand."

"When the salve's worked its magic and the wound heals, we'll be able to get a babe. Isn't that wonderful news?"

She nodded, looking closely at his flushed face. Twin spots of color blazed on his gaunt cheekbones, and his eyes glowed feverishly. Though his spirits were much improved, the fever was still with him.

"The wisewoman has had some experience with such matters. And she's sworn to secrecy. Are you not pleased?"

"Delighted," she agreed without emotion.

"Come, lie beside me until I go to sleep. The wisewoman's medicine has worked miracles. Already I feel stronger. And she promised I'd be in the saddle in less than a week."

Elena lay stiffly on the feather bed while Randle settled down to sleep. The wisewoman must have worked a miracle—he was a different person. Though she did not enjoy his childish outbursts, she enjoyed his lovemaking even less. Now that she belonged to Luis, the very thought of being touched intimately by another man disgusted her.

Elena lay in the darkening room, listening to a nightjar in the trees. Randle's labored breathing receded into the background as she relived this afternoon, the wonder of Luis's lovemaking filling her thoughts. Her heart lurched with love when she pictured his handsome face and virile body. The thrill of his kisses was still a source of wonder. Now at last she knew how it was to make love. It had been nothing like she had imagined. Though her body ached and she had begun to feel bruised between her legs, she was still possessed by the heavy languorous feeling of passion.

Chapter Five

For the next few weeks, all Elena's efforts to slip away to meet Luis were thwarted. The grooms, not anxious for further punishment, conscientiously followed Lady Locke's orders by mounting a twenty-four hour watch on the stables.

The entire household rejoiced and offered prayers of thanksgiving for the master's miraculous recovery. At the height of this rejoicing, there came an ominous new development. When Barton was combing his master's lank hair, several huge clumps came away in the comb.

"You damned fool, would you make me bald!" Randle shrieked hysterically. Seizing the polished steel mirror, he peered into its dim surface. To his horror, he saw a great bald patch. His ensuing wails brought his mother and a dozen servants racing to his aid.

That night Randle's fingernails began to turn black. And when he dried his hands, two nails came away on the towel. By morning, both his hands and feet were grotesquely swollen.

Randle had been ingesting large quantities of Mad Meg's remedy, the carefully guarded recipe given to a maid who had faithfully followed instructions. At first, no one suspected the wisewoman's cure was the cause of these alarming symptoms. In fact, so desperate did Randle's mother become, she tripled the medicine's dosage in hope of curing him.

Though Elena was relieved to have escaped her husband's unwanted lovemaking, she was shocked by the change in him. Randle lay staring shortsightedly at the windows, where sunlight filtering through the horn panes cast greenish banners across the rushes.

"She lied to me, Elena. She said I'd be able to ride. Now I'm worse than ever," Randle complained, examining his nailless hands on the covers, fat and dark as sausages.

"We all thought you were getting better," Elena comforted wearily. "Remember how well you felt?"

"Now I just puke and swell up," he complained, turning away. "Leave me alone. I'm tired. I want to sleep."

The following day, after Randle had scratched his feeble signature on some documents bequeathing land to the church, the elderly priest drew Lady Locke aside. Elena could not hear their muttered conversation for they kept their voices low, not wanting to wake Randle.

Lady Locke led the way downstairs. At the foot of the stair, they paused, and Elena heard the priest suggest he give Extreme Unction to Randle.

"By the Christ, you'll do no such thing!" cried Lady Locke, her face purpling. "He's going to recover, I tell you. Nay, Father, when we've need of the church's final rites, we'll send for you."

Bowing his head, the priest bade them good-bye.

"Damned papist, I should've known better than to have him in the house," Magdalen Locke muttered as she watched the dark-robed priest walking down the drive.

"It might be wise. There seems little hope of Randle's

recovery.''

Like a whirlwind Magdalen Locke rounded on Elena, her amber skirts swishing angrily. ''Don't ever let me hear you say that again,'' she cried, seething with rage. ''Any day now he'll be out of bed.''

Holding her steady gaze, Elena slowly shook her head. ''We both know he'll never leave his bed.''

Elena received a stinging slap across the cheek for her honesty. Taken completely by surprise, her initial reaction was to retaliate, yet mindful that she still lived under the other woman's roof, she held her anger in check. ''If you want me, Madam, I'll be in my room,'' she ground out, leaving Lady Locke alone to curse the cruelty of fate.

The next week passed without much change in Randle's condition. By now Elena, also, had begun to feel ill. Several times after eating highly spiced dishes, she had barely reached the privy in time to vomit. And the smell of her husband's sickroom, never pleasant, was becoming unbearable. The first whiff of that distinctive odor made her retch.

A sudden wave of nausea gripped Elena, and she leaned her sweat-beaded brow against the cold window till the feeling passed. Surely to God she had not contracted Randle's terrible ailment! Then a second chilling thought came to her—could she be with child? Dear God, was that the reason? Cold sweat prickled on her upper lip as she counted the weeks since her last woman's time. She had not had her monthly courses since her marriage. What irony that the babe for which her mother-in-law longed grew in her womb, fathered not by puny Randle, but by the Spaniard who had stolen her heart.

Fear and excitement mingled in Elena's veins. Eyes

filled with tears of wonder, she placed her hands on her abdomen. It was far too soon to feel life. Still, there seemed to be a new hardness present and her breasts were tender.

Elena began to grow desperate to see Luis and tell him what she suspected. Yet here she sat, bound by invisible chains to her dying husband's bed. Ill though he was, Randle took perverse delight in keeping her at his side through the waning summer. Aware of her longing to be outdoors, he decided with typical selfishness that if he could not leave his chamber, then neither would she.

Sometimes Randle pleaded for Elena to sing and play for him. While she sang sweet love songs and softly plucked her lute, she hugged the wonderful secret of her baby to herself. She pictured Luis riding along Lichborne Chase, looking in vain for her. Surely he would guess why she had not been able to come to him, for word of Locke Hall's dying master had spread throughout the countryside.

Mercifully, one quiet September evening when the haziness of the changing season enveloped the woods, Randle died. When Elena pulled up his bed covers before retiring to her own chamber, she found the rattling breathing to which she had grown accustomed was stilled. She gripped the bedpost till her knuckles whitened, stunned by the discovery. She was no longer Randle's wife—tonight she had become his widow! Overwhelming joy at having gained her longed-for freedom possessed her. That joy, however, was tinged with pity for Randle's wasted life, for the pain and suffering of his final days. She wondered if she should send for his mother, but decided it would be kinder to let Magdalen Locke make that terrible discovery for herself.

Sometime around dawn, Elena heard a horrified cry, its stridency penetrating her closed door. And she knew Lady Locke had finally been made to accept the truth.

Immediately following Randle's funeral, Magdalen Locke sank into a stupor of grief. For days she shut herself in her chamber, refusing to see anyone. When she finally emerged, bitterer, older, she declared a year of mourning during which time she would not leave the house nor entertain company.

Though it had not been stated, Elena supposed she, too, would be expected to observe this sentence. She had no intention of complying but, for propriety's sake, she decided it would be wise to observe a short mourning period. So queasy had she felt of late, it would be no hardship to forgo social events.

Elena was sure news of Randle's death must have reached Luis. Now that her husband was dead, there was no longer any barrier to their meeting. The manor house would seem like purgatory until she was in his arms again.

The two women coexisted in the gloomy house, the windows draped to indicate mourning. Lady Locke's nonstop recitation of Randle's virtues sorely tried Elena's patience. She had sympathized when, overcome with grief, her distraught mother-in-law wandered distractedly through the house. But Magdalen Locke's creation of Randle as saint was far harder to stomach.

With the passage of time Lady Locke's sorrow underwent a drastic change. She lashed out at whomever was convenient—Elena often being the unfortunate victim. Angered by the injustice of these unprovoked attacks, yet mindful of the older woman's shattering loss, Elena attempted to show tolerance.

One rainy September afternoon they were sitting

before the fire, embroidering a set of bed hangings. In an effort to please her mother-in-law, Elena suggested they share the task, aware these hangings had been intended for Randle's first wedding anniversary.

"Since the day you entered this house, Elena, we've never come close to friendship."

"Perhaps we understand each other too well for that," Elena ventured while she concentrated on her stitching. "Now that we alone share this house, can we not at least become better acquainted?"

"I need time. First I must try to forget it was you who killed my child."

"Me!" Elena jumped up, spilling the linen to the rushes. "How can you accuse me of that? Randle was ill long before we met."

"You robbed him of the last of his strength in the bedchamber. You should have refused him oftener."

"That's a novel suggestion from one who urged me to his bed at every opportunity," Elena reminded her through gritted teeth.

"Always the dutiful son, my lamb knew how much I wanted a grandchild. He sent himself to his grave trying to please me. Had he stayed unmarried, he might have lived to old age."

Elena seethed, longing to reveal the truth. Angry words formed on her lips, threatening to spill forth until she bit them back, remembering the babe in her womb. If she kept silent, the child would be accepted as Randle's posthumous heir. Far better the babe become Lord Locke than to divulge his true parentage. Though Luis gladly promised his heart, he might not as willingly give their child his name.

"Our name's dead now. His sacrifice was for naught. Had there been a babe, things would be different," Lady Locke said, her needle idle as she stared into the fire.

Then, turning spiteful, she snapped, " 'Tis likely you're barren stock for all your voluptuousness."

Elena gritted her teeth, battling her dislike of this aging woman whose tongue was sharp as a viper's sting.

"Perhaps I can cheer your heart, madam."

"Nothing can cheer my heart—it's broken beyond repair."

Making a supreme effort, Elena laid her hand on Magdalen Locke's bony shoulder, half expecting to be repulsed.

"According to Randle's will, I, and the heirs of my body, inherit Locke Hall. In view of that, could we not endure each other with a kinder spirit, madam?"

"Endurance, aye, perchance that's a happier choice of words than friendship. I'll endure you, daughter, as gladly as you endure me."

They looked closely at each other in the firelight. Elena was moved to compassion by the stark pain in the other woman's gray eyes. So low in spirits was Magdalen Locke that when Elena took her hand she did not pull away.

"Madam, your name won't die. I'm with child."

For the first and only time Elena saw a smile of sheer delight cross the other's gaunt face.

"By all the saints! Are you sure? A grandchild! The blessing for which I've prayed."

Elena smiled happily, her lovely face guileless.

"We'll call him Randle," said Magdalen Locke.

Within hours, Elena regretted divulging her secret. Lady Locke's melancholy lifted at the prospect of a grandchild, yet, to Elena's disappointment, her life was bound by increased restriction instead of new freedom. Lady Locke arranged every day like a general following a plan of battle. Not only was Elena forbidden to ride, now she was forced to alternate exercise periods with rest in a darkened room. This regimen was enforced by the servants, who had been drilled to safeguard their dead master's precious heir. Even reading was forbidden to her, for fear of tainting the unborn child's mind. All appeals for leniency fell on deaf ears. It was like a bad dream come true.

So restricted a life was punishment enough without Lady Locke's constant chat about the splendid deeds her grandson would one day perform. What "he" would look like constituted a vast portion of the conversation. Naturally, he would be the image of dearest Randle.

Tearful and generally out of sorts during these early months of pregnancy, Elena thought she would go insane if she had to endure the torment of the next seven months.

Signs of the coming autumn became daily apparent in the woods where, until mid-morning, the yellow-tinged trees lay enveloped in mist. Elena watched the changing season from her window, filled with the acute longing of a prisoner for freedom. Already, she had rebelliously exercised at times other than had been specified, earning even stricter surveillance for her defiance.

As she watched the mellow September sun burning off the dank mist, she found she could no longer endure the smothering confines of these walls. Seizing her cloak, Elena wrapped it about her shoulders and marched outside into the chill corridor. The maid who was supposed to watch her was flirting with a footman on the back stair, so Elena was able to move unrestricted through the silent house.

There was no use in her going to the stables for Artan. The head groom would bodily return her to her keeper. So instead, Elena set out on foot for the untamed woods edging Locke Hall's spreading acres. Here, creamy meadowsweet edged the fields and crimson sorrel brightened the autumn colors. Roadside brambles were heavy with ripe fruit, over which flocks of blackbirds squabbled.

Sighing with pleasure, Elena filled her lungs with crisp air tinged with that unmistakable autumn fragrance of woodsmoke and decaying vegetation. Suddenly, to her right, a rider emerged from the trees. Heart thumping, she quickened her pace, convinced he was Luis.

As the man drew closer, Elena was disappointed to discover a squat form wrapped in dun brown worsted. Then her spirits soared. It was Will!

"Stop, you oaf, 'tis me," Elena shouted as she raced toward him.

Startled by her unexpected appearance, Will's horse shied. Her half brother kept his seat. Good-naturedly, he hailed her. "What do you mean by coming from nowhere like that—see how you've startled Gelert. Come on, get up behind me, you wretch. We'll ride back together."

Elena happily scrambled up behind him, overcome by a burst of emotion. Clutching Will's substantial body, she gave him a great hug before she rested her head against his broad shoulder, fighting tears of joy. They chatted while they jogged along the path to Locke Hall. Elena had not seen a member of her family since Randle's funeral. Visiting Windland was forbidden. Lady Locke was afraid Will and Ronwen's uncouth country manners might adversely influence the unborn child. As yet, Will did not know about the babe, and Elena kept her secret to herself.

"You never came to visit on your birthday like you promised," Elena chastised. "To what honor do I owe this visit?''

''You'd best learn to curb that sharp tongue before Lady Locke finds out you're not all milk and honey.''

''It's much too late— she knows already,'' Elena admitted, pulling a face. ''Now, tell me what brings you here.''

''News the like of which you've never heard,'' Will answered mysteriously. Turning about, he winked at her. ''And whilst we're asking questions, why don't you visit us?''

''Oh, Will, I'm kept a virtual prisoner! You wouldn't believe the misery I'm forced to endure. I could clout you for arranging so bleak a future for me.''

''Bleak future—owner of Locke Hall? I'll be damned if I'd call that bleak.''

''That's because you don't have to live there with Lady Locke.''

To their surprise, it was Lady Locke herself who greeted them when they dismounted. Seeing that Elena was not alone, she forced a smile, though her eyes remained steely.

''Isn't it wonderful—Will's come to visit me?'' Elena cried in joy, anxious to forestall any arguments. ''May we please have refreshments in the blue room?''

Wrestling with her ill humor, Lady Locke forced a stiff smile and agreed to send a servant with wine and cakes.

Elena shooed Will inside her favorite room over-looking the south lawn, a small, blue-curtained drawing room which was bathed in light for much of the day. Huge vases of late-season flowers perfumed the air. Elena seated herself at the padded blue window seat, eager for her brother's great news. Before she was able to learn Will's secret, a servant arrived carrying a tray bearing a flagon of honey mead, two goblets, a platter of sliced mutton and a dish of rice cakes.

Will's eyes brightened at the sight of food, and he set to with gusto. Always a trencherman, Will was especially hungry when he was not footing the bill. He filled his goblet with wine, belatedly offering a goblet to Elena. Only two rice cakes remained, and he sheepishly held them out to her.

"Now that you've gorged yourself and drunk your fill, are you going to tell me your wonderful news?" she finally asked.

Smiling in satisfaction, Will dabbed crumbs from his scraggly brown mustache. He belched. "News . . . oh, it's not of much import, sister," he began teasingly, enjoying her ill-concealed impatience. "It's just that our prayers have finally been answered—Queen Mary's ordered you to court!"

"Court!" she gasped, clenching her hands till her fingers ached. "She's really sent for me?"

"Aye, do you doubt my word? Here it is, writ by her secretary and signed by her own hand."

The parchment crackled as he thrust it under Elena's nose. So excited was she that the Queen had finally recognized her petition that the letter's contents eluded her. The bold black signature, Mary R., was all she needed to see.

"Oh, Will . . . I don't know what to say."

" 'Yes' will suit well enough."

They exchanged smiles.

"When must I attend her?"

"No specified date, but as one never knows when a Tudor's likely to have a change of mind, you'd best leave on the morrow."

Then Elena remembered the tiny life growing in her womb. Clutching her abdomen, she looked wide-eyed at her brother.

"Don't gawk at me like some moonstruck jade. I know it's short notice, but the old lady will fall over herself to help you pack. She'd likely carry you there for a chance at Mary's court. Now, dress fine—'tis high time you shucked those rags."

"Will, listen to me. There's something—"

But Will went on, ignoring her protests. "Make yourself beautiful. Mary wants laughter, pretty faces, fine clothes—those things cheer a monarch. Well, what is it?"

"You won't stop talking long enough for me to say," she cried, seizing his hands in excitement. "Oh, I wish Ronwen were here. Will, I'm carrying a babe!"

"What!" Will staggered back a few steps, his face a study of disbelief. "Tell me you jest! By all the saints, you jest . . . don't you?"

"Would I jest about something as serious as that?" Elena was taken back by his attitude, having expected surprise, not total shock.

"No, sister, I suppose not."

"You don't sound overjoyed to learn you're to be an uncle."

"Oh, yes—I'm pleased. It's just a shock. You must understand, I was expecting you to be at court within the week."

"Surely you can see I can't travel till after the babe's birth. Mary will understand. They say she's compassionate. Don't worry, she won't change her mind because of this."

"Hopefully not," Will mumbled, pouring the last of the mead.

There was a strained silence. Possible reasons for her brother's strange reaction flitted through Elena's mind before her suspicions finally crystallized into one unpleasant answer. "Granted, my news was a surprise, but there's more to this than meets the eyes.'' Will kept his eyes downcast while she spoke. ''Assuming me to be a rich, eligible widow, and knowing you like I do—surely to God you're not already matchmaking!''

He turned to her, denial on his lips, before sheepishly glancing away. His expression betrayed him. Astutely, she had hit on the very reason for his displeasure.

''Damn it, Will, am I a prize filly to be sold to the highest bidder?'' she demanded angrily. Seizing his arm, she turned him about. ''Tell me what arrangements have been made.''

Will wanted to deny her accusation, but she knew him too well to believe a lie. Gruffly he shook off her detaining hand.

''You can rest assured that whatever's been done is in your best interest.''

''Then have enough backbone to tell me the truth. Are you negotiating a betrothal?''

''Yes, if you must know, I am.''

Eyes flashing tawny yellow, Elena swung about. ''No!'' she shouted, all the nerves in her body taut as springs. ''I'm a widow with lands of my own. I'll do my own choosing. How dare you bargain with first one man, then another—''

Will grasped her by the shoulders and shook her. ''Have done, you shrew! The man in question is Percy Morton—Lord Morton of Langdale Pike. Now, what do you think of that?''

''That you have a moneybag for a heart,'' she raged. ''Would you sacrifice your sister to a man old enough—''

''He owns half the north country, you fool wench.''

''It's not the north country I must bed.''

''Oh, I'll not listen to any more hysteria. I'm off,'' Will declared, picking up his gauntlets as he prepared to leave.

Elena raced to the door, spreading her arms to bar his way. "Listen to me, Will. I'm no longer your baby sister to barter for a purse of gold. I'm a grown woman. Don't try to rule my life. Just once allow me to choose for myself."

"Never! As long as you live you won't be free to do that. I'm still head of the Watkins family—besides, a woman hasn't brain enough to make a wise choice."

His final retort incensed Elena. Seething with rage, she hurled a fringed cushion at his head. Adeptly, Will ducked, allowing the satin missile to hit an urn of flowers and send it crashing to the floor. Water and flowers splashed across the rushes.

"Damn you, don't treat me as if I'm a simpleton! I can speak and read Latin. I can keep accounts. I ride as well as any man. Just because I'm a woman doesn't mean my brain's soft as coddled eggs!"

"Shut your mouth! How dare you speak so to me?"

"Because you insult me, brother. I'll not be dictated to. I'll choose my next husband for myself."

Face dark with anger, Will seized her and swung her about. Elena's face was set, her lips tight. When he tried to slap her, she swung first and caught him across the cheek. Suddenly, Elena looked over Will's shoulder, shocked to see Lady Locke standing in the doorway.

Puzzled by his sister's changing expression, Will also glanced about.

"I demand to know what's going on here."

"Oh, Lady Locke—naught but a silly family squabble," Will assured her, his smarmy smile in place.

"Your voices could be heard throughout the house. I think it better that you leave, sir. Elena's in a delicate condition which isn't helped by such angry outbursts," Lady Locke announced stiffly, her face grim.

"By all means, you see . . . I was preparing to leave." Will gestured toward the door with his gauntlets. "Good-bye, sister dear. We'll finish our business when you're in a calmer state of mind. 'Tis a sad fact of life, but what they say is true—breeding women are always tearful, madam."

Elena clenched her fist, listening to her brother's falsely confident tone fading away as he walked down the corridor. How dare he barter her a second time! What matter that powerful Lord Morton owned half the north country—that only made him harder to be shut of.

Chapter Six

"How dare you defy me by leaving the house! Then I find you screaming like a fishwife—in your condition. Are you addlepated, you fool wench?"

Lady Locke had barely taken time to show Will to the door before she returned to berate Elena.

"No harm was done. I merely want for a walk. And it was not my intention to quarrel. Will frequently rubs me the wrong way," Elena explained, standing her ground before her irate mother-in-law.

"Well, it won't happen again. Doubtless, you've not the wit for it, so I'll write Her Majesty to thank her for her kindness and explain why you're delayed. There'll be no further need of that ruffian's meddling."

Indignant protests sprang to Elena's lips before she wisely bit them back. "My brother's hotheaded. We often quarrel—there's no lasting animosity between us."

"Overexcitement can be dangerous. We'll take no risks with this child. He's far too precious."

"The babe hasn't been damaged by a few hot words."

"That remains to be seen."

Elena crossed to the window seat, her fists clenched in her velvet skirts as she silently cautioned herself to exercise tolerance. "At least allow me to walk in the garden, madam. You may set a servant to watch me.''

Lady Locke's scornful laughter filled the room. ''Aye, another foolish wench who can easily be bribed to turn a blind eye. Nay, daughter dear, from this day forward you're confined to your chamber.''

''No!''

''Shouting will avail you nothing. The menservants are strong enough to enforce my wishes.''

Eyes hard as flint, Lady Locke swung about to summon two menservants waiting outside the door.

''I'll not be kept prisoner in my own house!''

''Until I'm under the sod, this is still *my* house,'' reminded Magdalen Locke grimly. ''If you've not the wit to safeguard your child, then I'll do it for you. Pitkin, take Lady Elena to her room. She's very tired.''

Pride stopped Elena from struggling. Summoning great dignity, she shook off the man's hand and, head high, marched from the room.

Disappointed at being denied their tussle, the menservants used unnecessary force as they thrust her inside her chamber. The door slammed and the key grated in the lock. Elena was left to nurse her bruises.

Rage washed over her. How dare they treat her like a child! Despite Lady Locke's scornful declaration, this was her house. Provision for his mother's welfare had been made in the will, but Randle had left the land and house to her. ''Why then are you simmering behind a locked door?'' taunted a nagging inner voice. ''Summon your servants to release you.''

Her eyes filled with hot angry tears as she faced the bitter truth. She was merely the puppet mistress of Locke Hall. Magdalen Locke wielded the real power and not until she drew her last breath would she relinquish control.

Elena allowed a few tears of self-pity to splash on

her embroidered sleeve before she regained control of her emotions. Meekness was no weapon with which to fight Magdalen Locke. Filled with fresh determination, she thundered against the heavy wooden door until her hands were bruised; she shouted for the servants until her lungs ached. It was all to no avail. Defensively clutching her abdomen, Elena sank to the floor, unable to staunch her tears. This tiny life inside her ruled her days as effectively as any jailor.

With tear-glazed eyes, she looked toward the window, through which a cool breeze wafted. Birds chirped in the trees. Even the smallest sparrow had more freedom than she.

Blinking back her tears, Elena scrambled to her feet, fired by an idea. She had no wings, but she had two good strong legs, and her pregnancy was not so far advanced that she had lost her agility.

Elena leaned out of the casement, looking for a means of descent. There was a lead drainpipe at the corner of the building, and the manor's ornamental wood facade provided plenty of handholds. She would show Lady Locke she could not be kept prisoner in her own house.

Likely the grooms, considering her safe indoors, would relax their vigil at the stables. She might even be able to saddle Artan and ride to Lord Settle's mansion to see Luis. The idea sent a surge of excitement through her veins. The breath tangled in her throat at the mere thought of seeing him again.

Elena stepped out over the windowsill, her movements hindered by her voluminous velvet skirts. Grasping the lead pipe with one hand, she held on to a carved wooden boss with the other. The garden appeared so far below that her stomach lurched and she began to feel dizzy. Quickly she closed her eyes, fighting to maintain her balance until the feeling passed. As she slowly descended, the greenish lead pipe shuddered beneath her weight, sending her scrabbling for handholds in the gnarled ivy. Unused as she was to such athletic feats, her descent was not nearly as easy as she had imagined.

The garden looked much closer now, and Elena eagerly quickened her pace. Then, to her horror, a section of lead pipe came away in her hand. Grabbing desperately for something by which to save herself, Elena ripped away handfuls of ivy before she finally crashed into the herbaceous border beneath the windows.

Though shrubs and plants had broken her fall, Elena felt as if every bone in her body had been jarred from its socket. She had a strange taste in her mouth and she felt sick. Gradually nausea subsided and she struggled to her feet, shaken, but with no apparent injuries.

Elena made her way to the stables. As she had hoped, the building was deserted. In a matter of minutes she saddled Artan and soon they were pounding over the paddock to freedom.

As the miles between herself and Locke Hall lenghtened, Elena's spirits rose. Tender thoughts of Luis filled her mind, and she rode faster and faster, impatient to tell him about their babe. Luis would greet her with that special smile that had the ability to melt her heart. Oh, how she had longed for his arms, his mouth, the tenderness of his love. If only Artan were a mythical beast with winged hooves, the better to fly to Lord Settle's mansion!

A sudden breathtaking realization brought gooseflesh to her arms. Now that she was a widow, there was nothing to prevent her marrying Luis. Within the month she could be his wife!

its time!

Elena stretched out and lay still, desperately trying to halt this miscarriage by sheer willpower. The blood loss was slight, and for the most part the pains had stopped. Encouraged, she remounted. Now more than ever she was in need of Ronwen's aid.

She had barely reached the main road before the pains began again, becoming so severe she doubled over in the saddle. No longer trying to reach Windland, she turned back to a row of cottages beside the road. Hopefully at this late hour some of the women had already returned from the fields. Why had she foolishly risked the life of her child? Her fall must have begun this miscarriage.

Elena finally received an answer to her knock at the third cottage. The white-aproned woman who opened the door gave a startled glance at her white face and bloodstained skirts, needing only Elena's whispered explanation that her baby was coming too soon to set her springing into action.

Guiding Elena to a straw pallet before the hearth, the woman covered her with a coarse blanket. Elena was chilled and her teeth chattered. The woman drew a cup of water from the cauldron simmering over the fire and, after mixing in a pinch of herbs, she coaxed Elena to sip the hot liquid. Presently, the knotted muscles in her abdomen began to relax, and a feeling of goodwill followed. Even the colors around her brightened, and the small impoverished dwelling became mellow with soft yellow light. . . .

When Elena first woke, she did not know where she was. She focused her burning eyes with difficulty on an arras depicting a lady and a seated unicorn. How strange. A similar tapestry hung in her chamber at Locke Hall, yet it seemed highly unlikely that a poor cottager would possess such a luxury.

Her head felt so heavy that her neck would barely support it when she raised herself from her pillow to seek the source of light. To her surprise, she saw twin rows of mullioned windows through which sunlight cast blurred diamonds over the rushes. Surely the cottage windows had been unglazed.

A rustling sound in the corner captured her attention. A plump, middle-aged stranger was putting folded linens in a chest.

"Where am I?" Elena asked the woman through lips grown curiously dry and stiff.

"In your own room, lady. Now lie still, don't try to sit."

"My own room! Who are you?"

"The midwife. Be still—"

"Midwife! Oh, tell me, how is my babe? Is it—" Tears flooded Elena's eyes as the woman turned aside.

"Nay, don't fret. You're young. There'll be many more babes," the midwife soothed mechanically, this speech perfected through long practice.

"You don't understand," Elena explained in a choked voice. "There'll never be more babes like this."

"Shh." The midwife patted her arm soothingly, knowing that she well understood. The young lord was dead and now his son, too. Well, likely it was for the best. Folks did say the Lockes came from tainted stock.

For several days Elena lay in bed, barely conscious. The midwife administered regular doses of poppy tea and a second vile concoction to halt the bleeding. Before being given these soothing medicines, Elena's nights were tormented by nightmares. Then once the medicine began its work, she drifted into a blissful stupor where all pain and grief were erased.

Elena awoke to rain pattering gently against the windows. For the first time in over a week, she felt clearheaded. When she tried to sit up, she became aware of the pull in her stomach, an aching swiftly transmitted to her heart when she remembered there was no longer a tiny life inside her. Her tears splashed on the coverlet as she gave vent to her sorrow over the loss of Luis's babe.

Her tears dry, Elena rose and put on a furred crimson damask bedgown. Determined to shed the weight of sorrow, she knew it could not be done if she stayed up here alone wallowing in self-pity. She would go downstairs.

The house was deserted. No sound penetrated the upper floors. Not until she reached the lighted solar off the Great Hall did Elena meet another soul, and at this moment it was someone she had no desire to see.

"So, you're finally up and about. Damn you for your willfulness! You cost me the child!" spat Lady Locke from where she huddled beside the fire. "You've finally had your way of it."

"Madam, losing the babe was as great a pain to me as it was to you."

"By God, you mention it casually, as if it were a rotten tooth gone from your head."

Lady Locke jumped to her feet, anger visible in her thin face. She had been out riding, for she still wore boots and habit and carried a whip. Her shoulders were wet with rain.

"Madam . . . please . . . be not so cruel."

"How should I be then, daughter? Should I applaud you for your great wit in riding my grandchild to death?"

Elena could not answer. For once in their stormy relationship she felt bested and wholly defeated. There was no excuse she could make to explain away the truth; she had caused her own miscarriage.

"Had you not tried to keep me prisoner, mayhap I'd still have the babe," she retaliated as she came close to the fire to warm her hands.

"How dare you lay blame on me!"

Without warning the whip slashed out, curling about Elena's arm and her soft, vulnerable bosom. She screamed shrilly in shock and pain.

That scream seemed to bring Lady Locke to life. Eyes glittering black and evil in the firelight, she stood menacingly over Elena, her face contorted with hatred.

"You did it deliberately to punish me, you evil bitch. I can see the truth in your face."

"No, madam, have sense. Would I punish myself also?"

"You cared not a whit for the child. My poor Randle not cold in his grave and now you . . . damn you, you've robbed me of my heir!"

As the whip lashed out again, Elena tried to protect herself with her upraised arms. The leather thong wrapped searingly around her arms, retreating and advancing to inflict fresh pain. Scrambling backwards, Elena dodged behind the leather campaign chair beside the hearth, crouching low as the whip whistled overhead.

"Have done! You're insane!" she screamed. Then Elena shouted for help from the servants—but with little hope of being answered.

Face purple with rage, Lady Locke pursued her around the small room. Loss of blood from her miscarriage had made Elena weak. She stumbled dazedly about the room, trying to evade this madwoman. As she had expected, her screams for help went unanswered. She had only her own wit to save her.

Picking up a tall brass candlestick, Elena hurled it with all her strength at Lady Locke, who ducked and saved herself. The fact that Elena dared to fight back merely increased her rage. Fleeing from this renewed assault, Elena reached the door just as the cruel whip curled about her shoulders. She cried out in shock—but she did manage to open the door.

Elena ran into the dark hallway and down the stairs, stumbling, swaying, clutching the banisters to keep her balance. Enraged, Lady Locke pursued her, cursing the darkness, which brought her crashing into walls and furniture in her mad rage for vengeance.

Now it was Lady Locke who bellowed for assistance from her servants as Elena fled toward the outside door. Magdalen Locke lashed the whip through the rushes, against the panelling, striking anything in her path to vent her fury.

Panting and trembling from weakness, Elena struggled to open the door leading to the garden. To her horror, she found it padlocked. It was far too late to turn back. Lady Locke's heavy steps already pounded along the corridor. She was trapped!

Light from the nearby kitchen fires lit the arched passage with garish light, casting great menacing shadows over ceiling and walls. Her whip brandished high, Lady Locke bellowed in triumph.

"So, I've caught you at last. Now I shall whip you to within an inch of your life, you damned fool wench. This is for killing my lamb . . . this is for killing his babe . . ."

Desperately, Elena tried to fight off the relentless lash, which drew traceries of blood in its stinging passage. Trapped as she was against the locked door, she had but one weapon left.

"If you intend to kill me, at least let me go to my

grave with the truth on my lips,'' she cried, desperate
to capture Magdalen Locke's attention. "The babe was
no get of your darling baby boy—he wasn't man
enough—''

"What did you say?'' roared Lady Locke, eyes ablaze
with rage. "Not Randle's babe!''

"Not his.''

"You're lying. Who else could have fathered it?''
Though momentarily rigid with shock, whip frozen
overhead, Lady Locke suddenly came back to life. She
rained furious blows on Elena.

Trying to wrestle the whip from her mother-in-law's
steely grip, Elena refused to give up. They fought
desperately for possession of the whip in the narrow
passage, banging into the stone walls before finally
crashing to the floor, where they scrabbled amidst the
odorous rushes.

"He never took me once,'' Elena hissed repeatedly
in Magdalen's Locke's ear, wounding her with the only
weapon she had. In near glee she cried, "He was naught
but a sick, impotent baby, hand-raised by his doting
mother.''

"Be silent, damn you!''

"Never! Never!''

Shrieking in rage, Magdalen Locke fell on Elena,
sinking her hands in her thick hair, ripping, clawing.
Through tear-dazed eyes Elena saw the mask of fury
and hatred transforming the other woman's face.
Suddenly, the haggard features darkened as her blood
rushed through her veins.

"Damn you, damn you, for daring to say—''

The cry became a gurgle before it ended in mid-
sentence. Her grip gradually slackened and went limp,
her clenched fist striking Elena ineffectually against her

shoulder and breast before dropping, useless, to the rushes.

Face streaked with tears of pain and rage, Elena thrust at Lady Locke's inert body. Too dazed to properly understand what had happened, Elena kept struggling to be free of the weight until she was finally able to get to her feet.

She swayed against the cold stone wall. It was then she saw a semi-circle of startled servants crowding the entrance to the lighted kitchens. Afraid of their mistress's wrath, the servants had not dared interfere. A figure finally detached itself from the group and knelt beside Lady Locke's still form. Then the man called for a candle, which he held close to his mistress's face while the others crowded around to look. Her features were contorted with rage, drawn to one side as if she had been struck down in the midst of her frenzy. Magdalen Locke was still alive, but unable to speak or move.

Elena clutched her heart, aware of its pounding vibration against her hand. Without warning her knees buckled, and she slid down the wall. She could hardly believe her own eyes as she watched the servants carry the paralyzed Lady Locke up the stairs. Becoming aware of someone crouched beside her, Elena looked up to see a maid offering her a cup of wine.

"Here, my lady, take this to revive you. We was terrible sorry for what she done to you, but we was too afraid—"

Wearily Elena nodded. The watered wine was heavy and it clung to her parched mouth. "Yes . . . I understand. You were all afraid to cross her."

The maid nodded vigorously and kicked the whip lying in the rushes. "She's a vicious woman," she spat.

"You's not the first body to feel the sting of that whip."

Elena accepted the helping hand the girl extended. Leaning against the maid, she went inside the kitchen and settled on a cushioned bench before the hearth.

The stout cook, aware no one had befriended Lady Elena since her arrival, was afraid of reprisals. She ran to fetch cake and more wine in the hope of ingratiating herself with the young mistress.

Being far too weak for further battle, Elena did not take the servants to task for their cowardice. Meekly, she accepted the cake and forced the sweetness down her throat.

The cook breathed a great sigh of relief. With gratitude she sent the maid upstairs for pillows and blankets to keep Lady Elena warm.

Chapter Seven

The London church bells pealed a carillon in honor of the feast day of St. Simon and St. Jude. According to country sages, the date, Octobet 28, marked the end of the fine weather. Gray skies, torrential rains, storms and gales were bound to follow.

So far the day had lived up to expectations.

Elena peered through the small latticed casement overlooking a jumbled patchwork of carved gables, blackened chimney pots and tiled roofs. The lowering gray sky had begun to spit rain. She did not relish walking to Whitehall in the rain. London's malodorous streets were treacherous enough in dry weather. When it rained, the central kennels overflowed with filth; there was no way to escape the swirling deluge. Had she been more fortunate, she could have ridden to her audience with the Queen, but, lacking stabling or the money to provide it, Will had wisely taken Artan home with him.

Clasping her hands and trying to calm her nerves, Elena prayed for strength during the coming ordeal. For the two weeks she had been in London she had been summoned only once to Whitehall; there she had knelt before Her Majesty in the company of many other maids whom their generous monarch had deigned to honor.

Following that auspicious occasion, boredom had set in. Day after day she waited in her dreary lodgings for a summons that never came.

Even with her mother-in-law permanently confined to her bed, the house was still dominated by her presence. Elena could hardly wait to be free of Locke Hall. She had asked Will to oversee her property in her absence.

Elena pulled on her thick blue wool cloak and slid her feet inside wooden chopines to protect her leather slippers from the filth in the street.

As she picked her way through the fetid streets, Elena stayed close to the buildings to avoid the overflowing central kennel. By hugging the walls, she was protected by the overhanging second and third stories from slops emptied indiscriminately from the upper windows. Some dwellings leaned crazily against their neighbors, timbers creaking and groaning in the gusty wind. So narrow were the streets, that the tall timbered houses almost met overhead.

At times the mingled sounds of rough voices, vendors' cries, rattling wheels, clopping hooves, barking dogs and bellows and squeals of slaughter animals reached such a volume that Elena's ears rang. How different were London's crowded streets from the quiet lanes she was used to. In Lichborne, the most offensive sounds were the cackle of geese and Widow Smelford's barking mastiff. Here, no friendly voices greeted her, nor were there any welcoming smiles, for London's citizens hurried about their business with heads down against the steady rain. The smell of unwashed bodies encased in wet wool garments and ill-cured furs assaulted her nostrils. Pinned against the buildings by the sheer press of humanity, Elena had to virtually fight her way through the mob of pie and

rush sellers who gathered under the eaves to keep their
wares dry. Prentice boys, who normally waylaid
potential customers in the street, bellowed from their
masters' doorways, their voices raised even louder to
compensate for the added distance.

While Elena moved slowly toward the great palace
of Whitehall, she was highly aware of the Queen's
summons, the parchment crackling uncomfortably
inside her bodice. By the time the messenger finally
delivered this royal summons, she had almost given up
hope of being remembered by Mary Tudor. Elena
wished she owned finery suitable for a royal audience,
but she had traveled on short notice and had brought
only a few gowns with her. So eager had she been to
leave Locke Hall and its unpleasant memories, she had
not even wanted to take the time needed for seamstresses
to sew a traveling wardrobe. As she was still officially
in mourning, she wore her grandest mourning gown
of somber purple velvet lightly embroidered at the neck
with silver.

When she reached the palace, Elena had to wait inside
a chill anteroom. Though she presented her royal
invitation, the guards insisted she still must wait to be
summoned.

In an attempt to ward off the chill, Elena hugged her
arms about her body while she paced back and forth.
The prospect of actually speaking with the Queen made
her both nervous and excited. During her last audience,
there had been merely time to curtsy before she was
thrust aside by the next eager wench. All her starry-
eyed dreams of living in the lavish court and of being
reunited with Luis had dissolved on that disappointing
day. She did not even know if Luis was still in London.
For all she knew, he could have returned to Spain.

Whitehall Palace was very grand. The former London

residence of the Archbishop of York had been transformed by the Queen's late father into the greatest palace in Christendom. Elena had only heard about Whitehall's vast gallery hung with life-size portraits, its wondrous gilded woodwork and molded ceilings, its private gardens, tennis courts and tilt ground. Beyond that initial glimpse of the reception chamber, she had been given no opportunity to explore her surroundings. Still, even at its most boring, life in London was an improvement over her meaningless existence at Locke Hall.

At the memory, Elena grew uneasy. Locke Hall seemed so far away. Though she had lived there only a short time, they had been some of the most unpleasant days of her life. The events of the past month had all happened so fast, she could scarce accept the fact she had lost a husband and babe in the space of a few weeks. Yet only the loss of that nameless babe caused her grief. Tears threatened to fall as she reminded herself the little one was not nameless. In her heart she had always called him Luis.

Elena suddenly noticed a stern-faced woman beckoning impatiently from the doorway. The woman's plain garments of rustling black taffeta reminded her of a nun's habit. Thankful, Elena hurried forward. It was not good to have too much time to dwell on what might have been.

When Elena finally reached the Queen's private chambers, she blinked in shock at the sumptuous world of warmth and color unfolding before her. Instead of rushes, the floor of the Queen's firelit withdrawing room was covered in gaily colored Turkish carpets; the panelled walls were hung with bright tapestries. Elena shivered in pleasant anticipation of warming her icy limbs before the cheerful blaze leaping far up the sooty chimney. On the hood above the fireplace was a brightly painted coat of arms; even the molded ceilings were decorated with bright blues, red and greens, the embossed designs all magnificently gilded.

"Lady Elena Locke, Your Majesty." Without further ceremony, Elena found herself thrust inside the room.

A gray lap dog ran yapping to her feet. The Queen, who was seated before the fire, sharply clapped her square hands to summon the little creature back to its tasseled cushion at her feet. When Mary Tudor spoke, her voice was gruffly masculine.

"Greetings, Lady Elena."

"It's most kind of you to send for me, Your Majesty," said Elena, stumbling forward to curtsy. So badly did her knees shake, she feared she was going to fall at the Queen's feet.

Giving her a kindly smile, the Queen drew Elena from the floor. Then she motioned for her brightly garbed attendants to withdraw. The women curtsied to their mistress before obediently going into an adjoining room, leaving the Queen alone with her newest lady.

To Elena's amazement, once they were alone, Mary embraced her, clasping her tightly against her meager bosom.

"My heart goes out to you, Lady Elena. To have been so sore afflicted in the space of a month is a terrible burden for one so young. You mustn't stand. Here—sit beside me. You've barely recovered your strength."

Elena was quite overcome by the Queen's unexpected concern for her health. She sat as directed on a plump tasseled cushion before the fire. From this vantage point she could study the Queen closely. Mary Tudor was extremely plain and long past her prime. Her thin sandy hair was visible beneath the black velvet band of her French hood, which sat far back on her head, accentuating her high forehead. When Mary looked at

Elena, she narrowed her eyes, squinting in the manner
of the shortsighted. The Queen's lined skin had an
unhealthy pallor which, combined with her scrawny
neck, reminded Elena of an aging spinster. Even Mary's
sumptuous rose brocade gown, heavily trimmed with
marten, could not erase the impression. A huge square-
jeweled pendant with a single drop pearl the size of a
pigeon egg rested against the Queen's chest.

"Thank you for your kindness, Your Majesty," Elena
blurted, suddenly remembering her manners. "I'm still
tired from my journey."

Again, Mary admonished her lapdog for growling
jealously at her guest. "I'm sure you thought I'd
forgotten your existence."

"Oh, no, Your Majesty—"

"Come now, be honest."

Elena smiled sheepishly. "Well, I did think perhaps
Your Majesty was far too busy to think about me."

"Yes, always busy, there's so much evil to undo in
the land—but no, you were never far from my thoughts.
Where to house you presented no small dilemma. My
unmarried ladies all share a common room. In view of
your recent bereavement, it did not seem fitting to put
you with them. Then, as is often the case, our lord
solved the problem by returning a dear friend of mine
to court. Lady Anne was recently widowed, also. You
can share a room. You've so much in common."

Absently, Mary rubbed her brow, feeling one of her
frequent headaches coming on.

"Thank you, Your Majesty. You are too kind."

"It's the least I can do. I shudder to picture my grief
were my dearest Philip taken from me. He is my all."

The soft, almost tender, tone that crept into the
Queen's voice greatly surprised Elena. A bemused smile
lifting her old maid's mouth, Mary gazed into space,

contemplating secret thoughts. She's in love with him, thought Elena in surprise, hardly expecting that emotion from her royal mistress.

"I'm very glad Your Majesty is happy."

"Happy is hardly the word, Elena. For most of my life I've been deprived of someone to love. You must also understand—as a child I was forbidden to see my dear mother. I went from being my father's indulged darling to an outcast almost overnight. The years have not been kind to me—until now. It's as if sunshine has brightened my life and all's become perfume and flowers."

Elena's eyes shone. "Aye, madam," she whispered, her heart lurching. "I too have known that wonder."

Sighing for the burden she imagined the other woman endured, Mary sympathetically patted Elena's head. "Remember, Lady Elena, memories endure beyond the grave. No one can take them from you."

Then Elena realized the Queen assumed she had spoken about her love for Randle, and she was too embarrassed to enlighten her.

"Though I've no wish to open wounds, my heart aches for the loss of your dear babe," said Mary, clasping Elena's hand in her own square dry one. "Now, there's something I'm going to tell you which I've told no other. Something wonderful—I'm with child!"

"Oh, Your Majesty, that is wonderful news!" Elena cried, sincerely sharing Mary's joy.

"Yes, isn't it!" Mary sniffed and dabbed her eyes, overcome with emotion. "My darling Philip's given me what I crave most—what all England craves. Pray God it will be a son."

"Amen."

For those few emotional minutes their difference in

rank was put aside. The sheer joy in Mary's face told
Elena this expected child was the greatest gift she could
have been given.

"Now, remember, Elena, for the moment 'tis our
secret."

"No one shall learn it from me, Your Majesty."

Mary nodded, well pleased. Her smile had turned
indulgent as she looked Elena up and down, approving
of what she saw. "You're even more beautiful than your
mother. Doña Ana was devoted to my own dear
mother . . ." Mary swallowed, her recent emotion
making her unusually vulnerable. "Fate has given us
much in common, Elena. Our mothers came from
Aragon and our fathers were Welshmen. Mayhap our
likes and dislikes are of a sameness also."

'It is my dearest wish to serve you faithfully and
well."

Mary kissed Elena's cheek. Then, reaching to a side
table, she handed her an ebony and pearl crucifix. "This
was your mother's. It will forge a link to your Spanish
heritage. Please join us tomorrow at Mass."

"Oh, thank you. Yes, I will, Your Majesty."

Elena knew strict attendance at Mass was a require-
ment of the Queen's ladies. She had no particular
religious preference, considering the old church and the
new but different roads to the same place. Wisely,
however, she did not voice this sentiment, for she was
aware of the Queen's fantical devotion to her religion.
With the support of her Spanish husband, Mary intended
to return England to the Roman Catholic fold—not a
popular ambition with her fellow countrymen. It was
too soon after the denouncing of Catholicism to expect
an easy shift of conscience. Mary Tudor had never
pursued the easy road; firm in the belief there was but
one true faith, she proceeded in blind devotion. Her

conscience was her guide, and she turned a deaf ear to those who urged tolerance.

The Queen peered shortsightedly toward the open doorway, unable to see if anyone waited there. ''Lady Anne,'' she called gruffly.

A woman came from the other room to kneel at Mary's feet, kissing the Queen's proferred hand.

''Lady Anne—this is Lady Elena. Make her feel at home. She is in your care.''

''Welcome to court, Elena,'' said Lady Anne. ''I know we shall be friends.''

Lady Anne made Elena feel even more dowdy. Dressed in a black velvet gown over patterned black silk, Lady Anne scintillated with every movement, for the velvet overgown was crisscrossed with a design of brilliants. Plump, blonde and pretty, Lady Anne's pink cheeks dimpled as she smiled in genuine friendship.

When Elena looked back on her first day at the royal court, she realized Lady Anne had meant that greeting in all sincerity. During those first weeks at Whitehall life was difficult. Without Anne's help Elena would have been hopelessly lost in the reams of court etiquette she was expected to know, but which no one took any pains to teach her. Even Anne's rather bossy manner— she was six years her senior—she accepted in good spirits, thinking of Anne as the older sister she had never had. Instinctively, Elena knew Anne Shelton had her best interests at heart.

Out of necessity, Elena was soon taken into Anne's confidence. Though she, too, was a recent widow, Anne had already taken a lover. To her mind, Sir Miles Ravenscroft was the most handsome, charming gallant at Mary's court. She needed Elena's cooperation for the numerous secret meetings they arranged, which were always on the dangerous edge of discovery. Elena was tempted to tell Anne about Luis, yet never having had anyone except Ronwen in whom to confide her secrets, she deemed it wiser to keep her own counsel.

Because she and Anne were both officially in mourning, they were not invited to take part in the court festivities, nor were they allowed to mingle with the gentlemen of the court. They spent most of their days closeted in the feminine world of Mary's apartments.

As Elena became more familiar with the court, she began to make discreet inquiries about Luis. Several of the Queen's ladies shook their heads when they heard the name, while others laughed and said every third Spaniard was named Luis.

November spread a blanket of gloomy fog across the city. Nowadays the sun was a rare visitor; and when it finally made its feeble appearance, it hung low in the sky, its wan light barely penetrating London's warren of streets.

Elena longed for the country. How she missed riding through the misty woods and walking along hushed country lanes. When finally she confessed her acute homesickness, Anne sympathized with her and agreed a London winter was long and dreary. So far they had both been excluded from the laughing parties that rode beyond the city walls to hunt roebuck. Their exercise was confined to a portion of the privy garden, now bare of blossoms and shrouded in gloom.

During the first week of December, their royal mistress finally took pity on her two disconsolate ladies, granting them the right to lift their period of mourning in honor of the approaching Christmastide.

When Anne delivered this joyful news, Elena seized her by the hand and spun her about. They fell giggling on the bed like children, made giddy by the glorious prospect of freedom.

The following day Mary sent Elena a gown splendid enough to wear at the Christmas court. Yards of sumptuous crimson brocade, all trimmed with marten, spilled over Elena's arms as she admired the magnificent gown. The underskirt was of white velvet embroidered with red Tudor roses. Almost as wonderful as the gift was the accompanying summons to attend Her Majesty at a court function this very night.

As she hurried down Whitehall's chill, gloomy corridors on her way to serve the Queen, Elena was so excited her hands shook. Repeatedly swallowing and straightening her shoulders till her back became straight as a ramrod, she entered the vast reception room ablaze with candles.

Mary and her Spanish consort were seated on a dais at the far end of the crowded room. It took Elena a long time to thread her way between the jostling guests who stood sipping wine while they gossiped like well-dressed alewives. Men repeatedly snatched at her hanging sleeves in an effort to detain her, calling Elena "lovey" and "sweetest." So persistent were these rakish admirers, she was afraid she would have to call for help long before she reached the royal dais. Strangely, it was only the English courtiers who accosted her. The Spanish gentlemen ravished her with their eyes, fixing her with unblinking stares as they followed her passage across the noisy room.

When Elena finally curtsied to the Queen, Mary smiled and waved her to a cushion on the top step of the dais. So many other ladies were in attendance that Elena had little to do but enjoy the colorful spectacle as the courtiers formed lines for the dance.

When first he saw her, Philip fixed Elena with a probing stare until she was forced to look away in

embarrassment. Somehow, Elena had not expected the
Queen's husband to give her such an intimate appraisal.
Spanish Philip was not nearly as handsome as she had
heard. In comparison to dear Luis, he looked most
ordinary. From her vantage point, she surveyed Philip's
gentlemen, who were mostly attired in dark velvets
asparkle with jewels. With quickened heartbeat, she
sought Luis, but, to her disappointment, there was not
one gold head to be seen. Short of asking amongst the
Spaniards for Luis de los Santos's whereabouts, she did
not know how she would ever find him again.

Within the hour, Elena made the uncomfortable
discovery that not only did Philip not love Mary Tudor,
he viewed her with distaste. When Mary clasped his
slender hand, gazing shortsightedly into his fair-bearded
face, her emotions were an open book. The Queen's
obvious love and admiration for her husband were
almost embarrassing. While Philip treated his royal wife
with courtesy, his expression remained unfathomable.
No warmth lit his large eyes, nor was there a smile on
his full mouth when he looked at Mary. Beneath their
heavy lids his cold, calculating, eyes took in all and
revealed nothing.

Palace gossip said the mere thought of bedding Mary,
with her scrawny old maid's body and sagging breasts,
near turned the Spaniard impotent. Those same gossips
also whispered that Philip ached to return to his beloved
Spain, and, more specificially, to his beloved mistress,
whose arms he had reluctantly abandoned to wed the
English queen.

Though Elena knew such feelings were commonplace
amongst royalty, she was greatly annoyed with the
Spanish prince for his indifference toward her mistress.
Knowing the depth of unrequited passion Mary felt for
her young groom made Elena sad. She knew also that

the Queen compared her aging body to that of a younger woman, weeping in the privacy of her chamber because she was not beautiful enough for her beloved.

It took Elena only a matter of a few hours to assess the basic character of Mary's male courtiers. Vain, frivolous seducers all, the brightly garbed charmers roamed the vast room like predators searching for a victim. Beneath those bejeweled chests beat fickle hearts. Their very noses seemed to twitch at the scent of a new conquest. Apart from boasting of their sexual prowess, the courtiers' sole occupation appeared to be trying to entice pretty wenches to their bed.

Later, when Elena indignantly revealed her unflattering summation to Anne, her friend laughingly agreed. Of course Sir Miles was an exception, he being a man beyond compare. Hardly expecting less, Elena smiled, hoping for Anne's sake that emotion had not obscured her vision. Mentioning that the Spanish gentlemen held themselves somewhat aloof, she casually asked Anne if she knew Luis de los Santos. Elena hoped her brief explanation that the Spaniard had heroically rescued her groom on their wedding day had not revealed too much interest.

However, the sharp-witted Anne guessed Elena was far more interested in meeting the gallant Spaniard again than she admitted. And she promised to do all in her power to learn of Luis de los Santos's whereabouts.

Chapter Eight

On a rare December day of sun and thin, crisp air, Elena accompanied Anne on an errand for the Queen. They were to deliver gifts to a former lady-in-waiting who lay abed in her manor outside London. Mary also sent her regrets that she could not visit in person, assuring the ailing Lady Jane she would be missed at the Christmas festivities.

Everything sparkled in the frosty light. They rode across Moorfields' green expanse, and Elena paused to watch boys playing football until she discovered she was in danger of being left behind. In the country districts of Finsbury and Spittalfields, Londoners hunted and jousted. As they jogged through these pleasant hamlets on the way to Faverham, they passed several finely dressed parties returning to the city. The gentlemen bowed from their saddles and politely raised their hats to the two women.

Anne had been so vague about the details of their errand that Elena began to suspect she had arranged to meet Sir Miles Ravenscroft. Yet, when she accused Anne of using their royal errand as an excuse to see her love, Anne indignantly dismisssed the suggestion.

Elena's heart soared with pleasure as they rode

through the browning landscape. Here the air was tinged with wood smoke and smelled of decaying autumn leaves. Robins fluttered about the hedgerows, their sweet melodious song an anthem to ears long assaulted by city noise. They rode beside thick woods where wild boar lurked, and Elena pined for an early morning gallop through this prime hunting country. Like a bloodhound, she sniffed the wind laden with the scent of animals and damp vegetation, and her blood stirred at the thought of untrammeled miles of freedom.

Eventually they left the highway to follow a narrow road that ended at Faverham Hall's high stone walls. Only then did Anne reveal the truth.

"I should know it's useless to try to keep secrets from you. Yes, Miles is to meet me here. But that's not my only surprise. Now, come, say no more, for we're still about Her Majesty's business."

Laughing, Elena set spur to her horse, a white palfrey not near as spirited as Artan. Anne shouted for her to stop, alarmed by her recklessness. Unheeding, Elena ran the animal flat out across the grassy meadows surrounding Faverham Hall.

She reached the hall's oak-studded door just in time to meet a party of finely dressed gentlemen coming outside. Pausing in their chat, the men ogled her, finding Elena's appearance most arresting. The wild ride had brought glowing color to her cheeks and her hood had fallen back, revealing a mass of black curls framing her face and spilling about her shoulders.

The unexpected sound of Spanish voices coming from inside the house captured her attention, but Elena failed to catch what was being said. Now Anne joined her, laughingly chiding her for racing ahead. Their servants still plodded up the driveway some distance back. Many of the well-dressed courtiers hailed Anne as an old acquaintance. Then, as Elena had expected, Sir Miles appeared. The young nobleman, resplendant in saffron velvet, strode jauntily toward them, a long black cloak swinging from his broad shoulders.

Anne greeted him with modestly downcast eyes, continuing the charade they presented in public, for Sir Miles had an invalid wife at his Tetwood manor. It had also been suggested that his loyalties lay more with the Princess Elizabeth than with the Queen. This alone was reason enough for Anne, as one of Mary's ladies, to avoid having her name linked romantically with his.

Elena smiled at Sir Miles, and he returned her smile, aware she shared Anne's confidence.

"Lady Anne, Lady Elena, I'm sorry to have to tell you after you've ridden such a distance—my poor Cousin Jane begs to be left in peace. The flux still plagues her greatly," said Sir Miles as he politely assisted them from their horses.

Had Elena known Lady Jane was Sir Miles's cousin, she would have better understood Anne's desperation to be chosen for this errand. Naively she had supposed Anne, like she, merely pined for the freedom of the countryside.

They took light refreshment in the panelled parlor, where a welcome fire blazed. After consuming hearty tankards of mulled ale to wash down their greengage pasties, the travelers felt much revived.

Anne gave the Queen's letter and gifts to Lady Jane's housekeeper, relaying Her Majesty's message.

Casually, while he drank a second glass of sack, Sir Miles suggested that, as his party was also returning to London, they might escort the ladies home. The other men soon left the room to prepare for the homeward journey, leaving the three conspirators alone.

Elena went to the window at the far end of the room

to allow the lovers privacy. Again she heard Spanish voices accompanied by the tread of booted feet approaching the door. Instead of coming inside the room as she expected, the party continued through the house.

"Have no fear, sweeting," Sir Miles soothed, for Anne had quickly pulled from his embrace, "the Spanish merely rest their beasts and sup before heading back to court. They don't care about us."

"Be not so sure. I'm told these days spies are everywhere," said Anne, glancing uneasily at the closed door.

"I'll wait outside and make sure you're not disturbed," Elena offered, as once again the lovers resumed their whispered endearments.

The narrow corridor was deserted, though Elena could hear men's voices and laughter in the background. A few minutes later, heavy steps and the clink of swords against stone warned her that the party of Spaniards was returning. Not wanting to be discovered standing guard, she stepped into an alcove where she waited until they had passed.

Once the men were out of sight, Elena went back to the window and leaned against the sill. Bright islands of autumn flowers bloomed in a sea of grass. Gray mounds of lavender edged the paved walk leading to the old walled garden. A lattice, where the last roses of the season lingered, almost hid the gate from view. Sighing wistfully as she pictured herself walking with Luis in the garden, she was gripped by a sudden wave of sadness, and she wondered if they were ever to meet again.

"What, all alone, mistress?"

Elena jumped in surprise, startled by the unexpected voice. Yet when she would have spun about to face the man, strong arms pinned her against the window frame.

Elena's heart pounded. Though she longed to cry for help, she knew this courtier would consider her foolish if, at the first sight of a man, she began screaming for help like some little convent chit.

"What if I am alone, 'tis none of your affair, sir," she replied calmly, or at least she hoped she sounded calm.

"Beautiful women should never be lonely," the man whispered, his breath hot against her ear.

There was something disturbingly familiar about that voice, something that made the skin on the back of her neck prickle with excitement. Again she struggled to turn about; again he kept her prisoner.

"There's a difference between being alone and being lonely."

"Is that so?"

Elena shivered as his hot mouth slowly swept the nape of her neck. His fingers tightened on her upper arms as she struggled to be free of this unwanted embrace—or was it unwanted? Her boiling blood suggested otherwise.

"Please, sir, allow me to go. If you don't release me at once, I'll scream."

Laughing softly against her ear, he continued the tantalizing movement of his lips. Now he teased her delicate earlobe with the tip of his hot tongue and she shuddered. Her reaction made him laugh.

"Hypocrite," he whispered huskily, "your body betrays you."

Angry now, and desperate to be free of this forbidden, yet tantalizing courtship, Elena struggled wildly. Taken off guard, the man slackened his grasp. She was finally able to twist around, becoming even more intimately acquainted with her tormentor in the process, for he did not step back, merely stood his ground so that her thighs were pressed against his strong legs.

In the gloomy passage it was hard to see his face, hampered as she was by the blur of angry tears. Blinking rapidly to clear her vision, Elena looked up and gasped in shock.

"Luis! You! Oh, God in heaven, why didn't you say so? I thought I was about to be ravished!" Suddenly overcome with emotion, she crumpled in his arms. Luis supported her, cradling her face against his cheek, kissing away the tears spilling down her cheeks.

"Hush, sweetheart, you'll rouse the household," he whispered, anxious to quiet her sobs. "You have your devious friend to thank for our meeting. She sent word that a certain lady craved my attention—a lovely angel named Elena—"

"Anne arranged our meeting?" Elena gasped in amazement, trying to swallow the joyous sobs building in her throat.

"I need only steer my party to Faverham Hall. She promised to take care of the rest."

Luis held Elena slightly away from him in order to gaze on her lovely face. Those tawny eyes that had haunted his nights shone crystalline with tears. Gently he kissed her lids, soothing her, tasting salt on his lips.

"Are these tears of joy, or unhappiness?" he finally asked, holding her tightly in his arms as she threatened to swoon.

"Of joy and sorrow . . . Oh, Luis, how I've longed for you. So much has happened. I have to tell you—" The door at the far end of the corridor opened, and they quickly stepped apart.

"Tell me, Lady Elena, how fares Her Majesty? I've been gone from court over a month," Luis said, raising his voice slightly for the benefit of the others.

"She's well, and overjoyed that at last she's with

child,'' Elena replied, playing along with him. Two men
were walking toward them, one dressed in the long
robes of a cleric.

''Ah, Don Luis, we've been searching for you.
Come, the hour grows late,'' said the swarthy churchman, his eyes flicking over Elena as he tried to ascertain
what had taken place moments before. Tears stained
her cheeks, and Don Luis was agitated, for his hands
shook.

''Doña,'' said the other man, his dark eyes laughingly
appraising.

''This is Lady Elena Locke—one of the Queen's
ladies-in-waiting,'' Luis said, introducing her to his
countrymen. ''Ruy Gomez, Prince of Eboli and Duke
of Alba, and His Excellency Bartolemé Carranza, Archbishop of Toledo.''

Elena curtsied, somewhat overawed by the exalted
rank of these strangers. Ruy Gomez raised her from
the ground as he gallantly said, ''Come, ride with us,
Doña, then England will be made sunny as Spain.''

Luis clapped his companion on the arm and made a
laughing comment. Then they walked briskly toward
the house's entrance, where a large group of riders had
gathered for the return journey. Armed men as well
as servants accompanied the Spaniards. Considering the
open hostility of the English toward these foreigners,
men of their rank and importance were in need of
protection.

Elena noticed the dark-complexioned Carranza
studying her intently, feeling a chill as his black eyes
seemed to bore inside her brain. Carranza's reputation
had preceded him. Nicknamed the Black Friar both for
his swarthiness and his Domenican robes, Carranza's
presence in England was vastly resented. Philip had
appointed his archbishop as Mary's principal advisor,

anticipating Carranza's usefulness in bringing England back to the Catholic faith. In the short time he had been here, the hard, unmerciful Carranza had become both feared and hated.

Anne and Sir Miles finally came outside and walked to their mounts, not betraying their intimate relationship by either word or glance.

Somehow, as the party clattered toward London, the two distinct groups of courtiers blended until Luis rode beside Elena, Sir Miles beside Anne.

What appeared to have been a natural occurrence had taken much skillful maneuvering to accomplish, a fact not overlooked by the Archbishop of Toledo. Carranza viewed the scene with a jaundiced eye. He had little time for the English, their climate, or their land. Black eyes narrowed, he observed Don Luis's unseemly interest in the dark-haired wench on the white horse. Intimate relationships in this land of heretics were to be discouraged; it was especially unwise for the prince's confidant to be enamored of an Englishwoman. In Spain Don Luis's life had not been beyond reproach, but Dolores Mendoza, the voluptuous sister of Carranza's aide, had kept the Inquisition informed of his actions, and had finally become Don Luis's mistress. Fool woman. After she fell in love with the handsome don, her reports were most unreliable. Women could rarely be trusted. Still, were Doña Dolores here, he would feel more at ease. He must hope this fire would soon be doused. Hot-blooded men were seldom circumspect in their choice of bedfellows.

Surrounded as they were by others, there was little opportunity for private conversation. Elena must be content with the warmth of Luis riding beside her. The courtiers laughed and joked with their companions as they rode briskly toward London. No one wanted to be late for tonight's pageant.

Fortunately, Elena's horse docilely kept pace with the rest, for she gave scant attention to her riding, unable to think of much beyond Luis's disturbing presence. At times, passing farm carts or flocks of sheep halted the riders. Then Luis would slip his hand in hers, his touch burning through their gauntlets.

Elena admired Luis's handsome profile, finding things about him she had forgotten. The way his thick hair waved at the nape of his neck, and how it dazzled in the sun, glittering beneath the brim of his mulberry velvet hat. Nor had she recalled how his strong neck rose smoothly tanned from the frilled collar of his shirt. . . .

"Now you've even more to thank me for," Anne reminded her laughingly as they came abreast.

"I can never thank you enough for this. And I thought I was being so clever at keeping my feelings to myself—"

"Do you love him?" Anne interrupted, as their horses began to move apart.

"With all my heart."

" 'Tis thanks enough."

Smiling in satisfaction, Anne turned her attention back to Sir Miles, chatting amiably as if they had not seen each other for months.

The riders entered the city through the Moorgate. The party gradually grew smaller, shrinking as men dropped out to ride to their own houses. Many of the Spanish courtiers had lodgings in other parts of the city; Carranza, however, continued with them to Whitehall. The churchman's piercing black gaze was never far from Luis as, with mounting concern, he observed the don's obvious attachment to the English wench.

Aware of the archbishop's scrutiny, Luis considered

it wise not to betray his eagerness to meet Elena alone.
Though he did not expect them to remain celibate, Philip
demanded a certain propriety from his gentlemen when
they were in public. Luis could only hope they would
be able to steal some time together during the royal
masque.

When it came time to part, he politely asked, "Are
you to serve Her Majesty this evening, Doña Elena?"

"Yes. The entertainment promises to be most
exciting."

For just a moment Carranza's attention wandered.
Quickly, Luis raised Elena's fingers to his mouth. She
had withdrawn her gauntlet and his hot lips caressed
her flesh, making her shiver.

"It might be the most exciting night you've ever
spent," he mouthed silently, capturing her gaze.

Elena gazed into his light blue eyes, stunned by the
bolt of emotion that shot through her. She saw such
promise, love and desire in his arresting face, she could
scarce breathe for excitement. Finally, with a modestly
lowered gaze, she turned aside to follow Anne beneath
the stable arch.

The night was cold; ice had formed on puddles
collected in the cobbled courtyard. But Elena would
have shivered had it been summer. Hunched inside her
cloak, she hurriedly crossed the court beside Anne in
the company of a dozen other ladies-in-waiting.
Anticipation made her almost sick, and she had eaten
little at the late afternoon meal preceding this royal
masque.

Seeing the hundreds of people crowded inside the
high-raftered Hall, Elena's anticipation turned into tears.
How would she ever find Luis in this mob of merry-
makers?

On a dais at the far end of the room sat the Queen and her consort. Mary was not feeling well this Christmas season, plagued as she was by the symptoms of early pregnancy. She leaned on the arm of her chair, her purple ermine-trimmed gown merely accentuating the unhealthy pallor of her lined face. Beside her, Philip viewed the scene dispassionately. He wore his customary black velvet trimmed with ermine; pearls encrusted his velvet slippers and formed clocks down the sides of his black hose.

Nervously Elena smoothed her scarlet skirts and adjusted the stiff underskirt embroidered with Tudor roses. Tonight her lustrous raven hair was discreetly hidden beneath a French hood of black velvet and scarlet satin trimmed with gold.

Moving forward in a body, the late arrivals curtsied before the royal couple. As Elena took up her position behind the Queen, she became uncomfortably aware of Philip's cold gaze following her.

With jingling tambourines and reedy pipes, a troupe of brightly clad dancers skipped inside the hall to loud applause. After singing and reciting clever rhymes, the dancers formed a long serpentine line that twisted this way and that amidst the laughing guests.

A hand suddenly took hold of Elena's arm. To her surprise, she looked up and found the Queen's husband bending over her.

"They tell me you are of Spanish blood," Philip said, his voice low and attractively modulated.

"Yes, in part—my mother came from Aragon."

"Ah, yes, you have the classic Spanish features. Most true beauty comes from Spain." Smiling, he reached out to brush her cheek.

The touch, though fleeting, was somehow hot and possessive. Startled, Elena raised her eyes to his. For the first time she saw undisguised emotion smoldering there.

"You are a very beautiful lady, Doña Elena."

"Thank you, Your Highness."

"You remind me of much I've left behind. Sometimes one must make unpleasant sacrifices for one's . . ." He paused, his thick lips curving in an appreciative smile. "I trust we shall meet again." Philip turned then, stepping down from the dais to mingle with the courtiers.

Elena's heart thumped, not with excitement but unease. Did the Prince intend to seduce her? Naturally she would repel his advances—yet, was it possible to refuse the Queen's husband? Guilt over her thoughts brought the blood to her cheeks as she glanced toward Mary, who had been watching their exchange. The Queen's shortsighted eyes perceived little beyond two people engaged in conversation. Mary was so madly in love with her Spaniard that even if he forced his attentions on her, Elena suspected it would be she alone who would bear the blame.

Swallowing nervously, she rose and curtsied at the Queen's feet. "May I bring you some refreshment, Your Majesty? Or perhaps a muff," Elena added, noticing Mary's blunt fingers already swollen with chillblains so early in the season. The painful red swellings gave her hands the gnarled look of age.

"My dear, how thoughtful of you. Yes, I'd like a muff."

Though a great fire blazed in the hall and the mass of courtiers put forth much body heat, Mary, isolated as she was on the royal dais, felt only the searing draughts whistling through chinks in the rafters.

"Philip was delighted when he learned of your Spanish blood. He's understandably homesick," the

Queen added wistfully, her gaze following his black-garbed figure as he moved like a somber raven amidst the English peacocks.

"Yes, Madam, he told me he missed Spain."

"His gentlemen pine to go home. I'm afraid they'll persuade him to leave—but you've no wish to hear all my foolish fears." Smiling faintly, Mary leaned forward to stroke the soft velvet covering Elena's shoulder. "You look very lovely."

"Thank you, Madam, and thank you again for this beautiful gown. Tonight I feel almost as grand as a princess myself," Elena blurted before wondering if her choice of words had been inappropriate.

Mary shifted uncomfortably in her chair, resting her reddened hands on her noticeably protruding abdomen.

Elena realized she had been dismissed, and she backed away before thrusting her way through the noisy crowd to fetch the Queen's muff.

When she returned to the hall, Elena found the guests pressed close to the walls to make room for the masquers. The crowd rocked with laughter as seven men dressed in animal skins cavorted comically about the hall. Seven singing maidens wearing headdresses ablaze with candles entered the room. After a few wild capers, the beasts, feigning much canine subservience, were captured by the maidens, who led them by ribboned holly garlands to a papier maché kennel made to resemble Whitehall. Elena found the skit's significance puzzling, though the others roared with laughter.

Grateful for her muff, the Queen thanked Elena before plunging her hands into its warmth. Leaning close to Philip, she whispered something. The Prince patted her arm, treating Mary to one of his rare smiles before turning his attention back to the entertainment.

A group of maidens dressed in crimson satin and

playing beribboned lutes began a recital of Christmas carols. This sweetly sung piece was followed by a band of gaudily dressed gentlemen enacting a tableau, though Elena was far too busy searching the crowd for Luis to pay attention to the words.

Philip's favorite gentlemen stood about his chair, leaning forward from time to time to speak to him. Suddenly Elena's heart leaped, threatening to jump from her bodice when she saw a distinctive gold head bend toward the Prince. Philip grasped his friend's arm while they laughed at some private joke. Then Luis stepped behind the Prince's chair and allowed his gaze to rove over the assembly. Elena realized he was looking for her.

She made her way unnoticed through the crowd while the other guests were distracted by the capering antics of a troupe of fools who skipped about the hall, bells ajingle, shouting insults to whichever courtier caught their eye. Clever and biting, their wit did not please the victims, though the rest of the assembly enjoyed it immensely. Elena finally stood as close to the Spanish gentlemen as she dared, hoping Luis would turn in her direction after he had translated the fools' humor for his Prince. Several gentlemen noticed her immediately, and she grew uncomfortable beneath their unblinking scrutiny. When the fool's capers were ended, Luis joined the other Spaniards in polite applause. Being strangers both to current court gossip and the English language, the Spanish failed to appreciate the humor.

Suddenly, across that crowded, smoky hall, through the blazing pools of light, past shadowed corners, his gaze lifted and met hers. Elena felt as if a searing bolt of heat fused them. Her lips parted in a startled gasp.

Luis took her reaction as an invitation, for the tip of her pink tongue circled her lips suggestively. Shuddering, he quickly excused himself and turned to push his way through the crowd. Elena left the room, hoping he would follow. They had no more privacy in this noisy room than they had this afternoon on their journey to London.

A man's hand grasped Elena's waist, and she had no need to turn about to identify him.

"Beautiful One, your gown's brighter than the holly berries," Luis said huskily against her ear.

Elena slid into his arms and was pressed so close against his purple doublet that the pearl embroidery dug into her flesh. "At last," she whispered, growing faint with emotion. "I was afraid you weren't coming."

But he wasn't listening. Luis drew her rapidly into a cold, narrow corridor. On the way he grabbed two cloaks hanging from pegs on the wall, and wrapped one about her shoulders.

"Where are we going?" Elena asked in excitement, not really caring as long as he was with her.

"A place no one will think of looking," was all he said as he led her outside.

They walked briskly in the frosty air, staying close to the building. Pausing, Luis glanced about, making sure they were still alone before he pushed open the door of a low building. The warm fragrance of earth engulfed her, and the rare scent of tropical blossoms brought her to the realization that she was in the royal greenhouse.

"Luis!" she cried. "What a magical place. But surely we can be seen."

Luis said nothing. Instead, he took her in his arms, and soon his kisses swept all thought away.

Next he urged her to a makeshift bed of sacking spread atop straw used for mulch. Here, inside the greenhouse, all was warm and cozy. Exotic blooms, visible in the glow of charcoal braziers, surrounded them, while from an adjoining room wafted the scent of oranges. Wrapped about by a haze of scents and disarmed by her tumultuous emotions, Elena lay beside Luis. She gasped as the heat of his body engulfed her. No longer did she shake on weak legs, for now they lay side by side, their hearts pounding in unison.

"How many novenas I've made, how many prayers beseeching . . . oh, *querida, querida*, say you'll be mine."

Luis's husky invitation fired her blood. Mouths open, their tongues searched and met in searing union. Elena could not press close enough to him, longing to fuse muscle and bone, heart and soul. "Oh, Luis, my love, don't let this end. Let it last forever."

"Would that it could, sweet, would that it could." In the charcoal glow, his mouth quirked into a bitter smile.

"First there's something I must tell you. I've wanted to say this for so long. I—"

He placed a warm hand gently over her mouth. "Hush. Fortune has granted us only until the royal fanfare sounds. So make haste. Don't delay with senseless chat lest we run out of time. Oh, Elena, tell me only how much you love me—want me. You're the loveliest woman in all the world. A goddess—my goddess."

His lavish praise made her smile. His request had been so typically masculine. Pray God there'd be other times for talk. Besides, such secrets were not easily spilled and she would probably weep in the telling.

"Come, then, dearest Luis, make me forget speech. Make me feel only fire and passion."

"That's a pleasure I've lived for."

His hot hands caressed her shoulders, moving down to her breasts until she gasped. She grew impatient for his more intimate caresses. In the gloom, her bodice lacings were hard for him to negotiate, and she helped, giggling as he fumbled, hardly able to endure the suspense until his hot hands cupped her eager flesh. When he slid his thumbs over her hardened nipples, she shuddered as if she had the ague.

"Surely you have the most beautiful breasts in Christendom."

"Aye, Don Luis, they're a national treasure," she whispered throatily, enjoying his extravagant compliment.

Snorting at her conceit, Luis bent his head and warmed those golden buds with his eager tongue. Elena grasped his thick hair, imprisoning him there, shuddering with delight as his mouth engulfed her flesh, creating a fiery rush of pleasure.

When finally she dragged his face to hers, having become desperate for his kiss, she welded her mouth to his. The fire of their kiss ignited her very soul. Longing to caress him, Elena outlined his smooth face, smiling when he kissed her fingers. Then she traced the hard bridge of his nose and moved her fingers into his crisp golden hair. Again she imprisoned his face in her hands, forcing his mouth against hers while their searing tongues plunged deep in joyous abandon.

His own impatience mounting, Luis pressed her hand against the throbbing swell of his passion. Elena shuddered as her hand grasped his throbbing member. Though she had not forgotten how wonderful he felt, this reminder served to further inflame her desire. Impatient still, Luis moved her hand aside while he unfastened his codpiece, eager for her touch. For those few moments it took to unleash the secrets of his body, Elena shook with delicious anticipation. At last, she curved her fingers about the strength of his flesh, which swelled noticeably beneath her touch. That pulsing brand leaped in her hand, threatening to burst with pleasure as she caressed him. Slowly increasing the pressure, she marvelled at the strength of his manhood, which felt so hard she could scarce believe she touched flesh and sinew.

"Oh, Luis, you're like iron," she breathed in wonder.

"Then come, sweetest, you can change that," he invited breathlessly as he nibbled her earlobe. "You can make me soft as butter."

Elena pressed against him, thrilling to the heat that throbbed between them. If only there were more time, she thought for the hundredth time, if only they need not listen for that royal fanfare announcing the sovereigns' departure. Then she chided herself for squandering their precious time in idle dreams.

"Luis, darling, make love to me. It's what I've lived for," she whispered invitingly, her voice of the purest sweetness. And he shook with need. "You are my heart, my soul."

"Elena." His voice broke on a sob of passion as he welded his mouth to hers.

There was no more time wasted in speech, no more hesitation. He swept the ample curves of her breasts in a trembling caress. Lifting her crimson skirts, he slid his hand along her silk-smooth legs and curving thighs until he reached the throbbing portal he longed to breach. Elena gasped, squirming pleasurably at his touch, shuddering, sobbing deep in her throat. Luis could endure no more. With a groan he pressed her deep into their makeshift bed, his mouth on hers taking her breath. Quickly he parted her thighs, his eager flesh aflame with passion as he slid inside her.

"Oh, sweetheart, love me, love me," she beseeched

in near delirium as their bodies fused together. His kisses soothed her, his hands supported her; engulfed by blazing passion, Elena was swept from this time and place.

Raising her high off the rough sacking, Luis speared her deeper, filling her body with fire. Still, Elena strained upward, clutching his hard shoulders while she tried to control the tremors of delight shuddering through her body. Too deep in passion to take direction, Luis moved now by instinct. Plunging from the precipice, he took her with him to that dark world of sensual pleasure. Elena cried out in ecstasy. Her nails sank in his velvet doublet as she clawed his back. Luis took her to the crest of the world and back.

Gradually their mutual cries subsided as they sank deeper into the contoured mound of straw. Blood pounded through their veins, and their breathing slowed as gradual awareness of their surroundings seeped into spent, passion-weary minds.

Elena lay still in Luis's arms. They kissed gently, almost absently as they tried to collect their wits. In the distance came the sound of trumpets, the strident notes of that regal fanfare shattering their drowsy pleasure.

Cursing beneath his breath, Luis jerked to a sitting position.

Desperately, Elena fumbled with her bodice, smoothing her skirts, pulling her headdress into place. So many things to be done and her hands were still shaking so hard that she could scarce perform the simplest task.

"Come, love, make haste," Luis urged, pulling her up beside him.

Elena stood on weak legs. For a moment dizziness beset her, and she put out her hand, clutching him to steady herself. Luis slid his arm about her waist as he urged her forward.

The cold December air hit her like a bucket of icy water, the change shocking after the warm drowsiness of the greenhouse. Shivering with cold, Elena gladly pulled on the cloak Luis thrust into her hands. Holding the garment tightly about her neck and tripping clumsily over her skirts, she hurried after him as fast as she could.

Outside the door of the hall, before they returned to that bright inhabited world, he grasped her hand. "You beautiful creature, I love you far more than is either healthy or wise."

"I love you, too, Luis—oh, when can we meet again?"

"Soon, pray God. Now hurry. You go first. Slip amongst the crowd and try to catch up. Perchance Mary's still so calf-eyed over Philip, she'll scarce notice you've been gone."

Elena found herself gently thrust inside the hall where the guests were crowding about the entrance. No one could leave the masque before the Queen and her consort. Like bright-colored sheaves of wheat bending before the wind, the courtiers swept low as the royal couple passed. The fanfare was already over, the trumpeters having hastened outdoors to salute the Queen and her husband when they reentered the palace across the court.

With thumping heart, Elena tried to push her way through the press of tipsy guests to resume her place in the Queen's retinue. Panting, her face flushed, she finally tagged along behind the very last of Her Majesty's ladies, following the procession back outside in the December cold. She could barely draw an even breath, and her legs felt too weak to carry her. Though she looked for Luis amongst Philip's gentlemen, she did not see him.

How quickly Luis had regained his composure, she mused, staring at the trailing azure skirts of the wench in front of her. While hardly missing a beat, he had gathered his wits and quickly assessed the situation. Perchance his composure had been far too easily won. Was he accustomed to such swift departures after love-making? Though she wanted to think she was his first love, she was not so naive as to believe that. Jealousy speared her heart. In vain Elena tried to thrust out her disturbing thoughts. Suddenly a gruff voice cut through her jealous musings, and, gulping in horror, Elena realized the Queen was calling her name.

Her skirts clutched in her hand, she stumbled forward, arriving breathless and dishevelled before Her Majesty. Quickly she dropped a deep curtsy, nearly slipping on the cobbles underfoot.

"Lady Elena, why do you hang back so?" Mary inquired sharply. "You do me no good walking in the next county."

"My apologies, Madam. It won't happen again."

Mary harrumphed and turned away. Then tucking her hand beneath Philip's elbow, the Queen continued across the court with Elena following close behind.

Chapter Nine

"How was it with your babe, Elena? Did you feel such terrible bloat in the beginning?" asked the Queen, rubbing her side where a knife-sharp pain had made her catch her breath.

"In truth, Madam, beyond nausea, I had little discomfort."

"Would that I could say the same. Still, whatever God sends, I will bear. 'Tis nothing beside his glorious gift to me."

Without thought for the other's exalted station, Elena affectionately squeezed Mary's shoulder. Grateful for that loving, impulsive gesture, Mary reached out to pat Elena's slender hand, noting it was unadorned. She intended to rectify that matter at the Christmas court.

"Will you rest, Madam? Or perhaps you would like to walk in the garden?"

"No . . . no, I must wait here for Philip. He's bound to come before long." Mary sighed, her mouth tightening, the wrinkles under her eyes becoming more pronounced as she strained to see across the court, looking in vain for her husband. "Don't you think he'll come soon?"

"Assuredly, Madam," Elena mumbled as she

straightened Mary's lap robe. Her heart ached for her aging mistress, so much in love with a man who cared little for her. In truth, Philip had been absent many hours. It was said he did not greatly enjoy hunting, and it was not the hour for prayer—Elena could only guess what occupied the Prince's time.

"Did you enjoy the flowers you received yesterday?"

Swallowing uncomfortably, Elena nodded, surprised by the Queen's question. "Yes, they were lovely. Surely they were hothouse blooms, for lilies don't blossom in December."

Mary smiled. "You have a secret admirer."

"An admirer, Madam . . . oh, but who could he be?" Elena stuttered, feigning innocence while her heart pounded. The bouquet had been delivered late yesterday afternoon by a lad in unfamiliar livery. She assumed the flowers were from Luis, yet how could the Queen have known?

"Yes, Elena, an admirer! Doubtless the gentleman wishes to remain anonymous—yet surely no harm will be done." With a conspiratorial smile, Mary urged Elena closer. "My dear," she disclosed hoarsely, "it is Don Alvaro who burns with such devotion for you. Now, are you surprised?"

"Yes, most surprised," Elena gasped, as she searched her mind for a face to fit the name. Finally she asked, "Who is Don Alvaro, Madam?"

"You must remember him," Mary said, a note of irritation in her voice. "The distinguished gentleman who crowned the queen at last night's festivities."

Elena paled. Now she recalled the elderly Spaniard who had crowned the queen of the ball. He was grandfatherly, stern and forbidding.

Studying Elena's face, Mary nodded in satisfaction. "There, you do remember. He's a very worthy suitor, most beloved of my dear Philip. In his own land Don Alvaro's very well respected. The Escalante family is linked to many great houses. You could do far worse, my dear.''

''I'm not seeking a suitor, Madam.''

''Perhaps not, but suitors are going to seek you. As my lady-in-waiting you will need my permission to wed—oh, silly goose!'' Mary caught Elena's hand, pulling her close. ''You're making this so difficult. I'm trying to tell you, 'tis I who encouraged Don Alvaro in his suit.''

''Oh!'' Elena gasped in dismay. ''He's so old.''

''Mature. There's a big difference. Don Alvaro's a wealthy widower and desirous of a young wife. Philip speaks so highly of him and anyone Philip trusts, I trust also. You have my absolute approval of his suit.''

Elena lowered her eyes, staring at the hem of the Queen's blue gown as she said, ''Thank you, Madam, but I don't even know Don Alvaro, let alone choose him as husband.''

''Ah, you're too fainthearted. I didn't know Philip, and now he's the dearest part of my life. Allow Don Alvaro to make himself known to you. That's all I ask.''

Reluctantly, Elena agreed. There had been a hint of finality in Mary's voice. When she wanted something, the Queen could be very determined, and though she had not actually said so, Elena suspected Mary wanted Don Alvaro Escalante to be her future husband. Uneasily, Elena contemplated the Queen's anger when she rejected the old don's suit.

After Mary had dismissed her, Elena returned to the room she shared with Anne, which was tucked away in the sprawl of buildings on the palace grounds. Though it was only late morning, it was dark indoors, and candles had already been lit in the royal apartments.

The waxy long-stemmed lilies glittered in the gloomy room. Elena's stomach lurched at the unpleasant reminder of Don Alvaro's unwelcome suit. Yesterday the surprise bouquet had brought her joy, for then she thought it came from Luis; today the flowers depressed her.

Would all this matchmaking never end? Will sought to betroth her to aged Lord Morton and sentence her to a life in a frigid northern castle, while the Queen would pair her with an aging Spanish don. Were she to marry Don Alvaro, she would probably be kept in virtual imprisonment, for she had heard the Spanish had adopted many Moorish customs with respect to their womenfolk. Either way, the future proposed for her by these determined matchmakers was decidedly bleak.

Elena pressed her face against the cold windowpane, staring unseeing into the courtyard below. Why had she not told the Queen she was already in love with Luis? He was a Spaniard, Philip's friend—surely he would meet with royal approval. Yet the Queen had spoken of husbands and, though he vowed he loved her, Luis de los Santos had not proposed marriage. In fact, so secret were their meetings, she had begun to doubt their reality, sometimes wondering if they had all been rapturous dreams.

Her breath steamed the diamond windowpanes, and she cleared a patch with her sleeve. Gray clouds smothered the heavens, trapping London beneath an acrid shroud. How cold it looked outside, the sharp wind whipping cloaks and tossing horses' tails as visitors came and went, bundled to the eyes against the elements. Elena's attention was attracted to a rider who rode quickly into the courtyard. The man dismounted, his back toward her. He was muffled in a heavy cloak with his hat pulled low over his ears. A stable lad held his mettlesome black horse as it pawed the cobbles, impatiently tossing its head. After a brief conversation the man gave the lad something which he thrust inside his doublet, then the man remounted and rode briskly towards the Strand.

Elena rested her face in her hands, elbows propped on the windowsill. Her gloomy thoughts soon returned to Luis. He had not contacted her in more than a week. It was almost Christmas, and they had seen each other just twice since that stolen hour in the greenhouse. When Luis had returned to court, she had foolishly imagined they would spend part of each day together. In reality they merely addressed each other politely when they met, afraid to reveal their romantic attachment. As favorites of their royal master and mistress, they dared not steal away. The Queen's obvious displeasure the night of the masque had been warning enough for Elena. She must be content with whispered endearments, stolen handclasps and soulful glances.

Making a great effort, Elena finally tore herself away from the window, anxious to dispel her pensive mood. Briskly she moved about the room, straightening clothing and bed covers, stooping to retrieve a discarded fan from behind the door.

This morning Anne had left on important business, telling Elena neither where she was going nor when she would be back. She merely begged her friend to make an excuse to Her Majesty, for this had been Anne's morning to attend the Queen. Elena invented a splitting headache to explain Anne's absence, the lie readily believed since Mary herself suffered frequent headaches. The Queen's ready acceptance of her lie made Elena feel extremely guilty. She supposed Anne had gone to meet her lover, yet from her agitation she doubted they were keeping a passionate tyrst. Yesterday the court buzzed with gossip that Sir Miles Ravenscroft's life was in danger. Whether it was because of his reputed sympathy for the protestant princess, or his outspoken protestantism, she did not know.

Lately there had been much speculation at court that those who refused to embrace Roman Catholicism would be arrested. The queen believed England doomed unless the nation returned to the true faith. On this point she and Philip saw eye to eye. So fanatically did Mary believe this truth, she would go to any lengths to enforce her will. Speculation that the Inquisition could be established here no longer seemed improbable.

Before she knew Mary well, the suggestion that such a kindly middle-aged soul would reenact the ancient Heresy Act, whereby heretics were to be burnt at the stake, was unthinkable. However, since that time, Elena had seen the fantatical light transfiguring Mary's lined face, revealing the narrow bigoted side of her nature. Now Elena shuddered to think where all this would end. Already Carranza vigilantly observed the court, his piercing black gaze missing little. Elena herself had come under his scrutiny, and she found the surveillance unnerving.

A knock on the door startled her. Smoothing her skirts, Elena went to answer it. A lad stood outside. Politely touching his forelock, he asked, "Is you Lady Elena Locke?"

"Yes."

"For you."

The lad thrust a folded paper in her hand before hastening away in the gloom.

There had been something vaguely familiar about the messenger, Elena decided as she closed the door. Taking the letter to the window, she found there was not enough light to read it. She lit one of their precious candles at the small fire—Mary was not overgenerous with supplies, and good tallow candles were doled out sparingly.

The red wax seal crumbled and fell to the rushes as she unfolded the parchment. Then, with pounding heart, she read: "Beloved, my heart aches for you. Meet me today at the Angel and Child at the corner of Bread St. Come alone. I will wait until dark."

Clutching her chest, Elena read and reread the note. Strangely, Luis had not signed his message, but she knew it came from him. Could he, like Anne, have grown fearful of spies? Now she remembered where she had seen that lad before—he was a Whitehall stable boy. The cloaked man she had watched in the courtyard must have been Luis. It surprised her to discover she had looked at him and not known him.

With trembling hands, Elena changed gowns. Luis had not asked her to dress inconspicuously, but her own growing awareness of being watched prompted her to wear a modest dark blue woolen gown. Of late a feeling of unease pervaded Mary's court. Jokes about religion were no longer told, betraying the mounting fear of being labeled heretic. Soon she, too, would start glancing behind her, trying to catch spies who purportedly lurked behind every doorpost.

The thought made Elena smile as she thrust her hair inside a plain French hood. At the last minute she splashed her neck and wrists generously with rose water before pulling on her heaviest cloak and heading outside.

The London streets were heavily congested with afternoon traffic. A sharp wind blew off the river, and as Elena hastened along, she felt occasional snowflakes melting against her icy cheeks. Though it was some distance to the Angel and Child, she had decided it was wiser to travel on foot. To order her horse saddled

would have aroused curiosity, for the Queen's ladies
did not ride alone.

Of late the streets had taken on a festive air in honor
of the approaching feast. Many establishments were
decorated with holm and boughs of bay; even the
conduits and street standards were bedecked with
garlands of holly and ivy. As she passed a cookshop,
the tantalizing aroma of roast goose wafted outside.
Eager apprentices grasped her arms, trying to urge her
inside to sample their masters' wares, extolling the
virtues of steaming meat pasties, fruit-filled plum
puddings and spicy mince pies. Having eaten only a
slice of bread and honey this morning, Elena was vastly
tempted. Her empty stomach protested loudly as
increasingly succulent smells wafted in the cold air.
Resolutely, she shook off the beseeching hands; each
delay meant less time to spend with Luis.

The aroma of fresh-baked bread added to her hunger
pangs as she rounded the corner of Bread Street and
saw the Angel and Child. A sign depicting the Christ
child and an archangel identified the inn. For those who
could read, the name was spelled out in gold letters on
a beam spanning the narrow street.

When Elena opened the inn door, she was enveloped
by a blast of warmth from the hearth, and she stepped
into a room redolent of ale and damp cellars. She looked
around the gloomy panelled room for Luis.

Fortunately, Luis had been watching for her at the
window, his view of the passersby distorted by its dingy
horn panes.

"This way, sweetheart," he said, taking her arm.

Elena smiled with relief. Several of the inn's
customers had begun to eye her hungrily; unaccompanied women were always fair game.

She hardly recognized Luis, dressed as he was in a plain

russet doublet beneath a dark traveling cloak. Set low on his head was a flat velvet cap with a curving black feather. With the exception of his black leather boots, which reached to the thigh in the Spanish fashion, little about his dress suggested he was a foreigner. His fair coloring and typically English clothes made it easy for him to blend with the crowd.

"Good, you did not wear your court gown," he remarked with relief as he led her down a narrow corridor away from the common room. "I rented a room, but I couldn't see the street from there."

"I was afraid you wouldn't be here."

"You're always expecting me to desert you. You have such little faith."

"Perhaps it's because you act so mysterious—here today, gone tomorrow. What else should I think?"

"That I love you far too much ever to desert you."

His tender words gave Elena a warm glow, and she smiled happily as she clutched his arm beneath his thick wool cloak.

"I could listen to you say such things all day."

"And so you shall, but in the privacy of our room."

He led her up a narrow half stair, stopping before the door at the top. Fitting a key in the lock, he opened the door and ushered her inside.

Though small, the room was clean. A hearty blaze filled the hearth, and Elena hastened toward it, stretching her chilled hands toward the warmth. In her haste to meet Luis, she had forgotten her muff.

He closed the door and waited in the shadows. In this gloomy, low-ceilinged room, with the black voluminous cloak hanging from his broad shoulders, Luis appeared larger and somewhat menacing.

"Well, mistress," he said at last, when she failed to speak, "did you come merely to warm yourself . . .

or to sup?'' he asked, glancing toward the table where
covered dishes awaited them.

Taking a deep, steady breath for courage, Elena
prepared to tell him the secret about their child before
she could feel at peace. Yet today Luis seemed like a
stranger in his unfamiliar English clothes. The man she
knew always wore dark Spanish velvet adorned with
pearls and bore himself with the haughty arrogance of
the hidalgo.

The winter wind rattled the casement, and they
jumped, startled by the sound.

''Spies outside on the roof?'' Elena ventured
humorously.

''If they are, then pray God they freeze,'' he joked,
taking a hesitant step toward her. She did not move,
making him come to her. ''Elena, sweetheart, I know
I've deserted you of late, but it was not my fault,'' he
said, reaching for her. ''Surely you aren't angry with
me?''

''Never that. I just can't believe this is real.''

''Believe it. Oh, yes, sweetheart, believe it,'' he murmured, his face against hers. Impatiently, he captured
her in his strong arms, forcing her to relinquish her will
to his.

Elena had not intended to stand aloof, yet she seemed
quite unable to dispel the emotion that distanced them.
Not until his hot mouth covered hers, until he lifted her
off the rushes in the fervor of his embrace, did she come
alive. Heat tingled along each nerve of her body. She
shuddered, she trembled, she ached for him. Without
conscious thought her arms went about his broad
shoulders and she clung to him while they kissed open-
mouthed, their breaths mingling hot and fragrant.

''Dear God, how much I've wanted you in my arms,''
he finally whispered against her hair. ''Each day has

seemed like a week.''

Elena found herself set down on trembling legs, the rushes quaking underfoot. Yet, when he would have taken her again in his arms, she pushed against his chest, keeping him at arm's length.

''No. Last time and the time before you would not let me speak. Today I intend to tell you what's in my heart.''

Surprised by the unexpected determination in her voice, he honored her request, letting his arms drop uselessly at his sides.

''As you will. Can this vital discourse be exchanged over eel pie and malmsey, or is it of such seriousness—''

''Please, don't jest.''

''Forgive me.''

Solemnly he took her cloak, then pulling off his own, Luis pitched the garments across the bed in the corner. Pulling out a chair, he seated Elena at the small table with her back to the fire. He uncovered the plates and filled their glasses with red wine from a leather bottle before he took his seat opposite her.

''Are you not to speak?'' he asked finally as the minutes rolled by while she devoured a warm slice of spiced eel pie. Elena took a deep breath. This subject was not nearly as easy to broach as she had expected. The long rehearsed speech she intended to deliver forgotten, she fought for words, not wanting to betray the ragged state of her emotions. After taking a deep draught of malmsey, she finally began.

''Luis, please, don't interrupt. What I have to say isn't easy.''

He smiled faintly and nodded, before settling back in his chair to listen.

''I don't know how much you know about that last month I lived at Locke Hall. Randle was a long time dying. I was kept a virtual prisoner at his side. That was why I couldn't ride out to meet you."

"I thought perchance you'd lost interest."

"Oh, Luis," she reproached, tears stinging her eyes. "Surely you knew that my lord was dying."

Nervously he toyed with the stem of the glass beside his plate. "Yes, it was common knowledge."

"I heard nothing from you. When I rode to Nethergate and found you'd left for London without a word, I was shattered."

"How could I leave word? You were guarded like the royal jewels. I risked being set upon by the dogs every time I ventured on your land."

A wave of relief washed over her. "So you did try?"

"I tried, but obviously without success. I couldn't endanger you further by pressing the matter."

She reached across the table and took his hand, her eyes glistening with tears of relief. "Thank God. I was afraid you'd given no thought to me—"

His fingers crushed hers in sudden tension. "You certainly give me small credit—"

"Hush, be not angry. Just listen. There's more. The day I rode to Nethergate, I'd escaped—"

"Escaped! From your own home?"

"Lady Locke kept me a virtual prisoner, forbidden to walk, to ride . . . I . . . Oh, Luis . . ." Her voice broke, and she stared down at her hands, fighting for control. "At that time I was with child."

He exclaimed sharply in anger. Reaching across the table, Elena placed her finger on his lips.

"Hush, say nothing until I've finished. When I climbed from my window I fell—"

This time he would not be still. "Dear God! How far?"

"Not far, and at the time I thought little of it, so

anxious was I to get away to see you. I appeared unharmed. Only later I began to bleed . . . a cottager aided me . . . oh, Luis, I lost the babe.'' Now her lip trembled so much she could not go on. He patted her hand, holding it soothingly in his own until she could continue. ''Afterwards I was very ill. Lady Locke blamed me for killing the babe, just as she blamed me for Randle's death. She tried to whip me. I think she'd lost her reason. While we fought for the whip, she collapsed. She's bedridden now, no longer able to revile me.''

''Why didn't you tell me before? You should have told me that night—''

''I tried—you wouldn't let me speak, remember?''

Shamefaced, he looked down at his hands. ''I remember. If only I'd known about the babe . . . I might have hurt you.''

''It's too long ago for that. I'm quite recovered. Only in my heart does it hurt still.''

Luis's head snapped up, an unfathomable expression crossing his face. He saw pain in her eyes, her trembling lips, the shimmer of unshed tears hovering on her lashes.

''You grieve still for the loss of *his* child?'' he rasped uncomfortably. ''For, Christ in heaven, you surely don't regret his death.''

Fear gripped Elena as she saw the closed-off expression transforming his features. Quickly she tried to explain.

''Luis, don't judge me until you know—''

''I make judgment only by what you tell me. You say your heart aches still for the loss of his babe,'' he reminded, bitterness and pain apparent in his voice.

''Oh, Luis, now you make my heart ache for a very different reason,'' she whispered when he pulled his hand from hers. Pain wrenched forth her harsh words. "You're angry because I've wounded your manly pride."

"Nay, it's far more than that, Elena. You're grieving over the loss of the seed of a man you professed to hate—"

"Be still and hear me out! The babe wasn't his!"

"Then . . . you mean it was mine!"

"That's why my heart ached so. Randle never took me once. You were the only man I . . . Oh, Luis, I've kept this terrible secret all this time, longing to be able to tell you—" She could go no further. Elena laid her head on her arms and wept.

Luis hesitated before finally coming around to her side of the table. He took her in his arms. Kicking aside her empty chair, he leaned against the table, cradling her while she wept bitterly. He whispered soothing love words, holding her close until her tears finally ceased. Then he lifted her tear-stained face to kiss her swollen lips.

"If only I'd known. And to think you traveled to London when you were barely recovered—what risks you took. Would that things could have been different, beloved. Just think, you might have borne my son."

Gently he urged her to sit, handling her carefully as if it were only yesterday she had lost the babe. Kneeling before her, Luis held her hands, covering them with remorseful kisses. Looking up at her, his pale blue eyes glittering with moisture, he silently begged her forgiveness.

"If only I'd known," he kept repeating. "I understand why you dare not send such a message . . . yet if only I'd known. I could have cared for you instead of leaving you alone to endure your loss. To think you suffered such pain amongst those who loved you not

. . . Oh, dearest Elena, I'm sorry."

She stroked the bright gold head resting on her lap, moved by love that was almost maternal. "Luis, you're not to blame."

"You're too generous. The babe was mine and so was the responsibility."

"You forget—I had a husband. In the eyes of the law the babe belonged to him."

He winced at the painful reminder, and she bent to kiss his brow.

"I'd have endured much to bear your child. Oh, Luis, 'tis my turn now to ask forgiveness. I killed our babe by my own foolishness. Had I just stayed in my room—"

"No, no. Hush."

His arms went around her waist, and they clung together in the crackling firelight. Her tears wet his face until, at last, Elena's eyes were dry. Smiling up at her, Luis traced her soft mouth and wet cheeks with his forefinger, his gaze reverent as if he were looking at a holy statue.

"Dearest Elena, my biggest regret is that I didn't know, that I left you to face the ordeal alone. I'm so sorry. Say you forgive me."

"Of course you're forgiven. All that matters is that we're together now. That we stay together . . ." Elena paused as Mary's gruff voice speaking in praise of Don Alvaro Escalante echoed in her head. But she would not mention their conversation to Luis. After he had pledged his suit, there would be time enough to tell him he had a rival. Together they could approach the Queen—until then the unpleasant prospect would remain her secret.

"*Querida*, you're all the world to me," he whispered ardently, drawing her face to his to kiss.

For a few minues they lay content before the crackling

hearth. Elena felt safe within the circle of his arms, convinced of his love as she held him close, the scent of his body tantalizing her senses. "We couldn't have asked for a greater gift. I thought by now someone surely would have told you I'm a widow."

"Yes, I knew," was all he said.

Slightly taken aback, Elena waited for him to speak those words she longed to hear. Of course, she could not ask him outright to wed her. Possibly he still hesitated because as a foreign noble he doubted his ability to support a wife at the English court. The silence stretched interminably.

"Elena?"

"Yes."

"You're the most wonderful part of my life," he vowed sincerely, his face softening with love. "If I lost you I don't know what I'd do."

At those tender words her unease magically dissolved.

"You won't lose me, Luis. You're the only man I've ever loved. There could never be another."

"Do you swear?"

"I swear it."

"Beloved." Luis swept her into his arms. "Mine forever," he vowed as he hugged her tight. "Let me make love to you. Or should we not? I don't want to hurt you."

Playfully she cuffed him about the head. "I demand you make passionate love to me this instant," she cried. "What we did two weeks ago didn't harm me, and now I'm two weeks more desirous."

"Dear God," he exclaimed as he bore her to the bed, "then I'll be lucky to come out of this unscathed."

She smiled as she rested her cheek against his. Luis dropped her on the patchwork spread where she bounced several times on the soft feather mattress, giggling, wanting this wonder to never end. How she longed to feel him pressed against her, kissing her, loving her.

"Don't just stand there looking at me," she admonished at last. "Come prove to me what a worthy lover you are."

Together they unhooked and unfastened her garements, his hands trembling as he briefly skimmed the perfection of her breasts. But she would allow him no further privileges. Squeaking in protest, Elena scrambled hastily beneath the blankets to keep warm. Then in an imperative tone she demanded he undress for her.

Grinning at her unexpected command, Luis was only too pleased to comply. Slowly he unfastened his doublet, then his shirt; he was such a long time untying his points, she began to shake with anticipation.

"Oh, you're taking so long," she gasped impatiently. "I swear you're tantalizing me on purpose."

"Ah, you're far cleverer than I thought."

He struggled to pull off his tall boots. They thumped on the floor. He padded to the hearth and pitched fresh logs on the fire to keep the room warm. A few minutes later the fire flared high, bathing the room in orange light. With his back to the blaze, Luis slowly took off his doublet and shirt and peeled down his tights as Elena's heartbeat grew frenzied. Finally he stood naked before her, his muscular, perfectly proportioned body outlined by golden firelight.

"You're so beautiful," she whispered in awe, her voice catching in her throat. "Oh, come, be mine!"

His mouth crooked in a grin as he came into her outstretched arms. He was more than ready, his flesh darkly engorged with blood and fully roused in passion. Luis slid between the covers, his muscular arms going

around her, his hands stealing to her voluptuous breasts
while he drew her into a passionate kiss. Trembling as
his hot, hard body pressed against hers, Elena reached
down to cradle that pulsing brand that thrilled and fas-
cinated her, that brought her closer to ecstasy than she
had believed possible.

"I love you more than life itself," Luis vowed
ardently before his mouth covered hers.

When she was safe in his arms and fired by his
passion, Elena's happiness knew no bounds. She began
to tremble as he kissed her breasts, then moved down
to her navel, across her belly—she cried out as his hot
tongue flicked the sensitive core of her passion.
Shuddering, Elena fought to hold back as Luis brought
her tinglingly alive. Heat coursed between her thighs
until she doubted she could endure another minute of
torment. Just when she knew that if he did not stop she
was lost, Luis took away that heated pleasure. Slowly
he caressed the length of her with his hot mouth. He
moved painfully slowly, and she trembled with desire
when he finally reached her breasts, engorged and
aching for his touch. Gently he cupped those silken orbs,
his thumbs grazing her hardened nipples, making her
shudder. Luis trailed a fiery path of kisses across her
breasts until she sobbed with desire.

Seizing him, Elena welded her mouth to his while
fitting that bursting pleasure high between her thighs.
Shuddering repeatedly as their pulsating flesh touched,
she fought for control. Oh, today she wanted him more
than she had ever wanted him! His mouth seemed even
more wonderful than she remembered, his hard body
so much more arousing.

"Luis, sweetheart, take me," Elena begged desperately, running her hands over his smooth back,
feeling the muscles ripple beneath her touch. Seizing

him by the breadth of his square shoulders, she shook him, trying to hurry him as she urged him to heed her plea.

Effortlessly, Luis slid inside her, and she cried out in delight, clamping her legs about his slender waist, locking him there for her pleasure. He seized her hips and tilted her, diving even deeper into her hot core. Then Luis drove hard, making her gasp in delight at the hot invasion. Swirling darkness filled the room as Elena finally gave way to passion, releasing her pent-up pain and frustration, all the overwhelming love and desire she felt for this man. They moved rhythmically, straining limb against limb, muscle against muscle. Elena longed to be able to merge her being with his, to mingle blood, sinew, and flesh so that they need never part. This was the end of doubt, of loneliness . . .

Luis breathed her name hoarsely in a litany of passionate Spanish endearments as he strove to satisfy the torment of desire. Elena cried out in delight, but he didn't hear. His breathing grew labored, his mind far from this place as he plunged headlong into the darkness of passion, sweeping her with him to a climax so long and deep it became sweet pain. They drifted back to consciousness by degrees, fighting against the languorous weight of fulfillment. For a while they lay unmoving until Luis began to kiss her lips, his hands gently caressing her smooth back. Elena came back to the present with a great sigh of contentment, resting her face in the warm, fragrant hollow of his neck. Totally at peace, completely loved, she wondered if she would ever again feel the pangs of desire.

Yet a little later beneath Luis's slow caresses, while his sensitive hands swept her shoulders and back and traced the firm perfection of her buttocks, Elena's blood came jarringly to life. When she felt him roused hotly against her belly, she shuddered with delight, forced to admit the time might never come when she was satiated with his lovemaking.

Hours passed unnoticed. The crackling fire burned low; the light inside the room grew dim. And still they loved, lost in a world of their own making. Near delirious with happiness, Elena lay content in Luis's arms, waking and dozing until the gray sky beyond the windows grew dark.

Rousing himself at last, Luis jerked awake in alarm.

"Come, Elena, we must get back. The hour's late."

Reluctant and complaining drowsily, she finally thrust aside the covers and slid from the bed. He laughed at her stumbling sleepiness as he tossed her clothes to her. The rushes felt harsh underfoot, and the shocking chill of the room made Elena shiver. Her clothes stubbornly refused to fit, and finally Luis had to assist her before they were able to leave.

The street outside the Angel and Child was pitch black. Several shimmering pools of lantern light spilled into the narrow street, but vast stretches remained dark and forbidding. Luis's hand hovered about his dagger, for he was justifiably wary of the London streets. Their breath steamed in the cold air as he helped Elena to the saddle. A light snow had settled against the building and outlined tiled roofs and windowsills; even the holly streamers decorating the street standards wore crests of white.

Luis said little on the return journey, merely murmuring assent or absently kissing the top of her head when she spoke to him. Serious thoughts occupied his mind, for when she turned to look at him as they rode through a pool of lantern light, she saw his frown as he hunched down in the folds of his cloak. She did not ask what thoughts made him look so grim, for she was a little afraid to learn the answer. While they loved, safe and warm in the upper room of the Angel and Child, her doubts about the future had all disappeared. But now, as each minute brought them closer to the palace, closer to their duties and obligations, unease again gnawed at her peace of mind.

All too soon they reached Charing Cross. As they clopped along the Strand past the houses of the nobility, Elena's heart sank lower. The familiar mansions sped by in the cold darkness as Luis's horse picked up speed, impatient for its warm stable and bag of oats.

When they finally entered the precincts of Whitehall, Luis passed through a small side arch leading into a darkened court. He was not anxious to be identified, and his caution was necessary to preserve Elena's reputation.

From here Elena could find her way. He helped her from the saddle, and she clung to him, kissing his icy cheek before she reluctantly walked into the dark alley between the buildings. Flaring torches set in iron holders high on the walls lit her way as she hastened toward her quarters overlooking the adjoining court.

Tomorrow she must tell the Queen a second lie to explain her own absence. She prayed she had not been seen in Luis's company by some jealous courtier all too eager to whisper secrets in the royal ear. Unlike her father's, Mary's was not a licentious court; her ladies were expected to conduct themselves with decorum, and a secret assignation at the Angel and Child would meet with her stern disapproval. Elena knew that only Anne could be trusted with the truth. And perhaps her safety there lay only in her own knowledge of Anne's deepest secrets. The other ladies-in-waiting, though apparently friendly on the surface, were as false as their male counterparts, eager to discredit each other in hope of winning royal favor.

Weighing what she would say to Anne, Elena fitted her key in the lock. To her surprise she found the room dark and cold. Anne had not returned to fuel the fire, and only a few cinders glowed in the grate. Concern for Anne's safety overrode Elena's own fear of discovery. She prayed nothing had gone astray with her friend or Sir Miles.

Chapter Ten

The rollicking Christmas court was in full swing. The revellers hid their faces behind glittering gold and silver animal masks. Maidens, dressed in their finest, danced and laughed and grew tipsy. The Lord of Misrule presided over tonight's festivities, proclaiming many foolish laws and commands to the amusement of all present.

Branches of fir, holly and ivy festooned the rafters. The room was redolent with the pungence of evergreens, hot candle wax and the myriad perfumes worn by the courtiers. Spicy aromas from the recent feast also lingered in the atmosphere. Though long past, the groaning board was not forgotten. Many lolled on their benches, too full to move, while others lay snoring in the rushes, felled by an abundance of ale and malmsey. The main feature of the banquet had been an enormous glazed pie containing a dozen live white doves. When the pie was cut, the birds flapped about the hall before eventually perching on the rafters where they were forgotten until some lady squealed in indignation as bird droppings fouled her headdress.

Elena wore her crimson gown with a gilded red velvet headdress—Anne's gift to her. Tonight she had been the center of attention as first one, then another, of Mary's courtiers extravagantly praised her beauty. Best of all, Luis was here. And in the relaxed atmosphere of this Christmas revel they had openly exchanged kisses and embraces beneath the beribboned kissing bough. Luis partnered her for several dances, and they even contrived to sit together at table. If only they could steal away later, everything would be perfect.

Silver bells sewn to red ribbon streamers crisscrossed the room, tinkling sweetly at every draft. The mounting noise inside the hall soon drowned their music as the musicians struck up a roistering country measure. Several gentlemen sang a bawdy parody of the piece for the dancers' amusement. Already tired of the racket, Elena stepped outside into the chill December night in the hope the cold air would restore her senses.

Back and forth she paced, shivering in the darkness. She had expected Luis to follow, although that had not been her reason for stepping outside. Still, she waited expectantly. Elena's disappointment mounted as she heard no quick tread on the paving. This evening, many women claimed his attention yet, to give him his due, he had favored none above the rest. Merely watching him dance with others, or seeing the artful creatures trap him beneath the kissing bough, was enough to rouse her jealousy.

Leaning against the carved doorpost, Elena stared at the bright stars twinkling overhead. So far this had been a perfect Christmas. She fingered the large, rather awkward mounting of the gold ring set with topaz and pearls that had been the Queen's gift to her. Luis had given her a pair of pearl-embroidered kid gauntlets the exact shade of her blue riding buskins. Of exquisite workmanship, the perfumed gloves made the whole room smell of summer. When he presented his gift, Luis had kissed her passionately, repeating his vows of ever-lasting love. What more could she ask from life?

Yet at times a vague, uneasy feeling eclipsed her sense of well-being. Try as she might, Elena had been unable to conquer this periodic gloom. Was she uneasy because Luis had not asked her to marry him? Or was it more the Queen's championing of Don Alvaro Escalante as her prospective husband that caused her concern? At the Queen's urging, the old don had partnered her several times in the dance. And there was also the unpleasant reminder of Will's nuptial scheme. Only yesterday she had received a letter from him to inform her matters were proceeding well.

Deciding the noise and laughter of the hall was preferable to these unpleasant thoughts, Elena turned to go inside. She collided with a man who waited in the shadows. With a cry of alarm she put out her hand to steady herself, touching a stiffly embroidered doublet. The husky Spanish endearments that followed their collision quickly revealed this was no stranger.

"Luis! Why do you wait here in the dark? I expected you to follow me," she cried sharply. He had startled her badly, and she still felt cheated because he had not joined her outside.

"You've turned uncommonly shrewish."

"You've wasted precious time when we could have been together."

"Hold your sharp tongue till you find out what I was doing."

"After watching the prettiest wenches in the room flocking around you, I'm afraid to guess."

"So, you're jealous! *Dios*, that does my heart good."

Laughing he swept her in his arms and held her close while raining kisses on her cold face. Then Luis pulled her with him into the pitch-black depth of an icy alcove.

"Hear me out, then apologize. Your friend Anne says she'll take your place tonight in waiting on Her Majesty. And Philip, bless him, is already suffering from too much wine. He'll never notice if I'm gone. We're free! Free!"

They clung to each other, and Luis kissed her and kissed her until Elena made him stop so she could catch her breath.

"Where can we go? 'Tis too cold outdoors."

"Assuredly," he agreed, shivering. "My Spanish blood craves the heat. Come, give me no argument, just follow like an obedient child."

Elena pressed her silver cat's mask to her face, then, clutching the back of his stiff, jewel-embroidered black doublet, she let him lead the way. Luis also hid behind a mask, yet only the most casual observer would not guess their identities, if only by their distinctive garments. Along twisting stone corridors, up flights of stairs they went until, at the end of a damp passage smelling of must and age, they finally reached their destination.

Luis unlocked the door.

Elena gasped in surprise as she saw the inviting room. A glowing fire burned merrily in the hooded corner hearth, filling the room with flickering golden light. Though small, this panelled room was lavishly appointed. A great carved bed hung with gold-edged crimson hangings took up most of the space. She was further surprised to find the bedcovers had the Spanish coat of arms embroidered on them in gold thread. A decanter and two crystal glasses stood on a small oak table; a covered dish beside the glasses held slices of fine-grained, buttery Madeira cake glistening with sugar.

"How?" was all she asked as she turned to him with

a smile of delight. This luxury was more than she had anticipated.

"I, too, have useful friends," Luis replied mysteriously. "We have the use of these splendid accommodations until the small hours of the morning, when our worthy benefactor returns from Matins."

Surprised that the room's occupant kept monastic offices, Elena asked his identity.

"No, *querida*, he must remain anonymous. He wouldn't want it known he lends his room for sinful liaisons."

Pouting in mock displeasure, Elena abandoned her questions. It did not really matter whose bed, whose fire or whose wine this was, just as long as she shared them with Luis.

Elena sat on the ramswool rug before the hearth, knees drawn up, gazing into the rosy embers. If only she could count on a lifetime of nights like this. If only . . .

Gently, Luis nudged her arm as he handed her a glass of wine and a slice of cake. Though Elena had thought after tonight's banquet she would never want to eat again, she found the snack welcome.

Luis watched her eat, enjoying the rare privilege. The priest whose quarters they borrowed was aware he intended to entertain a lady, yet chose not to know her identity, merely telling him he would not need the room until after Matins. Bless you, Fray Tomas, for your hypocrisy.

"Wouldn't it be lovely if we could spend every night together like this," Elena ventured several hours later as she lay wholly at peace in Luis's arms before the glowing hearth. Twice they had made love, and they had dozed beneath the down-filled covers before returning to the warm hearth.

Though they had both slipped on their garments for warmth, they had not bothered to properly fasten them, and Elena's half-laced bodice was a temptation Luis could not resist. He traced the mound of her breast beneath the scarlet velvet, fingering her golden nipple through the soft fabric.

"Don't you think it would be wonderful to always be together?"

"Paradise on earth."

"When can we be together again?"

"I don't know. Must you always spoil our meeting by demanding a definite time for the next?"

She smiled. Then tracing her tongue along the hard outline of his jaw, she said, "You should be flattered I want to see you again."

"I am the proudest man in Christendom," he whispered, kissing the pulse beating in her throat. Very deliberately, he began to pull open her bodice.

"Oh, Luis, I'm happy and sad all at the same time."

"Don't be sad. We have each other for as long as I'm at court—"

"And then?" Elena sat up, staying his hands, wondering if this was the time to extract a lasting pledge from him. "What if you're sent home to Spain?"

"I won't be 'sent home,' as you put it. Philip values my friendship too much for that. I'll go home only when I choose. Now, no more foolish chatter. Come, let me make love to you one more time. No . . . stay here," he whispered when she started to get up. "Humor me— let us make love before the fire."

Shuddering in delight, Elena kissed him long and hard, thrilling to his arousing hands, hot and tantalizing as they moved softly over her breasts. Eagerly Luis thrust down his tights, freeing his aroused manhood. Elena could not keep her hands off him, fashioning the iron-hard shape before she bent forward to kiss the moist tip, rejoicing as he trembled beneath her caress, barely able to contain his passion.

"Your churchman would be shocked to think we're defiling his room."

"You're right," Luis rasped, "I doubt he'd believe what's taking place before his hearth. Frankly, I don't care what he thinks."

"Nor I." Elena pressed her breasts against his bare chest, enjoying the delicious feel of his crinkly gold hair prickling her flesh. "Oh, Luis, promise to love me forever."

"*Querida*, haven't I already made that promise a dozen times?"

"Then make it a dozen and one."

Blood pounded in her ears and she grew weak beneath the pressure of his hard, arousing body until she no longer cared if he even answered.

"I swear to love only you for as long as I live."

His earnest vow made her heart soar. The hot masculine scent of his body reminded her of all the other marvelous times they had made love. Suddenly overwhelmed by deep emotion, Elena buried her face in his neck and shed tears of joy.

Luis fondled her soft white breasts and her smooth, silky back, his hands arousing heat he had thought already spent. Overwhelmed by emotion, she kissed him hotly as she tangled her fingers in the hair on his chest, gently squeezing his nipples. A shudder of passion rocked him. Aware the hour for Matins was fast approaching, Elena rolled to her back on the curly piled rug, the coarse wool tickling her bare skin. Eagerly, Elena opened to him, and Luis breached that sweet portal, forcing her to lie still despite their mutual quivers of passion.

The time for speech was over. Hot blood swept them
to that secret place they alone inhabited. So sudden and
sweet was her release that Elena's teeth pressed into
his shoulder. She did not draw blood, but even if she
had, he would not have been aware of it. So perfectly
attuned were they to each others' needs that they writhed
as one and their cries of joy, their sighing descent to
earth, became a single pleasure.

Holding each other close, they lay still beside the fire,
which was burning low.

"At this moment I'd go happily to my death," Luis
murmured, holding her close.

"Please, Luis, don't say such things, even in jest,"
she admonished in sudden fear. Of late there had been
so much talk of punishment, spies and death, her nerves
were on edge.

"Silly little girl," he chided, tenderly kissing her,
moved by her concern. "Nothing's going to happen to
me."

"Luis, what if something should happen? I've no
claim on you. Oh, this is so difficult . . ." Elena buried
her face in his neck, realizing she had been on the verge
of asking him to marry her. The subject was so much
on her mind, she had almost blurted her thoughts aloud.
The realization embarrassed her.

Luis moved away, his face set.

"What are you trying to say?"

Her head snapped up, and she stared at him in
astonishment.

"Sweet Mary, are you that dense? Surely you aren't
going to make me actually ask you to—"

"Marry you?"

Letting out a painful breath, she lay back on the rug.
At last the subject that caused her such concern had been
broached between them. And, though it took some

prompting, he had named it himself.

"Now you mention it—yes, 'tis only natural for me to assume—"

Very deliberately, he set her aside. Elena was shocked by the change in his mood.

"I knew it would eventually come to this," he said.

He actually sounded angry! Defensively she pulled the unlaced sides of her bodice together, feeling suddenly ashamed to be bare-breasted before him.

"I didn't intend to anger you."

"It's just—oh, Elena, we were so happy. Isn't being together enough?"

"Perhaps for you. What if I'm with child? I've no convenient husband this time."

Shocked by the sharpness of her voice, his head snapped up, his eyes steely. "*Jesu*, I can hardly believe it's you speaking."

"What do you expect me to say? You vow you love me—"

"I do love you."

"Then make your suit public! I know it's not been long since Randle . . . Luis, we're already lovers. How much better it will be when we come out of hiding."

"Yes, it would be better. Unfortunately it's impossible."

Luis had already relaced his points and fastened his doublet. He went to the side table to pour himself a glass of wine.

Elena sat numbly before the hearth. Her trust, her love, had just suffered a terrible blow. And all because she had asked him to make an "honest woman" out of her.

"Why do you smile?"

"I was wondering if you intend to make me your wife. Obviously the answer's no. I satisfy well enough as your whore—"

In a moment he was beside her, yanking her up by the wrist. "Don't ever call yourself that again," he snarled, his face set.

"If you don't marry me, Don Luis, that's exactly what you make me."

Their eyes met, cold anger blazing there, the depth of their mutual emotion surprising them each in turn. Finally Luis released her wrist and backed away, his light eyes fastened on hers.

"Much as I want to, I can't marry you."

His shocking words struck like a knife in her heart. Elena reeled backwards, clutching the panelling.

"You're already married?"

Her tortured voice made him wince. He shook his head.

"Then why? Surely to God you love me enough to speak for me. Or are all those vows naught but passionate lies?"

"I've never lied to you, Elena, and I won't start now. You demand to know the reason and you shall. I can't speak for you because I'm betrothed to another."

"Betrothed!" she repeated, her voice shrill. "Betrothed is not married. Or in Spain does that mean something different?"

"Don't, Elena. Were I free, it would be the greatest delight of my heart. But it's hopeless. This is a betrothal that can't be broken."

"Why? Do you love her that much?"

"I barely know her. There are reasons you wouldn't understand."

"Ah, Don Luis, you underestimate me. I understand well enough. She waits for you in Spain whilst you make merry behind her back. 'But dearest, she was only an Englishwoman, a heretic, barely worth counting—"

"Enough!" he cried, blazing in anger. Grabbing her arms, he shook her. "I'll listen to no more."

"Is it too close to the truth?" she whispered, licking tears from her lips. Eyes glistening, she stared at him, his black velvet garments a menacing blur through the moisture.

"Never let me hear you say such things again. Come, it's time for us to go. You're overwrought. Tomorrow I'll explain everything. I was wrong to avoid the issue. You deserved the truth from the start. Forgive me, Elena, my love for you made me a coward."

"Damn you for your treachery," she hissed suddenly, her eyes flashing tawny yellow in the firelight.

"Elena, it's not what you think."

"Oh, of that I'm sure, Don Luis."

His name was a scornful hiss on her lips. His hand clenched white on the table. He had deserved as much, he knew, yet he had prayed this night need never come. That illusion had been merely a child's fantasy, not worthy of a man his age. Unwittingly, his cowardice had caused her more pain than the truth would have done in the beginning.

"Elena, please, listen . . ." he began, stopping when he saw she had no intention of hearing him out.

Stonily, Elena pulled her cloak around her body, not bothering to properly refasten her garments. Luis was more than a match for her—he stood already dressed, mask in hand. But then, she remembered painfully, he had always been the first to recover from lovemaking. And tonight he was spared the disadvantage of tears to slow his hands.

"I should enjoy nothing better than storming out of here and leaving you to your own devices, Don Luis, but I don't know the way. As a proper Spanish gentleman, perhaps you will show me back to the hall before you take your leave.''

Her cold, precise words speared his heart, for he did not realize they were spawned by pain and rejection.

''Assuredly, Mistress Locke. I'm still that much of a gentleman, though you possibly find that hard to believe.''

With that he opened the door and silently led the way down the corridor. Blindly, Elena followed, hardly knowing where she went, keeping only the dark blur of his body in sight—she would not deign to hold on to him now.

As they rounded the corner, laughter and many voices echoed in the distance as the drunken revellers revelled on. Avoiding the crowded hall, Luis led Elena outside, stubbornly insisting on escorting her to the very courtyard above which she lived.

''*Buenos noches, doña.*''

Emotions raged inside her as she looked at him— pain, hurt, rejection, anger, love . . . Dear God, love was still there in abundance. Elena did not reply, merely strumbled away in the darkness. When she thought he could no longer see or hear, she reeled drunkenly into the wall, crumpling against the cold stone. All her hurt spilled forth in hot tears. He had deceived her. Oh, how she longed to hate him, to be able to tell him in all honesty that she no longer cared what he did, that he could go home to his Spanish senorita with a clear conscience. She wanted to say that, but she had never been a good liar. Someday perhaps she could say it, thereby salving a little of her battered ego. Someday. But it would not be soon.

The cold gray sky was tinged with light as the Queen's ladies, muffled against the morning cold, entered the chapel for mass.

In the few hours before dawn Elena slept fitfully.
Anne came to the door and knocked to alert her before
going away again, probably thinking Luis had spent the
night. Surrepetitiously, Elena brushed tears from her
lashes. Try as she might, she could not stop crying.
The memory of his kiss, of his lovemaking, and
especially the hateful knowledge he was bound to
another, all started her tears flowing anew.

White-faced, Elena knelt to pray, unable to think of
anything except her pain. The priest's rose brocade
vestments indicating Advent was past, the nose-prickling
smell of incense, the carols from the sweet-voiced choir,
all were mockeries of her sorrow. This was the season
of joy, of celebration, yet she had no joy in her broken
heart and had little to celebrate beyond the loss of her
love. Mechanically, Elena made the responses, sitting,
standing, kneeling, her body alone participating in the
Mass while her mind floated free, pining for that
pleasant world of yesterday.

Those twelve days of Christmas feasting and revelling
were an ordeal to endure. No longer need Elena plead
lame excuses; daily her head pounded like a drum.
Nothing brought a smile to her set lips, neither the gaily
dressed mummers cavorting about the hall, or the pure
tones of the carol singers. Spiced dishes in mind-
dazzling numbers covered the groaning board and there
was much laughter and dancing, but it failed to cheer
her. Wine alone numbed her pain, though it did little
to relieve the throb in her temples. To make matters
worse, Elena was seated at table in a direct line from
Luis. He also looked grim, his dark-shadowed eyes
betraying restless nights. Only the assurance that he
suffered, too, brought her a spark of pleasure.

In the days immediately following her discovery of
Luis's betrothal, disillusion had set in. Was it possible

he was like the other men in this well-dressed throng,
ever ready with vows and promises that were nothing
but honeyed lies? His speed in redressing after lovemaking—his very skill at arousing her passion—
reflected long practice in pleasing women. These
thoughts merely compounded her misery, until Elena
began to wonder if this damnable Christmas celebration
would ever end.

"You don't look well, my dear," remarked Her
Majesty as Elena attempted to function in her capacity
as attendant.

"My head aches," she mumbled, biting her lip to
keep back tears of self-pity.

"Rest in a darkened room. Take no wine or food,
and perchance you'll soon be well," suggested the
Queen with a sympathetic smile.

"Thank you, Madam, I'll follow your advice."

Later, as Elena lay staring up at the wooden tester
hung with dusty green curtains looped back for day,
she wondered where it had all gone wrong. This was
supposed to be the happiest time of her life. She waited
on England's Queen, Luis was here at court, it was
Christmas . . .

Tears trickled down her cheeks and onto the pillow.
She was not the first woman to find her lover had
deceived her. Thank God it had happened before he
got her with child. She praised heaven for her
deliverance, for only this morning that blessed flow had
begun, releasing her from further obligation to him.
When Luis went home to marry his betrothed, only her
heart would suffer. And she could learn to overcome
that weakness.

Elena must have been dozing when a sharp rap on
the door shook her awake. Disoriented, she fumbled
on the rushes for her shoes before hastening to answer it.

A lad stood outside. When she asked him what he wanted, he handed her a note. Hastily, Elena closed the door, not wanting the messenger to see her tears. The note came from Luis, the wax seal identical to that other note she had read with fluttering heart. This communication would go unread.

How hard it was to cast the unopened parchment in the fire. With gritted teeth she watched the wax seal melt, the paper catch fire, his bold black writing crumble to ash. One word alone, *Querida*—beloved—caught her eye. And she wished it had not.

Though Elena pushed herself to take an active part in the Christmas revelry, the entertainment within this brightly decorated palace brought little joy. Concerned about her friend's distress, Anne repeatedly asked what was wrong. Elena could not trust herself with words and merely shook her head. Understanding, Anne asked no further questions, for lately she, too, had been burdened with painful thoughts.

On the tenth day of Christmas a party of Mary's ladies prepared to ride beyond the city walls. Though at first Elena declined their invitation, she finally accepted, thinking an exhilarating ride was what she needed to blow away the cobwebs of grief. One lady intended to light candles for a special indulgence at the church of St. Martins in the Fields; the others merely wanted an excuse for an outing.

The small party, accompanied by several grooms and maids, set out on a blustery gray morning. At the last minute Anne had gone to meet Sir Miles, so Elena was left with no special friend to talk to on the way. Chatting and giggling, Mary's ladies made a pretty sight as they rode briskly through the narrow streets, wrapped warmly in heavy cloaks and furs, harnesses jingling, palfreys stepping proudly. Passersby paused to watch them ride past.

Beyond the walls the riders picked up their pace.
Elena's blue habit and fur-lined cloak barely kept out
the harsh wind that seared across the open meadows.
creaking tree branches and whirling sodden leaves in
its midst. By arriving on the heels of a brief mild spell,
the return of winter was felt all the more acutely. Before
long everyone began to whine about the cold, complaining of frozen fingers and frostbitten noses. They
were a pitiful lot with their pinched faces and eyes slitted
against the cold wind. Eventually tiring of their
complaints, Elena rode slightly ahead, having no
company but her brooding thoughts.

Men often broke betrothals that did not suit them—
unlike women, they were free to do as they pleased.
For Luis to say he could not break his commitment to
the Spanish woman meant he did not wish to break it.
He loved Elena in his arms, in his bed—Elena
swallowed, fighting back tears—but not in his home!
She was not worthy to become a Spanish hidalgo's wife!
At court the arrogant Spaniards in Philip's entourage
made little effort to hide their contempt of things
English. The Spanish way was the ideal. Like most of
his countrymen, Luis de los Santos would not marry
an English heretic, considering no one but a proper,
convent-educated Spanish woman worthy to share his
proud name.

Bitter pain twisted her heart. Setting spur to her horse,
Elena rode faster and faster in an attempt to rid herself
of that horrid admission. Tall stone walls loomed ahead,
and she heard the others shouting for her to stop. This
must be Easterham Manor, where they intended to break
their journey. Sullen, she reined in to wait for them
to catch up.

The small, half-timbered manor belonged to one of

the ladies' brothers, so it was expected that they would rest their horses and take refreshment here. Fresh evidence of other riders marred the short drive, steaming in the cold. They could hear men's voices in the distance as they entered the stables.

The chilled travelers were quickly made welcome with mulled ale and bowls of steaming pottage of greens. Anxious to get back on the road, Elena nervously paced back and forth while the others, not sharing her impatience to venture outside in the cold, chatted on and on. Eventually, after making the excuse she must attend to her horse, she escaped to the stables.

It was such a relief to leave that tapestried withdrawing room, a relief not to have to smile charmingly and make senseless small talk. Elena's face ached from the strain. In the distance she could hear receding hoofbeats as a party of travelers departed.

The horses whickered in pleasure as she approached. Elena stopped at each stall, administering pats to gleaming hunches or velvety noses while whispering much soothing nonsense. At least she could be herself with the horses. No one here would report her actions, or criticize her ungracious manner.

"Greetings, *Doña* Elena."

She froze. His voice was the last thing she expected to hear. Her heart beat so fast, she could barely draw breath. Slowly she turned, her face working as she tried to compose her features into an indifferent mask. She failed miserably.

"What do you want?"

Booted and spurred, his full riding cloak swinging from his shoulders he moved from the shadows.

"You."

Raising her whip, she barred his way. "Don't come any closer. You can say what you have to say from there.''

He smiled sarcastically and gave her a short, mocking bow. ''As you will, *doña*. How fortunate that we meet in such unexpected circumstances—''

''Enough courtly nonsense—you followed me here.''

''Wrong. I preceded you. But the end result's the same.''

''What do you want?''

''To talk.''

''Oh, I hardly think so. Likely you've already spotted a secluded spot with clean hay—''

''Stop it!''

The sheer rage in his face halted her speech. Shamefaced, Elena looked down at her feet. ''I'm sorry,'' she mumbled. ''Say your piece and be gone.''

''It's not that easy. I've much to tell you. . . . No, you'll hear me out,'' he growled as he turned to leave.

''There's nothing you can say to alter the truth.''

''No, I grant you that. But there are things I intend to say that explain *why* it must be so.''

''I'm afraid I haven't time. I'm on my way to church, and my companions are waiting.''

He smiled, and the lack of humor in the expression made her blood run cold. ''Nay, *doña*, they *awaited* you. As it happens, the ladies have been told your impatience led you to join the party that just left.''

''How dare you!''

''I was desperate. You're going to hear me out if I have to bind and gag you.''

Fear shot through her veins. Determination to carry out that threat was revealed by his grim mouth and steely eyes. Perhaps it was for the best after all. This way there would be nothing left unsaid between them.

''Very well, I'm listening.''

''Not here. The things I have to say are for your ears

alone. There's an eating house in the grounds. It's sheltered from the wind. We'll go there.''

She contemplated his suggestion, wondering how wise it would be to accompany him. But she needed to hear his explanation and take what comfort she could from it. ''All right. I trust this won't take long.''

He did not answer, merely motioned her through the doorway. Glancing up at his face as she passed, Elena was shocked by the grim lines on either side of his set mouth. She had never noticed them before. In fact, she preferred to think they had not been there. Then she thrust the thought away, aware she was taking comfort where perhaps none existed.

The hectagonal supperhouse had latticed walls sparsely covered with withered roses. Inside the building was a rustic table with benches. Huddling in her cloak, Elena sat at one end of a bench, he on the other.

''Elena, please.'' Luis reached for her hand, but she hid it under her cloak, her fingers encased in the blue gauntlets he had given her. The memory of that gift-giving brought a lump to her throat.

''Go on, I'm listening,'' she croaked, swallowing rapidly.

Luis sighed over their lack of accord at this meeting. He had hoped she would come back to him once she knew the reason behind his apparent deceit. But he had not reckoned with Elena's stubborn streak.

''I've been betrothed to Leonora Fragoso for two years. She's the heir of a neighboring landowner. Much Fragoso land formerly belonged to the de los Santos family. Many years ago it was taken by treachery. This union will rejoin those lands. Once more it will become de los Santos land. No, listen, there's more,'' he snarled, grabbing her arm as she started to leave.

''I don't want to hear any more. So far you've said

nothing to enlighten me.''

"You will listen! Sit down!''

He thrust her back on the bench. Elena contemplated slashing him with her whip for his insolence, but allowed it to pass. While waiting for him to continue, she stared through the open doorway at the bleak winter landscape. Dead leaves clung to the tossing beeches, and heavy pine branches hung above the stable roof.

"I promised my father on his deathbed that I would marry Leonora Fragoso. His lifelong dream had been to restore what was rightfully ours. Don't you see, Elena, I agreed to marry her before I even knew you existed.''

She nodded, her mouth tight.

"In exchange for that promise . . .'' Now he paused, looking across the lawn spotted with blackened leaves, his eyes pale and bleak. "In exchange for that promise my father publicly acknowledged me as his son.''

At first his words did not register, then Elena gasped at his obvious meaning. Turning to him, she repeated incredulously, "Acknowledged you . . . Then . . . then you're a—''

"A bastard,'' he supplied, his mouth quirking to a bitter smile.

"As the Prince's friend I always supposed your bloodline . . . to be noble,'' she faltered, not knowing how to voice her thoughts.

"Oh, my bloodline's noble—my mother was descended from Aragon royalty. The only drawback was she didn't marry my father. She died in a covent giving birth to me. Until three years ago, Elena, I wouldn't have been allowed at Philip's court. All my life I believed my father to be the sea captain who raised me—Diego Gomez never told me my real father was the nobleman who owned his fleet. Not until Don

Gaspar lay on his deathbed did he send for me. And then he dangled more riches before me than I could earn in a lifetime at sea. In return for swearing that vow, he named me his heir.''

"And if you break the vow you forfeit your inheritance?''

"Yes . . . but, Elena, there's so much more to it than that. Say you understand, sweetheart. I love you dearly. Leonora means nothing to me—she's a virtual stranger.''

"She brings you great wealth.''

"I've my own riches now.''

"Providing you keep your bargain to marry her.''

"Agreed. My future depends on that marriage.''

"I have land, a manorhouse—if you stay in England you'll hardly be penniless.''

"*Dios!* Don't try to barter!'' He leaped up and went to stand in the doorway where he rested his head against the weathered wood.

"Nay, I don't barter for you, Don Luis. I'm not that desperate.''

Her icy words brought him about. They stared at each other, trapped in a mire of pain and injured pride. She stood very straight, straining to attain her full height, yet still she could not look him directly in the eye.

"Were it just the land, I'd gladly give it up for you. This vow was made before the Archbishop of Toledo. The Grand Inquisitor's aide, Arturo Mendoza, and his sister witnessed the oath. I swore on holy relics that, if I live, Don Gaspar de los Santos would have his dying wish. All Fragoso land will return to the de los Santos family. I'll own the largest bull ranch north of Toledo. Stock for the royal *corridas* comes from there.''

"Damn you, is that all your love's worth? You're casting me aside for the largest bull ranch north of

Toledo?''

"No! Oh, *querida*, listen to me. It's not just that,"
he groaned, catching at her arms when she leaned
sobbing against the lattice. "Don't cry . . . It doesn't
mean we can't see each other, that we can't belong
together."

From a great distance she heard his soothing voice,
felt the warmth of his strong arms supporting her. Much
against her will, Elena finally succumbed to the
temptation and let him take her weight against him. The
relief was blessed.

"Come back with me when I go home to Spain. I'll
buy you a magnificent house, blooded horses, gowns,
jewels . . . anything you want."

"Anything but what I really want."

"We'll still be together, Elena. I'll acknowledge
you—and any children God blesses us with. Don't you
understand? This need not come between us; we don't
have to part."

"And what will your wealthy Spanish noblewoman
say to that?"

"Do you think I give a damn what Leonora says?
If she wants me, she'll agree to it."

"And what, despite your obvious charm, makes you
so sought after?"

He hesitated a long time, and when he finally
answered, he did not look at her. "This marriage
ensures the security of her descendants. The Fragosos
are ambitious too."

Mustering all her self-control, Elena pulled away
from him. He did not stop her. "So, you're asking me
to come to Spain as your mistress?"

"Yes." He caught at her hands, but she evaded his
touch.

"No. If I'm not good enough to marry, I'm not good

enough to . . ." She stopped and glaced away, falling short of uttering that blunt word that flashed through her mind. "I won't come with you on those terms."

"Elena, please, be not so hasty. Don't you realize this is all I can ever offer you?"

"I understand that compared to the largest bull ranch north of Toledo, I'm rather a paltry prize."

Anger blazed in his face. Seizing her, he welded her against his body. Elena fought against his strength, afraid her back would break as he ruthlessly bent her to his will. His mouth came down hard and demanding on hers. Though she fought against his kiss, she could not keep a part of her from rejoicing in it, enjoying even this fierce battle of wills as he forced her to yield to him. Now Luis imprisoned her, turning her so that she was trapped against the wall. He shook her in anger, rattling her spine against the lattice.

"Have sense, damn you! What difference does it make if we're wed? We'll still be together. That's what you want."

She fought tears. His eyes burned pale fire as he glared at her, desperation making him rough. For just an instant she longed to succumb to him. The pressure of his thighs were against her, the throb of his blood tantalizingly close. Then, mustering every scrap of willpower, Elena held herself aloof, her head pressed back into the trellis. He panted; she could feel his hot breath fanning her brow, hear the rasp in his lungs. Tremors moved through his arms and legs, and she doubted they were still born of anger.

"Are you going to rape me?"

Her voice, so coldly controlled, surprised even her. Luis looked at her a long time without speaking, his eyes glittering in the gloom. Then abruptly he released her and stepped back.

"Go then. There's no more I can say."

"Good, you've wasted enough of my time. I heard you out and I've learned little, beyond the fact you remind me unpleasantly of my brother. He, too, sacrificed much for a dynastic union. Hearts and emotions mean little to him either. While Will cannot boast of having the largest bull ranch north of Toledo, I do believe he likes to say he has the biggest farm north of Winchester."

Stunned, Luis stared at her before his anger finally erupted. "Damn you, stop flinging that back in my face," he raged, his English heavily accented as he fought against using his mother tongue.

"How can you expect me to forget such a noble reward!"

Delivering that final taunt, Elena bent to retrieve her whip which had fallen to the floor, then turning, she walked blindly down the steps. There were three steps to the lawn, yet they were shallower than she expected, and her foot slipped on the springy turf, nearly causing her to fall. Walking in what she thought to be the right direction, Elena marched toward the stables. She did not know he ran after her until she suddenly became aware of his heavy breathing the instant before he grabbed her arm and swung her about.

"Tell me one more time we're finished. Tell me again you won't come to Spain with me," he demanded thickly.

Not daring to meet his eyes, which she suspected even now had the power to soften her heart, Elena repeated woodenly, "We're finished. And I'll not come to Spain as your mistress."

Luis stepped back, his face grim. Turning, he walked ahead of her to the stable. So jangled were her emotions—her heart thundering, her legs quaking—

that Elena fully expected to collapse on the grass. Pride alone kept her on an unwavering course. When she reached the stables, Luis was waiting with their saddled horses.

"Now, as I foolishly sent your party away without you, I'll have to take you back to London."

"No!"

"Have sense—'twill be dusk long before you reach the city. Do you want to be set upon by vagabonds? You need have no fear—I'll not touch you, nor attempt to sway your mind. You've made your decision and I accept it."

"Is that a promise?"

"You have my word."

"In that case . . ." Elena swallowed as she moved forward to the mounting block, disdaining his offer of help. She could not bear the touch of his hands just yet. Perhaps later she would have overcome her vulnerability to him. At the moment, given the right set of circumstances, she admitted even her fierce pride would crumble before the burning emotion she still felt for him. How could one both hate and love a man at the same time?

Luis, too, possessed more than his fair share of pride. Stonily, he made sure she was mounted before he swung into the saddle and headed out the yard.

That miserable return journey to London seemed a hundred miles long. Luis did not speak as he rode beside her, occasionally spurring his horse in swift bursts of speed that Elena was convinced were designed to leave her behind. Grimly, she kept pace with him, urging the utmost from her mount.

Several times as they rode along, she had begun to speak before thinking better of it. Let him be the one to break the ice. After all, it was his fault they had quarreled. Through his greed, so reminiscent of Will's obsession, Luis had lost her love. If he valued their love more than a fortune and his marvelous bull ranch, then he would have married her. Yet, even if he did ask her to marry him, she wondered if she would take him back now after all this heartache. How she longed to say no. But she was too honest for that. Luis merely had to ask and she would be his still.

Stubbornly Luis maintained his angry silence right up to the palace gates. Elena wondered if she imagined that his hand lingered overlong about her waist when he helped her dismount. Angrily she dismissed the weakening thought. As usual, she was grasping at straws. She should have realized a Spaniard's overwhelming pride would not allow him to apologize, or to make the first conciliatory move. Well, she, too, had her share of proud Spanish blood!

Mutually miserable in their prideful silence, they politely bid farewell. Then they turned their backs on each other, hearts aching for all that could have been and was not.

Chapter Eleven

In mid-January there was a grand procession to celebrate England's return to Roman Catholicism. Led by children of Christ's hospital and St. Paul's school, eight robed bishops and over 150 cross-carrying priests sang the Roman Mass as they marched through London's narrow streets. Huge bonfires were lit to mark the occasion.

In February of that same year great bonfires again were lit, but this time their purpose was to consume heretics. Bishops Gardiner, Bonner, and Tonstal, assisted by three priests, presided over St. Mary Overy's heresy court to select the victims. Now, more than the smoke from coal fires blackened the sky as the stench of human sacrifice hung like a pall over London.

The feared reprisals had begun!

It was both a subdued and a staunchly Catholic court that awaited the impending birth of England's heir. Philip himself had cautioned his wife to show more lenience toward the heretics, aware the English did not share the fervor of his own countrymen toward these horrid spectacles. To the English, piety and godliness were all very well, as long as they did not curtail too many of their pleasures. Of course, in time they would finally be brought to heel. Unfortunately, Mary was not prepared to allow her countrymen time to reawaken their collective conscience. Seized with great zeal, she was determined to stamp out all heresy without delay, using whatever method proved most successful.

This mounting religious persecution horrified Elena. It was unthinkable that English men and women could be burned alive merely because of dissenting religious beliefs. Nowadays, the shadow of the dreaded Inquisition hovered too close for comfort. It was hard for her to reconcile the Mary Tudor she knew with the zealot in whose name such cruel justice was dispensed. And though Elena strongly disagreed with the Queen's method of enforcing her religious beliefs, she quickly learned to hold her tongue. The merest suggestion of dissent brought an alarming change to Mary's face, narrowing her eyes, tightening her mouth, deepening her already harsh voice as she vehemently defended her principles. The English were to pay for all the insults delivered against her mother, Katherine of Aragon, upholder of the true faith. If men must die to achieve this end, then she took comfort from the knowledge that she had at least saved their eternal souls.

With the onset of spring, trees budded and mild weather coaxed flowers into bloom in winter bare gardens. Mary's condition worsened with the passing weeks. Elena pitied her royal mistress, understanding the degree of mental and physical torment the Queen endured during these final months of pregnancy. Mary's sallow, lined face was continually pinched with pain for her sick headaches had become an almost daily occurrence. The Queen spent much time weeping over her prayerbook, which, by now, opened automatically to prayers for deliverance of women in childbirth. Mary also beseeched her Maker to guide her in her mammoth task of converting her heretical subjects.

Never a beauty, these trying months robbed Mary Tudor of any pretense of physical attractiveness. Her feet and legs swelled, while her distended belly was grotesquely at odds with her stringy old maid's body. Hardest of all for Mary to bear was the pain of Philip's indifference. She wept because she was not beautiful enough to make him love her. His neglect during these miserable months cut her to the quick. Though privately Mary beseeched him not to desert her, Philip spent less and less time in her company.

"Is Philip come?" she would ask a dozen times a day, only to be told, "Not yet, Your Majesty."

One bright afternoon in March, when puffy clouds scudded across the rain-washed sky, Mary felt well enough to sit before the open window where the sunshine warmed her pain-wracked body. Between sips of a chalky mixture prescribed by her physicians for her numerous digestive complaints, Mary announced to no one in particular, "Though Philip hunts late with his gentlemen, he promised to return in time for tonight's revel. This will be our last function before leaving for Hampton Court."

With a curt nod, Mary dismissed the three ladies-in-waiting hovering about her chair. Turning around, Mary sought out her latest lady-in-waiting, who was replacing her jewel boxes in an ornate chest. "Do you suppose Philip will be happier there, Elena?" the Queen asked.

"I've never been to Hampton Court, Madam, though I'm told it's lovely beside the river. I'm sure His Highness will find much pleasure there."

"Would that he found much pleasure in me," Mary muttered, twisting her swollen hands in agitation.

"Once the babe comes, things will be different," Elena comforted hopefully.

Mary smiled and rubbed her abdomen, momentarily satisfied with the promise.

Elena replaced the rest of the Queen's rings in their velvet-lined boxes; Mary's hands were too swollen to wear them. Though her ladies-in-waiting had used goose grease in an effort to get off the rings already on her fingers, the Queen's rings stayed firmly embedded in her soggy flesh.

"Tonight's revel will be merry—surely that will cheer his mood. Philip's so homesick for Spain." The Queen sighed, dabbing away the tears trickling down her cheeks.

Elena dreaded the coming ball. This final diversion before the court adjourned to Hampton Court for the Queen's lying-in would force her into Luis's company. For most of the winter she had deliberately avoided him. Whenever she saw him dance with another, or laugh with the flirtatious women of the court, her heart ached. To her jealous eyes it seemed as if every pretty woman in England had set her cap at him! And not just in England. Ever fond of gossip, the court ladies eagerly repeated stories about Don Luis's past loves, including an exotic beauty who spied for the Inquisition. The women's careless tattle deepened her anguish. Oh, how she hated him! She never wanted to see him again.

The Queen had been delighted with Elena's new devotion to duty. Out of misplaced generosity, Mary frequently thrust Elena into Don Alvaro Escalante's company. Unable to refuse the Queen's matchmaking, Elena treated the old don politely. Don Alvaro was attentive and fatherly toward her—she would not have minded his company were it not for the unwelcome intent behind it. None but a blind man could fail to notice the Queen's scheme to seat them close at table. Lately, he had even been ordered to escort Elena on the royal pair's walks about the rose garden. Elena began to long for the birth of Mary's babe, if only to direct her mistress's energies elsewhere.

For tonight's grand ball, Elena intended to wear a sumptuous gown of moss green brocade over a kirtle of green satin. The gown's full, turned-back sleeves were trimmed with rows of ruched ribbon and silver lace. Her springy hair would be concealed beneath a green velvet French hood banded with white satin ribbon. Her low-heeled shoes were silver satin. When Elena received this gown from the Queen as an Epiphany gift, she was thrilled, but since she had avoided most court gatherings rather than confront Luis, she had yet to wear it.

To her surprise, Don Alvaro had also given her an Epiphany gift, so perfectly matched to the gown she could only assume it had been chosen to complement the Queen's gift. Though Elena protested the great worth of the gold earrings and matching necklace studded with emeralds, Mary quickly shushed her. The Queen later confided the Spaniard would have been highly insulted had she refused to accept his gift.

Stomach churning in apprehension for what the night might bring, Elena quickly secured her thick hair with bone pins before putting on her headdress. The French hood's stiffened frame set so far back on her head that a large expanse of hair was revealed. To her chagrin, the dark, curling mass refused to lie smooth, forming a springy halo about her face. As she placed the beautiful emerald necklace about her slender neck, Elena shuddered. The jewelry was cold as death against her flesh.

Laughter and music drifting down the corridors of the palace could be heard long before the Queen's ladies-in-waiting entered the gaily decorated hall. They laughed and chatted, caught up in the air of excitement surrounding this farewell ball.

The solemn-faced Queen moved ponderously along the Palace corridors, her flowing gown of purple silk brocade worn over black velvet making her complexion appear muddy and faded. Some wag suggested the colors had been chosen as mourning for the many lives she had taken in the name of God. Though her courtiers silently shared the speaker's sentiment, few dared laugh at his sally. Whispers of condemnation were no longer uttered in the sovereign's presence. Many a nervous glance was cast in the Queen's direction as she slowly passed between the rows of bowing and curtsying courtiers—Mary's sight might be poor, but there was little wrong with her hearing.

The vast timber-beamed hall shone bright with torch-light. Garlands of beribboned greenery festooned the wooden pillars and hung from the smoke-blackened rafters. Tonight the royal dais resembled a spring bower. Mary clapped her hands in childlike pleasure, delighted with the display of bright yellow daffodils, frilly pink and white apple blossoms and spikes of gold forsythia decorating the platform draped in Tudor colors of green and white.

Elena's gaze was drawn like a magnet to Philip's gentlemen who stood somber as ravens amidst the spring blossoms. While Philip assisted his clumsy wife up the shallow steps to her throne, Elena saw Luis watching her. She swallowed nervously, her heart thumping and her stomach churning. She had hardly expected to have to stand barely three feet from him. Tonight Luis was splendidly dressed in silver-embroidered black velvet over tawny satin, the brighter color puffing through slashes in his sleeves, which were fastened to his doublet by pearl clasps. A winking diamond pin fastened a jaunty orange plume to his flat black velvet cap.

To her surprise, she found Luis appeared older since their quarrel, his hard face almost cynical in repose, his mouth set in an unyielding line. Yet this betrayal of his apparent pain brought no satisfaction; Elena's own hurt went too deep for that.

Once Mary was comfortably settled on her throne, Philip turned to Elena, catching her sleeve to detain her.

"*Doña* Elena, where have you been? Many's the day I've looked in vain for your pretty face."

That same, warmly seductive light shone in his eyes, and Elena did not doubt that Philip had sought her out. How fortunate for her he had not found her. "I've not been well of late—and Her Majesty has required a great deal of my time."

"Yes, of course," Philip agreed, curling his thick lips distastefully at the mention of his wife's current indisposition. Quickly changing the subject, he asked if Elena was looking forward to the coming move to Hampton Court.

She quickly mumbled that she was, then curtsied to the Prince before assuming her position behind Mary's throne.

The Queen soon dismissed her younger ladies, insisting she would have far greater pleasure in watching them enjoy themselves. Instead of racing to join the dance with the others, Elena stayed behind to wait on her mistress.

"You go as well, Elena. I can manage without you for one night," Mary urged kindly, gently pushing Elena toward the dancers. "You're going to miss all the fun."

Stiffly Elena smiled, longing to decline the Queen's generosity, yet realizing she could not. Suddenly she saw Luis moving in her direction and she panicked, desperately seeking a means of escape.

Magically on cue, Don Alvaro stepped forward to take her hand. With a deep bow he asked in his heavily accented voice, "*Doña*, will you honor me by dancing this measure with me?" The request was formally made, and he took great effort to pronounce the unfamiliar English words correctly.

Mary beamed—had she arranged this invitation herself she could not have wished for better.

Seizing any opportunity to escape, Elena smiled charmingly at Don Alvaro and accepted his invitation. Luis's brows drew together in an angry line when he saw what she had done.

Fortunately the measure was slow. Though he stood straight and moved with a younger man's lithe step, the gray-haired don found the fast-paced English dances far too taxing for his advanced years. Elena's hand rested lightly on his cool dry palm as they moved stiffly down the middle of the room, elegantly bowing and curtsying at the designated spot before continuing the stately measure. When Don Alvaro spoke, it was usually to deliver reams of praise to her beauty. Elena barely listened to what by now had become routine.

"You seem so remote, my lovely lady," Don Alvaro said when he bowed over her hand at the dance's conclusion. "I'd almost think you did not hear me."

Elena smiled, her eyes modestly downcast. "Nay, Don Alvaro, your lavish praise renders me speechless."

He smiled with such delight at her words that Elena felt quite despicable. To her great relief, Luis was nowhere to be seen. Elena politely refused several further offers to dance from gaudily dressed courtiers whose usual goal was to persuade her to their beds. Gratefully, she accepted a cooling cup of wine from a server at a side table. While she sipped from her cup,

shrieks of wild laughter, followed by a flurry of crimson
satin skirts streaking across the hall, attracted her
attention. Gartwright Lane, her golden hair straggling
untidily from beneath her headdress, had raced across
the room to join her four sisters. They stood heads
together, screeching and cackling while the flighty
Gartwright relayed some scandalous tale.

The women kept turning to look at someone across
the room and, to her dismay, when Elena followed their
gaze, she discovered Luis was the object of their
attention. He caught her eye and smiled with grim
satisfaction. Whether his expression was because he
realized she had observed the commotion, or for what
had just taken place with that giggling wench, Elena
did not know. A bolt of anger shot through her, swiftly
diffused by the nausea of jealousy. How dare he dally
with that strumpet beneath her very nose! She virtually
seethed with anger. Yet Elena knew the emotion was
unjust. She had been the one to discard him, not the
other way around. It had been futile to expect him to
remain celibate while awaiting his Spanish bride. How
foolish to believe that his anguish over losing her love
would temporarily quench the fires of lust. She could
not bear the sight of Gartwright's flushed cheeks and
sparkling eyes, the mop of golden curls falling about
her face where likely his fingers had recently strayed.
And where else had his fingers strayed? Elena glanced
pointedly at the girl's amply filled bodice, her sharp
eyes noting that several ribbons appeared to have been
hastily tied.

Clenching her fists in jealous anger, Elena stalked
from the hall.

The darkened corridor was shockingly cold after the
heated hall. Perhaps this chill was just what she needed
to calm her blood. Braving the iciness, Elena penetrated

deeper into the labyrinth of corridors, marching back
and forth in an attempt to dispel her anger. On her fourth
pass along the screened passage behind the vast hall,
she became aware of the someone standing in the
shadows. Heavy steps revealed the intruder to be male.
While having no actual fear that a courtier would try
to force her to his will outside the crowded hall, Elena
felt a flicker of unease as she drew closer to the
menacing male bulk.

Before they came abreast she spoke out, wanting to
let the man know she was aware of his presence. "Are
you to let me pass, sir?"

He gave no answer. Then suddenly he seized her cold
hands, gripping them tight. Elena's heart lurched.
"Luis!"

"Come with me. We must talk."

"No, we've nothing left to say."

"There's much left unsaid. Come quietly. Don't
make a scene."

"Why should I make things easy for you? Let go my
hands."

"You'll do as you're told," he ground out, yanking
her toward him.

Elena stumbled. She righted herself, but now it was
far too late. He stood so close his breath fanned her
brow. Luis grasped her, crushing her against his velvet
doublet. She could smell the warm, heady perfume of
his clothes, musk and roses mingled with a mysterious
fragrance from the east. The arousing scent of his body
she knew so well, her poignant memories threatened
to undo her. Angrily, she thrust at his chest,
uncomfortably aware of his steady heartbeat. She
shuddered, recalling how often she had lain against his
chest, listening to its strong rhythm.

"Elena," Luis breathed before his mouth came down

hot over hers. The pressure of his lips was so inviting she could barely stand against the assault. Softening alarmingly beneath his kiss, her lips opened slightly and she tasted the intoxicating fragrance of his mouth. She felt as if she were drowning. Desperately groping for a handhold before passion swept her under, she forced herself to picture Gartwright Lane's china blue eyes and foolish simper.

"No! Let me go," she exclaimed, thrusting in earnest at his chest.

Luis slackened his grip, but he would not set her free. "Elena, dearest, come," he coaxed, his voice soft.

Angrily she kicked at his shin in an effort to be free. The blow from her soft slippers was ineffectual. "Let me go or I'll scream."

"No," he snarled, all his warmth and tenderness vanishing.

The change was so sudden and unexpected that Elena gasped. "You don't think I'll scream, do you. Just—"

Luis clamped his hand across her mouth. Struggling, Elena tried unsuccessfully to bite his hand.

"You're coming with me."

Purposefully, he marched her along the icy corridor to where a flaring torch illuminated a deserted bench. The smoking torch cast them in a flickering pool of light, which she supposed was his way of assuring her he intended no harm. She sat stiffly on the narrow bench, and they looked at each other in the wavering light. His face was hard with anger and pain. She was forced to admit to seeing that pain, yet it was more likely caused by the thwarting of his desires than any lack of her love.

"You've had ample time to change your mind. Are you coming home to Spain with me?"

"No. I already gave you my decision."

"And you've not relented?"

"Why should I?"

He began to speak, paused, then mumbled, "I hope . . . prayed . . . No matter."

"Surely you didn't think by seducing Gartwright Lane you'd bring me to heel," she snapped, unable to keep from blurting the pain of her discovery. "Damn you for your treachery! Not content with your women in Spain, you dally under my nose. And then you've the gall to suggest I might have changed my mind about becoming your mistress. You must be insane!"

Her speech delivered, Elena tried in vain to still her trembling lips. An annoying twitch had also begun in her eyelid. Though she bit her lips hard, there was little she could do to hide the other. She need not have been distressed—Luis was mired too deep in his own anger and pain to notice.

"Insane—yes, perhaps I am to assume you're capable of love. You're ever ready to damn me—I damn you threefold for your falseness, your hard heart and your damnable pride!"

"Pride has nothing to do with it. You never made me an honorable offer of marriage."

"Only because I cannot."

"Because you *will* not!"

"I can't so easily discount my sacred vow, or all that rests upon this marriage."

Finally regaining her composure, Elena rose, holding herself stiffly erect to attain maximum height. To her annoyance, she found her low heels only brought her level with his chin.

"Do forgive me, Don Luis, I'd forgotten you must compare my worth to the largest bull ranch north of Toledo. How could I ever hope to match that?"

Her icy condemnation delivered, Elena stalked away.

Blinded by tears, she waited only until she was out of his sight to lay her head against the cold stonework and give way to wracking sobs.

Unknown to Elena, her sorrow did not go undetected. Luis had followed her, pausing in the shadows, the sound of her tears a knife in his heart. Dear God, if only he could change her pain to pleasure, if only she would allow him to comfort her. He longed to give her hope for their future together but, short of lying, he knew hope was one gift he could not offer.

Sadly, Luis turned on his heel, gritting his teeth against his conflicting emotions. Tonight had been a disaster. There was so much he had intended to say. He had not even told her he must return home sooner than expected, the surprise royal command having been issued at Carranza's urging. He had wanted to assure her, wherever he went, whatever he did, no other woman could ever take her place. Yet she had never given him time to voice his deepest thoughts. From the beginning her heart was set against him. The simple solution he had proposed with no intention of dishonoring her had become an impenetrable barrier between them.

Long after Luis reentered the lighted hall, he could hear her sobs echoing in his ears. His mouth set grimly as he clenched his jaw against the pain.

For many months to come, Luis was still to fancy he could hear those tormenting sobs moaning in the rigging of the galleon bound for Spain and wailing in the ocean's crashing waves. Even when he rode about his spreading lands, her voice seemed to whisper in the breeze blowing off the winding Tajo. Never again would he experience the same pride in these vast holdings guaranteed to him by his marriage to Leonora. Now when he heard the boastful phrase "the largest bull ranch north of Toledo,'' his stomach churned and his throat went dry. Elena's scorn had turned his most cherished possession into a hateful mockery.

Even the beautiful Hampton Court brought no solace to Mary Tudor. Her physicians said they must have miscalculated by perhaps two months the due date of the child. A false rumor that she had given birth to a son on April 30 set the London churchbells ringing and *Te Deums* were sung in thanksgiving. London's joy gave way to mass disappointment when it was learned there had been no royal birth.

Several foreign dignitaries swiftly put their own interpretations on the strange events surrounding the Queen's lingering pregnancy, suggesting in their letters home that the English Queen had been delivered of a fleshy mole or a hideously deformed child.

Meanwhile Mary's terrible vigil continued. June, July—the summer months passed slowly in Wolsey's former palace beside the willow-screened Thames. Everything was in readiness for the long-awaited lying-in. Again the physicians announced a miscalculation, then another, until the court came to realize there may never have been a babe in Mary's shrivelled womb. The Queen was thirty-nine and rapidly approaching the end of her birthing years. Whatever had swelled the royal belly had not been England's heir. Stubbornly, Mary refused to give up hope. She was convinced there would be a child.

In an effort to cheer their sovereign's lagging spirits, the courtiers arranged for middle-aged women holding either their own or borrowed infants to be brought before the Queen.

Finally, as the uneventful summer became autumn, Mary, too, was forced to accept the truth; her pregnancy had been false.

Long believing that her personal happiness and the future of her country depended on producing a child, the Queen was inconsolable. While she wept and prayed long hours on her knees, the flock of ladies she had gathered for her confinement made merry in the luxurious palace with its dazzling blue ceilings appearing as a glimpse of heaven visible through gilded fretwork. Unhappily, the door had just been slammed on Mary's glimpse of heaven. She was old, barren, unlovely—and Philip did not love her.

When the court moved upstream to the former royal hunting lodge of Oatlands, Elena followed. Her former pleasure in the luxurious trappings of royalty had long since faded. Luis's departure without even a word of farewell had cut her to the quick. How could he have left without telling her? This was so like the other time when he pleaded he was prevented leaving word of his departure; now she wondered if that story had been merely a glib lie. Most damning of all was Gartwright Lane's reaction to the loss of her Spanish gallant. The loose chit wept gallons of tears, her behavior convincing Elena that all her worst fears about Luis's fidelity were well-founded. This discovery merely deepened her bitterness. The Queen's funereal demeanor mirrored her own. It was almost a comfort to see Mary's tears and unhappy face—she could not have borne great cheerfulness when her heart ached so much. She wondered how much longer she could endure the pain.

Mary's unhappiness deepened when Philip received an urgent request from his father, the Holy Roman Emperor, asking him to return to Spain. The joy that suffused his features as he read those blessed words became an added burden for the Queen to bear. Mary collapsed in grief, her misery complete. Her failure to produce an heir had brought Anne Boleyn's redheaded daughter uncomfortably close to the throne. Philip was leaving, and with him went her hope of conceiving. Not only had she failed as a Queen, she had failed as a woman. Her desperation to prove she was still young enough to please her husband, to bear his sons, had been futile. The light of her life was leaving. And he did not even try to hide his pleasure over the impending separation.

Locked in bitterness, the Queen sat brooding before the sunny window, her narrow mouth hidden in her clenched visage, her chin resting on her bony chest. Many hours of weeping had rendered her eyes little more than lifeless slits.

Elena tried to concentrate on her embroidery while she took her turn at attending her mistress. Mary's demands were few. Unfortunately, inactivity had given Elena too much time to dwell on Luis. Back and forth her emotions waged—pain, anger, longing. Now, with all those miles between them, pride seemed a poor substitute for his arms, his kisses. . . .

"Elena, please come."

The urgently whispered summons turned Elena's head. Mary, locked in her own misery, had not heard. Anne Shelton stood in the doorway, her face white as a ghost. Wringing her hands in agitation, again she beckoned for Elena to join her.

Hoping the Queen would not miss her, Elena tiptoed from the room. Her heart went out to Anne, who looked so devastated she could not imagine what woes beset her.

"What is it?" she asked, slipping her arms around the other woman. Anne crumpled against her, sobbing quietly against the shoulder of Elena's marigold yellow gown.

"Oh, Elena, he's taken," she wailed piteously.

Elena's stomach pitched. Anne could mean but one thing—Sir Miles had been arrested. During these fruitless months of waiting for the Queen to give birth, the court had buzzed with rumors of a manhunt for Sir Miles and his brother, Thomas Ravenscroft, pastor of Ravenscroft parish church, and an outspoken opponent of Mary's religious policies. Few knew the fugitives' whereabouts, and those who did kept their mouths shut.

Finally, shaking Anne gently to quiet her sobs, to try to halt the tears, which soaked through the shoulder of her gown, Elena scolded, "Come, Anne, tears won't save him. What can we do?"

"There's little," Anne sniffled, raising her tear-wet face. "Unless . . . unless you are willing to help us?"

"Oh, Anne, you know I am. I can't bear to see you in such torment. What must I do?"

"Come outside where we can talk."

"You know I can't leave Her Majesty," Elena protested hoarsely, glancing through the open door to see the Queen kneeling before her *prie-dieux* and weeping for the cruelty of fate.

"Yes, you can—say you withdrew to allow her privacy. We must go where we can't be overheard."

They quickly stepped through a side door to stand in a patch of sunlight on the green lawn, just far enough from the shrubbery to forestall any eavesdroppers.

"Miles is under guard, 'tis true, but he has sympathetic friends. I've already squandered my last guinea to see that he's fed and decently housed. Elena, sweet, help me buy a passage aboard ship for the Netherlands."

"I've not near enough money at such short notice. How long before you need—"

"Tonight."

"Heavens! That's impossible. I have to send home for it. We must go to someone else."

"No, I can't trust anyone but you. Oh, help me, dearest Elena. You too have loved and know the heartache I feel. I swear, if Miles is executed, I'll kill myself. There'll be nothing left to live for."

"Don't talk like that!" Elena seized her friend's arm and drew her close, hugging her in an effort to quiet her sobs. For the first time she felt older than Anne and much wiser. However painful, life went on. One did not kill oneself because a lover was gone.

"Elena, help me, please," Anne beseeched again, clutching Elena's hand where the Queen's heavy ring cut into her flesh. "What about this," she exclaimed suddenly. "Sell it."

"I can't sell the Queen's Christmas gift! She'll notice it's gone. How would I explain?"

"Tell her 'tis lost—stolen. You must, Elena; his life depends on it. I know where I can sell the ring for cash. Maybe not much, but surely enough . . ."

Elena glanced at Anne's own hands and was surprised to see them devoid of jewels—even her pearl drop earrings had gone to help her lover. Sense told her not to yield to Anne's pleas. Surely there was something else she could use to raise money. To sell the Queen's gift could have far-reaching consequences.

"So you're condemning us both to death?"

Anne's bleak summation cut through her thoughts. "No, not that. I'm just trying to think of another way."

"There is no other way. Friends intend to set him free. I must leave within the hour. There's barely time left to secure a passage."

Anne's big eyes glistened reproachfully, and Elena squirmed, shivering in the late summer sunshine. Anne's tears finally melted her heart. "Here, take it," she cried, pulling the heavy ring off her finger, feeling lighter the minute she was freed of the symbolic gift.

"Oh, Elena, bless you, dearest. Oh, God bless you!" Anne hugged her, depositing a flurry of wet kisses on her cheek. "You're assured a place in heaven."

Elena stood in the shadows of the building, watching Anne flying across the lawns toward the stables. Uneasily, she wondered how she could explain the ring's absence to the Queen. As she stepped inside the building, she suddenly realized Mary was calling her. She ran back guiltily into the room, dropping a hasty curtsy before the Queen.

"My apologies, Your Majesty. I thought you'd rather be alone," she mumbled self-consciously.

"Were you talking to someone?"

"Yes."

"Was that Lady Anne in the garden?"

"Yes, Madam."

"How strange," Mary said, peering through the diamond-paned window. The scarlet-gowned figure she had seen running over the grass had gone. "Why didn't she come to speak to me? She's been away from court a long time." Then Mary's face tightened and her mouth formed a hard, narrow line as she swiftly supplied an answer to the puzzle. "Ah, doubtless she's just discovered her paramour has been arrested."

Elena gasped in shock, not merely because she was alarmed that Mary knew about Anne's love affair, but because of the terrible transformation the Queen's face had undergone. The tired, lined expression she knew so well had given way to something malignant.

"She did tell me Sir Miles had been arrested, Madam. There must be some mistake—he's ever been loyal to you," her voice faded, struck down by the anger blazing on Mary's embittered countenance.

"How dare you criticize me!"

"No, Madame, I don't seek to criticize. It's just that those rumors that he plots against you are unfounded."

"I know that."

"Then why?"

"Sir Miles is a heretic. Perchance he will recant—he and that evil brother of his who preaches against me throughout the land. No, Elena, you've been misguided. From now on I forbid you to have aught to do with Anne Shelton. She's been a disloyal friend to me by associating with the Ravenscrofts. And after all I've done for her. Well, 'tis as well to know one's friends."

Seeing the hurt on the younger woman's face, the Queen took Elena's hand in hers.

"Poor Elena. I'm sorry to have spoken so sharply to you. You're new to court and must find our ways strange. There's much you don't understand. . . . Tell me, how do you feel about Lord Morton's suit?"

All Elena could do was gasp. Mary's question was completely unexpected. She had no idea the Queen was familiar with Will's ambitious scheme to snare the northern lord as her husband.

Mary managed a slight smile at Elena's shock, though her lined mouth had trouble with the expression. "There, have no fear, my reaction to the match is similar to yours. You have my word—you shan't be forced into such an unsuitable match. Your brother's already been informed of my feelings in the matter." Such a beam of delight suffused Elena's face, that the Queen said, "Oh, my dear, you thought I'd said yes, that I'd sentenced you to imprisonment on the frigid moors. Nay, I love you too well for that. This brother of yours seems mighty ambitious, but let's not fault him for that. He's merely aware of the worth with which he bargains. Don't you realize you're a choice marriage prospect?'' The Queen patted her shoulder. ''Are you not desirous of marriage?''

''No, Your Majesty. I was married once and I—''

''Oh, of course, how clumsy of me. I've allowed my own misery to addle my wits. Your marriage ended so tragically.''

Elena swallowed guiltily, allowing the Queen to rhapsodize over what in truth had been a hateful arrangement.

''You might feel differently in time. Given an understanding older man, someone who'd take good care of you.''

Elena's stomach lurched. It took little imagination to put a name to that ''older someone.'' Lowering her gaze, she waited to be dismissed. As usual the Queen gave with one hand and took away with the other.

''Don Alvaro Escalante will soon return to Spain—possibly when Philip visits his father.'' Mary's mouth tightened at the painful reminder. ''Be not so cold toward him, Elena, he's a very fine gentleman. You could not ask for better. Now you may go—send my other ladies to me.''

Elena was dismissed. Squeezing her hands together, she was reminded of the lack of her ring. She knew she had been a fool to allow Anne's grief to overrule her better judgment, especially after hearing Mary's bitter condemnation of Sir Miles. Pray God the Queen never found out the intended disposition of her ''lost'' ring. Mary's sight was poor, and of late she had been so preoccupied that Elena hoped she would never notice that the ring was missing.

Chapter Twelve

The Queen passed the remainder of the waning summer at the former royal hunting lodge of Oatlands. Summer heat always brought plague to the airless warren of squalid lanes adjacent to the palace; so, to safeguard her health, and the life of England's future heir, Mary had chosen to spend the entire summer in the country.

One perfect sunny day Elena accompanied two of the Queen's ladies to the nearby woods to pick ripening bittersweet berries to brew a rheumatism remedy for their mistress. They laughed like children about their errand. A carpet of ferns, starred with yellow wood pimpernel and magenta campion, lay underfoot; scolding birds circled overhead as the women wreathed their unbound hair with fragrant honeysuckle. Any passing stranger might have taken them for wood sprites had they been seen joining hands to dance and sing a country air beneath the quivering trees.

For the first time in months, Elena realized her heartache had begun to ease. Though these surroundings were a poignant reminder of that time Luis made love to her in Lichborne Forest, today those memories did not rend her heart. Her pain had grown bittersweet. And she thanked God she was finally starting to live again.

221

Last month Sir Miles's dissident brother had been burned at the stake, while Anne's handsome lover escaped to the Netherlands. Though at first Elena had regretted her hasty decision, now she was glad she had helped Anne. Out of gratitude for her part in Sir Miles's rescue, Anne gave Elena a hand-decorated New Testament translated into English. She treasured the tiny work, ignoring the possible danger of possessing a forbidden book. She hid the gift amongst the clothing in her oak chest.

So wracked with sorrow was Mary as she contemplated her husband's departure, she never noticed Elena no longer wore her ring. The court buzzed with preparations for Philip's journey. The Spaniards could hardly wait to be free of this chilly, dismal land. The palace corridors rang with excited Spanish voices, every laugh, every smile, plunging the knife deeper in Mary's heart. Though she did not intentionally make others suffer, the Queen's despair accelerated her religious zeal, until she grew near insane with her deadly purpose. Now smoke blackened skies over other cities besides London.

Unhappily, Elena's newfound peace was to be short lived. Her returning high spirits were quickly dampened when she entered Oatlands in the late afternoon sunshine. Mary's despair seemed to have permeated the house's very atmosphere. Although Philip was not to depart for several days, the Queen already mourned the loss of her beloved.

Mary had left word that Elena was to be brought to her as soon as she arrived. Barely given time to change her soiled gown, Elena was hastened to the Queen's chamber. The excited voices of Spanish courtiers and their servants could be heard in the background as they stacked bags and boxes ready for the journey. Elena had to squeeze past a mountain of goods before she was able to continue along the oak-panelled passage leading to Mary's suite.

When she walked inside the room, Elena saw the Queen seated before the window, prayerbook in hand.

"Ah, so you've finally returned, Elena."

"Yes, Your Majesty."

"And did you enjoy your outing?"

"Yes, Madam. It's lovely in the woods."

A wave of unease gripped her. Elena found these innocent questions somewhat disturbing. While she waited for Mary to continue, a nervous pulse began to flutter in her throat.

Finally the Queen rose and came toward her, her gray face tight with strain, her hands clenched about her prayerbook; an ivory rosary dangled from her fingers.

"Do you love me well, Elena?"

"Oh, yes, Madam."

"You lie!" The Queen exploded with anger.

Elena backed away in self-defense. "No, Your Majesty, I'm ever loyal—"

"You betrayed our friendship—I'd always considered it special because of our shared heritage. I trusted you, Elena, and you betrayed me! Oh, why have I never learned how easily affections can be withdrawn!" The Queen stopped, her face working. When she was somewhat more composed, she said, "You recently sold an item of great value?"

Elena's face went parchment white. Should she try to brazen out matters by lying, or tell the truth and trust in the Queen's mercy? Uneasily she recalled that Mary Tudor had rarely displayed that virtue in recent months. "Sold something, Madam?" she asked, desperately playing for time.

"Do you take me for a fool?" Mary snapped, her

hands shaking as she fought to control her anger. Great
veins swelled in her scrawny neck and her skin was
flushed. "You betrayed my trust by aiding a heretic.
Oh, don't lie, don't try to deny—"

"I didn't intend to lie, Your Majesty."

"You sold the ring I gave you to aid Ravenscroft. . . . I see you're surprised by my knowledge.
Your treachery was discovered when the ring fell into
the wrong hands and was recognized."

"Oh, please, Your Majesty, hear me out," Elena
cried, dropping to her knees and seizing the hem of
Mary's brown velvet gown. "Anne begged me for
money . . . she was threatening to kill herself. At the
time, I had naught else of value. I succumbed in a
moment of weakness—later I regretted the action, but
by then it was too late."

Mary looked down at her stonily, her face a mask.
"I never dreamed you'd betray my trust. A heretic goes
free because of you. He should have burned with the
others."

"Oh, Madam—please try to understand! I never
thought of the consequences of offending you. It was
done so quickly!"

"You can plead till Michaelmas, but you won't
persuade me of your innocence."

Tears spilled down Elena's face, her emotions in a
turmoil of fear, shock and sorrow for having seemingly
betrayed her mistress.

Angrily Mary dragged her skirts out of Elena's grasp.

"You realize you can no longer serve me after this.
The sight of you will only remind me of your
treachery."

"You're dismissing me?"

Mary did not answer. She stalked away to the window
where she gripped the sill, her knuckles white. Finally

she turned about to see Elena crouched where she had left her.

"I've not decided what to do with you," she admitted honestly as some of her anger subsided. "You do not deserve my pity, or my mercy—that's not to say you shall not receive it," she relented when Elena gasped in shock. "Go to your room. We leave for London in two days. By then I'll have reached a decision. . . . How could you desert me, after all I've endured?" Mary whispered. Then, holding her hand to her brow, she cried, "Dear God, I feel so ill."

But when Elena sprang to assist the Queen to her chair, she was thrust away.

"Leave me, you wretch! I can't bear you near me. Send in the others."

Eyes bright with tears, Elena summmoned the Queen's other ladies. Little passed unnoticed at court, so she assumed the others were aware of her disfavor. They had probably listened at the door and could repeat the Queen's exact words. She knew she did not imagine their sly smiles and nudges, their somewhat condescending manner when addressing her.

Miserable, Elena watched the ladies-in-waiting hasten to the Queen's bidding before she turned away to retrace her steps through the twisting corridors to her room.

It was the morning of departure. The court was to travel to Greenwich Palace, from where Philip and his entourage would sail downriver to await the tide to carry them home to Spain. Mary was prostrate with grief and unwell in the bargain; she was to be carried into her capital on a litter.

Elena dressed and made ready for the journey, still unsure whether she should join the other ladies-in-waiting, or make separate arrangements for travel back to Lichborne. She already held her cloak, awaiting someone to collect her trunks, when a manservant tapped on the door and told her the Queen wished to speak with her.

Stomach knotting in apprehension, Elena tried to thrust from her memory the lurid descriptions she had heard of burnings and torturings, for in truth she did not know what Mary would consider just punishment for her crime.

The Queen lay propped against a mountain of pillows on her curtained bed. She was dressed for travel, her face white as the starched linen edging of her black headdress.

"Come inside and shut the door. We would be alone," Mary commanded, and her attendants obediently departed. "So, you are awaiting my judgment," Mary said, her voice rasping with fatigue. "And I suppose you expect to be forgiven."

"I expect to be dealt with as you see fit, Your Majesty."

Mary liked that answer, though she did not comment on it. "Are you aware someone I respect has pleaded your cause?"

"No, Madam, I am not."

"Even my dearest Philip asked me to spare you dismissal out of concern for the health of this gentleman. . . . I'm sure you can guess his name."

Elena nodded, wondering if now Mary would offer marriage to Don Alvaro as an alternative to harsher punishment.

"The poor gentleman is distressed to hear of your foolishness. Nevertheless, he has reminded me you are still young and impressionable."

Elena hung her head, listening to the Queen's grating voice and wondering what would be forthcoming. She could only hope and pray the sentence would not be too unpleasant. "If you wish, I can arrange for transportation home to Lichborne," she offered when the Queen stopped speaking.

"That's not necessary. I have other plans for you. First, I will remind you that you can avoid any dishonor by marriage. Are you aware of that?"

"Yes, Madam."

Mary looked stonily at Elena, waiting in vain for her assent. "So you still refuse?"

"I will obey your orders."

Mary's mouth tightened. She had hoped the wench would have enough sense to seize the easy way out. "I will never order you to marry against your wishes, even to someone as worthy as Don Alvaro Escalante." Mary paused to run her ivory rosary beads through her fingers, her lips moving slightly as she mouthed the accompanying prayers. It was almost as if she had forgotten Elena's presence. Yet, when Elena began to rise, Mary's head shot up and she snapped, "I didn't give you permission to stand."

"Forgive me, Your Majesty, I thought perhaps you'd forgotten—"

"I'm old, but not that old," snapped the Queen in displeasure. "Do you know a wench from Essex named Annis Jesmond?"

"Slightly, Your Majesty."

"I've decided you shall act as her companion on her journey to meet her groom."

Elena's head snapped up. There must be some mistake! She had heard Annis Jesmond was to marry one of Philip's courtiers who had already returned to Spain.

"A companion, Your Majesty? Maybe I've not heard the true story. They say she's to marry a Spanish grandee.''

"They speak the truth."

"You're banishing me to Spain?"

"Banish is too strong a word. You're merely to accompany the Jesmond wench—poor wench, she will find Spain foreign enough, yet your presence will help smooth her transition. Your baggage is already in the wagon, so you need not fret over it. Don Alvaro will act as your escort."

Elena reeled in the doorway, gripping the gilded doorjamb with whitened knuckles. So that was the Queen's scheme! By thrusting her in Don Alvaro's company, she hoped to persuade her to accept the Spaniard's suit. Face set, Elena turned to Mary, who had returned to fingering her beads. She curtsied.

"Thank you, Your Majesty, you've been most generous."

"Aye, generous, forgiving, merciful—all virtues your heretic friends accuse me of lacking. Mark that well, Elena Locke, when next you have discourse with them. Remind them Mary Tudor is ever just."

"Madam, I beg you listen. I have no discourse with heretics. I merely helped Anne—"

"Silence! You're done pleading your case. The sentence has been passed and it is a most lenient one. A word of warning—in Spain the ears of the Inquisition are everywhere; their arms encompass the length and breadth of the land. Take care, Elena, for they show no mercy toward heretics. Now go. At some future date I will recall you to court. Until then, pray for guidance. And be not blind to the merits of those who follow the true faith."

The wind off the river blew fresh. Elena stood on the deck of the huge Spanish galleon, watching all that was familiar slip slowly into the distance. Though around her many English wept to be leaving their homeland, her own tears had long since dried. White-faced and tight-lipped, she forced herself to look one final time at the London skyline, tiny as a child's building blocks against the blue sky.

For five days Philip had waited for favorable tides, days he might have spent with his wife. Mary had wept bitterly as his barge passed beneath her window at Greenwich Palace. Elena pitied the aging Queen who must surely guess Philip wanted no part of his amorous wife; but pity for her mistress could not soothe her own feelings of being unjustly served. For all she had thought the Queen loved her well, Mary had treated her as coldly as she would a stranger. The one gesture she had made for which Elena gave thanks was to place her aboard Philip's companion vessel. When Elena considered Mary's action, she concluded the Queen might not have been as blind to her husband's amorous intent as she had thought.

"Elena, how can you stay so calm?" whispered Annis Jesmond, her heart-shaped face pinched with grief, her brown eyes red and swollen from weeping.

Elena slid her arm about the younger girl's narrow shoulders.

" 'Tis not calm, Annis, love, 'tis pride. I do my weeping alone," Elena revealed bitterly. "Cheer up, you're not exiled for life. Likely you can visit your family from time to time."

"Alejandro . . ." Annis smiled wanly as she struggled to pronounce the unfamiliar Spanish name. ". . . My betrothed appears to be kind. He's handsome, too. But I barely know him, Elena. If only I were going to friends, I wouldn't feel so lonely."

"I'll be your friend for as long as I'm able. Now come, smile, we've a long journey ahead. Best not to look like a wet weekend for the entire journey."

Annis smiled and hugged Elena's arm against her side.

"You are a kind wench. Thank heaven I have you as my companion. I was so surprised, for we barely know each other. I thought the Queen would choose some horrid old spinster to chaperone me."

"Well, there you are, sweeting, you never know what surprises heaven has in store for us."

Aye, surprises aplenty, Elena thought later, as she clutched her aching stomach while the vessel pitched relentlessly on the tide. Seasickness beset many aboard. They were three days out, and Elena hoped her ailment was on the wane, for in truth this morning she felt somewhat restored. Poor Annis still groaned and vomited, feeling so ill she begged for death. The four women Lord Jesmond had sent to serve his daughter were useless, for they, too, lay prostrate on their hard pallets, praying to their Maker for deliverance.

After Elena had made Annis comfortable, she told the least ailing of the wenches to minister to her mistress if needed. Then, pulling on her cloak, she struggled up on deck, desperately clutching the iron handrail on the narrow stair, tottering and reeling as she tried to keep her balance on the rolling ship.

As soon as he saw her, Don Alvaro hurried to her side. The motion of the ship did not affect him. He was his usual dignified self, spare of body and hair, ramrod-straight, and clad from head to toe in black velvet decorated with silver lace.

"Doña Elena, my prayers have been answered. You are still pale, but looking more like yourself."

"Thank you, Don Alvaro. I am feeling a little better. The air on deck is so much fresher. Perhaps I'll soon be revived."

He gave her his quiet smile, which reflected far more

of his inner feelings than he was aware. When he gazed at her, love brightened his hazel eyes. Elena blinked in alarm, taken back by the unexpected revelation. Dear God, this romance was no longer a figment of Mary Tudor's old maid's imagination—he was truly enamored of her! Having no wish to cause him pain, Elena had tried not to encourage his attentions, nor to give him false hope, yet every hour spent in her company merely strengthened his resolve to claim her for his bride.

Elena quailed when she contemplated the future. Though she had no desire to marry Don Alvaro, neither had she any wish for Will's cherished suit with Lord Morton. In a recent letter received the day before departure, Will had bluntly stated her choice lay between the two. Mary's lack of sympathy for his selection angered him, yet it had not deterred him from his purpose. Elena wished there had been a message from Ronwen in the stilted letter. She was aware her sister-in-law did not write well and usually left correspondence up to her husband, yet if she had received a note from Ronwen, perhaps she would not have felt so isolated from all she held dear. Though Will scribbled a postscript, "Ron sends her love and bids you take care, for London's a hotbed of vice," she doubted those sentiments had ever passed Ronwen's lips. They were too much like Will's thoughts to be believed. Had Will known she was bound for foreign shores, he would have added several pages of warnings heeding her to safeguard her virtue. Her letter informing them of her journey would not reach Windland until long after she had left English waters.

As the days spent aboard the Spanish vessel passed, Elena managed to lock her unhappiness in a corner of her heart, dwelling on it only when she was alone. Her fierce pride proved a godsend. Once little Annis

Jesmond recovered from the worst of her sickness,
Elena devoted her attention to her charge. She proved
to be such a cheerful companion, Annis vowed to keep
Elena beside her for as long as Her Majesty would
allow. Of course, Alejandro's consent would be needed
for that. Elena suspected the little wench's husband
would have far different ideas of a suitable companion
for his child bride, but she kept those doubts to herself.

They finally reached Corunna on a warm autumn day
when the sun shone bright in a clear lapis sky. Sunlight
dappled the silver water until it seethed and shimmered
like endless miles of satin.

All round her Elena could hear excited voices
jabbering in Spanish. Though she had formerly prided
herself on her knowledge of the language, she found
she could barely understand a word. The rough-voiced
sailors spoke so many dialects, their speech lazy and
ill-formed, she eventually gave up all hope of understanding them.

On this important day Don Alvaro wore a fine black
cloak and tall crowned hat on which a great diamond
buckle winked fire in the sunlight as he strode
impatiently about the deck.

The unloading of the baggage seemed to take hours.
Elena leaned on the rail and gazed at the huddled
buildings edging the docks. The port of Corunna spread
many miles, its light-colored buildings alien to her eyes.
She would have given much for the sight of London's
murky streets and timbered dwellings overshadowed
by rain clouds instead of this brazen sky, which in
autumn still burned with the intensity of midsummer.

They had arrived ahead of the Prince's own vessel,
which could barely be seen tipping the horizon. Spanish
galleons traveled in a fleet as a safeguard against pirates.
Don Alvaro had revealed Spain's coastal waters were

infested with infidel pirates, and not wanting to offend her, he failed to mention some of the pirate ships flew the English flag.

"How long before we reach our destination?" asked Annis Jesmond, nervously clutching Don Alvaro's arm. Out of loneliness she had made a substitute father of the gray-haired don.

"The best part of a week, *doña*. But we'll travel easy to make your journey pleasant. Your betrothed impatiently awaits your arrival—waiting is hard when the heart burns with love."

Elena glanced away, the naked emotion in his eyes making her uncomfortable. Though Annis was unaware of it, Elena knew he spoke not about Don Alejandro's impatience for his bride, but rather about his own unrequited love for her. To her surprise, Don Alvaro had not yet proposed. Not sure how she would handle his proposal when it came, Elena wondered if she would dare to speak honestly and tell him she turned him down for lack of love. That decision was far longer coming than Elena had expected.

They toiled across the vast Castilian plain parched by the hot sun. Yellowish earth blew in spirals before the horses' hooves, whirling heavenward. The sky shimmered above them, bright blue and brazen. Elena had never seen such a vast land. England could be fitted in one corner of this desolate, sun-baked place. Her heart lurched painfully when she recalled this alien land was home to Luis. Riding long hours beneath the unrelenting sun, thoughts of him were never far from her mind. First she must find the ancient city of Toledo; from there all she need know was the direction of the largest bullranch.

"Come, Doña Elena, let us rest," suggested Don Alvaro, interrupting her tormenting thoughts. They had reached a cluster of buff-walled dwellings perched beside a stunted olive grove. "There's good water here. And we can rest in the shade. We've not much farther to ride."

Though Elena was anxious to reach Madrid, she welcomed this opportunity to dismount. She staggered when she set foot on the hard-baked earth, her legs stiffly unresponsive. The refreshing water was surprisingly cool. So many wells were tainted that Don Alvaro chose their watering places with great care; likewise their nightly lodgings. At times they were forced to camp beneath the stars, for even crude wayside hostelries did not exist in the more remote regions. Their servants made them comfortable with blankets and pillows. Elena found these makeshift arrangements preferable, for the inns generally crawled with vermin and their rooms were stale with the odors of garlic and rancid cooking oil. At times during the journey, Don Alvaro was often strict; and though this grated on her nerves, Elena learned to be thankful for his stubborn insistence on getting his own way. He knew this land well, often having journied back and forth from Corunna. The location of each good well and honest inn along their barren route was stored in his mind, for he used no map to guide them. Before their journey was done, though she had never expected to admit it, Elena found herself grateful for Don Alvaro's company.

Fanned by the branches of a stubby, wind-stunted tree, Elena wiped her dusty face with a water-soaked cloth.

"We're fortunate to have your knowledge, Don Alvaro. Without you we'd be a sorry sight indeed."

He knelt beside her to offer another cup of water, his thin, lined face intent. "All I have done has been done for love," he revealed, his eyes boring into hers.

"I've never spoken to you of my deepest feelings, *doña*. Soon we'll reach Madrid. Don Alejandro lives nearby. You are my guest and as such shall be treated with all respect, yet . . . Oh, *doña*, would that you consented to be much more—that you consented to be . . . my wife!"

Elena gasped and looked away from the naked emotion in his eyes. Deep lines, pouched eyes and sagging features all betrayed Don Alvaro's advancing years, yet at this moment he had the lovelorn expression of a lad with his first sweetheart. A strange, sick feeling washed over her. She had not wanted to hurt him—he had consistently done his best for them. It was not his fault she did not love him.

"What can I say?" she mumbled lamely, wishing herself many miles away.

"I realize this is sudden. . . . Forgive me." He stood, the sharp creak of his knees an unpleasant reminder of his age. "Later, when you're more refreshed, we can discuss it further."

Elena smiled, forcing the expression. He nodded and turned away, busying himself about his saddlebags. He swiftly produced a handful of sweet dates, which he divided between Elena and Annis, who had skipped over to tell them about the lizards she had spied amongst the rocks. With a sigh of relief Elena realized the embarrassing situation was temporarily resolved—until they reached Madrid!

Chapter Thirteen

A warm breeze fanned Elena's brow. She sat before a high, narrow window overlooking the square where, during the course of the day, all Madrid seemed to pass. These past two weeks she had seen much of the town, yet she tired of merely being an onlooker, longing instead to take an active part in life.

She sighed, fingering the spicy geraniums that spilled from the window box, their scarlet blossoms contrasting brightly with the black iron railings and white stucco wall. This was one of the few windows in Don Alvaro's house that was not overshadowed by iron grills, and therefore her favorite place from which to watch the world go by. At times Elena felt like a prisoner, forever behind bars. Even the door leading to the street was covered by a massive iron gate which was kept locked, opened only to visitors after their approval by the gate-keeper. Don Alvaro was a wealthy man and this provincial town of Madrid was lawless; he was taking no chances with his treasure.

For two days Elena had been the guest of Annis Jesmond's Spanish groom in his palatial home outside town. As she suspected, he had already chosen a suitable *duena* to chaperone his bride until their marriage next

month. Annis wept piteously, pleading to be allowed
to keep her new friend beside her, but fearing he would
offend his elderly relative, Don Alejandro refused to
yield.

To Don Alvaro's great delight, Elena then became
his houseguest. To Elena's relief, they spent little time
alone, strict propriety being observed within his household. Instead, the elderly don bombarded her with love
notes in his native language, for, as yet, he did not write
English. Again he broached the subject of marriage;
again she looked down modestly at her hands and
demurred. The situation could not continue.

Desperately, Elena wrote to the Queen asking to be
allowed to come home. She supposed if Mary chose
to be laggard in answering, she would be forced to beg
before her request was considered.

The elderly woman who served Elena as her maid
rose to open the door as steps outside alerted them to
Don Alvaro's arrival.

Elena's spirits soared. Today they were to visit Don
Alvaro's estate south of the city. She was already
dressed for riding in her sapphire velvet habit, impatiently awaiting her host. Though after their arduous
journey from Corunna she had thought never to want
to ride again, she could not wait to be in the saddle.

"Don Alvaro! I expected you an hour ago," Elena
cried excitedly, hurrying to greet him as he came inside
the room.

Don Alvaro wore a padded brown velvet doublet, and
a great diamond and gold chain glinted about his neck.
His black hat had a soft white plume curling above its
steep crown.

Solemnly he bowed. "Dear Doña Elena, forgive me
the delay. I've been making further arrangements for
your pleasure. We're to visit the lands of my niece

who's a recent bride. It's customary to pay her a congratulatory visit.''

"Oh, so we aren't to visit your estate?''

"Our lands border each other. Come, we have much distance to cover before the afternoon heat.''

They soon left the town behind as they rode beside the Manzanares, little more than a trickle at this time of year. From a distance Madrid looked even more provincial with its unpaved road and shabby buildings.

As they followed the dusty road south, Don Alvaro's conversation became more personal. He finally stated his resolve to make her his wife, hoping to win her love if not before, then at least after their marriage. Elena flatly told him she had no desire to become any man's bride. Infuriatingly, he ignored her statement, merely smiling in a knowing fashion, his eyes fixed on the distant horizon.

They continued their journey in silence. The road through this barren countryside broken by patches of thick forest seemed never-ending. Elena simmered angrily over Don Alvaro's refusal to take her seriously. He must be taking her to visit his newlywed niece in the hope she would become so envious, she would virtually agree to marry him on the spot. For a sophisticated courtier, his strategy was so naive that she could not keep from smiling. Her amusement successfully chased away her ill humor.

Their small party of eight spent the night at a monastery in a range of bleak hills south of Madrid. After a sparse breakfast of thick bread fried in olive oil and washed down with sour wine, they prepared to ride the final leg of their journey.

A snatch of conversation overheard at the monastery made Elena's stomach lurch. She discovered they were close to Toledo. With churning stomach, Elena viewed the sunny but desolate landscape through which they rode, wondering how close she was to Luis's estate. This grassy land rolling to the horizon, divided by streams and dotted with scrub and thickets of trees, seemed no prize worthy of being sacrificed for!

Before noon they had reached their destination. A long, low dwelling could be seen ahead, partially shielded by willows, which also blanketed the banks of a stream. In every direction herds of black cattle grazed the rolling grassland.

Don Alvaro reined in. "We are here, Doña Elena. Is this not a wonderful spot—the best bloodstock in all Spain!" he pronounced proudly, shielding his eyes against the sun's glare.

"This is your estate?" Elena voiced in disappointment. She had been expecting green-treed vistas broken by flower beds and pathways, a facsimile of an English country estate.

"Yes. Beyond the trees on the higher ground begins my niece's land. Some of the bulls you see in the distance belong to her. Come, let me show you what magnificent stock they are," he urged, his voice quickening with excitement.

Don Alvaro surged forward, breaking into a gallop; his servants followed. Not anxious to be left behind, Elena spurred her horse to catch them.

So these were Spain's feared fighting bulls! They were most disappointing. Elena had envisioned great weighty animals with rolling eyes and ponderous hooves, like the bulls chained in English farmers' fields. These creatures, though their eyes rolled fiercely enough, were only half the size of an English bull. But not wanting to insult her host, she allowed him to think she was impressed.

They finally entered the white painted house, which

felt pleasantly cool, its dim interior a relief after hours in the glaring sun. Don Alvaro's country home was far more rustic than she had expected. He had proudly revealed that Casa Escalante was Madrid's finest dwelling, but this house was more like a yoeman farmer's house. The wood plank floors were swept clean, devoid of valuable Moorish carpets or even scented rushes. A few massive dark wood pieces sparsely furnished the rooms. Plain wood crucifixes were prominently displayed on the starkly whitewashed walls, reminding her of the monastery where they had stayed last night.

A servant brought them a refreshing orange-flavored drink, which Don Alvaro revealed was a secret recipe of the former Moslem ruler of the area. Elena found the chilled beverage to be a marvelous thirst quencher. She also ate some delicious date-studded cake and a handful of a sticky almond confection. Their snack complete, they were ready to set out for Carmenilla to visit Don Alvaro's niece.

From his sparse conversation as they rode slowly through the hot, still afternoon, Elena deduced Don Alvaro's niece and her husband oversaw this land in his absence. It was so lonely here. There seemed no end to the grazing land. As they rode farther south, the terrain became greener, criss-crossed with streams along which thickets of trees were clustered. How homesick she was for England's trees, grass and flowers, for the green vista of rain-washed countryside! Blinking back unexpected tears, Elena offered a silent prayer that Mary would soon relent and summon her back to court.

They approached a castellated stone dwelling, which appeared to be a small fortress set on high ground, affording unobstructed views of the surrounding countryside. They rode inside the outer walls, and here,

as if in answer to her prayer, Elena found a courtyard
full of flowers and trees hidden behind a huge iron gate.
Shady Jacaranda trees, fragrant oranges and red and
white flowering vines cast their shadows over a fountain
tinkling merrily in the center of the tranquil courtyard.
Tears again pricked her eyes as a fresh wave of homesickness wrenched her heart. How different from
England was this land with its fierce, stark beauty.
Moorish arches and fretted stone, whitewashed stucco,
the vast riches of its nobles in contrast to the dire poverty
of its peasants—all these elements made Spain an alien
world.

A young woman dressed in black, sunlight catching
her many jewels, came out to meet them. Her walk was
stately and dignified until the last few paces, when she
broke into a run, arms outstretched to greet her uncle,
who had just dismounted.

Elena waited uncomfortably in the saddle, wondering
what she should do. It was as if her presence had been
forgotten during this emotional reunion. Don Alvaro's
niece wept loudly as she hugged her favorite uncle. How
beautiful she was! So startlingly blonde, her hair like
spun gold beneath the black lace headcovering hanging
loosely down her back. An exaggerated pointed stom-
acher accentuated her tiny waist. For a woman, she
seemed unusually tall, her heavy velvet skirts barely
ruffling as she walked.

Suddenly remembering their guest, Don Alvaro
turned back to Elena. "Come, poor child, you're all
but forgotten," he apologized softly as he helped her
dismount. "Meet my beautiful niece, Leonora."

"Welcome to Carmenilla, *doña*," said Leonora,
smiling charmingly as she dabbed away her tears of joy.
"Oh, Uncle, you surprised me. Why did you not send
word sooner? When your servant arrived, I could hardly

believe—there's barely been time to prepare. So this is the lady from the English court.''

Uncomfortably, Elena wondered if Leonora assumed her to be her uncle's affianced bride. But when she tried to explain their relationship, Don Alvaro quickly interrupted, making the introduction in rapid Spanish.

''A lady-in-waiting to the English Queen!'' gasped Leonora, genuinely awestruck. ''Such an honor.'' She dropped a sweeping curtsy to Elena.

They walked inside the house, uncle and niece chattering excitedly. Elena followed, finding the welcome shade of the building a change from the bright outdoors. She glanced with interest at the interior of this small fortress. Tapestries and elaborate crucifixes adorned the stone walls of the corridor down which they walked. Leonora led them inside a small central hall where two vast iron and wood chandeliers hung on chains from the blackened rafters, adding greatly to the room's feudal appearance. After they were comfortably seated on red velvet padded settles facing the lush courtyard, their hostess excused herself to oversee the preparation of refreshments.

Though Elena welcomed a cooling drink—she had never been as thirsty in her life as she had been since coming to Spain—she hoped they would not expect her to eat again. She had barely had time to digest the rich food taken at Don Alvaro's table.

''Isn't my niece beautiful?''

''She looks as if she stepped from a holy painting,'' Elena observed sincerely. Leonora moved with such grace, she barely seemed mortal; her cloud of golden hair and heavenly blue eyes merely added to the illusion. ''She does not look Spanish,'' she added, regretting the remark as soon as it was made.

Don Alvaro laughed. ''Does she look more English,

then? Perhaps it is you who look the most Spanish of us all, eh, Doña Elena?'' And he chuckled in amusement.

Leonora returned, gliding almost soundlessly over the stone floor at the head of a string of servants each carrying carafes of wine or trays of food.

Politeness forced her to sample the food, and Elena tried a dish of beef cubes floating in a spiced red sauce. She washed down the meat's hot, tangy flavor with a milky almond drink, which effectively soothed the fire in her throat. Between sips she made small talk with Don Alvaro's niece who spoke and understood much English. The gray-haired don listened, smiling at their women's talk, but he did not join in.

Leonora told Elena her husband was riding about their property on his weekly inspection and would not return before sundown; she also confided that as yet she had not conceived a babe, a lack she mourned, for she was anxious to give her husband an heir. Without intending to, Elena found herself telling Leonora about her lost babe. To her surprise, she felt little pain in the recounting. It was as if recent events had numbed her emotions.

Finally, Don Alvaro interrupted the women's chatter to suggest they ride out to meet Leonora's husband, showing Elena the estate on the way. Instant displeasure marred Leonora's classic features, the expression so fleeting Elena was not sure it had actually been there. Leonora quickly agreed a late afternoon ride would be most pleasant. Perhaps Elena also imagined the strain in their hostess's voice when she courteously invited them to spend a few days at Carmenilla instead of returning directly home.

Leonora led them down a dimly lit corridor toward the rear of the dwelling. Portraits covered the walls of a wide gallery where they were to await their hostess's return while she went to change clothes for riding.

Elena amused herself by walking up and down, inspecting the paintings of Leonora's ancestors stiffly encased in armor, or draped in what appeared to be religious habits. While she read the names either painted on the canvas or engraved on the frames, one name, repeated often, made her heart miss a beat. She stopped before a portrait of a fierce mustachioed warrior, her heart pounding uncomfortably.

"Don Miguel Alcante Fragoso Menares Escalante." Her throat went dry, her eyes glued to that third name. "Fragoso," she repeated, her voice strangled. "Don Alvaro, is your niece Leonora Fragoso?"

He smiled as he stepped to her side, glancing up at the portrait on the wall. "She was," he agreed. "After her marriage she became Leonora Fragoso de los Santos . . . ah, here she is."

Throat dry as parchment, Elena raised startled eyes to the blonde vision appearing out of the gloom. So this was the hated Leonora—the woman for whom Luis had spurned her. Leonora looked like some heavenly apparition, clad in form-fitting dark blue velvet embroidered with seed pearls, her cloud of blonde hair caught in a pearl-encrusted net beneath a blue hat. Elena stared speechlessly at her rival, who had stopped and was eyeing her quizzically.

"*Doña*," Leonora asked in concern, "does something ail you?"

Realizing she was attracting unwanted attention, Elena quickly tried to mask her shock. Finally finding her voice, which croaked, she explained, "Nay, Doña Leonora, I felt a little faint, that's all. No doubt 'tis the heat . . . I'm not used to this weather."

"And what heat we've had this year! It's like July

instead of October. But soon the freezing winds will
blow over the plain and make us long for summer.''

Leonora placed her hand on Elena's shoulder, guiding
her toward the tree-filled courtyard.

Moving like a mechanical doll, Elena allowed herself to be led to torture. Within the hour she would come
face to face with *him*. She did not know if she could
bear the sight of Luis and his lovely wife together.
Perhaps she should plead illness, she thought, moving
as if in a dream. They would not remark on that, for
she was unused to this climate. Yet that part of her that
still loved him would not sanction such cowardice. She
would go forth to meet him, mustering all the pride in
her blood. Then he would know she had finally overcome her weakness for him, that her blood no longer
ran wild at the thought of his kiss . . . Dear God, how
could she perform such a miracle? Blindly, Elena
followed the chattering Leonora, mounted her horse and
rode to her doom.

The Carmenilla ranch covered thousands of acres.
Like a child eager to show off her most treasured
possession, Leonora pointed out each stream, each
pond, the spreading woods marring the rolling
grassland. Peasants touched their forelocks, or doffed
their hats, bowing low to their *señora* as she rode by,
her head high, shoulders back, spine ramrod straight.

Unconsciously, Elena copied Leonora's unbending
carriage, calling on her own pride to see her through
the coming ordeal. She must not let Luis see her pain,
her shock. Would he betray their relationship by word
or glance? Or would he greet her as a stranger? She
suspected that, being Luis and having his own vast store-
house of pride, he would reveal nothing at that treacherous moment of meeting.

She was wrong.

They rode up a slight incline toward a group of men who stood discussing some serious subject, heads down in concentration. Elena was blinded by the late afternoon sun until she crested the grassy rise. Then, suddenly, without warning, she saw him! Luis stared at her, his face blanching as if he saw a ghost.

"Luis, we have guests," called Leonora, swiftly dismounting and hurrying toward her husband and his men.

Luis stared at Elena, transfixed, not seeing Leonora or Don Alvaro. For a brief, unguarded moment their eyes met and held. Elena saw his pain. She tried to ignore the stab of recognition, the surging emotion. But it was all in vain. So weak did she feel, she thought she would fall from the saddle.

Dear Lord in heaven, nothing had changed! For all her high-flown lies, for all those convincing arguments she had made, nothing between them had changed.

"Welcome, Don Alvaro . . . *doña*," Luis said, coming suddenly to life. They were all staring at him, wondering at his stupefaction. He explained quickly with forced humor, "I thought I was seeing a ghost. When last I saw you, Don Alvaro, 'twas in England's green land."

Don Alvaro chuckled as he helped Elena from her saddle. She was relieved that Luis had not offered her his hand, for she did not think she could touch him without revealing the torment in her heart. Numbly, she stepped toward him, aware of Leonora frowning at him. His wife could not know there had ever been anything between them; her ill humor must stem from jealousy at having another woman on her land.

"May I present Doña Elena, one of the Queen's ladies. I'm sure you remember her, Don Luis, she's a lady not soon to be forgotten," said Don Alvaro, proudly bearing Elena forward.

She curtsied stiffly to Luis, who politely brushed her
hand with his mouth. For all the heat of the afternoon,
his hard mouth felt chill against her flesh. Elena
shuddered, wishing she could prevent her telltale
reaction. Fortunately, no one seemed to have noticed.

"Welcome to my land, Doña Elena. I never expected
to see you in Spain."

While he spoke, he looked her full in the face, a
dawning smile in his eyes. *Oh, no, Luis, not that,* Elena
screamed silently. Quick, lest he form the wrong
impression, she said, "Her Majesty commanded me
to accompany an English lady who was traveling to
Spain to be wed."

Her explanation given, Elena stepped back, refusing
to look at him. She did not know if he registered surprise
or disappointment, she only knew she could not let him
think she had accepted his terms. *As long as you are
married to her, I won't become your mistress,* she
repeated silently when she found the courage to look
at him again. Luis stared back at her, his face a mask.
She could not begin to guess his thoughts.

Like players in some dignified tableau, all four walked
back to their horses for the return ride. Luis assisted
Leonora to her saddle. And Don Alvaro, panting slightly
from the exertion, helped Elena to mount. Luis sprang
agilely astride his own horse and raced down the incline
into the shadowy, sloping meadows as the sun dipped
low on the horizon. Elena realized she had been holding
her breath, preparing to endure his touch. However,
this time she had not needed to call on her extra reserve
of control. Instead of gratitude, perversely, she felt
disappointment because he had shunned her in favor
of his wife. Each time she pictured Luis holding
Leonora in his arms, Elena grew nauseous with

jealousy.

Luis wore a simple dark leather jerkin and white shirt, a flat black cap with a red feather atop his blond hair. His skin was browner than when last she had seen him, the dying golden light burnishing his hands and face until he looked dark as a Moor. He galloped ahead, the breeze whipping his full white shirtsleeves and tossing his horse's black mane and tail. Oh, how handsome he was, how disturbingly virile. She was not the only woman present to appreciate those qualities— she had already noticed Leonora's adoring gaze as she followed her husband's swift descent of the long slope. Worse than that—Leonora had a right to him.

The rest of the evening was misery to endure. Luis spoke little to Elena, avoiding her whenever possible. She longed to retire to her chamber where she might indulge herself in the luxury of tears. This had been one of the worst days of her life. She never dreamed Don Alvaro's niece would be Luis's wife. Leonora was a common Spanish name, there had been no reason to suspect she was *that* Leonora. Oh, why had she been such a fool! She should have guessed the wonderful estate about which the old don rhapsodized was that same parcel of land for which she had been exchanged. They were all obsessed with this land. Even Leonora spoke about the accursed place as if it were a lover, extolling the virtues of their fine bloodstock being raised for slaughter in the *corridas* of royal Spain.

It was almost more than Elena could endure as she watched Leonora brush Luis's arm, her pale gold head sinking against his. Uncomfortably, she overheard her whisper that it was past time to retire. Clenching her hands in the folds of her skirt, Elena tried to force down the rising nausea that threatened to choke her. It took little imagination to guess what prompted Leonora's fatigue. Likely she was not yet surfeited with her groom's expert lovemaking. Regardless of her angelic qualities, not for one moment did Elena suppose Leonora to be half as saintly as she appeared. Picturing them entwined in each other's arms in some great bed made her stomach lurch dangerously. In alarm Elena's hand flew to her mouth.

"I'm feeling a little faint and terribly weary," she mumbled weakly when her hostess looked questioningly at her.

"Yes, I'm exhausted myself. I'll show you to your chamber, Doña Elena. Or would you prefer the maid to do it?" asked Don Alvaro, stifling a yawn.

"Don't trouble yourself, Don Alvaro. This has been a long, tiring day for us all. Goodnight, Doña Leonora . . . Don Luis." There, the name was past her lips, yet not spoken without great difficulty.

"Sleep well, *doña*. I trust tomorrow you will feel much revived. Teresa, show Doña Elena to her chamber."

A dark-haired maid came from the shadows to do her master's bidding. The girl carried a lamp to light their way through the gloomy fortress overlooking the mighty Tajo.

Without a backward glance, though it cost her much effort, Elena followed the maid.

They wound their way up and down short flights of stairs, round seemingly endless corners, until she stumbled wearily on the uneven stone floor. Would this terrible day never end?

At last they reached her bedchamber. A fire blazed in the grate, for the night air had chilled the house. The maid spoke no English, but she seemed eager to please. She turned down the bed, showed Elena the warm water for her ablutions, the chamber pot, a carafe of wine;

then, after handing Elena a ribbon-tied bouquet of jasmine, she backed from the room.

Finally, given the luxury of privacy to indulge her pain, Elena relinquished all pretense at bravery. Burning tears welled in her eyes. Her heart threatened to burst with grief as she threw herself on top of the velvet bedcover and wept as if she would never stop.

Chapter Fourteen

Elena examined the ravages of last night's tears in a venetian hand mirror on the chest beside the bed. Her eyes were swollen, her face blotchy; given the choice, she would have preferred to spend the day in her room.

Though she saw their guest had been weeping, the maid pretended not to notice. Yet, when Elena had eaten her small meal of bread and sweet wine, Teresa made her lie back while she placed cold compresses over her swollen eyes. Surprised by the maid's unexpected attention, Elena lay there without protest, enjoying the unusual luxury of being pampered.

Later, when she went downstairs, Elena discovered Don Alvaro had risen at dawn to join Luis on a tour of their combined lands. She was left alone with her hostess.

After their few mutual interests were explored, the women fell into an uncomfortable silence. Sitting idly by while Leonora embroidered an altar cloth, Elena became so tense, she could barely endure it.

"May I go for a ride, Doña Leonora?"

"Certainly. I'll send someone to accompany you," said Leonora, allowing herself a sigh of relief. She no more welcomed this strange woman's company than

the Englishwoman did hers. She was glad to ring for
a servant to escort their guest to her room to change.

Wearing her sapphire riding habit and blue kid
buskins, Elena walked briskly outside in the warm sunshine. Two grooms mounted on donkeys were waiting
to serve as her escorts.

Some of Elena's terrible tension evaporated as she
galloped over the rolling grassland, the hot breeze
whipping at her hair. How could she endure much more
of this torment? Luis could not contrive to be absent
during her entire visit, yet she was grateful that he was
purposely avoiding her. This way she was not forced
to test her limited acting ability when they met.

The hot sun beat down fiercely on her bare head,
reminding her she should have brought a hat. Elena
glanced about, seeking a shadier place. To her left the
ground rolled uphill toward a grove of trees where
tangled shrubbery thickets lined the banks of a winding
stream. Thankful, she headed for the welcome shade.
Though the ground was steep, her horse pulled ahead
eagerly, anxious to reach water. Suddenly the horse
shied; Elena clutched the reins and fought to maintain
her seat. She patted the animal's neck to quiet him,
though he still snorted and tossed his head. She was
wondering what had frightened the beast when one of
the grooms yelled a warning. Elena was startled to see
a huge black bull emerge from a nearby thicket to stand
squarely in her path. Nostrils flaring, the heavily
muscled animal slowly switched its tail before finally
losing interest and ambling away.

"You must take care, *señora*. It's unwise to startle
an animal from its *querencia*. Are you all right?"

Elena turned, seeking the speaker. A few feet away
a broad-shouldered man sat astride a white stallion, his
black hair gleaming in the sun. The bareheaded stranger

was dressed in a white peasant shirt with loose dark
britches covering the tops of his rough leather boots.
He was handsome in a coarse way, his dark, sun-
bronzed skin stretched taut over high cheekbones; a
prominent hooked nose gave him a predatory look.
When he smiled at her, his dark lips drew back to reveal
strong white teeth. His coal black eyes were alight with
admiration.

"Thank you, sir, but I'm not in need of rescuing.
Fortunately I was only startled."

The man rode forward and bowed to her from the
saddle.

"Who are you, *doña*, that you ride through this
land?"

"An English guest of the . . . the *Señora*."

"Ah, so that explains matters. You're unfamiliar with
the habits of the bulls. Allow me to escort you back
to the house and on the way, I'll explain."

He motioned to the grooms to leave and, doffing their
hats, the lads rode away.

Elena did not know whether to be angry or grateful
to her would-be rescuer. "You presume much by
sending away my escort. Who are you?"

He grinned broadly, his teeth flashing against his dark
skin. "Cristobal Santos . . . You must be a stranger
if you've never heard of me."

Elena bristled in annoyance at his supreme conceit.

"Oh, so you're that famous?"

"Around here, yes. I'm the leading *torero* of the
district." Discovering his boastful claim was lost on
her, he scowled as he tried to explain. "You are
English, so perhaps you do not know. A *torero* fights
the bulls. I'm a grand champion."

"Oh, like a knight in a tournament?"

"*Si*, something like that."

"So you are looking over the bulls for your next tournament."

He laughed. "I look them over every day of my life—I've had charge of this land since I was a boy."

They were moving swiftly across the scrubby grassland stretching uphill toward a long ridge dotted with shrubs and spiky grass. At the crest of the ridge, Cristobal reined in. Pointing into the distance, he explained, "As far as you can see is de los Santos land. It's a great birthright." He paused, a scowl drawing his heavy brows together over the bridge of his nose. The expression gave a sinister cast to his striking features.

Despite the hot sun, Elena shivered. What a fool she was to be riding alone in such an isolated area with this man. For all she knew, he could be a common criminal. She glanced uneasily at the twin daggers thrust beneath his belt, the blades winking in the sun.

Almost as if he sensed her unease, Cristobal turned toward her with a disarming grin. "Have no fear, *doña*, you are safe here. The bulls respect me. Every animal has his *querencia*—his haunt, and it's unwise to startle him or drive him from it. But this place is *contra-querencia*. No bull will ever set foot here. The land is cursed. My mother is to blame for that."

"Your mother! Is she a witch?"

"She was a gypsy—to many it's the same thing. Here she gave birth to me and died the same day, cursing both the bulls and the *Señor*."

"The *Señor*?"

"The old man—Don Gaspar de los Santos. My mother may have been gypsy, but my father was a great nobleman."

Elena's breath caught as she grasped his proud words. Was this black-haired, bold-eyed ranch foreman Luis's half brother? He had never mentioned a brother, yet, to give him his due, during their heated discussions she had given him little chance to elaborate on his story.

"Don Luis is your brother?"

Cristobal turned in the saddle, his thick lips twisted in a sneer. "Don Luis de los Santos, king of all he surveys—yes, he's my brother, for what good it does me. His mother was a noblewoman, so Don Gaspar chose him to inherit the kingdom . . . his favorite bastard, as it were."

Cristobal's wild laughter echoed in Elena's ears as he spurred his horse forward, racing down the incline. Afraid she would be left behind, she spurred after him.

They galloped side by side for a few minutes until Cristobal slackened his pace. "You never did tell me your name, lovely one," he said at last, his anger vanished. He glanced sideways at her, his thick lips curved in an appreciative smile.

"Elena Locke."

"Elena . . . Spanish?"

"My mother came from Aragon."

Again Cristobal scowled. At first Elena did not understand his anger until he said, in that same sneering manner, "You must be related to the great Don Luis. His mother's family is Aragonese."

"Oh, no, I'm a guest of Don Alvaro Escalante. He brought me here to meet his niece."

Accepting her explanation, Cristobal relaxed visibly. A few minutes later he even began to hum beneath his breath. They were riding beneath a grove of arching trees whose heavy leaves fluttered noisily in the hot wind. Here Cristobal dismounted and held up strong bronzed arms to her.

"Come, Elena, I want to show you a waterfall. It's known as a lover's meeting place."

Elena allowed him to lift her from the saddle, trying not to take exception to the length of time he held her before placing her feet on the ground. Instinct told her to beware of Cristobal Santos and his overwhelming ego.

Walking at her side, he led the horses down a path worn in the grass and weeds. Soon they came to a rocky formation overgrown with moss and ferns; here a small waterfall cascaded into a rock basin, swirling like a whirlpool, crystal clear and inviting.

"Sometimes I swim here at dawn. The water's pure and icy. It banishes the sluggishness of sleep and prepares me to face the bulls. Have you ever seen a *corrida*?"

"No."

"Then I invite you to attend the next *corrida* as my guest. I will dedicate my kill to you."

Elena was sure Cristobal intended to do her great honor, although she had little desire to watch bulls slaughtered in the name of sport. It would remind her too much of the cruel bull and bearbaiting Mary's courtiers enjoyed. She thanked him stiffly, aware of the undercurrent of emotion he emitted. A disturbing mixture of violence and passion simmered just beneath the surface; each word, each movement of his lithe, dark-skinned body, suggested barely contained energy.

"I'm very good with the bulls."

"So you've told me."

"And also with the women."

Elena stepped back quickly toward her horse, but Cristobal was too fast for her. His arms shot out and he pulled her against him. Overpowered by his strength, Elena became aware of the heat of his skin, the prickle of his hair, before he covered her lips with his burning mouth. She was so surprised she barely had time to struggle, although, anticipating her resistance, he had imprisoned her hands behind her.

"Your mouth is sweet as ripe cherries," he declared ardently. "It was made to be kissed."

"But not by you! How dare you! Let me go!" Elena struggled to free herself, and Cristobal laughed, secure in the knowledge he would soon charm her into acquiescence.

"One kiss is not such a sacrifice. I've much more to offer, *señora*, something you've probably missed in your frigid homeland. Heat and passion . . ."

He was so sure of himself as he prepared for the next kiss that he slackened his grip. Elena managed to free her hand and gave him a resounding slap across the face.

"Don't touch me again! I demand to be taken back this instant."

Cristobal had retreated a pace to nurse his stinging cheek. Barely discouraged, he grinned ruefully. "You're a she-cat. I'm surprised . . . but then, I like spirited women. Come, Elena, let me love you. I promise you won't regret it."

"I've no desire for your lovemaking, your kisses or your company," she blazed, seizing her horse's reins. "Guide me back to the fortress at once, or your employer shall hear of your audacity."

"You disappoint me. Surely you're not going to turn down Cristobal Santos. *Dios*, half the women in Toledo pine for my kisses."

"Fortunately for me, I don't come from Toledo," Elena snapped as she scrambled unaided into the saddle. "This is one contest you've lost, Don Cristobal."

Anger darkened his face and his mouth turned sullen. Without another word, he swung into his saddle and turned his horse about. He headed down the narrow path, picking up speed as he neared the trees.

"If you'll be so good as to follow me, *señora*, I'll show you the way back." He flung the words at her as he abruptly quickened his pace. Once on the flat, he kicked his horse's flanks, forcing him into a gallop. When finally he reined in, he turned about, surprised to find Elena still on his heels.

"You're a good rider," he admitted grudgingly. "What else are you good at?"

"That, Cristobal, is something you'll never discover."

"Oh, I shouldn't be too sure—you'll soon regret today's actions. I'm convinced of it."

Beyond the trees Elena saw the gray outline of the fortress; she had no further need of an escort to find her way home. "Time will prove you wrong," she said sweetly, preparing to gallop away.

Rolling clouds of dust above the trees alerted her to a party of riders who suddenly came into view. The leader shouted a greeting, and Cristobal raised his hand in acknowledgment.

To Elena he said, "Ah, you're honored, *señora*. The great Don Luis comes to save you."

Elena's stomach pitched in dismay as she recognized that straight, broad-shouldered figure astride a sleek black horse. Blood flushed her cheeks, and she turned her back on Cristobal, not anxious for him to discover her weakness. When Luis rode close enough for recognition, she saw his face was set in anger.

"What's the meaning of this? The boys came back alone."

"I sent them home, Don Luis. The *señora* is safe with me. She wished to see the estate, and who knows the bulls better than I?"

"That I don't dispute, yet you've not been appointed official escort of Carmenilla. If the *señora* wishes a tour

of the land, I'll escort her. Now, get back to your
duties."

"But, Don Luis, you were busy elsewhere."

Luis's mouth tightened and his eyes grew steely. "I
don't choose to argue the point, Cristobal. Do as I say.
From now on confine your exploits to the *corrida* . . .
and the women of the streets."

Uneasily, Elena glanced from one to the other, aware
of the undercurrent of emotion crackling between them.
There was far more to their hostility than a simple
dispute over who should guide her about the estate.

Without a word, Cristobal wheeled about and
galloped in the opposite direction. Tight-lipped, Luis
watched him until he was no more than a rolling cloud
of dust on the horizon. Then, with a brisk wave, he
dismissed the party of men who accompanied him.

"You'd better go indoors, Elena, it's far too hot to
be riding without a hat. This is siesta time."

"Luis . . ." Elena swallowed nervously. There was
so much she wanted to say to him. Yet, when he looked
at her, his eyes pale and remote, he appeared so closed
off, she had no encouragement to continue.

"I'd have thought you'd have had better taste than
to ride with the get of a gypsy whore!" he snarled as
they came close to the fortress.

"A bull startled me and Cristobal took command of
the situation. There was no more to it than that."

"Indeed. Had you stayed out much longer with him,
I'm sure he would have remedied that. He has a sizeable
reputation with women as well as bulls."

Enraged by his failure to give her any loving gestures,
or even to speak civilly to her, Elena snapped, "Does
it outweigh yours, Don Luis?"

He twisted about in the saddle, his face tight with
anger. "I haven't asked you what relationship you share

with Don Alvaro, nor have you ever bothered to explain it to me. I can only surmise . . . but with that gypsy bastard there's no need for speculation. I know what would take place."

"Are you suggesting I'd lie with any man who asked me?"

"You never hesitated with me!"

His cruel taunt wounded her beyond belief. Elena gasped, glaring at him. "Damn you for reminding me of that! 'Twas the last thing I expected to have flung in my face."

Shamefaced, Luis glanced away. He wanted to apologize, and had even begun to voice his sentiment when Leonora hailed them from the gateway.

"Ah, so you found her, Luis. I thought perhaps our pretty guest had been trampled."

As she rode past Leonora, Elena was surprised to see a flash of malicious pleasure cross her face as if she contemplated that satisfying fate. The discovery added nothing to her peace of mind.

"Fortunately no harm was done. Cristobal was bringing her home. As the lady of the house, Leonora, it's your responsibility to see to our guest's welfare. I've more important tasks at hand. Good day." Abruptly, Luis wheeled his horse about and headed back to the fields.

Hurt by his sharpness, Leonora watched him ride away, her lip trembling. Finally turning to Elena, she snapped, "You cause much trouble for my husband. Stay indoors in the future."

A sharp retort sprang to Elena's lips, but she wisely let it go unsaid. The atmosphere at Carmenilla was tense enough; there was little need to further antagonize Leonora.

As they walked indoors from the stables, Elena asked

her hostess, "Why does Luis hate his brother?"

'I wasn't aware it was that obvious—especially to a stranger."

"But you are aware of their feelings?"

"One could not live on this land and not be aware. Don Gaspar chose Luis as his heir—that's the root of their hatred. Luis was the eldest son. Besides, a gypsy's bastard could never inherit. Cristobal has never forgiven Luis for that. And Luis can't forgive Cristobal for being born. He considers his honor was tarnished when the old don gave him Cristobal as his brother. Luis knows Don Gaspar only acknowledged Cristobal as his son to allow him to fight the bulls, to bring honor to our name—but it makes no difference. You see, only the nobility can take part in the *corrida*. As a gypsy, Cristobal would have been barred—as the younger son of Don Gaspar de los Santos, he can display his skill. Sometimes I think Luis is jealous because he never learned to fight the bulls."

"That's because he spent much of his early life aboard ship."

Leonora's head snapped about, her eyes narrowing at Elena's unexpected knowledge. "Yes, so he did. He never had the chance to learn the art like the sons of other nobles." Leonora stopped, considering Elena quizzically. "Did Cristobal tell you about his mother?"

"Only that she was a gypsy who died giving birth to him."

"They say her spirit haunts this land. When a de los Santos's death is imminent, she appears. The servants swear they saw her and heard her laughing when the old don lay dying. . . . Oh, I didn't intend to frighten you," Leonora added sweetly as she saw Elena pale. Yet her gleeful smile revealed the opposite.

They entered the flower-filled courtyard where the

fountain splashed musically in its marble bowl.

Leonora was highly pleased at having distressed Elena. Though Luis had betrayed little during these past couple of days, she suspected he habored more than a passing fancy for this woman. Fury possessed her at the mere thought he admired another woman. He was hers, her handsome, virile Luis. No one else should have him. She even begrudged this Englishwoman one hour of his attention. Leonora agonized jealously over her husband's past relationships with women, and her instinct told her there was far more than met the eye to this particular "acquaintance." She would be relieved when her uncle and his guest were safely on the road to Madrid. Never again would she invite another woman to stay at Carmenilla. Luis was far too precious to risk losing him!

They took cakes and a refreshing glass of cool wine in the courtyard beneath the shade of the flowering trees. Presently, Leonora suggested that Elena should go to her room to rest and that she would do the same.

By evening black clouds had rolled in from the west. The air became so oppressive, Elena could scarcely breathe. This impending storm merely deepened the crackling tension in the air as she sat under the arched roof surrounding the courtyard and attempted to make polite conversation with her host and hostess. She could feel Luis's gaze on her, his pale eyes glittering in the light of a candle burning inside a glass dome.

The wind increased, sending the branches of the large jacaranda crashing against the shutters. Thunder rolled, and a dazzling sheet of lightning suddenly lit the sky.

"Perhaps this will be a blessed end to this hot weather," Leonora remarked hopefully. She glanced up at the turbulent sky, awaiting the first raindrops.

"No, the storm's not intense enough. Tomorrow will

be another sultry day,'' predicted Don Alvaro.

Luis said nothing. Elena could hear his glass clink as he poured more dark red wine from the decanter. This wine came from grapes grown on their estate, and the resulting heavy wine was named *Sangre de Toro*, blood of the bull.

"Our guest sounds tired,'' Luis remarked at last as Elena stifled a yawn. "Let me call a servant to show you to your chamber, *doña*.''

"Oh, no, the cool breeze feels pleasant,'' she protested feebly. Her head throbbed with the tension of being so close to him and not being able to say what was on her mind. "Storms often clear my head,'' she added lamely.

A sudden downpour erupted, splattering their clothing as the deluge splashed off the veranda's wooden railings.

Leonora squealed, jumping back against the wall. She shook raindrops from her embroidered velvet skirts. "Let us go indoors, Luis, I'm getting wet.''

"Not yet. You may go inside if you wish.''

Leonora hesitated, not anxious to leave her husband alone with this women. Don Alvaro was also on his feet, gallantly offering to escort her indoors. In a quandary, she finally decided it would be wise not to make an issue of the situation lest her jealousy arouse Luis's anger. Her handsome husband might feel compelled to flirt with the Englishwoman to reassert his masculine pride.

"Very well. Don't be long, dearest. I'll wait for you.''

Leonora's sweet smile was for Luis alone. The knife in Elena's heart twisted another turn. His wife's eagerness for his company led Elena to draw but one conclusion—she had not forgotten his expert lovemaking.

For a few minutes after Leonora and Don Alvaro left, they sat in silence. Tears filled Elena's eyes and spilled down her cheeks. It was so beautiful out here in the dark, fragrant night, yet they acted like strangers. The pattering rain had brought alive the scent of flowers and leaves. This evening could have been so romantic; instead it was a torment to endure.

"Elena . . . about this afternoon," Luis began, his voice gruff with emotion.

"There's no need to explain," she dismissed, her tears making speech difficult. "I understand well enough."

"You understand nothing!" His words were ground out in anger. Seizing her wrist, he gripped so hard she thought the bone would shatter.

"Stop it, Luis, you're hurting me."

Obediently he slackened his grasp, but he did not release her. "How much longer can this go on?" he demanded angrily.

"If I have my way it will be over tomorrow," she cried, leaping to her feet. Wrenching free of his grasp, Elena stumbled blindly through the curtained archway into the silent room beyond, grief and pain squeezing her heart.

Luis did not follow. Had she really expected him to? Trying to gather her wits, she heard Don Alvaro's approaching steps and she forced her mouth into an artificial smile.

"Don Alvaro, I've wanted to speak to you all day," she said as he came inside the room. Fortunately he was alone.

"Dare I hope . . ." he began eagerly, but she cut him short.

"It's not about marriage. I want to return to Madrid."

"But we've been here such a short time. We must

stay a week or two at least.''

"There's nothing for me to do here. I long to return to England. Only then will I be happy.''

In the gloomy candlelit room she could only guess at his expression for he had turned from her.

"You forget, you cannot return until your Queen summons you. After we're wed, you'll not dislike Spain as—''

"How many times must I tell you—we're not going to be wed!''

"That, *doña*, remains to be seen. Remember . . . your Queen may command it.'' With that he walked stiffly outside to join Luis, the subject dismissed.

Anger replaced Elena's pain. Would he never take her refusal seriously? A prolonged stay in Spain would give him false hope. That was why she must leave as soon as possible—that and the terrible pain of seeing Luis wed to another!

Determined to find her own way by the dim light of the sconces flaring on the stone walls, Elena marched rapidly to her room. A lone candle burned on the table and the covers had been turned down for the night. But Elena's thoughts were far from sleep.

Taking parchment, quill and ink from her leather trunk, she drew the feeble flame closer and began to write.

"Dearest Majesty: I pine to be back in England. Please, have pity on me, the lowliest of your subjects. Never have I knowingly betrayed you, or given you just cause to doubt my loyalty. I am ever your faithful servant. I beseech you, dearest Majesty, allow me to return to all I hold dear. My heart is breaking in this alien land.''

A large tear fell on the parchment, and Elena fiercely dashed it away. Dear God! Was she to be exiled for the remainder of her days? Was she never again to see her own land? The dreadful finality of the thought was so devastating that it sapped her will. Wearily, she laid her head on her arm while tears dampened her brown velvet sleeve.

Below, in the bougainvilla-scented courtyard pale with waxy jasmine and night-blooming flowers, Luis waited. How she longed to go to him. Perhaps he was alone, for Don Alvaro retired early and Leonora had gone to her chamber some time ago. If she went to him, if she confessed the pain of her love, he would take her in his arms. She ached for his embrace, for his sweet endearments, his kisses. It was likely his heart ached as much as hers.

Clenching her fists, she raised her tear-wet face. ''No!'' she ground out through gritted teeth. She would not beg, not after he had virtually accused her of being a whore. Never again would she give him the opportunity to wound her so severely. The strength of her injured pride would ensure that.

Chapter Fifteen

After a fitful night's sleep, Elena rose at dawn to finish her letter to the Queen.

As Don Alvaro had predicted, the day was hot and oppressive; the least exertion raised a film of sweat.

Deciding it might be cooler outdoors, Elena went to the stables to saddle her horse for an early morning ride about the estate. To her surprise, none of the sleepy grooms attempted to stop her as she cantered over the parched grassland.

Even morning at Carmenilla was hot. Tendrils of wet hair were soon plastered against her brow, and Elena grew uncomfortably aware of riverlets of sweat trickling between her breasts and down her back. It was still hot as mid-summer—did the seasons never change in this land? In England, autumn would have tinged the trees russet and gold, bringing heavy morning mists to blanket the woods. The poignant reminder produced a great surge of homesickness swiftly followed by the choking pressure of unshed tears. Angrily, Elena steeled herself against weeping. Of late she had become little more than a whimpering fool. Pray God, Mary would recall her soon while she still possessed a few of her wits.

Teresa had assured her that her letter to the Queen

would travel aboard one of Don Luis's ships bound for
England. When Elena discovered Luis had ships sailing
to England, she began to formulate a wild plan of
escape. Surely he would take pity on her and allow her
passage aboard one of his vessels. But that hope soon
died when she remembered Don Alvaro had been
charged with her safekeeping. Until Mary summmoned
her home, she was not welcome in England. The Queen
might have no intention of recalling her—she had much
favored a match with Don Alvaro. It was possible that
Elena's consent to marry the Spanish don would be
Mary's requisite for forgiveness.

The realization closed around her like a trap.

Defiantly, Elena galloped across the scrubby land as
if by some miracle this mad ride would rid her of hurt.
She longed to go home, it was true, but her yearning
for England only left her more vulnerable to experience
the full force of heartbreak. Try as she might to convince
herself her pain sprang from homesickness, seeing Luis
again and knowing he was not hers was the cause of
much of her grief. The terrible finality of seeing him
with his wife gave her far more anguish than the
Queen's displeasure. In England she could forget him,
she told herself fiercely. There she would not be
reminded of Spain at every turn. Now that the Queen's
Spanish husband was back in his homeland, most of
his retinue sailing with him, the court would have
become refreshingly English again.

Slowing her pace to a canter, Elena reconsidered
those wild ideas of escape still seething in her brain.
So isolated was Lichborne from the mainstream of
English life, little that happened there ever reached
Whitehall. Why could she not live quietly on her manor,
leaving Mary none the wiser? But sense told her she
must eventually be discovered. The Queen would punish

her for disobedience, and a Tudor's wrath could be
terrible to endure. The fact was, she was no longer plain
Elena Locke. As lady-in-waiting to the Queen, her every
move was contingent on her royal mistress's good
graces.

Besides, after some consideration Elena decided
Lichborne was not such a safe haven after all. Will was
not beyond forcibly carrying her off to wed Lord
Morton. There would be little to choose between
imprisonment in bitter Northumberland or in the Spanish
city of Madrid.

Elena urged her horse over the higher ground, trying
to reconcile herself to the unpleasant truth. Whether
she chose to admit it or not, she was already a captive.
And though her jailor was congenial, Don Alvaro
Escalante would be reluctant to set her free. With
Mary's support, he already considered her his.

The unpleasant feeling of being trapped continued as
Elena rode beside a stream tumbling over boulders in
its mad race to the valley. She was close to the small
waterfall Cristobal had shown her yesterday. Uneasily
she wondered if any bulls lurked in the dense undergrowth. When nothing more dangerous than twittering
birds emerged, Elena took heart and, casting caution
aside, clattered recklessly beneath the shady trees. The
resulting breeze stirred wet tendrils of hair against her
face and moved deliciously through her heavy velvet
habit, cooling her damp skin.

As the splashing water grew louder, a wonderful idea
occurred to her. Why had she not thought about it earlier
and come prepared with soap and towel? She would
bathe in the crystal pool. She had not been provided
with a bath since her arrival at Carmenilla, and in this
hot climate that was a luxury long overdue.

Making sure no one was about, for Cristobal had said

he sometimes swam here, Elena dismounted and tethered her horse to a branch overhanging the stream. Glancing about one final time to satisfy herself she would not be disturbed, she eagerly peeled off her sticky garments. In this heat her heavy velvet habit was suffocating, and her lawn petticoats clung damply to her legs. How light she felt, how free and unhampered by all those yards of velvet and lace-trimmed lawn.

Laughing like a child, Elena danced a few steps, then she flapped her arms, rejoicing in the blissful feeling of weightlessness.

Speading her clothes on a tree branch to dry, she stepped to the brink of the pool where the silver cascading water played a ceaseless melody. Gingerly dipping her foot into the water, she grew bolder, shivering as the refreshing chill inched up her shapely legs. Elena suddenly plunged to her hips in shockingly cold water, her resulting shriek bringing her horse's head up in surprise. How much farther dare she go? If only she could swim, she would plunge into the heart of the whirling foam.

Underfoot lay a flat rock bed, which on inspection proved to be a flight of steps hewn in the rock. This made a perfect place to sit, allowing her to trail her legs safely in the swirling water. Elena pulled the bone pins from her thick curling hair, letting it hang loose about her face. Leaning back against the rocks, she allowed the water's spray to play on her hair until it draped about her shoulders like a gleaming black cloak studded with diamonds.

The hot sun beat down on her upturned face, tempering the water's chill. The constant stream gently caressed her lower body, pushing her back and forth. It was so peaceful here, even the running water became soothing. Lulled by the ceaseless movement of water and warmed by sunshine, Elena's eyes grew heavy, gradually closing as she gave herself up to this novel, sensual experience. She emptied her mind of painful thoughts and floated pleasantly in space.

For how long she lay there, Elena did not know. Reluctantly opening her eyes, she realized she had dozed. Last night's oppressive heat and her own tormenting thoughts had robbed her of sleep. And though the nap had been refreshing and the sun warm, Elena felt chilled. She pulled all but her feet out of the water, basking happily in the sunshine. She wrung out her heavy hair, allowing the water to stream in crystal rivulets over her full breasts. The sun's rays soon evaporated the gleaming drops of water beading her silk-smooth skin and made her feel drowsy all over again.

Elena was not sure why she glanced toward the trees. Perhaps it was to reassure herself her horse was still tethered there. From under half-closed lids she saw a sleek brown hide. Squirming pleasurably on her warm, rocky bed, she sought a different position. Basking nude in the sun made her feel decadent and sinful, like some pagan princess. Fortunately, none but her horse bore witness to her shamelessness. Again she glanced at the trees. Something was wrong! A black patch blocked her view of waving willow fronds.

Elena jerked upright. Her eyes were not playing tricks on her. There were two horses tethered to the tree! A muscular black stallion nuzzled her gelding in friendship.

Someone was watching her! Gasping in shock, she submerged herself completely, belatedly trying to hide her nakedness. The cold water made her shudder. Eyes slitted against the sun's glare, Elena scanned the area but could not see no one. Turning about, she examined the rock face, glimpsing a man who quickly dodged behind a boulder.

In great indignation, and forgetting to use Spanish, she yelled, "You up there, how dare you spy on me?"

Naturally there was no answer. Elena could feel her cheeks growing hot as she wondered how long he had been watching. Uneasily she wondered what to do. She had to come out of the water to reach her clothes. If the man intended to ravish her, the water would provide little protection.

"You can't hide up there, you coward, I know you're still spying on me," she finally shouted in anger. It had to be Cristobal. He was the one who showed her this spot, and now it was most likely he who skulked in the rocks. Though this was something she would never confide to Luis, she hoped that Cristobal would believe her.

"I warn you—if you don't go away, I'll tell Don Luis."

"You'll tell Don Luis what, *doña*?"

An unexpectedly familiar voice sounded at her elbow. Her blood froze as Elena turned to see not Cristobal, but Luis crouching beside the water.

"You!"

"Yes, it's me—though I've had warmer welcomes. Come out, I must talk to you."

His voice sounded strangled, but perhaps it was only because he was trying to make himself heard above the splashing water.

"No," she cried, shaking her head. "Go away."

He smiled then, but his expression was decidedly unpleasant.

"I've witnessed your nakedness for over an hour— and with unforeseen wonder I must admit, considering all we've shared. Here are your clothes. To get them you have to come out of the water."

''Not while you're here!''

To her dismay he plucked her drying garments from the tree branch. Holding out her blue buskins and velvet habit, Luis grinned triumphantly over her predicament.

''Leave them alone! I'm not coming out till you're gone.''

''Stop playing the fool, Elena. Come out.''

''No!''

He stood there looking at her, anger darkening his face. Elena sank as low as she dared in the water, aware he could still see her white shoulders. Her hair streamed like a banner behind her, floating on the water. There was something frightening about Luis's expression, yet at the same time it was highly exciting. As she looked at him, she was aware of blood coursing madly through her veins in delicious expectation.

''For the last time—are you coming out?''

''Not until you leave.''

''Then I'll have to join you.''

Elena shrieked in alarm as he flung down her clothes and began to pull open his shirt. ''Don't you dare! Stay where you are!''

''This is my land, and here I do as I please.''

She stared at him in shock, aware he had every intention of carrying out his threat. His shirt hung unfastened, and he quickly peeled off both leather jerkin and shirt. Bare to the waist, a challenging half smile on his face, he was devastatingly attractive. The arousing sight of his broad square shoulders, of his deep chest matted with curling dark gold hair brought her memories vibrantly to life, making he shiver.

''No!'' Elena cried again, realizing her protests were useless.

Luis leaned against a tree while he tugged off his tall leather boots. Tossing them aside, he began to unfasten his hose. Absurdly, Elena closed her eyes.

"Isn't your modesty somewhat belated, Mistress Locke?" Luis remarked sarcastically as he noted her action. "You've seen me stripped before."

Pink suffused Elena's cheeks and blood pounded hotly through her veins. She did not deign to answer him. What would happen next was something she dared not contemplate. Her mind went numb. She should do something, yet she could think of nothing to combat Luis's fierce determination to have his way.

"You can safely open your eyes now—your modesty won't be affronted."

His sneer roused her to anger. "How dare you mock me!" she spat, stepping backwards as he moved toward her through the water. She was angry, hurt, furious with him—and what's more, she had very badly wanted to see him naked! This honest admission shocked her into silence.

"How much longer are we to play these foolish games, Elena?"

"Don't come any closer," she warned, jumping away from him as he reached out a muscled arm to grab her. To her horror, there was nothing underfoot. Panic-stricken, she trod water, eyes wide with shock, then, screaming and flailing her arms, she went under.

Luis grasped her firmly and pulled her head out of the water, holding her against him as he swam with her to the safety of the rocky steps. The heat of his body was comforting, his supporting strength her salvation. Elena's eyes filled with tears of fright and gratitude.

"That's enough foolishness," Luis growled, stopping on the far side of the rock wall away from the splashing water. Here it was quieter, and he could make himself heard without shouting. "Enough, Elena—God knows, these past days have been purgatory."

Everything that happened next was like a dream. Elena consciously fought against him, yet her heart, her soul reached out to his. When she shouted at him, insisting the release her, Luis only pulled her closer, fitting her supple body against his. All the marvelous angles and curves of their bodies matched so lovingly— she thrilled to his touch. Seizing handfuls of her wet hair, Luis drew her face to his and kissed her deeply. The touch of his lips set her on fire. Dear Jesus, how long she had ached for that kiss, dreamed of it, pined for it. Much against her will, Elena kissed him back.

Gently pulling back her head by her sodden hair, Luis buried his face in the soft white curve of her neck, his lips burning like fire against her chill wet skin. Slowly he moved upward, and again he claimed her lips. Elena cried out, sobbing with need and rousing anger.

"No, Luis, stop! I won't be yours whilst you're still married to her," she managed to say, wrenching her mouth from his though he was temptation beyond endurance.

"You will be mine, Elena, wed or not. I'm only human, woman! For this past hour I've watched you until I was driven nearly insane. It was a battle to allow you to stay untouched—a battle I fought valiantly. But see how well my blood obeys the call of your flesh."

Seizing her hand, he crammed her fingers about the throbbing brand clamoring eagerly against her thigh. She sobbed, desperately trying to extricate her hand, fighting an overwhelming surge of desire.

"Watching you bask in the water like some beautiful water sprite, remembering how wonderful it is to make love to you and knowing it's denied to me—*Jesu*, I could scarce endure the sight of you," he murmured ardently, fondling her chill flesh until she shuddered. Moving lower, Luis took her nipple in his mouth, drawing on it until it rose hard and quivering to meet him. "Oh, Elena, I want you so! Dear God, haven't I loved you better than any man alive? You torment me with your beauty, then think to order me away like a pet dog."

"We mustn't make love again," she cried, trying to push him away, yet only succeeding in drawing him closer. With great effort she ignored the thrusting insistence of his manhood, though her body ached for him.

Pulling away slightly, needing the distance in order to think, he frowned down at her. She was so lovely sparkling with crystal drops, her full white breasts upthrust like some ancient fertility goddess. As he watched her from above, he had to exercise his utmost willpower not to seize her and bend her to his will. He knew he still hovered dangerously on the brink of taking her, even without her consent. Never before had he been in such a high state of arousal and failed to act on that instinct. Steeling himself against her possible answer, Luis held her rigid, his hands biting into her upper arms.

"Answer one question, Elena Locke."

Mutely she nodded, not trusting herself with words. Hot tears blurred her vision, thankfully eclipsing the arousing sight of his hard, broad shoulders and strong sun-bronzed arms, of that burning brand betraying his great arousal. This was no stranger to repel; this was Luis, the man she loved, the only man she had ever really wanted.

"What is the question?" she whispered, gulping down her choking emotion.

"Do you still love me?"

When she hesitated, he shook her, irritation clouding his face. "Now tell me the truth, damn you. There've been enough lies between us—"

"I've never lied to you. I won't start now," Elena defended stiffly, wishing herself a thousand miles away from his virile, intoxicating presence.

"Then tell me true—do you love me still?"

"Yes."

"*Querida*, I was so afraid the answer would be no— oh, Elena." Now he reached for her, and still she tried to resist, but her defense was weak and ill-timed.

Ignoring her turned head and her set mouth, Luis held her against him, making her aware of that insistent warmth against her thighs, making her acknowledge the rush of passion consuming her chill lips as he pulled them from that set line and warmed them to fullness again.

Elena gasped as he slid his hands over the prominence of her full breasts, cupping the flesh, inflaming her passion until she found it difficult to stand.

"I've never stopped loving you. Even when you called me whore."

"I didn't mean that—God knows it was a cruel thing to say, dishonorable to taunt you with something that brought us such delight. Oh, sweetheart, let there be no more harsh words between us. Only words of love. And I do love you. I love you, love you, love you . . ."

His voice died away as he buried his mouth in her neck, his hot lips tracing a passage along her cheek, her brow and down her nose. Trembling, Elena seized his shoulders, finally giving in to that clamoring emotion that recognized neither matrimony nor pride, that knew only that the man in her arms was the most arousing man alive. She no longer had any power to resist him. With a sigh of surrender, Elena molded herself against him, letting him take her weight in his strong arms.

Luis placed her on the rock above him so that she stood higher than he, and he slowly kissed her breasts until she trembled. She sank her fingers into his springy gold hair, keeping him there for her pleasure. She rained kisses on the top of his head, finally pulling up his face, desperate to taste his kiss.

"Oh, Elena—all the things I intended to say can wait."

Luis seized her so swiftly, Elena gulped in surprise. Turning, he stepped out of the water and she slipped to her feet, finding the mossy grass soft as velvet beneath her bare feet.

He gazed in adoration at her beautiful alabaster body gleaming in the sunlight, the sheen of water droplets sparkling like strings of crystal girding her hips and breasts. Elena's hair fell in dark waves over her smooth back and shoulders, sending gleaming rivulets of water slithering seductively between her full breasts. Luis shuddered all the way from his head to the depth of his toes. Dear God, how much he loved and wanted her, the clamoring emotion so strong, he could scarce draw breath.

Elena did not speak, afraid to break the wonder of this moment. It was as if they moved together in a dream, limbs heavy with passion, hearts heavy with pain for all the things left unsaid between them.

"*Querida*," Luis murmured at last, shattering the silence, "no one else ever made me feel this way. My blood throbs for you alone—oh, come, say you'll be mine."

He held out his arms to her and, though it was only seconds, it seemed hours before she reached that haven. Suddenly afraid to breach the invisible wall between them, Elena trembled as she recalled another woman's adoring gaze.

"Leonora," she croaked aloud, "do you tell her also that you love her?"

His gaze never wavered from hers, that luminescent

quality she had always found so fascinating softening his blue eyes until she felt as if she were drowning in them.

"Not for one minute of one day have I ever loved Leonora."

And Elena knew he spoke the truth. A sob escaped her lips as that final invisible barrier was shattered. She nestled against him. He slid his strong arms around her and she sobbed for the pain of their thwarted love. Heightening desire licked through her veins, speeding her blood as she felt the eagerness of his arousal against her belly. They stood before each other with no place to hide their nakedness of either body or heart.

"Oh, darling, I believe you," she whispered against his neck, trying to draw him closer, longing to become one in sinew, muscle and blood.

"You're cold. Come into the sunshine," he urged remorsefully, for he had forgotten they both were wet.

"My tremors aren't from cold," she revealed huskily as they lay on her skirts, basking in a patch of sunlight.

"Nor mine. Oh, Elena, when I saw you unclothed, your lovely breasts, your curving hips," he murmured, stroking her until she shuddered with delight at the touch of his warm hands on her chill flesh. "I was beside myself with longing. Yet, after our differences, I wasn't sure you still welcomed me. I watched you, knowing I should leave, yet unable to go. I can honestly say I've never wanted any woman as much as I wanted you."

Luis glanced away. Touched by his honesty, Elena smiled, tracing her slim fingers along his hard jaw. Slowly she turned his face to hers.

"If you'd told me this morning this would have happened, I'd have called you liar. Yet, at this moment there's nothing I want more than to lie in your arms," she said shyly, realizing so much time had passed, she had to reacquaint herself with her lover before she would feel wholly at ease with such confidences.

Smiling, Luis pulled Elena against him, nestling her softly in his arms, fighting his raging desire. It was too soon and, though he knew she was already aroused, they had been apart too long to take her hastily.

"There's something else I must confess to you," he admitted, glancing away from the penetrating gaze of her dark-lashed, tawny eyes. He could see himself mirrored there, and his conscience pricked. "Had you told me nay, I still think I'd have taken you."

She gasped, partly from shock, partly from arousal.

"You meant to rape me?" she whispered against his ear.

"That's not my usual way—but yes, today I think I could have. I've endured such torment since we've been apart. Then seeing you like this—I couldn't help myself. Say you forgive me. I've never wanted to hurt you before."

"Nor did you then. You merely wanted to take me."

"I still want to take you—but not like that."

"Then how shall it be, my darling?"

A tremor shot through him at her throaty invitation. He gazed down at her in wonder, tracing his trembling hand across her high cheekbones, lifting strands of ebony hair from her brow. Luis smiled tenderly at the woman in his arms. All the pain, the tormenting thought that she no longer welcomed him were left behind in that swirling crystal stream. Elena still belonged to him. And he thanked God for the wondrous gift.

"*Mi vida, mi alma*," he breathed huskily, his hands whisper soft on her breasts, which seemed to swell beneath his touch. "I ask no more of life than this."

"Oh, Luis, my heart's ached for you—only I thought . . . that you took much pleasure in Leonora."

His caresses slowed. "I won't lie and say I don't take her—after all she is my wife. No, Elena, please, hear me out," he said when she turned away. Gently he stroked her face, aware that tears glistened in her eyes. "I don't say this to be cruel, just to let you know the way it has to be. Leonora must bear my heir. And, I admit on occasion out of faceless, soulless need I've taken her as a man takes a whore, with no thought of a child . . . sweetheart, don't," he pleaded remorsefully as tears trickled down her cheeks. His heart wrenched for having caused her pain.

"Please, Luis, don't tell me any more," she begged at last, feeling the knife twist yet again in her heart. "I know that's how it has to be. Let it be a silent truth between us."

He nodded, tenderly stroking her cheek, his thumb grazing her high cheekbone as he vowed tenderly, "I swear I'll never love another, nor give myself to another out of love." Pressing a kiss into the palm of her hand, he added, "I swear also to stay faithful to you in my heart until the day I die."

Her eyes shone with tears of deepest emotion as he pledged his undying love. Elena clung to Luis, pressing against him, marvelling at the smoothness of his skin and the throbbing heat of his flesh. How hard and protective was his embrace as his arms went around her back, holding her safe and secure as if he would never let her go.

"I love you, Luis, I've always loved you. No less, no more than at this moment."

Her sincere words moved him deeply. He bowed his head, burying his face in the soft perfume of her neck. Absurdly, he felt moisture gathering in his own eyes, and he swallowed the growing lump in his throat. So deep was his emotion for the woman in his arms, he marveled at the tenderness that disarmed him. With Elena he was vulnerable, all pretense and masculine bravado stripped away. He came to her with soul bared, desperately seeking her love, aching for her body. And, wonder of wonders, she accepted him wholeheartedly as if nothing had ever come between them.

Luis smiled tenderly at her, thinking at this moment she must be the most beautiful creature on earth. ''For ever and ever,'' he whispered, his face close to hers, his hot breath fanning her brow and making her shudder.

''Please, Luis, make love to me,'' she whispered at last, unable to endure another minute without taking him into her body. For what seemed like years, she had awaited this time of trust and loving abandon, of coming together in naked beauty, totally without shame, hearts as well as bodies bound in love.

''Do you think I was waiting to hear you beg?'' he asked, amusement glinting in his eyes.

Elena chose not to reply. With a low and throaty laugh, she laced her hands behind his head, bringing his face down to hers. Luis whispered endearments in impassioned Spanish she could not translate. As his mood grew ever more passionate, his hands, his mouth, his muscular body translated those unknown words into tongues of fire. Elena abandoned herself to the delectable fires he aroused. If she should die this moment, she would be the most contented woman alive, she mused. This was her last conscious thought as his hip bones ground against hers in passionate caress.

Luis moved his hot mouth down her neck and over her breasts, his tongue drawing a vibrant response from her body. He caressed her firm buttocks, sending a burst of flame through her body as he gently slid his fingers inside that secret cleft to explore the moist urgency of her passion. Straining upward in mute appeal, Elena's body craved his. When Luis placed the swollen proof of his arousal gently against her throbbing mound, she cried out with desire. How smooth, how full he was, promising such delight, she wondered if she could endure it.

Those passionate words were a prelude to his entrance into the secret chamber of her body. Fiery, insistent, he explored the innermost reaches of her being. When Elena would have seized Luis's firm, sloping buttocks to drive him deep inside her, he forced her to a more leisurely pace, determined to extract the ultimate pleasure from her desire. He moved slowly back and forth, drawing that blessed probing heat across her every nerve until Elena sobbed in ecstasy.

Finally, when Luis reached the point where he could no longer maintain that delicate balance between arousal and assuasion, he grasped her silky buttocks, raising her high to allow himself complete penetration. Like a great burst of fire, he thrust deep inside her, bringing the whirling magic giddily within reach. For Elena there was no more holding back, only total surrender.

She cried out as she was consumed by fire. The driving, blazing force of his body sent her to the highest pinnacle. She soared through velvet blackness, through dark and light, through pain and pleasure until finally she was drifting back to earth, drained and whimpering softly with fulfillment.

For a long time they lay joined in each other's arms. Gradually, like sleepwalkers they became aware of their surroundings and of the vulnerability of their position. Luis raised himself on his elbows to survey the area. Thank God, they did not appear to have been discovered.

Smiling in sheerest pleasure, Elena reached for him

and drew him back to her. They kissed, their lips softly
vulnerable with spent passion.

"Though I'd like to stay with you all day, I must leave
soon," Luis finally said with great reluctance. "Come,
sweetheart, let us get dressed."

He had given her a full half hour of recovery, yet
so deeply shattering had been their lovemaking that
Elena stumbled on weak legs when she tried to stand.
Laughing, Luis supported her against his body before
ruefully setting her aside when his flesh responded
magnificently to her nearness.

"No, we must stop—I could make love to you all
day."

"I wish you could."

"So do I."

She heard the undisguised regret in his voice, his sigh
as he moved from her. Still shaking weakly, Elena
leaned against a nearby tree for support, watching Luis
as he gathered their clothes. How perfectly his body
tapered from broad shoulders to taut, narrow hips; his
high buttocks, smooth and hard, his back firmly
muscled. She shuddered, longing to caress him. When
he turned, and Elena saw his barely diminished passion
for her, she had to bite her lip to keep from crying out
in longing. She must not keep him here any longer.
Already the others might have grown suspicious about
his absence. Luis must always guard against discovery,
for he was married to another.

A chill went through her veins as she acknowledged
Luis was a Spanish Catholic to whom marriage meant
a lifetime commitment. Until Leonora was in the grave,
he would never be free to offer the woman he loved
respectability. Hypocrite that she was, while wildly
loving and desiring this man, with virtually the same
breath she had reviled him for marrying another.

"What deep thoughts make you frown?" he asked softly, kissing her damp brow. "Come, help me dress."

Swallowing the pain of her swift return to reality, Elena smiled up at her lover. His face was shadowed, his eyes dark as he studied her intently. She wondered if he guessed her thoughts.

"I'll take a distinct pleasure in that task, though perhaps not as much pleasure as I would in undressing you."

He grinned, his hand gentle on her hair. "Ah, *querida*, that you shall do also. We must be very, very clever from now on. You'll never know how much I bless this day."

His mouth grazed her brow as he bent to put on his clothes. With shaking hands, Elena helped him tie his points and fasten his shirt, highly aware of the hard, throbbing body beneath the fabric. The steady beat of his heart shuddered his frame beneath her forearms, making her pulses race as she fumbled blindly with the fastenings, tears of longing clouding her vision.

"What . . . tears?"

"Of joy. And of pain, for the need to lose you again after only just finding you."

"You'll never lose me," he assured her, smiling down at her lovely face. "I promise we shall meet whenever and wherever we can."

In turn Luis helped her dress, finding it difficult to keep his arousal in check as he touched the soft curves of her delectable body. Fighting against the hot renewal of passion, he knew there was no more time to make love to his beautiful Elena. When she was ready, he helped her wind her thick damp hair in a knot at the nape of her neck. Her bone hair pins had been lost in the frothing water.

"You leave first," he suggested when they prepared

to mount. "I'm supposed to be meeting with a neighboring landowner who by now has probably drunk much of my finest wine. Ride back to the fortress—I'll be at the winery. Till this evening, Elena, *luz de mi vida.*"

Their lips met, the sweet poignancy of their forbidden love contained in that kiss. Eyes bright with tears as she reviewed the hopelessness of their situation, Elena rode away.

Light of my life, he had called her. Turning in the saddle, she gazed at him, and Luis waved to her in farewell. Sunlight burnished his springy hair, making it gleam like a halo of gold about his finely shaped head. The lump in her throat threatened to choke her as she returned his wave. No other man had ever moved her like he. As long as she lived, she would want no other. Luis was her world.

Chapter Sixteen

For all Luis's reassuring promises, during the remainder of the week they were able to share little more than stolen kisses. Though now he needed no longer absent himself from the fortress to avoid Elena, a steady stream of guests and business associates took up much of his time.

Carmenilla's most recent guest was the bearded captain of one of Luis's galleons. Wistfully, Elena wondered if this man commanded the vessel bound for England. An absurd idea of hiding aboard ship flashed through her mind, followed swiftly by the shocking realization she could never return to England. If she left Spain, she left Luis! Ironically, the two things she desired most in life could not be had together; to keep one she must relinquish the other.

The long, noisy evening finally drew to a close, the guests departing to their chambers after much talking and feasting.

It seemed to Elena that Luis's wife was watching her closely during the meal. Yet how could Leonora know what had taken place at the waterfall? Likely this heightened interest existed only in her own guilty conscience.

Don Alvaro had been unwell these past couple of days. Too much rich food, he had explained, too much wine; yet his sallow skin, shaking hands and dull eyes suggested an ailment of more severity than a billious attack. Tonight, however, he had rallied and, after taking a light meal, had entertained their guests with colorful stories of court life.

"Soon you shall have your wish, Doña Elena," he said as they sat alone in the courtyard after the guests had departed. It was a warm, scented night, a thousand stars pricking the black velvet sky overhead.

"Wish," Elena mumbled after a long silence, realizing the elderly don had been speaking to her. As usual she was engrossed in thoughts of Luis, which made her hands tremble and her limbs ache with longing.

"Yes. Did you not say you were anxious to return to Madrid? We're bound there on the morrow."

"No! Oh, no—leaving so soon!"

Don Alvaro gaped at her in amazement. Afraid she had betrayed herself, Elena mumbled apologetically. "I'm only thinking of you. Don't endanger your health by giving way to my silly whims. Rest, Don Alvaro. Next week, or later, will be soon enough to travel."

The elderly don smiled and, taking her hand, pressed it against his dry lips. "What sweetness. Nay, Doña Elena, my heart beats merely to satisfy your whims. I'm not ill—a little liverish, perhaps, nothing more. I'm as vigorous as a man half my age. Perchance my youth would be fully restored if only you'd agree to marry me."

Elena tried to draw back her hand as he pressed his lips ardently against her palm. The timely sound of Leonora's voice from across the courtyard blessedly spared her from further impassioned declarations.

"That man's so tiresome! All he does is recount his conquests and boast about his wealth," complained Leonora, stepping into the courtyard.

Elena's heart lurched, before beginning a frenzied beat as she saw Luis's white shirtsleeve gleaming in the darkness behind Leonora.

"He's young. Give him time," Luis muttered tersely as he crossed the courtyard.

A decanter of wine and several glasses stood on a tray beside the stone bench. Elena watched as Luis filled a goblet and raised it to his lips. Feeling her gaze upon him, he turned, their eyes meeting above the gold rim of his goblet. The smoldering look that passed between them, fraught with love and denied passion, made Elena gasp. Quickly she glanced at the others, convinced they must have sensed that unspoken communication. To her relief, neither Leonora nor her uncle seemed to be aware of the exchange. The gloomy courtyard, pierced only by the light of two candles in fretwork holders, had kept their secret.

Leonora leaned over to pat her uncle's hand. "So you're determined to leave us. Can't I dissuade you, uncle? I'll never forgive myself if you're taken ill on the road."

Luis's head snapped up. "Leave?"

"You were so busy, there wasn't time to tell you. Don Alvaro wishes to return to Madrid." Leonora flashed Elena a spiteful glance. "It seems his English guest finds life here somewhat boring after the court."

Elena swallowed uneasily, aware of the sudden change in Luis's demeanor. Don't be angry, she pleaded silently. Surely he understood those words had been spoken before they made love. She did not want to leave now, yet how could such a rapid change of heart be explained without exposing their relationship?

"I know what a determined man you are, but this once won't you change your mind?"

"No, niece, my mind's made up. Rest assured, Leonora, I'll return in plenty of time for branding in December."

Luis's breath rasped audibly at the don's remark.

Leonora glanced in surprise at her husband and asked, "Luis, is something wrong?"

"No—I'm surprised, that's all. You're most welcome to return for the branding, Don Alvaro. Bring your guest with you. She'll find it an interesting experience."

"Rest assured, Luis, unless her Queen recalls her, dear Doña Elena will be my guest in the new year— longer if I have my way."

The others finally went indoors, leaving Elena alone in the perfumed darkness. She waited, praying Luis would come back to allow her to explain.

On this warm night the atmosphere inside the fortress was close; the spicy aroma of their evening meal lingered in the corridors. The terrible realization that Elena would leave tomorrow made Luis unbearably tense as he strode up the broad stair. Outside his chamber door he became aware of Leonora clinging possessively to his arm, her sometimes haughty features soft with invitation.

"Come, spend the night with me," she urged, inclining her head toward her own chamber at the end of the corridor.

Luis allowed her to draw him away from the closed door. He needed to talk to Leonora, yet what could he say? That he was in love with another woman? Or could he perhaps demand that their English guest stay? The old don could return to Madrid—it was only imperative that *Elena* stay. The sheer impossibility of making any of those statements brought a bitter smile to his mouth.

Leonora stood expectantly beside her white-curtained bed, slowly unlacing her gown. Tonight she had dispensed with her maid's services, which meant only one thing. With the torment of his love for Elena uppermost in his mind, Luis doubted he could be aroused sufficiently for her purpose.

"Not tonight." He dismissed her gruffly as Leonora pulled him toward her. Luis shook his head, ignoring the flash of anger that crossed her face. Leonora was arrogantly aware of her own beauty. The rippling cloak of her thick, honey-colored hair fell past her knees now that she had discarded her black headdress. She thrust forward her pink-tipped breasts and swayed her curved hips in an effort to arouse him. His wife was the perfect embodiment of Spanish womanhood—and she left him cold.

"Leonora, don't you understand? You're wasting your time. Some other night."

"Some other night! *This* is the night!" she cried, eyes flashing at his stubborn resistance. Sliding her hand over his black velvet doublet, across the broad sweep of his shoulders, down the long point at the waist, she sought that heated swelling. Her snort of anger revealed her annoyance at finding him soft.

"I told you—this has been a trying day," Luis apologized, "I'll be no use to you tonight."

"Yes—I'll arouse you," she cried, the light of challenge gleaming in her eyes.

Scowling, Luis moved away from her. "Would that I could arouse you," he retorted gruffly. He deliberately sought to provoke her anger, for tonight he had no stomach for their abortive lovemaking.

"You do arouse me—at first."

"Then what makes you turn cold as a nun toward

me?''

"Stop demanding answers, Luis—I've told you, I don't know!" Leonora covered her face and turned away. "You're my husband and I love you. Many have not such a good foundation for marriage. I long for a babe—maybe I'm a woman who has no need of passion from a man."

Leonora still did not look at him, her face flushing as she considered her guilty secret. The truth was that Luis aroused her fiercely. Her fantasies were filled with erotic visions of her handsome husband. Yet she did not warm to actual lovemaking. Though he often excited her, when his body swelled majestically, she chilled and went rigid. There seemed too much similarity to a seed bull about him, and the thought of mating with one of them filled her with terror. Afterwards, he stormed angrily from her room, leaving her free to indulge herself in that shuddering secret pleasure that afforded such sweet release. At those times, she revelled in that glorious sensation that was hers alone. The thought that her handsome husband wanted to give her that same pleasure never crossed her mind. Luis always made her sore. But with God's help the hot seed he shot inside her belly would produce the child she longed for. Naive though she had been at the onset of her marriage, even Leonora knew without this spilling of seed there would be no child.

After a long silence Luis demanded angrily, "Is this to be the pattern of our days?" He wondered why Leonora had not dissolved in a gale of tears and fled to the safety of her curtained bed. That childish reaction usually irritated him—tonight he prayed for it.

"I always allow you your satisfaction," she retorted hotly. "What more do you want?"

"Leonora, you say you dreamed of taking me for

your husband from the first time you saw me, that you
begged your father to let us marry—''

"That's true. I did."

"Then why are you so cold to me?"

"You ask too much I—I can't do *that*, Luis. I never
knew such things would be expected of me."

"How did you think to get a babe?"

"I did not think about it. I thought only how
handsome you were, how you made my heart race . . .
the prince of my dreams."

Leonora turned away, clenching her trembling hands,
loath to reveal she had thought babes came from kissing.
When she learned Luis wanted to put that part of his
body inside her, that he wanted to probe and split her
apart, she felt nauseated. Yet she drew a perverse
pleasure from looking at the dreaded force that
threatened to tear her asunder. She preferred looking
at him when he did not know she watched. Then he
truly became the prince of her dreams instead of turning
into something from a nightmare when his thwarted
desire made him rough. By dwelling on memories of
Luis unclothed, by reliving the heat of his kisses, the
sensation created by his fondling hands, she could bring
about that hot shuddering pleasure. Leonora had kept
this sinful secret since she was a girl at the convent of
Nuestra Señora de Carmenilla. Now Luis added so
much fuel to her erotic fantasies that her formerly mild
pleasure had become an explosion.

Composing her features, Leonora finally turned back
to Luis. "I demand you give me a babe. As your wife
it's my right."

He ignored her. His hand on the door latch, he merely
said, "Good night, Leonora."

"No," she cried, her legs going rigid. "You're not
going to leave me alone. If that English wretch wanted

you to give her a babe, likely you'd jump at the chance.''

Her words hit him like a cold splash of water. Luis spun on his heel, his voice brittle as ice. "What did you say?"

"You heard. Don't ask me to repeat it."

Defiantly, she stood her ground, glaring at him, her hands trembling in the folds of her half-open gown. When Luis's brows drew together, when his blue eyes went pale as the winter sky and his sensual mouth turned hard, she grew deathly afraid of him—not merely because she feared a physical attack, but because she knew she drove him away with her spite. Oh, Luis, don't leave me, she wanted to cry. He was so beautiful, so perfect . . .

"Never say that to me again."

"It's true, isn't it?"

"What if it is?"

"Ah, so you admit it!"

"I admit nothing."

His hand turned on the latch. She looked at his slender fingers through the veil of tears that clouded her eyes, wanting his caressing hands on her body. "You're my husband in the sight of God," she shrieked hysterically. "Until death parts us—don't forget that, Luis."

"It's something I'm aware of every minute of every day," he snarled, opening the door and striding outside.

Leonora stood, her hands clenched, fighting tears. Damn that English bitch! Damn her for coming here, for casting her yellow cat's eyes at Luis. He's mine, Leonora thought; he has always been mine. Why couldn't he stay in her safe fantasy world, there only for her pleasure, biddable, obliging? If she had not desperately needed a babe, there had been times when she was tempted to tell him to go satisfy his terrible

lust on some gypsy *puta* as his father had done before
him. Thank the Holy Mother she had never said such
things, for then even the pleasurable part of his attention
would be lost to her.

Angrily, Leonora kicked the door closed, listening
to his boots thumping as he went downstairs. Now he
was gone and she would spend tonight alone. Why had
she the knack of making him so angry? She did not mean
to drive him away. If she dared tell him about her secret
pleasure, if she dared ask him to relive her erotic
fantasies, would he? They could kiss and caress until
that trembling delight possessed her. . . . Never! She
could not confess her terrible sin to another living soul,
not even her own husband.

Guilt-ridden, Leonora spun about, looking beseechingly at the large crucifix on her chamber wall. Surely
she would burn in hell for her wickedness. Try as she
might, she had been unable to give up that childhood
vice. Now, by having handsome Luis as her husband,
her fate was sealed. Recalling his kisses, his hot hands
on her sensitive breasts, made her sin impossible to
resist.

Face buried in her hands, Leonora sank to her knees
before the crucifix, desperately begging for mercy as
she tearfully asked God's forgiveness for her vile sin.

When Luis reentered the tree-shadowed courtyard,
he thought it was deserted. Then he heard a muffled
sob and rustling behind the jacaranda tree.

"Elena?"

She started, thinking she was still alone. "Luis?"

Quickly he came to her side, his hands resting warmly
on her shoulders.

"Move farther back into the shadows," he urged
tensely. "Now, what's all this nonsense about returning

to Madrid?''

"Oh, Luis, surely you realize it was said when I thought you loved Leonora. I wanted to leave because I couldn't bear seeing you together and knowing you weren't mine.''

Quietly Luis considered her explanation, tension easing in his shoulders. "You alarmed me, *querida*. I thought perhaps you were having second thoughts.''

"Never,'' she whispered, licking her trembling lips. His hand slid in hers, the hot strength vastly comforting.

"While we're answering questions, perhaps you'll tell me exactly what the old don means to you?''

"Absolutely nothing. He was appointed as my escort on the journey. The Queen favors a suit between us— he's convinced he'll eventually win me over. That's the extent of our relationship. He's never even kissed me.''

Luis's sigh of relief was audible. He drew closer to her in the perfumed darkness and wrapped his arms about her to pull her close. Elena rejoiced in the hot, hard pressure of his body against hers.

"*Madre di Dios*, how I've tortured myself—I should have had sense enough to know.'' He placed a kiss on top of her head, his hot mouth burning through her stiffened headdress.

"What a pother of misunderstandings we've brewed between us,'' she said regretfully, laying her head on his shoulder.

"Let us put them all behind us. Oh, *mi alma*, how can I wait until December to see you again? I'll lose my mind riding about the *estada* remembering, yearning.''

She gazed up at him in the darkness, barely able to distinguish his features. The fountain tinkled incessantly and a soft breeze stirred the perfumed vine climbing the whitewashed wall behind them. Luis had stopped speaking now, and she became aware of the growing tension between them. Elena gasped as the unspoken force of his passion communicated itself to her and made her tremble.

"Elena, Elena," Luis whispered hoarsely, his arms so tight around her that they lifted her from the floor. "I'll wait a thousand years for you, if necessary, my *bella amada*. Promise you'll think only of me, that you'll want no other."

"You had that promise long before you asked for it."

He sought her with his hot mouth, and Elena drowned in the fragrance of his kisses. She slid her hands about his neck, her fingers moving up into his crisp gold hair. Pulses racing, blood pounding, she clasped him against her. When she was safe in Luis's arms, nothing else mattered.

"I love you with all my heart and soul," she vowed earnestly, her lips moving against his ear.

"You've made me the happiest man alive."

They clung together, kissing deeply, their blood surging with awakened passion. Elena grew aware of the mounting tremors in his arms and legs, of his rising arousal burning through her velvet skirts.

"If only tonight could last forever."

"Don't remind me that this is all we'll have till December," he pleaded huskily. Glancing over his shoulder, making sure they were not observed, Luis allowed himself to consider a reckless, insane idea. Smiling at the sheer danger involved, he whispered, "*Querida, querida*, let me make love to you one last time."

She heard his joyous invitation, his voice husky with emotion. Sexual tension quivered through his muscular body. Elena did not remind him that they might be discovered, that his proposal was sheer insanity; instead she pressed her mouth against his, her lips opening beneath his probing, their tongues uniting in mock union. His anxious mouth was on fire. A terrible ache spread through her limbs until she could barely stand. Arrows of fire shot through her veins as the heat of his hand covered her right breast. Lovingly cupping the swelling flesh, Luis fumbled for entry into her velvet bodice. When he negotiated the fastening, they uttered mutual sighs of delight, Elena gasping as his thumb and forefinger imprisoned her swelling nipple.

"I prayed you'd want to love me," she whispered breathlessly against his ear. Her honesty was rewarded by a crushing embrace that robbed her of breath.

Luis moved Elena back against the stone wall. All the while she stroked his neck, his ears, playing with the tendrils of golden hair curling over the collar of his shirt. So aroused was he, he could barely endure as he pushed up her heavy skirts and slipped his hand inside the secret warmth cradled between her thighs.

Lovingly stroking the silky flesh, his finger probed, hot and insistent. Elena tensed, shuddering at his knowing touch. Mouths welded together, Luis devoured her lips, her tongue. Never had she known love to be such an all-absorbing, burning passion. As long as she was in his arms, she did not care if the world came to an end.

Now Luis fumbled impatiently with his own clothing, finally releasing the throbbing, aching brand she longed to caress. Like molten steel, the force of his smooth flesh pressed against her body, making her moan in delight. Taking the soft velvet tip lightly between her thighs, Elena allowed the most intimate part of their bodies to touch in sweet caress. Luis groaned, too, no longer content to touch and kiss.

His breath burned against her cheek as he pleaded

hoarsely, "*Now*, Elena, before I die of passion."

Her mouth curved in delight at his impassioned plea. Fondling the swollen heat of his body, marveling at its strength, at the bursting veins apparent beneath her fingertips, she positioned him exactly where she wanted. Luis groaned in anguish as their flesh joined. Braced against the wall, she opened to receive him. She was aware of Luis's supporting hands gripping her buttocks, lifting her higher against the vine-covered masonry. Then her body was speared with fire, and Elena clung to him, moaning in abandoned delight as the throbbing heat completely filled her being.

Stolen as it was, this swift passion was all-consuming. Luis swept her away in the delicious shuddering momentum of his magnificent body. Elena moaned in total surrender. Never before had the heat of their love-making been so shatteringly fulfilling.

Clinging to his hard shoulders, Elena buried her face against his neck. Her hair fell free, tangling them both in a perfumed black cloud as her stiffened headdress fell to the ground. Her bruised mouth trembling against his burning cheek, she whispered again and again, "I love you, Luis, I love you."

His hands still enmeshed in her midnight hair, he slowly allowed her to slide down against the wall until her feet touched the tiles. Leaning against the cold masonry, his breathing labored, he fought to control the tremors of passion still wracking his arms and legs. So swift, so intense had been their lovemaking, he could hardly believe the sheer insanity of his actions in taking her out here in full view of his household.

"Dearest angel, sometimes you make a madman out of me," Luis whispered as he rained kisses on her soft cheek.

"Yours is a brand of insanity that appeals to me."

She slipped her hand inside his shirt collar, rejoicing in the touch of his smooth flesh burning beneath her fingertips.

An unexpected sound in the shadows made them freeze, waiting, alert. There was no further sound. Relaxing slightly, Luis pulled Elena against him, kissing her brow, her cheek, her trembling lips.

"You're mine and I'm yours till death."

The beautiful sentiment of his tender vow mingled with the perfumed night and the winking stars to create a mood so charged with emotion that Elena was moved beyond belief. Trembling, she laid her cheek against his velvet doublet. Luis lifted up her face to kiss away the silver trace of tears on her soft cheeks.

"Good night, my darling Elena, *mi vida, mi alma.*"

In the deep purple shadows beyond the fountain, Leonora pressed back against the whitewashed masonry, her heart racing in sickening tumult. She could not believe what she had seen and heard. In these few unguarded minutes her life had been upended. Her wonderful, handsome Luis had dared call that English bitch his life, his soul! Damn him! Damn them both! Hot, furious tears rained down her cheeks as she swayed weakly against the bouganvillea spilling down the trellis. This was why he did not want to give her a babe tonight. He could not wait to come out in the darkness to rut with her! All the time this woman had been at Carmenilla, they must have been doing that. Some days Luis had been gone from sunup to sundown. No wonder the English bitch had taken a fancy to riding. They must have met in the winery, the cellars, out in the open—who had seen them? Who else knew the terrible shame that had befallen her house?

Leonora's fingernails bit into her palms as she clenched her fists, trembling in outrage over his deception. How could her beautiful Luis touch that creature so intimately? How could he delight in her caresses, allowing her to fondle the part of his body that belonged to his wife alone?

Face flaming in impotent rage, Leonora shrank farther back into the shadows as they passed on their way indoors, the Englishwoman's velvet skirt sighing against the stonework, his leather-shod feet making a dull thump on the azure tiles. Leonora stood with fists clenched in the darkness, calling down vengeance upon them for her betrayal. Eyes glittering with malice, she looked up at the twinkling heavens, calling the power of the saints to avenge her. Luis would pay for his treachery— the Englishwoman would die for hers.

Chapter Seventeen

Clouds hid the sun. This gloomy day, so unexpected in such a sunbaked land, reflected Elena's bleak emotions. She stared through the tall narrow window of her room overlooking the rolling acres of Luis's *estancia*. How long it would seem till December. At least she could take heart from the assurance he would await her return with open arms.

A knock came on the door, and Elena carefully composed her features before answering.

It was Leonora, magnificently robed in darkest blue damascene, diamonds sparkling fire in her blonde hair and about her slender neck.

"Doña Elena, Teresa tells me you're not yet packed."

"I'm almost finished."

Though it was almost more than she could manage to look upon this woman and not scratch out her eyes, Leonora's voice remained pleasant. "Let me help you," she offered.

"Oh, no, Leonora, in truth I've little to pack. Just two trunks."

"Go downstairs, there's food and drink waiting. Teresa can finish this. Don Alvaro's looking for you."

After some hesitation, Elena finally accepted her

hostess's suggestion, surprised by Leonora's unexpected solicitude. "Very well, I am rather hungry."

Leonora gritted her teeth. Yes, the wretch would be in dire need of sustenance after last night's demands. Grimly Leonora waited until she heard Elena's steps on the stairs before turning to the open trunk on the rushes beside the bed. She had come seeking condemning letters written by Luis to this woman. Perchance the foolish creature carried his love letters with her. Leonora intended to confront her husband with the evidence and see how cleverly he could lie out of this corner.

Last night she had longed to plunge a blade in the Englishwoman's heart—this morning cold, calculating hatred replaced her rage. A surge of fresh anger made her long to shred the woman's pretty embroidered petticoats and her silver-striped bodices. Forcing herself to remain calm, Leonora methodically turned over stacks of neatly folded linens and voluminous gowns of vibrant damascene. Nothing. She should have known Luis was too clever to put such sentiments on paper. Those words were for dark nights and hurried whisperings.

Leonora took a pile of folded silk stockings off the bed and dropped them in the trunk. In stooping to rearrange the garments, she noticed a book lying at the bottom of the trunk. Triumphantly she seized it, hoping this was the wretch's diary.

"To my dearest Elena, your loving friend, Anne," read the inscription inside the blue leather cover.

As she turned the pages, Leonora gasped in shock. A lifetime of Catholic teaching compelled her to fling the abomination to the farthest corner of the room. Then, while murmuring prayers for forgiveness for her terrible sin, she retrieved the heretical volume with trembling hands. Not only had the Englishwoman stolen Luis from her, she was a vile heretic to boot! This was an English bible. There was enough damning evidence here to sentence Doña Elena to death! She could hardly credit the woman's stupidity in bringing such a thing to Spain. She must be totally ignorant of the far-reaching power of the Inquisition. Even the whisper of heresy was sufficient for arrest, let alone the condemnation of possessing such a book.

Heart pounding with excitement, Leonora hid the book inside her gown. Quickly, she flung a heap of shifts and velvet slippers atop the other garments before latching the trunk. She would tell Teresa to pack the rest of the things, leaving Doña Elena none the wiser to her theft until it was too late.

As she sped downstairs, Leonora's face glowed with triumph. Her pleasure was marred only by the knowledge she could not tell Luis what she intended to do. It would have given her the greatest satisfaction to see him tremble in fear for his paramour. Yet she dared not reveal her plans. Luis was not beyond breaking her arm while forcing her to relinquish the damning evidence. Nausea rose in her throat as she recalled the tender endearments he had spoken to his mistress. Well, she would ensure that he whispered no further words of love to his Elena; he would utter only cries of anguish as he watched her devoured by the flames of Toledo's grand *auto-da-fé*.

Glancing up at the silver crucifix glinting above the stair, Leonora quickly reminded herself she was not denouncing Doña Elena solely out of jealousy—the Englishwoman was an abomination in the sight of God! By reporting her heresy she was actually saving Doña Elena from eternal damnation. This pious reminder effectively overcame the niggling doubt that she might not be justified in what she intended to do. That wretch would thank her with her dying breath for showing her the way to the true faith.

A party of horsemen came toward the fortress, raising great clouds of dust above the trees. Don Alvaro and his servants, already mounted in the stableyard, watched the approaching party with interest as they waited for Elena.

Walking stiffly toward her horse, Elena fought tears, calling on pride to see her through this anguished parting. Luis was tense also, his face set in lines she did not remember seeing yesterday. The wonderful sensuality of his mouth, which made her long for his kisses, was locked behind a straight, unyielding line. Even his eyes lacked their characteristic allure, that indefinable look that made her heart leap whenever he turned his soft gaze upon her. Today the blue glittered as pale and metallic as the overcast sky.

"Good-bye, Doña Elena. Have a safe journey."

"Do not push yourself," Luis added gruffly to his wife's polite good-bye. "Though it's not hot today, the journey will still be tiring."

"Luis, you sound like an old wife." Leonora gave a brittle, forced laugh. "I'm sure Doña Elena's old enough to be aware of that."

Luis effectively silenced his wife with a dagger-sharp warning glance. Stepping up to Elena, he placed his hands about her small waist, painfully aware of the shudder that wracked her body at his touch. He lifted her to the saddle. They exchanged only a brief handclasp before he stepped back.

"Go with God," he pronounced gruffly.

At his words, several members of their party quickly blessed themselves. Then, at a signal from Don

Alvaro, the riders turned their horses' heads toward the dusty road.

Steeling herself against showing emotion, Elena turned to wave to Luis one final time. Unable to stop the tears misting her vision, she rode blindly beside Don Alvaro, her back ramrod-straight.

They must cross a wide stretch of grassland to reach the road. The road's dun ribbon wound past thickets of ash and maple, its surface dry after the summer drought. Great yellow swirls of dust bowled along beneath the horses' hooves.

A stinging shower of dust and grit bit into their lips and eyes as the approaching party of horsemen rounded the bend and drew abreast of them. Several churchmen in rich clerical robes led the riders; much gold in the form of crucifixes and elaborate horse trappings proclaimed their exalted station.

Don Alvaro doffed his pumed hat, delivered a polite greeting, but did not stop. Elena was somewhat surprised, for it appeared the heavy-faced man leading the riders had been expecting them to dismount.

Glancing back, she saw the doll-sized figures of Luis and Leonora kneel to kiss the proferred hand of the heavy-set churchman when he dismounted before the gates of the fortress.

"Come, Doña Elena, 'tis not wise to tarry," reminded Don Alvaro, tugging her sleeve to draw her away.

"Who are they?"

"High clergy of Toledo and their spies about one of their fact-finding missions. The Inquisition already knows who we are and where we're bound, you can be sure of that. And I don't want to excite any further interest on their behalf."

"Why should they be interested in us?"

The aging don turned in the saddle, an expression
of sheer astonishment on his face. "My dearest Doña
Elena, the Inquisition make it their business to know
where every man of note goes and whom he sees. They
employ an army of clerks to keep up with the paper-
work. It's not yet that way in your homeland, I know,
but don't forget—you're in Spain now."

The prospect of the Church's constant surveillance
was chilling. Surely these spies of the Inquisition were
not privy to *every* move made by one of their flock.
Uneasily Elena wondered if there were spies in Luis's
household. Had they reported those stolen hours beside
the waterfall? Her face flushed at the thought that such
a private moment might be recorded for posterity by
some inky-fingered cleric. At court she had heard it said
that Carranza knew what a man was thinking before
he thought it, yet until now she had always considered
the remark a joke. Don Alvaro's revelation about the
far-reaching power of the Inquisition had somehow
robbed the statement of humor.

They rode in silence, skirting the spreading pasture-
land of the de los Santos *estancia*, each contemplating
the unsettling appearance of those holy envoys of Rome.

"Are you leaving us so soon?" shouted Cristobal as
he thudded toward them, sending up billows of tawny
dust as he finally drew rein.

"We're bound for Madrid. How are the new season's
bulls? Fierce as the devil, I'll be bound," Don Alvaro
remarked amiably. "You'll heap more honors on your
name in the new year. I promise I'll be there to watch
your victories."

Cristobal grinned in pleasure at the old man's praise,
inclining his head in thanks. His gaze was hot and
penetrating, and his scrutiny made Elena vastly
uncomfortable.

"You will come, too, Doña Elena? Remember, I promise to dedicate my kill to you."

"I've not forgotten."

"It's an occasion to which I'll look forward."

Abruptly Cristobal swung from the path and, slouching in the saddle, he watched as they rode on. When they reached the next bend in the road, Elena glanced back to see if he was still there. He sat immobile as a statue, his shirtsleeves ballooning in the rising wind.

"Cristobal's the bravest of men. Foolhardy, some call him," remarked Don Alvaro, picking up speed as they reached the highway. "You'll enjoy the bullfights. All Toledo will be in holiday mood. Everyone flocks to watch Cristobal kill the fiercest stock in the land."

As they rode through the barren countryside, eventually all thoughts of the grim Inquisition, and even of Cristobal Santos and his slaughtered bulls, dissolved. Sinking into a rosy, trancelike state, Elena thought only of Luis. When her body reacted unexpectedly to vivid memories of his lovemaking, she squirmed in the saddle, seeking a more comfortable position. Dearest Luis. How much she regretted those lost months when she wallowed in her injured pride. She would waste no further time in recriminations. All that mattered was that they had found each other again.

Don Alvaro's party had been on the road several hours when the sky began to darken and raindrops blew in the rising wind. Suddenly the cold deluge descended, whipped by gale force winds. Their servants shouted to each other in alarm before galloping for cover at a tumbledown roadside hostelry. So heavy was the rainstorm that all hope of travel had to be abandoned until the skies cleared.

It took them over a week to reach Madrid. On his arrival, Don Alvaro immediately took to his bed. His

previous malady had been aggravated by repeated
dousings at the beginning of their journey. Now his
chest wheezed and rattled with every breath, and his
repeated chills shook the canopied four-poster. An army
of black-robed physicians came to bleed him. They
shook their heads gravely over his steadily worsening
condition and went away, leaving the elderly don ever
weaker.

Elena spent much time singing to the old man,
accompanying herself on a beribboned lute she found
in the solar. At times Don Alvaro was content for her
merely to sit beside him. These long idle hours served
as an unpleasant reminder of the days Elena had spent
chained to Randle's sickbed. Was she always destined
to be a nursemaid to old men and half-grown boys?

Daily, Elena awaited a letter from England. It was
too soon to expect a reply from the Queen, but she
hoped Will would send her news of home. She had
written to him when she landed on Spanish shores and
had yet to receive one word from Windland. Given
much time to think while the aging don dozed away his
days, she began to form a plan that daily grew dearer
to her heart. Luis could accompany her to England.
Surely his royal master could find business at court to
merit the appointment. That way she could have the
two things she wanted most in life.

Before the month was out a letter arrived, but not
from England. Leonora wrote from Carmenilla to
inform her uncle that a deadly plague had struck the
herds.

Don Alvaro's face blanched as he read and reread
his niece's letter. "I can't believe it," he gasped, "all
was well when we left. Now here's Leonora begging
me to return. I'm not nearly well enough for travel.
She must realize that. I wrote telling her I was confined

to my sickbed . . . why does she ask me to come? She knows I'm ill. . . .''

Elena shut out the old man's querulous voice as he continued to think out loud. She stood looking down on the sunny square, the scene divided into four sections by the ornamental iron grill over the window. Since the don's illness, she had become more of a prisoner in this grand house. Dark figures moved in the shadowed doorways at the perimeter of the square. An army of beggars virtually lived on the mansion's doorstep, their gaunt, diseased presence a constant reminder of Spain's terrible poverty. Elena knew there were beggars aplenty in England, yet these beggars seemed more diseased, more ragged. Their plight was made even more noticeable by the vast wealth of the haughty nobles, bedecked with diamonds, rubies, and pearls who traveled about the land. The Spanish preference for dark colors was born out of a desire to better display their priceless gems, making the nobility look for all the world like life-sized jewellers' showcases.

Elena's longing for freedom mounted by the day. If only she could travel to Carmenilla to investigate this sickness. Even if Luis had not been waiting for her, she would welcome the opportunity to leave this shrouded house.

Trying to appear calm, though her heart raced with excitement, Elena turned to Don Alvaro. As shafts of clear afternoon light fell across his bed, she was shocked to discover how much he had changed. This illness had aged him twenty years. Though she had not wished him ill, her hopes had soared as his strength dwindled. Providence may have stepped in to spare her from a second loveless marriage. An ailing old man was not nearly as anxious for a young bride as one who sought to prove his unflagging youth.

"Don Alvaro, let me go to Carmenilla for you. Send your best men with me so they can make a report."

"Never!" he cried, summoning the last of his strength. "I'll not hear of it—a lady riding unaccompanied about the land—never."

"I won't be unaccompanied. You can send your most trusted men with me. I'll take maids, chaperones, whatever you will, only let me go. I pine for freedom. I feel like a caged bird inside this house."

"I can't ask you to do that for me," he decided at length, clasping her soft hand in his yellowing claw. "You're far too generous—a saint, Doña Elena. I can't ask you to do more."

Ask me, please God, ask me, she pleaded silently. Disappointment overwhelmed her as she feared his mind was already made up. Then, out of sheer desperation she said something that later made her conscience prick. "When we're wed, the herds will be mine also," she reminded him. "Isn't this the perfect time, whilst you're ill, for me to take responsibility for our household?"

The sheer joy that lit Don Alvaro's sunken features made her feel thoroughly despicable. Elena glanced away from his watery gaze, unable to face those hollow eyes filled with hope.

"Dearest Doña Elena, dare I hope . . . that you . . . It's too wonderful to believe—you've agreed to marry me!"

Smiling, Elena stooped to place a cool kiss on his age-spotted hand. She did not say yes, nor did she say no; she merely let him assume what he wished. If it meant seeing Luis again, even this cruel ruse was justified.

"You've made me the happiest man alive."

The reminder that those sentiments had been spoken by another man merely deepened her guilt.

"But I can't let you travel alone. It's too dangerous. You must stay safe within these walls. You are most precious to me."

Though she was not allowed to travel across the country, Elena did at least bargain for some time outside Casa Escalante. Beneath a blue sky stretching achingly bright to the horizon, she rode on the outskirts of the city accompanied by a party of armed servants. By recklessly hinting she would accept his suit in hope of buying time with Luis, Elena had created a difficult situation. It was possible Don Alvaro would not live out the year, she told herself. So why not let him die happy? She had been a fool, yet for a few days with Luis she would have defied the Pope himself. And because she was in Spain, with the power of the Inquisition an unseen presence throughout the land, she glanced quickly over her shoulder. She half-expected to find a spy recording her thoughts, and the absurdity of the idea made her laugh.

Kicking her heels in the horse's flank, Elena flew like the wind along the tree-lined banks of the trickling Manzanares. The vast Castilian plain lay between her and her love. She must find a way to leave Madrid.

Fate stepped in to fulfill that desire, though with a more terrifying solution than she'd ever dreamed possible. Throughout the next week Don Alvaro fretted over Leonora's letter. He even struggled to dress for the journey, only to fall back in his bed, shaking and feverish. Defeated, he sent a messenger to Leonora explaining there was no possible way for him to travel.

To their surprise, a messenger arrived shortly thereafter informing him the plague had miraculously abated. Elena was roused from sleep by his shout of joy over the welcome news. She stood clutching her bedrobe while he relayed the contents of the message. Presently

a thunderous racket below disturbed them. The door-
keeper's raised voice could be heard floating upstairs.

Elena went to investigate the commotion and found
the muttering servants standing about in groups with
shocked expressions on their faces. Wondering why
they did not admit the visitors, she herself took the key
and unlocked and unchained the door.

"Who's there?" she cried, unable to distinguish the
knot of men who stood in the shadows.

"The Holy Office," came the reply.

Behind her the maids clutched each other and shrieked
in terror. Unaware of the ominous meaning behind those
words, Elena threw wide the door. Three robed men
stood outside, a fourth hovered beside the street corner,
holding a shrouded lantern.

"Doña Elena Locke?" asked one of the men.

"I am she."

"Come with us. You are under arrest."

"Arrest! For what? I demand to know the charge,"
she cried, pulling back as the man reached for her.

"Suspicion of heresy."

"I'm an Englishwoman. You've no jurisdiction over
me. I am the Queen's lady-in-waiting," she cried, trying
to wrestle free. To her horror, none of the servants came
to her defense.

"All the more condemning," snapped a man in a
monk's hooded habit. "Come, you're wasting time. It's
a long ride to Toledo."

Fear gripped her. Screaming for help from someone,
shouting Don Alvaro's name, Elena fought wildly as
the men dragged her into the dark street. A large hand
was clamped tightly over her nose and mouth,
effectively muffling her screams.

The watchers knew what this innocent did not; when
the Holy Office paid a night visit, no human aid was

possible. The only hope lay with God.

Racing upstairs, the servants tearfully recounted the frightening events to their master. Weak though he was, Don Alvaro had to be restrained to keep him from going to Elena's aid. He called for pen and paper to dispatch urgent letters for assistance. Over and over in his brain swirled the puzzling discovery that Elena was being taken to Toledo where the warrant had been issued. None of this made sense.

His hand shaking with weakness and rage, Don Alvaro wrote to Philip, beseeching royal intervention. Then he wrote briefly to the English Queen, also asking her aid in obtaining the release of her lady.

Exhausted, the old man lay back, trying to quiet his thundering heartbeat. That she should be taken now, when she had promised to be his wife, was the cruelest blow of all. Muttering prayers, he shut his eyes, struggling to overcome the shock of this latest calamity.

Thus he lay in the dawn's light, hands joined in prayer, eyes closed, when his servants came to wake him. Their efforts were in vain. Don Alvaro was dead.

Elena's throat ached from crying and shouting as she banged futilely on her cell door in hope of attracting someone's attention. She had been taken on a dreadful journey to Toledo the night of her arrest, dressed only in her bedclothes. Her exalted position at Mary Tudor's court had earned her no special privileges. Here she was merely a recalcitrant soul, completely under the power of the Spanish church.

A lengthy session of questions and accusations had produced no answers as to why, or how, she had become a prisoner of the Inquisition. Her Inquisitors, tiring of her lack of cooperation, finally brought her to this cell with only a cold stone floor for a bed.

Rats scrabbled in the corner beneath a heap of dirty straw. Elena tensed in dread, awaiting the emergence of those squeaking creatures whom so far she had kept at bay by flapping her bedrobe. Her accusors had not allowed her to dress respectably, or even to send for her trunks. She wore only her nightgown and her furred velvet bedrobe. Her black hair tangled around her shoulders; her feet were bare.

Though Elena had explained over and over who she was and which authorities should be contacted to verify her identity, her pleas fell on deaf ears. She wondered desperately how she could get a message to Luis. Without money, she could not even bribe the jailor. The man had told her they were in Toledo—that much she knew. So close to help, yet so far away from it. Tomorrow, they kept telling her—tomorrow she would have justice. Tomorrow never came.

Sometimes terrible screams echoed through the stone corridors. Elena shuddered as she pictured poor souls being tortured in an effort to make them recant or reveal the names of their fellow heretics. The Spanish jails must be bursting at the seams with Lutherans—this is what the Inquisition had accused her of being. They said they had evidence against her, but of course that was nonsense. She had told them so, then she cursed them and laughed in their faces. Now Elena regretted her actions. Perhaps, had she been meek and humble, they would have dealt easier with her. It was too late now. Humbling herself was foreign to her nature, and she doubted she would be given a second chance.

Sometimes she wept over her plight, praying she might wake to find this a terrible nightmare. Those cherished deams of being reunited with Luis had ended in this cold cell. It was so dark she would not have known day from night had it not been for the man who

emptied the slop pail and brought her meager rations.
Each time he came clanking and rattling to the studded
door, it marked the beginning of another day. She had
been in the dungeons of the Inquisition over a week.

A distinctive cough, rattling keys and the hollow clank
of feet on stone announced her jailor's arrival.
Suddenly, light flooded the cell, and Elena cried out,
shutting her eyes against the pain.

"Here she is. You can be together. Don't say the
Holy Office has no heart," chuckled the asthmatic
jailor, wheezing and coughing as he set down pans of
food and water.

Balls of fire still bounced before Elena's eyes. She
squeezed her lids, trying to stop the pain. When she
opened her eyes again, darkness surrounded the fiery
spots seared indelibly on her tortured eyeballs. There
was someone else here. With her senses acutely honed
by fear and deprivation, she could hear breathing, smell
the warmth of another human being.

"Who are you?"

"A friend who has risked his life for you."

At the sound of a male voice, she shrank back against
the wall, jumping away in shock when she encountered
icy manacles and chains mounted in the stone. The voice
was familiar, though she could not place it.

"Who are you?"

"You disappoint me, *doña*. I admit, I never expected
us to meet in such unpleasant circumstances—Cristobal
Santos, at your service."

"You! In my cell."

She heard him laugh bitterly in the darkness.

"You almost sound insulted."

"Why are you here? Have they arrested you too?"

"I stand condemned with you."

"Why?"

"Because, when I heard you'd been taken, like a fool I raced to save you. I protested their accusation indignantly, saying you had no secrets from me—*ai*, what a fool! I didn't know I was condemning myself. You did not tell me you were a heretic, *amita*."

"Nor am I. They've no evidence to prove it. I've made no heretical statements, nor have I consorted with heretics. I don't even know a Lutheran. Unless it's because I'm English, I can make no sense of it."

"Foreigners are ever suspect. And you had a condemning book in your possession. They needed no more than that. Why, little fool? I thought you wiser than that."

"A book? I have no book," Elena protested adamantly. Then she remembered Anne's gift. "Dear God—surely that hasn't condemned me," she whispered aloud.

"So you admit it! *Cristos*—I'd hoped they were wrong."

"The book was a gift from a friend. I thought nothing of it. Oh, I should have known! But how did they find it?"

"The Inquisition has eyes and ears throughout the land."

Elena wrung her hands as she paced the floor. "We must get word to Luis. He'll come to set us free."

Cristobal laughed scornfully at her hopeful suggestion.

"No, *amita*, the great Don Luis is aboard ship somewhere off Cadiz. He has no idea of our predicament."

"At sea!" Elena gasped in horror, clapping her hands to her face. All this time that she had thought he was awaiting her at his *estancia* he had been at sea! Fighting tears, she said in a quavering voice, "Then Don Alvaro will vouch for me.''

"Even more impossible—the old *don* had been dead over a week.''

Shock and horror gradually gave way to grief, and Elena began to weep piteously, rocking back and forth, her sobs deep and heartrending. When Cristobal reached for her and pulled her roughly into his arms, she was so distraught she did not repel him. He offered the only comfort available in these chill tombs of the Inquisition. Eventually, after she had wept herself dry against his linen shirt, she realized in whose embrace she stood and struggled to be free. He allowed her to go.

"There's little point in wondering how they got the book. They did and you and I are condemned by it. I've already sent a message to Don Luis. Hopefully it will reach his ship in time. Until then, *amita*, we have each other for company."

Alone in this cell with Cristobal Santos. A flicker of fear began in her stomach. She was completely at his mercy. Cristobal's open admiration for her, coupled with Luis's warning of the bullfighter's reputation with women, compounded her unease. Elena withdrew to the farthest part of the room. She heard him chuckle in the darkness as he read her uneasy thoughts.

"You need not fear me. I swear on my mother's grave—while we're in this cell, you're safe as a nun."

He sounded as if he meant it, yet she did not know if she could take his vow seriously. Tentatively, Elena drew a little closer. "Why did they put you in my cell?" she asked suspiciously, not wholly convinced of his innocence. This sounded like a perfect opportunity for him to do with her as he pleased. He could even have bribed the jailor to admit him.

"That, too, is my fault. Thinking to better your cause, I told them we were lovers. Even the Inquisition has some heart. They decided to let us spend our final days together.''

Elena did not know whether to be angry, or to thank him for his duplicity. The more she considered their curious plight, the more humorous it became. Finally she began to laugh, her laughter growing louder and more out of control. Cristobal caught hold of her and slapped her sharply across the cheek.

Screaming in rage, Elena wrenched away from him, nursing her injury. ''Damn you! How dare you hit me?''

''I'm sorry, *amita*, but it's what you needed. Hysterics will get us nowhere. I bribed the old man to bring you some clothes. They said you'd been taken in your night clothes.''

''Aye, they virtually dragged me from my bed.''

''What wicked irony that I, who would have killed for such a sight, should be with you now in perpetual darkness.''

Elena failed to see any humor in his observation, though Cristobal continued to chuckle.

Elena picked up the wooden porringer of cold gruel the jailor had left beside the door. She took a hunk of barley bread, which would have done justice to the tanner's art, and attempted to soften it in the broth. Belatedly, she offered some to Cristobal.

''No—though it's generous of you. I've supped already.''

''This is the best it gets.''

''I was afraid of that.''

For several hours they shared an uneasy silence. At first Cristobal tried to engage her in conversation, but finally abandoned the idea and retreated to his corner. Elena knew they could not remain incommunicado. She just needed some time to adjust to this new and most alarming development. She had no inention of encouraging his friendship lest it lead to other familiarities; she was all too aware that inside this cell she was completely at his mercy.

Though she began to grow drowsy, Elena was afraid to sleep; she even hesitated to use the slop bucket, though she knew she would soon be forced to abandon that delicacy. The full impact of her hapless plight was brought home to her as the dark hours crawled silently by. Tears of self-pity trickled down her cheeks as she huddled against the door, finding the wood warmer than the icy stone walls. Elena wrapped her robe tight around her, trying to tuck her feet inside the hem of the garment. Finally, unable to keep her heavy lids open any longer, she allowed her head to droop on her chest. And she slept.

As the days passed, Elena's confidence in Cristobal increased. He said he had no intention of raping her, and, so far, he had been true to his word. They now huddled close together at night for warmth. Long ago Elena had been forced to overcome her fastidiousness over the sanitary arrangements in the cell. And she gave thanks for the perpetual darkness to hide her blushes. Before the week was out, she had begun to grow mildly fond of him, though she was reluctant to call it that. Cristobal entertained her with stories of his childhood, of the gypsy tribe from which his mother came and of the glory of fighting the bulls.

The jailor brought her a warm gown, a shift, stockings, shoes and a cloak. Elena was overjoyed at being able to dress in warm clothing again. The garments were still not heavy enough to counteract the dank chill inside the cell, but they enabled her to endure confinement in greater comfort.

Twice their inquisitors took them singly from the cell for interrogation. As yet, torture had not been used.

It was an inevitability they did not discuss, each privately realizing it was merely a matter of time before the Inquisition brought its deadly arsenal into use. Cristobal had seen the condemned brought out to be burnt, wracked beyond humanity, poor broken creatures unable to walk. He chose to allow Elena the comfort of ignorance—she would learn the truth soon enough.

Luis received the appalling news of Elena's arrest on the feast of the Epiphany.

The crew of *Nuestra Señora de Carmenilla* had put into port to celebrate the holiday, and Luis was preparing to return home. Unavoidably detained by unfriendly tides, he had come ashore weeks later than he had intended. The time for branding had come and gone. The thought that Elena had waited for him while he was a prisoner of the sea gnawed at his peace of mind until he could hardly wait to feel solid ground under his feet.

He was lodged at an inn close by Cadiz's harbor, when a scabby rascal delivered a crumpled, wine-stained letter. Quickly Luis broke the seal, surprised to find the letter came from Cristobal.

"Don Luis, return as soon as possible. Doña Elena has been arrested by the Inquisition. I will do what I can to free her. Cristobal."

So short and yet so deadly. Luis felt the blood drain from his face. His hand shook, spilling wine on the scarred table so that it trickled to the rushes, red as blood. He shuddered at the terrible news. It was not true! Elena could not have been arrested. Again he read the brief message, hoping against hope he had misread its contents, yet knowing he had not. Many unanswered questions swirled through his brain. The wine he had drunk this evening dulled his senses, though harsh reality was quickly sharpening them again.

Swaying to his feet, Luis steadied himself on the edge of the table as he looked for Captain Diego Gomez.

"*Mi padre*," he called thickly, searching for the gray-bearded seaman amidst the woolen caps and grizzled faces crowding the smoky *taverna*. From long practice he still referred to Gomez as father, a practice Don Diego did nothing to discourage. For was not Luis loved like his own son?

Hearing the strain in Luis's voice, Diego Gomez turned from watching a game of hazard. "Here I am. What is it?"

"Read this." Luis thrust the crumpled, wine-spotted missive in Diego's gnarled fist. With difficulty the message was read, for though Gomez had sailed the world, he was not a man of much learning.

"I'm no scholar," he excused with an embarrassed shrug, "but this sounds serious."

"Serious—by Christ, it's a calamity!"

"So this is your lady?" During the long nights at sea Luis had spilled forth the tormented secrets of his soul. Diego had advised him to follow his heart, for it pained him to see his foster son so troubled.

"To think I took ship to dispel the boredom until we could be together again—*Cristos*! I must go to her at once." Luis ran his hand across his brow, which ran with sweat.

"Take care, Luis, the Inquisition is dangerous," warned Diego, clasping Luis's hand. "Don't let your heartache make you careless."

Riding north, Luis smiled grimly as he reviewed Diego Gomez's parting words. Dangerous was a gross understatement. Few who were enmeshed within the Inquisition's web had lived to tell of it. While furiously covering the miles that separated him from his beloved, he alternately puzzled and cursed over Elena's unexpected fate. How had she run afoul of the Holy Office? A stab of suspicion linking Leonora to the event came to mind. His wife had revealed her jealousy of Elena on several occasions, yet what could Leonora possibly learn to condemn her? Besides, Elena had been safely in Madrid with the old don. Though Cristobal had not said she was being held in Madrid, he assumed it was so.

Luis made good time by frequently changing horses, rarely stopping for food and managing with but a few hours of rest each night. He arrived at Carmenilla before dawn on a frigid January day, his horse lathered from hard riding. The cold wind seared his face; sleet had pelted his hat and clothes as he galloped across the stark plain, relentlessly pushing forth, driven by one thought—he must save Elena!

A sleepy Leonora met him at the door, wrapping her bedrobe tight around her waist. She looked wide-eyed and pale.

Shaking Cristobal's letter in her face, Luis demanded, "Why was I not told of this? Why did you leave it for *him* to write?"

Leonora swallowed nervously, wondering how to explain this latest development to Luis. Licking her lips, she smiled tentatively at him.

"Welcome home, husband." Then, as his brows drew in an angry line and he impatiently grasped her shoulder, she said, "How could I tell you while you were at sea? Had you not gone off on your pleasure voyage, you'd have been here to prevent it happening."

He glared at her, jolted by her reminder. She was right. And that fact made him even angrier. "Damn you, how long have you let her lie in that stinking hole? Why couldn't you do something? Enlist your uncle's aid, anything—''

''You've not heard then,'' she whispered, her eyes filling with tears.

''Heard what?''

''Poor Don Alvaro . . . he's . . . he's dead, Luis.''

''My God! Then she's been there without anyone to plead her cause. I'll go to Madrid at once. Where's Cristobal?''

Leonora clasped her hands nervously, wondering how to tell him. Luis's blue eyes sparked fire. In this mood he made her deathly afraid. ''Wait, Luis, first let me explain,'' she said, catching his arm to detain him.

He suffered her restraining hand, his nostrils dilated like an angry horse's, his mouth hard as he awaited her explanation.

''Cristobal's been arrested also.''

''What!''

''When he heard they arrested the Englishwoman he galloped off to rescue her. They arrested him, too.''

''*Dios mio*—what next!''

Luis paced the darkened hall, trying to decide what to do.

''And, Luis, you've no need of riding to Madrid,'' continued Leonora quietly. ''They're here in Toledo.''

Luis raised his accusing eyes to hers. ''The warrant was issued here? I don't believe it. On what possible charge?''

Leonora turned away, made uncomfortable by his piercing gaze. Dear God, if he ever guessed her part in the denouncement, her life was worthless. Trying to quiet her thundering heart, she whispered,''They're both accused of heresy.''

''That's preposterous!''

Her husband's angry cry tore through her, mutiplying her fear. She had never intended Cristobal to be

arrested. Poor fool, he had innocently gone to rescue
a lady in distress, unaware of her guilt. Leonora had
wanted to tell the Inquisitors the bullfighter was
innocent. He was their own *estanciero* and, despite his
gypsy blood, a good Catholic. She had wanted to tell
them—but her courage failed. Short of revealing her
own part in their arrest, she could do nothing. Besides,
if she pleaded for Cristobal to be set free, that might
mean the Englishwoman would be released also. She
would not risk that. If necessary, Cristobal would have
to be sacrificed.

"It's preposterous, I tell you," Luis thundered, his
face white with anger.

"Then go tell that to the Inquisition," she snapped,
pushed beyond endurance by his open display of
emotion over the Englishwoman.

"That, wife, is exactly what I intend to do."

Luis emerged in the pale winter sunshine of the
January afternoon enraged and frustrated, his hands
fiercely clenched. He wanted to pound on the walls of
the nearby building to vent his rage. Hours of
petitioning, of waiting for audiences, of pleading the
victims' innocence had all come to naught. He already
knew the Inquisition never revealed the name of the
accuser. He was not sure what he had expected to
learn—certainly not what the holy brothers had told him.
They said Elena possessed an heretical volume that
proved she was a Lutheran. Could someone have
planted such evidence to discredit her? Again he was
reminded of Leonora's jealousy. But how could his wife
come by such a book? The idea was ridiculous. Surely
poor, trusting Elena had not actually carried such condemning evidence with her. The more he considered
the latter, the more sure he was of its likelihood. In

England, though times were certainly changing, to possess such a book would not constitute a sentence of death. In Spain, things were woefully different.

A dark-eyed girl selling good luck charms pulled at his arm, begging him to purchase her wares. Impatiently, he shook off her detaining hand and began walking rapidly down the street, not knowing where he went, just walking and thinking.

Several hours later Luis found himself on the banks of the Tajo, desperately forming a plan of action. The cold wind whipping across the water chilled his face, but he remained oblivious to its blast. There was only one avenue of help left open to him. He would visit Dolores Mendoza, sister to the Inquisitor's aide. In the past they have been lovers. Perchance, because of that old relationship, he could save Elena's life.

Chapter Eighteen

"Luis! I can't believe it's really you!"

Luis stood in the shadows near the door. Dolores, seated at a long oak table, was bathed in candlelight. Time might have stood still. She was just as seductively beautiful as ever. Was it really three years since that torrid summer of passion? Early in their relationship he had discovered she spied for the Inquisition, but she was beautiful and he had had little to hide. It had been her possessiveness and demands on his time that finally became too much to endure. He had met her when he was merely Luis Gomez; when he had returned to Toledo it was as the scion of the de los Santos family. That had been a tumuluous year. Perhaps it was the last time he had been completely sure of who he was and what he wanted from life.

"Dolores, you're as lovely as ever." He smiled, stepping toward her.

"*Querido*," Dolores whispered, jumping up and holding out her arms. "Where have you been all this time?"

"To court. To England and back. Much has happened these past couple of years."

"Much indeed. Now you're not just a sea captain's

get, but a grand *hidalgo*—owner of the famous Carmenilla *estancia*, no less. Fate's been kind to you, *chico*.''

Slightly put out because he ignored her outstretched arm, Dolores sucked on her full lower lip, studying him intently. "Older, better dressed and even more handsome," was her throaty observation.

"May I?" Luis motioned to the wine decanter before her on the table.

"By all means. I also hear you're married to Leonora Fragoso. Congratulations. That milk-and-water woman brought you half a country with her marriage bed. You were ever a man to seize opportunity."

Aware of the spite in her tone, Luis allowed it to pass. Dolores never held anything back—passion, rage, anger all bubbled to the surface.

"You're probably wondering why I'm here."

"Perhaps," she agreed with a sly smile, slipping a ruby ring back and forth on her slender finger, "and perhaps not."

Luis stood looking down at her. Dolores boldly met his gaze. She ran the tip of her moist pink tongue over her full red lips. Huge dark eyes, catlike above her high cheekbones, examined him curiosly. Her black hair tumbled loose down her back, for she had flung her headdress on the settle. She was all seductiveness and passion with a venomous bite; at the sight of Dolores, every man's thoughts turned to passion. Full breasts, tiny waist, amply curving hips and skin like golden honey inspired men to fight for the privilege of kissing her ruby lips. And Dolores revelled in their sacrifice, patronizingly bestowing her favors on the victor. Not one for sentiment, she did not expect it from others.

"Cristobal's been arrested by the Inquisition on a charge of heresy," Luis said.

"Yes, that's why I thought you were here. You want me to get him released?"

"Not exactly."

Dolores popped a grape between her sharp white teeth, biting into the flesh, letting the juice trickle onto her dimpled chin.

"Surely you're not here to make love to me," she suggested archly, the throbbing pulse at the base of her throat betraying her interest.

Luis was left in no doubt she would welcome him. Her unslaked passion would serve his purpose well, yet he was surprised she still wanted him. After all this time he assumed Dolores would have found a man more to her taste, someone meeker and more biddable.

"Are you saying you'd let me?" he parried, pulling out a high-backed chair and sitting down.

"It's you who are here to talk."

A grin twitched Luis's mouth. No, she had not changed. Dolores still liked to fence with words. "I'm here to ask your help. Arturo is still in high places. You need only ask—"

"You don't realize how times have changed. Now it's harder to get out of a charge of heresy."

"But you can do it?"

Dolores smiled slyly and flicked his cheek with a long oval fingernail. "I might."

Short of sleep, of food, but mostly of patience, Luis found this game tiresome. While they sat here bandying words, Elena languished in the Inquisition's rat-infested dungeons.

"No more games, Dolores," he rasped suddenly, seizing her slender wrist. It felt virtually boneless in his strong hand as he exerted just enough pressure to let her know he meant business.

"All right. You want me to have the bullfighter

freed."

"There's something else."

"Oh."

Luis hesitated. If Dolores even thought his interest lay in another woman he would get no help from her. How then to tell her he wanted Elena freed most of all?

"As you know, Cristobal was ever one for the ladies."

Dolores laughed and rolled her eyes. "Everyone knows that. A bullfighter never need pay for a woman—there are plenty who'll pay him. So?"

"Cristobal tried to rescue some English wench. That's why he was arrested. *Dios mio*, heresy—you couldn't ask for a more devout Catholic. Those who fight the bulls ever keep Our Lady close to their hearts."

Dolores nodded. "Yes, I heard about that. This Englishwoman—is she pretty?"

A barbed question. Answering carefully, Luis said, "I'm sure Cristobal considers her an angel."

"And you?"

Luis shrugged. "Englishwomen are Englishwomen," he allowed noncommittally. "My taste usually runs to hotter blood."

"Ah, how well I remember." Dolores was warming rapidly to the subject. "So you also want me to free Cristobal's whore?"

Had he managed to hide his reaction to her words? Luis hoped so, though his hands sweated copiously as he clenched them beneath the lace table cover. "That's right."

"And what, Don Luis, am I to be paid for this favor?"

"Name your price."

"You want him out that bad!"

"The new bulls will soon be ready. I'm no fool. I

can't risk having a man like Cristobal in prison at the height of the season.''

''Agreed. As there's much money to be made on wagers, your *estanciero* is a brave man.''

''So . . . will you do it?''

Dear God, how much longer was she going to play this out? Moisture beaded his upper lip, and he grew aware of sweat trickling between his shoulder blades. Nervously, Luis shifted his feet as he sipped red wine, somberly likening the liquid in his glass to blood.

''Name my price, eh?'' Dolores said after a long, thoughtful silence. Licking her lips with the tip of her pink tongue, she looked for all the world like a cat contemplating a juicy mouse. ''And you'll agree to my terms, Don Luis?''

''I've said as much.''

''For the bullfighter—and his whore?''

''Yes.''

''Well, Don Luis, I'm not a greedy woman, so my request shall be simple.''

''Anything.''

He leaned toward her, grasping her hand on the lace table cover. Luis crushed her small hand in his, unaware he was hurting her as he waited for the magical words that would set Elena free.

''Then I shall ask for you.''

''Me? I don't understand. How do you mean—me?''

''Oh, I think you understand well enough. Even when you were only a poor seaman you were no one's fool. You're to be my price. I'll settle for no other.''

Luis swallowed as a hot wave of nausea curled up from his belly. ''You realize I'm married to Leonora?''

''Pooh, what do I care for that blonde madonna. I'm more woman than she ever dreamed of being. I want you in my house, in my arms and most important—in my bed!''

He stared at her, his pupils dilating. ''And that's to be your price—a night of lovemaking?''

''Who said anything about a night. I want you to be my husband.''

''Impossible. You know I'm already married.''

''But if Leonora were gone, you'd be free then.''

''Yes, I suppose so, but she's young and in good health. There's no point to this questioning. Are you going to help me or not?''

''I've already told you my price for the bullfighter—''

''And don't forget his woman. Cristobal would never forgive me if I didn't bargain for her, too.''

Dolores nodded. Cocking her head to one side, she asked, ''Why this sudden brotherly love? I always thought you hated him.''

''As you said before, I'm no fool. Cristobal knows how to kill bulls. He'll win much money and many honors for us.''

Dolores accepted his answer, and Luis breathed easy once more. ''So, Don Luis, for the bullfighter *and* his woman I ask your services whenever and wherever I require them. I also want your sworn oath that if Leonora dies, you'll marry me.''

Abruptly Dolores pushed back her chair. Going to a side table, she returned with a large gold reliquary. Taking Luis's slender bronzed hand, she spread his long fingers over the embossed gold lid.

''Now, *querido mio*, repeat after me.''

Luis hesitated. Fire blazed in her black eyes, which burned with a fervor approaching insanity. This was not the first time he had doubted Dolores's reason. A shudder went through him as he encountered the evil gleam of her eyes.

''I, Luis de los Santos, promise in the event of my

wife's death, to take Dolores Mendoza to be my wife.''

Eyes downcast so she would not see the mockery there, Luis repeated her words in a low voice. Fool woman! Did she really think he would keep such a vow? She might have to wait a lifetime for Leonora's death. There was no way she could hold him to this promise. It was such a small price to pay for Elena's freedom, he almost laughed aloud in relief.

"And now, *querido mio,* for the rest of the bargain."

Dolores reached for him, her fingers tantalizing on his face. Up into his crisp golden hair her small hands smoothed and ruffled. With a sigh, Luis grasped her hands and pushed them down.

"Much as I want to make love to you, I'm tired unto death. I've ridden with little sleep from Cadiz—"

She placed cool fingertips on his lips. "Hush. No more excuses, Don Luis. I know you're tired. Do you take me for a fool? First you will bathe and sup—I'll even let you sleep a few hours because I'm so kind and generous. Then you'll make love to me until I'm satisfied. Only after that will we go to the chambers of office to talk to Arturo."

The February dawn was late. Soft golden fingers sliced across the paneled wall of Dolores's bedchamber, and she stirred indolently beneath the covers. Beside her, Luis stirred also, flinging his arms across the pillow. Dolores lay watching him, reacquainting herself with all the things about him she had loved and longed for since he had been gone. Once she had thought he would marry her—they had even discussed the prospect, though whether it was seriously meant on his part, she did not know. When Luis left her, she had wanted to kill him. Furious over his desertion, she had vowed never to speak to him again, never even to admit him

if he came whining at her door. Of course she knew
Luis whined at no woman's door. He had no need. They
were far more likely to come whining at his.

Dolores sighed in contentment as she watched him
stir on the point of waking. In a few minutes Luis would
arouse that part of her that had lain dead for three years,
the fierce emotion he alone could kindle.

"Luis," she whispered, her breath soft against his
ear. "*Querido mio*, wake up. I grow impatient for your
kisses."

Luis stirred. His eyes flickered open, soft, scintillating
blue at first awakening. A shiver of delight shot through
Dolores as she remembered those other mornings long
ago. He blinked in surprise when he saw her leaning
over him. Then, as the cobwebs of sleep gradually
cleared, Luis remembered just why he was here. His
gaze turned wary and his mouth tensed.

"Are you well rested?"

"I've not been awake long enough to find out."

Dolores stroked his face, allowing her long black hair
to fall in a cloud about him. "Now you're trapped. And
I'll never let you go," she promised throatily. "Oh,
Luis, Luis, how I've prayed for this."

Her eyes smoldering with passion, she bent to kiss
his mouth. At the touch of her hot, moist lips, Luis tried
not to tense, forcing himself into the role he had chosen.
Inwardly asking Elena's forgiveness, he caught Dolores
by her abundant hair and rolled her over, pinning her
to the pillow.

Raising up on his elbow, Luis said, "It's I who'll
play the lover, Dolores."

A tremulous sigh went through her, and she closed
her eyes, waiting for it to begin.

Luis looked down at her, trying to reawaken those
feelings he had once felt for this ripe spitfire of a

woman. They did not come easily. Trying to forget she was Dolores Mendoza, instead he imagined she was a nameless whore for whom he, being long at sea, had desperate need. Offering up thanks that at least she was clean and beautiful and not some dockside slattern, he allowed purely bodily cravings to possess him.

As Luis eased her thin shift from her round, brown-tipped breasts, Dolores laughed throatily. When he finally buried his face amidst those soft perfumed pillows, Dolores, unable to keep still, unable to fully carry out the role of subservient wench, grasped his shoulders and locked him against her. Their mouths welded together as the lovers fought and strained. Their tongues probing, she writhed in delight beneath him. Deep in her throat she murmured words of love and seduction. Luis was deaf to her impassioned speech as he called on the primitive responses of his nature. By having Dolores Mendoza in his arms he would one day hold Elena again. Though perhaps Elena would not view it in quite that fashion, Luis was using Dolores as women often used men. She was a means to an end. By making love to her, he was ensuring Elena's release.

Impatient, Dolores reached down between their heated bodies, her hands trembling in anticipation as she touched the swollen magnificience of his engorged brand. The contact made her gasp in wonder, setting the blood pounding through her veins.

"Ah, *querido*, there was never another man like you," she crooned deliriously. She kissed his shoulder, took his nipples in her soft lips before slowly moving downwards, her mouth following the triangular curling golden pelt where it merged with that most treasured of places. Dolores gently brushed his swollen flesh with her mouth, tipping the velvet head of his manhood with her hot tongue.

Grunting, Luis yanked up her head, impatient with desire. Not for her the long, slow awakening, the drawn-out lovemaking.

"Would you have me useless before we start?" he rasped, rolling her over and spreading her legs.

"Useless—since when were you able to do it only once?"

But Dolores obeyed without further protest. She had waited so long for his lovemaking, she herself could not endure extended loveplay. That would come later. Oh, yes, she was not going to excuse him after one performance. Luis was being granted a great favor and Dolores was a woman who liked to have her money's worth.

When Luis next roused himself, the sun was high. He felt so exhausted, he could scarcely drag himself awake. Someone was singing and clattering pots across the room. Turning his head on the soft pillows, he saw the outline of a woman in the dim shadows, dark hair billowing about her shoulders. For an instant his heart leaped as he allowed himself to hope—then, just as quickly, that hope was dashed as Dolores said, "Come, *querido mio,* Arturo leaves within the hour."

And it all came back to him. Reality settled like a lead weight in the pit of his stomach. Luis could smell the hot, rank scent of lovemaking all around him in the bed.

His mouth twisted in a bitter grin as he considered his choice of words—there had been nothing of love about it. That emotion he reserved for the precious woman whom he would barter his soul to free.

"First let me wash off this stink," he growled, leaping from the covers.

"Stink! That's a delightful way of putting it. There's water over there," Dolores snorted, her eyes narrowing

as she considered him. Yes, Luis had changed, she
decided with an uneasy stab. Once, he would never have
referred to the precious juices of their mutual passion
as "stink." Perhaps he was just more fastidious now,
she thought, trying to soothe her uneasy heart. Involun-
tarily she shuddered, thrilling as she watched him cross
naked through shafts of golden sunlight. The muscles
rippled in his perfectly tapered body as he bent to reach
for soap and sponge, preparing to wash away all traces
of their lovemaking.

Turning back to the carved table, Dolores frowned.
She dabbed a generous amount of jasmine oil between
her breasts and behind her ears. She kept forgetting—now Luis was a fine *hidalgo*. The frown
deepened as she considered he was also forgetting she
was the sister of Arturo Mendoza. If she chose, she
could bring the finest *hidalgo* to ruin!

Luis dressed quickly, eager to have this interview
behind him. Dolores lay on the bed, watching him, her
tongue playing about her full lower lip as she
pleasurably anticipated returning to this chamber.
Tonight she would insist he go slowly. Last night he
had taken her like some bought woman. She would not
allow that again. Her cherished dream had been of his
fine lovemaking, not merely a swift assuagement for
the fire between their legs. Apparently handsome Luis
needed to be taught a lesson. But there was plenty of
time for that. A whole lifetime . . .

"Come, Luis, we don't want to be late."

"I'm ready. Do you think they'll release them
today?"

"Today! *Dios mio*, what's your hurry? The bulls
won't be ready for another month."

Luis smiled grimly as he followed Dolores outside.
If he was fortunate enough to have Elena set free today,

this would be the last Dolores Mendoza would see of him. He and Elena would reach Carmenilla long before sunset.

It was not to be.

Arturo Mendoza, older and even more pompous than Luis remembered, seemed in no hurry to accept his statement of Cristobal's exemplary practice of his religion as proof he was no heretic.

"That's all very well, Don Luis. But you understand—I must have more than this. Half the heretics burnt at the stake faithfully attend Mass. That's no assurance," protested Arturo, stroking his silky beard, then lovingly fingering the pearls encrusting the sleeves of his purple doublet.

"Come, Arturo, *I'm* telling you, this bullfighter's no heretic. The English wench was his reason for coming here. His blood's hot for her. Men like Cristobal Santos would tilt with Lucifer himself for a piece of skirt," Dolores interjected in exasperation. When Arturo still refused to be swayed, her temper soared and she retorted angrily, "Your position's gone to your head, brother."

Arturo's mouth opened and shut like a fish as he thought better of retaliation. Sometimes he was afraid of crossing his volatile sister.

Luis looked from one to the other, waiting. Dolores's explanation for Cristobal's arrest came too close to the probable truth for comfort. Why had Cristobal gone to free Elena? It would not be because she had recently been their houseguest, nor even that he believed she was innocent. Luis well understood Cristobal's interest in pretty women.

"Do you want money?" he snapped, reaching to his purse for gold.

Feigning shock at the suggestion, Arturo drew himself

up to his full height. "Don Luis, dare you suggest the Inquisition would accept a bribe? That's very grave—"

"Damn it, Arturo, you know as well as I do how things are done," Luis growled, not expecting to run into any resistance now he had come this far. "How much for Cristobal and his woman?"

"I'll have to consider the matter," mumbled Arturo, shuffling papers on his desk and trying to appear busy. "Now go. It's late and I have more important tasks."

Dolores linked her arm through Luis's and marched him away when he would have stayed to argue the point.

"Shut your mouth, fool," she hissed once they were through the door. "He's as good as done it. Even Arturo's not immune to spies. Things must be done according to rules."

"But he didn't say—"

"Had he not intended to grant our petition, he'd have called the guard. Where's your wit? I think you lost most of it once you became a grandee, eh, *chico*?"

Luis bit back an angry retort, forcing himself to walk quietly behind her out into the pale winter sunlight. He drew his black cloak close about his body, finding the wind cold. Today his velvet finery seemed devoid of warmth. A chill, more of foreboding than that of winter weather, gripped him as he turned the corner and walked a few doors down the narrow cobbled street to Dolores's house.

"How long must we wait?" he demanded of her as they stood outside her door.

Dolores shrugged. Turning to him, she slipped her arms about his neck and pulled his mouth to hers. "Just long enough for me to know if you're sincere," she whispered, and there was no accompanying softness in her dark eyes.

A servant opened the side door, admitting them inside

the gloomy house. The air smelled sweet with incense and the fragrance of oranges.

Dolores turned to him, her high cheeckbones bronze as a gypsy's in the murky daylight filtering between closed shutters. Her full mouth was languid, her lids drooping seductively over brilliant liquid brown eyes as she twined her supple arms about his neck. Pressing close, her breasts like twin points of fire against his chest, she smiled wickedly.

"Now, *querido mio*, you will make love to me as if you meant it."

More than a week passed before that glorious day of redemption arrived. On awakening, Luis stretched languidly, then jerked upright as he found Dolores already dressed. She was holding two crackling papers in her hand. When she leaned over him, she purposely allowed him an unobstructed view of her breasts as the black embroidered bodice of her gown gaped unfastened.

"See, your prayers have finally been answered—as have mine," she added huskily as she reached for his manhood beneath the mounded covers. Finding what she sought, Dolores tried to tease him into readiness. When she failed, her derisive laughter pealed harshly. "What, limp as a wilted stalk, *chico*? You should be ashamed!"

"No man who's performed as I have this past week has any need for shame. Now give me that," he growled, snatching the papers from her hand.

Just as Luis had hoped and prayed ever since his arrival in Toledo, he finally held the release for the two suspected heretics. God be praised, Luis thought, offering heartfelt thanks for the intervention of the Almighty.

''What are we waiting for?''

''Are you to go naked? I agree, it would be a stirring sight. In fact, Luis, I'd enjoy it immensely.''

He had no time for humor. Scowling, Luis pulled on his shirt, his hose, then fumbled as he tied his points. Dear God, he was all thumbs this morning. Excitement made him quiver, and he kept reminding himself to mask his eagerness from Dolores. She was not quite as gullible as she had once been. There was still time for her to go back on her word. Until Elena was safe, he could not afford to give himself away.

''Come, help me, Dolores. You sap so much of my strength I can barely dress.''

That was an invitation much to her taste. Laughing, she came and deftly assisted him. When he was dressed, she knelt to kiss what she hoped to arouse beneath his gold-flecked tights. Pouting when he refused to allow her the intimacy, she flounced away to fetch his cloak and boots.

Luis shaved quickly, nicking his cheek in the process. Crying out in distress, Dolores ran to staunch the wound, sucking the blood, swallowing, repeating the process until his face ceased to bleed.

''This is an omen, *querido mio*,'' she whispered passionately. ''Your blood and mine have become one. This is the beginning of our future together.''

It was oppressively warm inside the chambers where Arturo Mendoza received them. This morning the pompous little aide wore mulberry satin and black velvet and his fingers were covered with rings. Luis wondered which poor soul had lately sacrificed his wealth, for the jewels were new this week.

''We're here to take the prisoners home,'' Luis announced as he strode inside the room. He stood over a head taller than the dark-haired Mendoza, and Arturo

strove to make himself taller, teetering before him on
tiptoe.

"All in good time, Don Luis. As yet the accused have
not been wholly—"

"Now listen here, Mendoza, I'll not be fobbed off
with any more excuses. Here are the papers for their
release. Bring them out!" Luis growled, his face
darkening with anger. Behind him he was aware of
Dolores disapprovingly clicking her tongue while she
tugged at his doublet. He was damned tired of playing
the good boy; it was time to take action.

"This way," said the Inquisitor's aide, ignoring
Luis's angry outburst as best he could. Two dark-robed
clerks followed at a respectable distance as Arturo led
Luis down a corridor leading to a narrow flight of stone
steps.

Dolores stayed behind, hoping Luis would not allow
his temper to get the better of him. Arturo could be
manipulated, but one pushed him only so far. The
promise of fine horses and of wine to stock his cellars
for the next five years had gone a long way to soften
his heart, but the prisoners' release was not wholly
settled. Still, she could not waste time worrying about
how Luis controlled his temper; she had more important
tasks ahead.

Two men dressed in brown homespun, their dark
cloaks slung about their shoulders, were waiting for her
below in the courtyard. At Dolores's approach, the men
removed their hats and bowed respectfully.

"Good day, Doña Dolores. You sent for us?"

Glancing about to make sure they could not be overheard, Dolores beckoned the men to the very center
of the cobbled courtyard. The many windows of these
tall buildings overlooked the square, yet surely such
a brief meeting would not arouse suspicion.

"I outlined my plan last week. Do you recall, Gonsalves?"

The shorter of the two men grinned and nodded, his one good eye trained on the voluptuous sister of the Inquisitor's aide.

"Good. You are to ride to Carmenilla at your convenience and carry out the plan. There should be no difficulty."

"Oh, no, *doña*, no difficulty. We're merely gathering information. It's scheduled for us to ride through that district," said the other man. "Only this time our token of remembrance will have a bitter taste."

"Make it not too bitter," cautioned Dolores, "lest she suspect." Then she walked briskly away.

Safely inside the building once more, Dolores twisted her hands together in agitation until the small bones cracked. It was hard to believe that this time next week Luis would be in a position to marry her. Poor fool man, she knew he considered her mad when he agreed to her proposition, though he had tried to hide it. Becoming a widower was the furthest thing from his mind. That was last month—this month the situation would change.

Dolores hurried back upstairs to the dark, panelled reception room where a small group had gathered. At her entrance, a tall black-robed monk stepped forward to greet her.

"Doña Dolores, the woman is here."

"Thank you, Fray Tomas. I'll see her alone if I may."

The monk hesitated, then nodded. He and the other men withdrew to the adjoining room, purposely leaving the door ajar.

As she passed, Dolores deliberately kicked the inner door closed, then went to admit the trio waiting outside in the gloomy passage. A dishevelled black-haired

woman huddled inside a thick cloak. She was flanked
by two helmeted guards.

"You're the Englishwoman?" Dolores asked slowly
in case the woman did not understand much Spanish.
She was not surprised when she received an answer in
English.

Waving the guards away, Dolores led the prisoner
to the table, where she motioned for her to sit. Offering
wine and sweet almond cakes, she seated herself across
from the prisoner to study her.

Far too beautiful, she thought peevishly, even after
weeks of deprivation. The woman's tangled ebony hair
framed her pale face and tumbled in a curling mass over
her shoulders and down her back. And what a face! The
flesh was sculpted like marble and appeared as flawless.
High cheekbones, full lips, a Spanish nose. But it was
those tawny, wild animal eyes Dolores disliked most.
Now she could see what the gypsy bullfighter had found
appealing about the woman. She had puzzled over what
some foreign woman could have to make a man like
Cristobal Santos risk his life. Now she knew. The discovery did not please her. Though Dolores had no
romantic aspirations concerning Luis's *estanciero,* like
many beautiful and possessive women, she resented any
woman taking a man's attention from her.

"You were hungry, eh!" Dolores remarked, finding
the woman had emptied the plate of cakes.

"Your table usually leaves much to be desired."

Even that swift, witty answer annoyed her. Eyes
narrowed, Dolores leaned forward. "Are you a
heretic?" she asked suspiciously.

"You know I'm not."

Elena blinked rapidly, her eyes finally focussing on
the woman seated across the table from her. Haughty,
buttoned to the neck in black velvet embroidered with

pearls and gold thread, this was someone of importance. Up till now her inquisitors had all been male. Shuddering, she tried to put those hideous interrogation sessions from her mind. Brothers in hooded robes, coarse guards with wandering hands, fanatical public officials, all bent on the same course—to prove she was a heretic.

"I am not a heretic," she repeated loudly and firmly, the wine and cakes having imparted a new sense of strength and courage.

"Do you know who I am?"

Elena shook her head. She held her shoulders back, her defiant chin high, determined not to be cowed by her accusers. These Spaniards had an overwhelming dignity and pride, arrogance if you would, but she was more than a match for them.

Dolores rose from her chair, towering over the seated prisoner. "I am Dolores Mendoza. My brother is the Grand Inquisitor's aide."

"I see," murmured Elena, awaiting further enlightenment. She did not know why this woman had asked to see her. The guards told her she was to have a private audience with someone of much importance. Cristobal had also been taken from the cell; she had not seen him since. Uneasily, she wondered what had become of him. This black-haired woman probably knew, but she would not give her the benefit of knowing she cared, or give her anything to hold over her.

"Your lover must be madly in love to risk his life."

She must be speaking about Cristobal, for he had told the Inquisition they were lovers, thought Elena, trying to keep the facts straight in her muddled brain. Too many hours of darkness, of not knowing the day, or even the month, had taken their toll.

"Cristobal is innocent also," she said.

Dolores ignored her and walked to the windows.

Below she saw Gonsalves and his companion mounted
and moving toward the archway. Excitement fluttered
in her breast. It had begun—the road to destiny was set.
There was no turning back now.

"I know what it is to love," said Dolores at last, her
voice unsteady with emotion. "I'm shortly to be
married. The bullfighter will never marry you, though.
I think you should realize that."

Elena's mouth tightened at the smug note that crept
into the other woman's voice. Presently, Dolores
Mendoza walked back to the table and stood stiffly at
her side. "You've been absolved of your crime. You
are free to go."

The words floated about the dark, airless room. At
first Elena thought she had imagined what the Mendoza
woman had said. It could not be. Not salvation after
all this torment, this deprivation . . .

"You said . . . free? Free to go?" she croaked, tears
chocking her voice.

"Yes, you and your lover. Wait over there. I'll have
him brought in."

Pushing Elena none too gently as she rose on unsteady
feet, Dolores indicated she was to sit on a bench in the
far corner of the room.

It was dark here. Elena was glad of the seclusion
because tears were flowing unchecked down her cheeks
and dropping to her cloak. A wave of weakness flooded
over her until she doubted she could stand if she had
to. Free! That word had become almost meaningless.
Free to go to Carmenilla, to Luis, to safety. With Don
Alvaro dead, there was no further purpose to Mary
keeping her in Spain. Pray God she would soon recall
her, that Luis would come with her to England. . . .

An inner door opened, and a party of robed men
walked inside the room. Dolores went to them, and they

conversed in tones too low for Elena to hear. The monk named Fray Tomas she recognized as one of her more zealous inquisitors. He looked at her, his dark eyes burning with righteousness, eager in the name of God to ferret out all who erred.

"My child, you will be watched. We are still not wholly convinced of your sincerity. We want to believe, oh, yes, we would like to believe . . ." He made the sign of the cross over her, his thin, almost transparent hand like a shadowy claw in the candlelight.

Elena shuddered as he continued to stare at her, dread gripping her body. Fray Tomas exuded evil. She had always suspected that one slip would give him a welcome excuse to rack her, to administer the water torture or any number of other horrors he had described to her with relish.

Impatiently, Dolores Mendoza ushered the dark-robed men from the room. Again they were alone, but now the Mendoza woman seemed to have lost all interest in her. Elena sat in the corner, waiting to be told what to do next. She wondered if Luis had come to claim her, or if Cristobal would escort her to Carmenilla? Surely she would be given back her trunks. Everything had been confiscated at her arrest, and she had nothing but the clothes on her back.

Footsteps sounded outside the door, and Dolores hastened to open it, disappearing into the corridor.

"*Querido mio*, you have him?"

A muffled male voice answered her. There were more steps followed by a second male voice. Elena leaned back against the tooled leather paneling and tried to think about what she would do now.

"Soon, my love, you'll be mine in the sight of both God and man," promised Dolores huskily.

Silence followed, then whispering and smothered

laughter. Elena guessed Dolores must be kissing someone. This must be the man she was shortly to marry.
Closing her eyes, Elena tried again to concentrate, to
form some plan.

"Ah, you are the most wonderful lover in the world.
I'd move heaven and earth to keep you beside me,"
Dolores said, opening the door again.

Steps echoed over the room's polished floor.

"Come, Dolores, this isn't the time, or the place,"
replied a man irritably. Dolores snorted with indignation, her skirts swishing as she clacked across the bare
floor.

The man's voice sounded vaguely familiar. Elena sat
up and opened her eyes. Blinking rapidly, she tried to
focus. The two lighted candelabras cast grotesque
shadows dancing through a blazing halo. Finally Elena
made out two figures—Dolores Mendoza and a man in
a long black cloak. The man stepped inside the pool
of candlelight, his hair dazzling like beaten gold. Then,
as he turned toward her, Elena's breath caught in her
throat. The instant cry of delight she had formed upon
seeing Luis died on her lips as she saw his hand lying
possessively close to the magnificent swelling inside
Dolores Mendoza's black velvet bodice. Now, as
Dolores pressed her full red lips against his, Luis swiftly
embraced her.

Sickened by what she saw, Elena squeezed her eyes
shut. Surely her mind wandered, or perhaps her sight
had been affected by all that time in perpetual darkness. Again she opened her weak eyes, praying she
would find the room empty. The only change was that
now Cristobal stood in the doorway, his black eyes
glittering with malice as he looked at the couple standing
before the hearth.

"So, Don Luis, it is you I have to thank for my

release?''

"You are my *estanciero*. I have need of you at Carmenilla—besides, we both know you're innocent.''

"You disappoint me, Don Luis. I'd thought you rescued me out of brotherly love.''

Luis's mouth tightened in his hard face. "Brotherly love has always been in short supply between us. Enough talk, let us be on our way. Where is . . . where is . . . your . . . woman?''

How hard it was for him to get out that question, to publicly acknowledge Cristobal's interest in Elena. Luis strode toward the bullfighter; in his outstretched hand lay Cristobal's glittering knives.

"If you'll promise not to cut out my heart, I'll give you back your knives,'' he said with a feeble attempt at humor. Eyes narrowed, Luis directed his gaze down the gloomy corridor behind Cristobal, wondering where they were keeping Elena. He had not seen her all morning. Finally turning to Dolores, he demanded gruffly, "Well, where's the woman?''

Dolores smiled slyly as she motioned toward the dim corner. "Both you men must be blind. She's been here all the time.''

Luis froze, the twin blades quivering in his hand. Sickened, he saw Dolores lead a cloaked figure from the gloomy corner, and his heart swooped into his belly. Dear God, she had been there all along, had seen, heard . . .

"Doña Elena! I'd no idea you were there,'' he said in a strangled voice.

Cristobal stepped forward, his arms outstretched. "Elena *mia*,'' he cried jubilantly, "we're free as the air.''

Luis winced as he watched Cristobal embrace Elena. Of course it was necessary—he had made such a point of calling her Cristobal's woman. It would have seemed most unusual had he not embraced her. Yet it did not make it any easier to watch.

Elena stood in a trance, unable to fully take in this morning's events. Freedom, so long cherished, at last had been granted. But it was that other heart-rending sight that rendered her speechless. Never in a thousand years had she thought to see the man she loved caressing another, enjoying another's kisses. She had endured the sight of him with Leonora, being forced to accept that unpleasant fact. Besides, Luis had so eloquently pleaded his cause . . .

Luis grasped her shoulder, propelling her to the door.

"Don't leave Toledo just yet *doña*," cautioned Dolores. "Fray Tomas asks that you remain within—"

"Easy striking distance of the Holy Office," Luis completed savagely. "Are the prisoners free or not?"

"Perhaps paroled would be a better description," offered Dolores, hurrying to catch up with him.

"No, Dolores, I'll attend to matters now."

Surprised, Dolores stopped, angry questions springing to her lips.

Luis was in no mood to fence with words. He had to get Elena away from here, had to explain that what she had witnessed did not mean what she suspected. And how was he to manage that feat? One glance at her stricken face told him she had already put the worst construction on that chance incident. Grimly, he had to admit that he could not blame her. Damn Dolores for her thoughtlessness; had he not known otherwise, he would have thought the maneuver deliberately planned.

"Where are you taking them?" Dolores called, coming out into the corridor.

"The inn close to the cathedral. I'll contact you

tomorrow.'' Then, before she could protest further, Luis took Elena's arm and marched her down the corridor. Dolores would have followed had not Fray Tomas been stalking toward them. It was the first time in his life Luis had been pleased to see the old vulture.

''Ah, Don Luis, I see you have your *estanciero*. I trust Doña Dolores told you our terms?''

''We'll be at the inn close to the cathedral, Fray Tomas, should you need to reach me.''

The brother nodded and passed them. Taking Dolores's arm, he took her with him back inside the room and shut the door.

When Elena stumbled blindly on the stair, Luis and Cristobal caught at her arms, united in a common cause.

''If it's agreeable, Don Luis, I'll spend the night in my own house,'' Cristobal said as they made their way toward the cathedral through the narrow congested streets.

''Whatever you wish. Don't leave Toledo.''

''I assure you, I'll be most visible.''

Aye, in all the *tavernas* and whorehouses in town, Luis added silently. Still, he did not care what Cristobal did, for he had a far more pressing concern. Dear God, how was he to explain what Elena had seen? Even if he told her the truth, he doubted she would accept it.

The ancient inn bowed out over the narrow cobbled street, its facade adorned with delicate stone fretwork and narrow Moorish columns of twisted stone. The entranceway was brilliant with cobalt blue tiles; the ceiling honeycombed with filigreed stone.

''I'll have water sent up for washing. I managed to reclaim one of your trunks, Elena. Your room's at the head of the stair.''

Numbly, she heard Luis's voice, saw the concern on his face, but all she could think about was his hand under

Dolores Mendoza's breast. Again she heard the woman's sultry crooning praise—"You are the most wonderful lover in the world"—the sentence dashing all her hopes to bits. There was nothing left. Her home was far across the ocean, her aging patron dead, her Queen had forsaken her and even her brother no longer cared enough to write. Yet all those things she could have endured had not that final crushing blow been dealt—the man she loved was untrue!

Chapter Nineteen

Externally, the warm scented bath soothed and comforted her, but Elena knew nothing could ease the ache in her heart. Clean and decently clad, she felt more able to face the world. Dressed in russet velvet over an undergown of cream damascene, she again looked like Elena Locke, though inside she doubted she was ever capable of feeling quite the same again. A maid from the inn had tried without success to dress her hair after it had been washed and dried. In exasperation Elena had finally thrust the curling mass inside a brown velvet French hood edged with cream satin. Now she was ready to face him.

Down the narrow stairs she went, feeling as if she went to her doom. Luis had said he would be waiting for her in a private room at the rear of the inn. She hoped Cristobal would not be there, for she needed to speak to Luis alone, to settle once and for all this matter between them. She walked down the narrow white-washed stone passage to the rear of the inn, wishing herself a thousand miles away. Steeling herself for battle, Elena was prepared to discount the easy explanation she suspected Luis would present. Didn't he always attempt to soothe her, to sway her to his way of thinking? Likely honeyed lies would drip from his lips.

Elena stiffened her shoulders, her mouth set in a grim, determined line. There he was, seated at a table, waiting for her. On the point of entering the room, she finally panicked, longing to flee so that she need not face the truth. But she forced her feet forward—she had never been a coward!

"Elena, sweetheart, how lovely you look."

The softness of his expression wrenched her heart. Stiffly, she smiled. "You need not have waited for me," she said, indicating the untouched food.

"I wasn't hungry. Sit down."

Luis drew out a high-backed chair, and Elena sat erect, spreading her russet skirts about her. And she waited. There was so much tension between them, the room virtually crackled.

"They brought me word of your arrest just after I'd docked at Cadiz. I rode here as fast as I could—dear God, I couldn't believe you'd been arrested! Thank heaven you weren't harmed. Forgive me, *querida*. I didn't mean to desert you. I thought to take a short voyage to help pass the time till you returned to Carmenilla." He stopped, aware of her grim expression.

"What is she to you?" Elena demanded. And they both knew to whom she referred.

"Years ago Dolores and I were lovers."

At his easy explanation, something snapped in Elena's brain. How dare he calmly say that, as if what she had witnessed this morning had never happened? Her eyes flashed tawny yellow in anger. "Stop it, Luis! Don't play me for a fool. I didn't ask about years ago—I'm concerned with now."

He looked down at his hands, wincing at the ill-concealed pain and anger in her voice. "Very well, suppose I owe you an explanation—"

"And damn you, Luis, make it the truth!"

Unable to face her, he rose from his chair and went to the window. Across the alley a craftsman hammered on an anvil, pounding gold into an elaborate damascened sword. Focusing his attention on the man's brawny arms, Luis began. "I went to Dolores to obtain your release—the Holy Office wouldn't listen to me. Her brother is aide to the Grand Inquisitor—"

"So she told me," Elena interrupted sharply. Turning in her seat, she addressed his broad back, angry that he dared not face her. "After what I saw this morning, don't insult my intelligence by pretending she granted this favor on the strength of past relationships."

"Had you been patient, you'd have learned I had no intention of deceiving you," Luis said stiffly. He stared at the leather-aproned craftsman, every blow to the anvil a hammer to his heart. "Elena, please believe me when I say Dolores means nothing to me. I love you. I'd do anything to save you. Without Dolores's help you might have burned at the stake. We have her to thank for your freedom—"

"And for stealing the man I love."

"For Christ's sake—I wasn't stolen!"

"Nay, from the look of it the pleasure was all yours. I saw your wandering hands, the eager way you—"

"Damn it, Elena, enough!" Angrily Luis rounded on her, fists clenched. "I'd have done anything to set you free. Dolores Mendoza was an easy penance."

"Penance—Oh, God, I can listen to no more of this," she cried, choking. Leaping to her feet, Elena tried to run from the room, but he caught her and swung her back in the chair.

"Sit down, damn you, and hear me out!"

Elena fought for control, gasping for breath. Luis

towered menacingly over her, so angry that he was
white about the mouth. Imprisoned as she was, she had
little choice but to listen.

"I warn you, Elena, she's a powerful, jealous
woman," Luis began, his voice low. "Do not cross
her. She considers herself in love with me."

"Aye, she told me you were soon to wed."

Luis spun away, throwing up his hands in exasperation. "That's a figment of her imagination. How can
I wed her? You know I'm married to Leonora."

"Did you promise her marriage?"

Pacing the floor, Luis refused to answer. He was
handling this badly. If only he had known Elena was
in the room this morning, none of this would have been
necessary.

At last he said, "I promised much to save your life."

"So you did promise to marry her!"

Wearily he thrust his hair off his damp brow,
wondering how to tell her what he knew he must. He
owed her that much, though he wished to God he could
have kept it secret. "In return for her promise to set
you free, I did what she asked. I had no other choice."

Elena leaped to her feet. Eyes narrowed, she grasped
the sleeve of his doublet. "And that was?"

Again he could not look at her, unable to face the
accusation he knew was in her tawny eyes. "I love you.
Whatever else I do doesn't change that."

And she understood what he was trying to say.
Blanching, Elena gazed at him beseechingly, looking
into his pale blue eyes glittering in the sunshine reflected
off the courtyard. She had asked for the truth. Now she
wished she had not.

"Even when you make love to another?" she
whispered, the words falling like lead on her heart.

"There was nothing of love about it. But yes—even

then. Oh, Elena, I'm sorry. I never intended you to know.''

"Of that I'm sure.''

"It's not like it's been with us.''

"Enlighten me, Luis. Tell me how it was.''

"I love you, Elena. No one else matters. I can say no more.''

Her heart thundering, her weak legs shaking with emotion, Elena grasped the windowsill to steady herself. When Luis tried to take her in his arms, she thrust him away, eyes blazing. "No. Don't touch me, not after being with her! To think I prayed you'd rescue me, that you'd find a way. Never once did I think my freedom was being paid for in another woman's bed.''

"That was her price,'' he repeated dully, knowing he had lost. "I did what I must to set you free so we could be together.''

"Do you take me for a fool? She has no intention of handing you over to me—she considers you hers.''

"She doesn't know about us.''

Shocked by his revelation, Elena's head snapped up. That explained much. Dolores Mendoza believed she was Cristobal's woman. "And you, desirous of pleasuring yourself, didn't dream of enlightening her.''

"Not if I expected her help. Have sense, woman—would you have freed my mistress? Dolores is no fool. I—''

"No, and neither am I. How convenient that she named a price so dear to your heart. Well, Luis, you're free to return to your panting obligation. In the past I was forced to accept Leonora, lulled by the tale of your loveless marriage.''

"It's the truth.''

"After today's discovery, forgive me for wondering how much is truth and how much convenience.''

Luis seized her arm, wrenching her toward him. "Stop it! I saved your life. *How* is not important."

"Not to you perhaps—to me it's devastating."

"Would you have had me stay meekly faithful while you burned at the stake? I thought not."

Luis glared at her bent head, knowing she wept. So unjust had been her reaction, and so deep his own guilt, he felt anger instead of tenderness. Grasping her chin, he forced Elena to look at him while he ground out, "I took her not for pleasure, but to buy your freedom. And that is the truth of it."

"The truth?" she repeated scornfully, trying to keep the quaver from her voice. "Surely you aren't pretending your noble sacrifice was without pleasure."

"We'll discuss it no more," he avowed angrily, crossing to the table. "Dolores Mendoza belongs to the past. Come, you must eat something. I hope to get permission for us to leave for Carmenilla in the morning."

"No."

He paused, a chunk of bread and honey in his hand. "What do you mean, no?"

"I'm not going to Carmenilla—I'm not going anywhere with you ever again."

"*Dios mio*—I don't believe this. Have sense, Elena. What is done is done."

"Curse all you want. My mind's made up," she declared stubbornly. Her heart was consumed with pain as she whispered, "You may sleep with Dolores tonight and every night—"

"Stop it!"

"You sound angry," she croaked, licking tears from her lips. "You should thank me for making your life easier. There's no further need for deception, no need to pretend you lie with her out of obligation. Go, Luis, enjoy your whore. I'm giving you your freedom."

After delivering that final tearful declaration, she fled from the room. His steps came thundering after her. Desperately, Elena wrenched open the nearest door and darted outside. Catching her toe in the hem of her gown, she stumbled over the uneven cobblestones as she tried to escape him. Luis captured her easily and wrenched her about. Blinking rapidly to clear her vision, she saw his face was a grim, angry mask.

"You're not going anywhere."

"I'll seek lodging in town. Fray Tomas suggested somewhere I could make restitution for my sins—Santa Maria la Blanca. It's a refuge for fallen women. Except for the fact that he accused the wrong man of leading me into sin, perhaps he is right."

"I'll not allow you to go there like some woman off the streets."

"You have not the choice."

"Elena, sweet, if you won't come home with me, at least let me arrange lodgings in Toledo. You'll be comfortably housed. In time I know you'll see things differently," he soothed, swallowing his anger. Elena was close to hysteria, her wild eyes, her rapid movements, all warned him to be careful. Though so far he had handled matters poorly, at least in this perhaps he could right the wrong. "Come, you've been through much."

"And I have you to thank, my darling, for giving the final *coup de grace*. You can imagine how much it cheered my heart to watch you fondling that woman. And now to know you paid for my freedom in her bed. How does it feel, Luis, to play the whore?"

Mustering what was left of her pride and dignity, Elena left him standing in the courtyard. She fought building grief, stumbling against the wall as she tried to negotiate the narrow passage, the steep stairs; the worn treads seemed never ending. Finally she reached the sanctity of her room and slammed the door. Hearing his steps on the stair, she quickly shot the bolt.

He thundered on the door, shaking it on its hinge. His angry voice demanded she open to him. She ignored his demands. Yet a few minutes later, as he continued to bang and shout, she realized it was foolish not to speak to him. He would never go away. In fact he was threatening to break down the door.

Raising herself on her elbow, Elena tried to find voice enough to end this horrid scene. "Luis, thank you for your sacrifice. Now go, please, leave me in peace. Your obligations to me are fulfilled. Tonight I'll stay here. Tomorrow I'll seek charity from the nuns."

"No, Elena, don't be a fool."

But she refused to enter into further conversation with him.

"All right, stay here the night," he said, finally relenting. "I'll be back at first light. Then we'll talk some sense."

Elena did not respond. A few minutes later she heard his heavy steps as he bounded down the stair to the accompaniment of groaning timbers. Then silence.

Dear God, at last! He had finally left her in peace. Fighting for breath, she tried in vain to stifle her tears. Too weak, too long deprived of comfort, she could not battle the pain. Burying her face in the pillow, Elena abandoned herself to deep, wracking sobs, awash in a river of grief as she mourned the loss of that which she had held so dear.

It was pitch-dark when she heard the rap on the door. Startled from sleep, she sat up quickly, her heart lurching. Luis was back. Yet surely it could not be dawn.

"Go away."

"Eh, *chica,* open the door. It's I."

Cristobal! Hastily thrusting her sweat-damp hair off her face, Elena fumbled in the darkness for her headdress before finally abandoning the search. The door latch was stiff. With a struggle she opened the door. Cristobal stood outside, holding a candle; in the wavering orange flame he looked dark as a Moor.

"No light? Surely you don't miss your cell," he joked, striding inside the room. Quickly he located two candles in terra-cotta holders and lit them from his own. "Well, shut the door. We don't want all the world to listen, do we?"

Obediently, Elena shut the door. Why was he here? Fear churned in the pit of her stomach as she realized her own vulnerability. Tonight Cristobal was finely dressed in a dull red velvet doublet and tights; gold rings glinted in his ears; his tall black boots had a gold design tooled in the leather. With his long hair combed back and falling over his collar, his fierce profile cast in grotesque shadow across the whitewashed wall, he reminded her of a pirate or an evil gypsy king.

"Pleased with what you see?" he asked, grinning at her stupefied expression. "This is the *real* Cristobal Santos, the man the people of Toledo know, not the subservient *estanciero* in peasant shirt and britches. Here I'm a man of substance. I've come to invite you to dine with me."

"Dine? Surely it's the middle of the night."

"Close to midnight, but no matter. We dine when we are hungry. After the sumptuous fare we've been used to of late, you must be hungry."

Elena forced a smile. "No, Cristobal, that's kind of you, but I don't feel well enough to go out."

He peered closely at her face, finding it blotchy with weeping.

"There's no need for tears. You're free now. This is a time for joy."

If he only knew. Elena took a deep breath, squaring her shoulders as her hand stole to tidy her unruly hair.

"Leave it. This way you look more like the gypsy girls I'm used to instead of a grand *señora*," said Cristobal with a grin.

"I can't come with you."

"Elena—*amita*, I've waited long for this night. The food grows cold."

"No, Cristobal. Thank you for your generosity."

"Tomorrow then?"

Taking a deep breath, Elena said, "Tomorrow I intend to seek shelter with the sisters of Santa Maria la Blanca."

Cristobal muttered an oath, his face darkening with anger. Leaping forward, he cried, "*Dios* . . . that bastard! Don Luis suggested you lodge there!"

"No." Amazed by his anger, she looked into his black eyes agleam in the golden candlelight. "Why should he suggest it?"

"I thought perhaps because we . . . we shared a cell. No matter. You can't go there. It's no place for you."

"I've little choice. The sisters will give me sanctuary until I have permission to go home. Surely the Inquisition won't deny me travel for long. Once I'm gone, I'll no longer be a thorn in their side."

When she said "home," he gasped, the reaction unconscious. Elena was touched.

"Oh, Cristobal, you can't imagine how much I long to go home to England," she whispered tearfully. And her weakness made her angry. Damn Luis for reducing her to this idiotic state! Damn him for betraying their love, for daring to try to reason with her about his affair with Dolores Mendoza.

Cristobal reached out to catch the tears trickling down her cheeks. "I understand. It's too soon after your ordeal. I should have realized—but I'm a man of action, not thought. Come, *amita*, come here."

Blindly she allowed him to comfort her, desperate for the warmth of another human being. Only after a few minutes, when that warmth became too comforting, did she withdraw. They were no longer in the cell, and the vow he had sworn to her did not bind him here. A curious expression played over his dark face as, with a lopsided grin, he released her.

"Ah, you've a long memory. But I suppose you have a right to be wary. My vow didn't extend to the entire city of Toledo, merely to the cells of the Inquisition."

Against her will, Elena gave a weak smile. "Thank you for being such a good friend to me, Cristobal. I never thought I'd be able to say this, but without you I don't think I could have endured."

He gave a nonchalant shrug, yet he did not deceive her. His expression revealed how immensely pleased he was with her praise.

"So, *chica*, life goes on. Are you going to act the poor downtrodden prisoner for the rest of your days?"

She shook her head, uncomfortably fumbling with her skirts, wishing he would leave. If only he knew the shattering events she had recently endured, he would have no need to question the state of her emotions.

"Where will you stay until you're given permission to travel?"

"I'll stay here tonight. Tomorrow I'll beg the sisters' charity."

Turning her back on him, Elena went to the open chest to find her hairbrush. Cristobal muttered something under his breath that she suspected was a curse, then suddenly he was beside her. Seizing her wrist, he turned her about, making her drop the hairbrush back in the trunk.

"Now listen, I own a modest house near the old Jewish quarter. It's not a grand fortress like Don Luis has, nor is it a sop thrown to me by my guilty father. I've purchased this property with my own sweat. For a gypsy I've not done bad, eh? Come, stay there until you're free to travel."

"I can't stay with you!"

"Why not? What if I promise to behave like a gentleman? How do you say it—you have no obligations to me. Of course, *chica*, if you ever change your mind, I'll welcome you with open arms," he added with a grin, unable to keep his true feelings hidden. "Doña Elena," he continued gravely, his voice trembling with suppressed emotion, "I have much love in my heart for you."

Elena gasped, her expression of shock so apparent, he laughed.

"Eh, it's not such a strange thing. You look as if a performing bear has just confessed his love for you." As he spoke, his amusement faded and his face took on a decidedly hostile expression.

Elena quickly tried to explain. "Cristobal, I've always known how you felt, only then I didn't think it had much to do with love."

"Well, I won't deny I want you—I always have. I'd be less of a man if I didn't want a lovely woman like you," he explained matter-of-factly. "You can safely live in my house. I promise not to rape you. Give me your decision tomorrow. My house is far more suitable for you than Santa Maria la Blanca, whatever our high-and-mighty don thinks."

Again he made that bitter assumption. "Cristobal, Don Luis has no idea we shared a cell."

He paused on his way to the door. "You didn't tell him?"

Elena shook her head. In the face of what Luis revealed, that fact had not seemed important.

"You don't know how much pleasure I'll get from enlightening him." Still chuckling at the thought, Cristobal opened the door. "Don Luis has always considered me a base gypsy without sense or refinement. This news might change—"

"Please, Cristobal, wouldn't it be better to keep that to ourselves?"

"I won't pretend I took you—there's no need. Don Luis's own imagination will be punishment enough."

Long after he had gone, Cristobal's parting words rang in her ears. Naturally, Luis would assume the worst given Cristobal's reputation with women. The realization gave her a flicker of warmth. This was a weapon to wield against him, a means to extract small payment for her own hurt. How much more wounding would it be if she accepted Cristobal's offer of hospitality? Luis's jealousy would know no bounds. In taking that action, she would convince him Cristobal was her lover, and his near hatred of his gypsy half brother would merely fuel the fire.

As Elena paced the small room, her desire for vengeance mounted. Her heart ached for payment for the pain she had suffered. Luis had betrayed her. Let him suffer the heartbreak of betrayal. Let him think she, too, had found solace for her loneliness as he had done in Dolores Mendoza's arms. To think he had tried to insult her intelligence by suggesting he took no pleasure in it, that lovemaking had been the price of her freedom. One look at the Mendoza woman abrim with sensuality, coupled with her knowledge of Luis's nature made the suggestion ludicrous. Undoubtedly, the pious reminder that he made love to Dolores merely to save Elena from the fires of the *auto da fé* had gone a long way to absolve him of guilt. That outlook reflected the curious paradox of Spanish conscience, where enforced piety was ever at war with an inborn sensuality.

When Elena opened the door to Luis in the early morning light, she almost wavered in her resolve to give an eye for an eye. Dressed in embroidered dark green velvet so dense the color appeared black, his gleaming hair in bright contrast to his clothes, he was achingly handsome. The heavy gold chain around his neck flashed fire as it caught the rays of the rising sun, which burnished his springy hair until it shone like a cap of gold.

Her heart lurched and skipped a beat as he smiled at her. Elena swallowed, steeling herself against his charm. She was already dressed for outdoors, her belongings packed. When he saw this, Luis smiled in relief, his eyes brightening expectantly. Tentatively he held out his hand, that seductive softness transforming his face. How blue his eyes, how tempting his lips— and how easily he lied, she reminded heself grimly. She dared not touch him.

"Good morning, Luis."

"God be praised, you've changed your mind," he said, stepping inside the room.

"Yes," she said, watching him as he bent to hoist the chest. "I'm not going to Santa Maria la Blanca, after all."

"See, I told you—a little time, some sleep . . . oh, sweetheart, you don't know how happy you've made me."

Elena clasped her hands so tight they hurt. "I'm going to stay with Cristobal."

Luis paused in the act of swinging the trunk from the

rushes, frozen like a statue. Slowly he turned, his face parchment white. "What did you say?" he croaked.

"I said I'm going to stay with Cristobal—only until I have permission to travel," she could not help adding, though she wished she had held her tongue. Let him sweat, let him suffer, she thought vindictively, trying to quiet her racing heart. Be calm, she admonished, the victory's yours.

"You're mad!"

"Why? Do you think you're the only person who grows lonely these nights? There's obviously no room for me in Dolores Mendoza's house—I doubt she'd welcome a *ménage à trois*—though you might find it a fillip for a jaded appetite. This way I won't be a burden to you. The Inquisition will be happy, and Cristobal most assuredly will be happy."

He moved menacingly toward her. She watched him as if in a dream, unable to move though the sheer white anger on his face warned her to flee. Gripping her shoulders, Luis shook her until her headdress came loose, until her hair spilled down her back.

"Damn you, Elena, don't be such a fool! Don't do this to me—not now, not after all we've been through," he cried in an agonized voice.

"It's done already. A boy is coming for my trunk. Go home, Luis, perhaps Leonora wonders what you're doing these nights. Poor woman—at least I'll *know*."

Stopping short of hitting her, he gradually let his hands drop to his sides. His face hard, his mouth a grim slash above his tense jaw, he rasped, "Does this mean you don't love me anymore?"

Unable to answer that terrible untruth, Elena turned away.

"Answer me!"

"It means I'm going to live with Cristobal. Make of

it what you will," she said, trying to push her hair inside her headdress. "At least I'll not be in the company of common streetwalkers. You should be pleased. You're a strange man, Luis. Of late there's no way to please you. Granted, Dolores Mendoza may be to blame for that . . ." She broke off her taunting speech as she saw two men approaching. The men nodded at her, and she pointed behind her to the trunk. "Good-bye, Luis," she said, stepping toward the door.

"Elena, don't do this. Give it time . . ." He stopped, his painful words broken off, thrust like a jagged sword into his heart. Elena had deftly skipped before the servants, placing their lumbering bodies between them.

"This is entirely my own decision. Cristobal had nothing to do with it."

Numbly he watched her go downstairs, still trying to thrust her curling hair inside her stiff headdress. She stepped through the doorway into the orange sunlight skimming the tiled rooftops, and a great lurch turned his stomach upside down. He could not believe what he had heard.

Luis stumbled to the head of the stairs, determined to go after her and bring her back. She turned to look at him one final time, her face remote, bleak in her pain. And he held back. He had lost her. Dear God in heaven, how had it happened? How?

Finally he clattered down the stairs, taking them two at a time. She was standing in the courtyard, watching the men put her trunk on a handcart. Sensing his presence, she turned. For a long time their eyes met and held, hers flickering yellow, hard, fierce; his blue and soft with pain. Her lips parted as though she was about to speak, and he stepped forward expectantly. Then she deliberately turned her back on him.

Had it been his imagination? Just before she turned

away, he could have sworn her eyes glistened with tears. Injured pride kept him from following the little procession as it wound its way down the alley and past the cathedral. Fierce anger bubbled inside him as he considered what she had said. Damn Cristobal! He wanted to slit his throat. To think he had expended such effort to free them. And for what? To send her into that gypsy bastard's arms. Someday he would have his vengeance. Yet right now the thought of soothing, numbing red wine was most appealing.

Smashing aside the inn's wooden door, Luis strode inside, yelling for service.

Chapter Twenty

The hot wind stirred the tall dried grasses, rustling the browned leaves and swirling the dust.

Leonora rode slowly along the spine of the ridge, fighting tears. She felt completely deserted. There had been no news of either that wretched Englishwoman or her beloved Luis. Everything had gone terribly wrong. She never dreamed Luis would get the creature released. Why did he not send word? Three weeks ago she had received a brief note telling her the prisoners were free, but must remain in Toledo. Since then— nothing!

Angrily she picked up speed, galloping over the dry ground, sending up great clouds of dust. It was hot today, far too hot for early spring. The lonely sameness of each day without Luis made her feel like a prisoner. Doubtless he sported with his Englishwoman in Toledo, giving no thought to his wife. She had suffered much of late, enduring blinding headaches without any sympathy from her husband, not even one line inquiring about her health.

Reining in, Leonora ran her hand across her brow, wiping away trickling sweat. All morning she had been feeling queasy. At times her vision blurred, creating

waves over the brown winter plain. Had Luis been more
amorous these past months, she would have thought she
was pregnant. Dear God, how much longer must she
wait for a child? Countless Masses had been offered, a
sea of candles lit, all to no purpose. Heaven seemed
deaf to her pleas.

Weak tears trickled down her dusty cheeks.
Viciously, Leonora dug her spurs in the horse's flanks,
thundering over the open fields. The wind blew away
her tears of self-pity, stinging her eyes, her cheeks.
Suddenly she pulled on the reins, bringing the animal
to a sliding, skidding halt. Again her eyes blurred,
creating those shimmering waves until the undulating
miles ahead looked like the ocean. A figure had
appeared from nowhere. Who could it be? This land
was uninhabited; no local peasant would even approach
this cursed spot.

The clouds of dust gradually settled. Leonora wiped
her face on her sleeve, positive someone walked ahead.
There, still as a sentinel on the ridge, a dark figure stood
outlined against the blazing sun. Turning her horse's
head about, Leonora followed the track up the ridge.

"You—what are you doing here?" she shouted,
unreasonably angry at having her solitude disturbed.

There was no reply. Again she shouted, drawing ever
closer. Suddenly her horse shied. Whinnying in fright,
the animal pawed the air and danced backwards. With
a curse, Leonora held him in check. Now she could
see the interloper was a gypsy woman swathed in a
shawl.

"You—get off this land! This is de los Santos land,"
she shouted, stiffly regal in the saddle, her crop raised
to strike should the creature prove abusive.

The gaunt figure turned and started toward her, her
black hair blowing in the wind, her faded crimson shawl

blending with the indeterminate colors of her tattered gown. A few feet away the woman stopped and raised her head.

Leonora gasped, a bolt of fear shooting through her body. The woman fixed her with a look of sheer hatred, the malicious black eyes old as sin in her gaunt gypsy face. The wide gold bands in the woman's ears reflected the sunlight, blinding, flashing like great beacons until Leonora could no longer see. With a cry of distress, she put her hand to her face, beset by dizziness. Nausea rose in her throat; her ears roared. Toppling sideways, Leonora grabbed her horse's mane, trying to regain her balance. All was in vain. The jarring impact of dusty earth suddenly met her face; she tasted grit in her mouth.

Finding itself riderless, her frightened horse bolted. She called out weakly, but the thud of fleeing hooves told her she had been ignored.

Leonora lay motionless on the barren ground, terribly aware of her thudding heart. The sun's hot rays beat down relentlessly on her unprotected face. Her tongue was swollen in her parched mouth. She must have water. She felt so ill out here alone with no one to aid her.

Out of the corner of her eye she saw the gypsy woman's bare feet less than a yard away. With renewed hope she stretched out her hands, pleading for help. "Water. Please, help me, I'm Leonora de los Santos— the *señora* who owns the land. Don Luis is my husband . . . please, gypsy, help me."

The gypsy woman swished her skirts out of Leonora's weak grasp and spun on her heel, scornfully kicking a shower of dust in Señora de los Santos's face. The last sound the Señora of Carmenilla heard was the gypsy's sharp, evil laughter as she walked away, leaving her to die alone.

The wind blew chill as Luis stood bareheaded,
listening to the monotonous Latin verses. His wife had
been buried in the family vault in the grounds of the
chapel of *Nuestra Señora de Carmenilla*. The shock of
Leonora's sudden death had still not worn off. He had
been dining in Toledo when they brought him the news.
Riding hatless in the unseasonal heat had been the
physician's verdict, yet Luis could not wholly accept that
explanation for her death. Leonora was a child of this
land. The heat never bothered her. Likely it had been
some malady the physician lacked the skill to detect,
for her maid had said the señora had not been well
recently. Or then again, could it have been that accursed
spot? Leonora had been found beside the ruined hovel
where Cristobal's gypsy mother had died. The local
peasants never ventured there, for they swore the gypsy
still wandered the land. It was nonsense, of course, but
every time he thought about Cristobal's dead mother,
a chill went down his spine. Superstitious nonsense,
Luis repeated, automatically making the sign of the
cross. He discovered the prayers were at an end.

Luis still had much unfinished business in Toledo.
In fact, he had spent much of his time there since Elena
deserted him, hoping she would finally come to her
senses. As yet, that hope had been in vain. Luis had
confronted Cristobal only once, discovering at that time
he had somehow managed to ingratiate himself into
Elena's cell. It was all Luis could do not to plunge a
dagger in Cristobal's treacherous gypsy heart. Since
then he had avoided his half brother, not trusting himself
to keep his hands off him.

Mechanically moving forward, Luis laid a great
bouquet of white lilies on the cold marble slab; then
he turned and walked quickly toward his horse. The

other mourners watched him respectfully, allowing him his privacy, for clearly he mourned. Sadness was apparent in his every step.

Luis thundered away, taking the road south to Toledo. And he smiled bitterly. Aye, he mourned, but it was the loss of Elena, not his wife, that stilled his heart.

Laughter and singing filled Toledo's narrow cobbled streets.

Elena leaned over the edge of the wrought iron balcony of this tall, narrow house, the better to see the colorful procession passing below. Gaudy silken banners worked in gold and silver flapped in the warm breeze. A gloriously dressed and bejeweled religious effigy was being borne aloft. Singing girls scattered handfuls of scented flowers on the cobbles as the dazzling figure of Our Lady of Carmenilla was carried past. Barefoot children skipped along behind the effigy, chanting as they passed beneath the balcony, their childish trebles echoing between the tall stucco houses. Behind the singing children walked a dozen pretty young women clad in their magnificent best, brilliant red carnations fastened in their black hair. The procession marked the feast day of Our Lady of Carmenilla. This was the first festival following Holy Week. Now that somber Lent was past, all Spain rejoiced with singing, feasting, dancing in the streets and the inevitable bullfights.

Elena rested her arms on the cool iron railing, watching the colorful parade without actually seeing it. As usual, her thoughts turned to Luis, and she quickly tried to force her mind to other things. She must not think about him; the pain of his betrayal was still too fresh. Last month the shocking news of Leonora's sudden death had reached them. By some quirk of fate

Dolores Mendoza's prayers would now be granted. Luis was free to marry her. Daily, Elena awaited news of their impending nuptials. She had even asked Cristobal if he had heard that Don Luis planned to remarry, but he said he had not. She must not take false comfort from that—Luis would hardly give his half brother the good tidings. No communication passed between them now, all necessary instructions being relayed through a third party. And she knew she was the cause of their final rift.

The sweet perfumed warmth of April was spreading across the land. Warm sunlight stretched golden fingers along Toledo's narrow streets and forgotten alleys. Each evening the populace paraded about the plazas in their best, meeting and greeting friends as they enjoyed the new season.

Elena saw Luis and Dolores walking arm in arm near the cathedral, the shocking sight rendering her motionless. She had been quickly overcome by a hot wave of nausea and she was forced to retreat into the blue shadows of the cathedral walls, where she quickly parted with her dinner. From that day on she had purposely stayed away from any place or event where she expected them to be. To be confronted by Luis's open infidelity was more than she could endure.

The culmination of this festival would be a grand tournament and bullfight in the central plaza, which Cristobal had made her promise to attend. Elena was dreading the event. All the city notables would be present—it was too much to expect Luis would not take Dolores to see the spectacle.

Even the thought of watching the bulls slaughtered made Elena's stomach queasy. The bloodthirstiness of the age was curiously lacking in her makeup. Memories of a hideous bearbaiting vastly enjoyed by Mary's courtiers still made her shudder. Bear and bullbaiting, blood-spattered cockfights and public executions, all considered grand entertainment by her peers, chilled her to the bone.

During the first bullfight of the season, wherein Cristobal dedicated his kill to her, she had felt sick. It had been nothing but a noisy melee of galloping horses, shouting men carrying gleaming lances and hideous screams of pain as gored horses went down. The poor beasts thrashed in their death throes, entrails dragging in the dirt. The smell of blood was everywhere.

Elena had begged permission to leave the bullfight, aware of Cristobal's anger. Grudgingly, he allowed the servants to escort her back to his house. Yet later, bristling with anger, he rounded on her, accusing her of dishonoring him by her weakness. Never again was she to leave a bullfight. All her arguments were overturned. If the sight of blood nauseated her, then she should close her eyes; if the screams of pain offended her, then she should stop her ears. He did not understand. Long ago she had given up trying to explain. She would attend the bullfight as promised, praying for strength to endure. Most Spanish women appeared to enjoy the spectacle, demonstrating the same fervor they displayed for religious ceremonies. Those dreaded *autos da fé* likely sparked a similar response.

Cruel, pious and sensual, the complex nature of the Spaniard often eluded her. She had decided Luis was a true son of Spain, for those same emotions ran hot in his veins. How could he be so tender, so passionate, yet suddenly turn heartless and cruel. . . .

"It is not a grand spectacle?"

Startled by the unexpected voice, Elena spun about to discover Cristobal had come silently to stand behind her.

"I think they'll celebrate all night."

"That's quite possible. Elena, will you dine out with me tonight? This could be my last night—"

"Don't say that."

"It's the truth, whether you wish to face it or not. For one who fights the bulls it's always that way," he explained quietly.

They went back inside the room. Bars of orange light splashed the pale walls, but Cristobal's face remained in shadow. Elena had noticed a strange intensity to his hard angular features that made her shiver in apprehension. So far he had respected her wishes to be treated as a guest within his house. Only once had he come close to destroying her trust. That had been on the night before he fought the bulls during Holy Week. He had seized her and kissed her savagely, releasing her only after she put up a violent struggle. Cristobal apologized profusely, but the incident stood between them. Realizing this might be another such night, she moved warily away from him.

"Still afraid of me?"

"Should I be?"

Cristobal shrugged and grinned, though his eyes were hard. Her question had not pleased him. "I'm only human, Elena," was all he said.

He went to the table and poured wine. Bringing back two crystal goblets, he handed one to her.

"Let us drink to bravery and honor during tomorrow's ordeal," he said, lightly touching the gold-rimmed goblets.

His words evoked an unexpected chill as Elena realized this time tomorrow he could be dead. "Is there really that much danger?" she asked in a small, tight voice.

Quirking his eyebrow in astonishment at her question,

Cristobal laughed scornfully. "Ah, spoken like a true Englishwoman. Danger—*Cristos*, we walk hand in hand, he and I. I thrive on danger, *amita*. Didn't you know that? If there was no danger involved, I wouldn't fight the bulls. Now, no more of it. You will be there tomorrow? You promised."

"Yes, I promised."

"For you, I will excel. You know, *chica*, I've been considering something for a long time—someday I will fight the bulls on foot like the ancient gladiators. Just me, the bull, and a sword. What do you think?"

"No! Don't be a fool," she cried, her face paling. "You'll be killed."

He laughed and drained his glass. "I hope not. Imagine what a spectacular feat that would be—the great Cristobal Santos meeting *el toro* on his own ground. I've long had visions of that glorious day. And you are going to make it possible for me, Elena. For you, I'll have the courage of ten men."

His hand stole to her neck, slipping up into her hair. Moving her head, Elena tried to elude his touch. Gently stroking the nape of her neck, he rested his blunt, brown-skinned hand on her shoulder. An unusually soft expression transformed his hard face, for Cristobal's features were usually a study of hawklike ferocity.

"No, Cristobal, please don't," she protested at last, when his fingers strayed dangerously close to the swelling of her breast. "Remember our agreement."

"You mean your agreement, *chica*. To tell the truth, I'm getting damned tired of it," he retorted sharply, but he removed his hand. "You don't know what you're missing."

He walked to the door. Pausing in the doorway, he gave her a strange, tortured look. "I'd hate to die without ever having tasted you," he said as he walked into the corridor.

His parting words still haunted Elena as she undressed
for bed. She wished there were a bolt on the door. In
the beginning she had gone to great lengths to guard
her virtue, pushing a chest behind the door. Then, if
Cristobal went back on his word, she would at least
have warning. Lately she had given up that practice,
though tonight she was tempted to return to it.

She lay in the darkness, puzzling over Cristobal's
strange mood. Had it been solely because tomorrow
he faced the bulls, or was he simmering with resentment because she continued to reject his advances?
Though they had never been lovers, she knew he
considered her his. Her understanding friend from the
cold dark cell and this man of violent moods were two
separate beings. Once they had emerged into the light,
he had abandoned that newfound personality, becoming
once more the Cristobal Santos she did not like. At the
time it had not been generally known that he had been
arrested by the Inquisition. Once the news was made
public, the crowds welcomed back their idol with
renewed enthusiasm, accepting the gossip that a
woman's jealousy had put their darling behind bars.

Elena wondered if Cristobal had approached her as
the same caring friend who had encouraged her during
that black time, would she have welcomed his lovemaking? Perhaps it was as well he had reverted to his
arrogant, swaggering self. That way her choice was
simplified. When she rejected him, he had exploded
in rage before stalking out of the house in search of
an eager woman in the *tavernas* that dotted this quarter.
Yet how much longer could this explosive situation
continue? Daily she prayed she would soon be free to
leave Toledo, to leave Spain, where she had buried all
her dreams of love.

Tears burned Elena's eyes when she considered that not once had Luis tried to contact her, though he was aware she was living in Cristobal's house. He must find Dolores most satisfying.

The painful indulgence of memory was so sharp, she felt physically ill. How much she had loved him—still loved him. Licking tears from her lips, Elena forced herself to honesty. Whatever Luis did, that feeling would never die. It was as if, of all the men in the world, he was the one destined to bring her joy. And pain . . . dear God, and pain. For, of all the men alive, he had brought her that in full measure.

After she lay tossing for some time, Elena finally fell asleep, the singing in the streets, the bursts of laughter and the strumming of lutes all fading into the background.

Suddenly a shaft of light spilled across the bed. Elena stirred, aware of the unexpected brightness on her face. Moonlight flooded through the high, arched window, casting a giant shadow of iron railings over the wall. All was quiet, Toledo had finally gone to sleep.

An unexpected movement in the room captured her attention. Turning her head on the pillow, Elena tried to pierce the gloom. The dim light of a votive candle burning in a niche beside the door mingled with the moonbeams. She could easily identify the tall carved clothes press, the ebony crucifix, the fringed shawl hanging on the wall beneath a lute—then ice shot through her veins. A tall, unfamiliar shadow fell beside the chest, motionless and unmistakably human.

"Cristobal," she whispered, knowing before she spoke it was he.

"Dare I hope your dreams were of me?" he asked thickly, stepping from the shadows. He was drunk.

Elena gasped as the silver sheen of bare skin shone

in the moonlight flooding through the window. Clutching the covers, she pulled them up defensively to her chin.

"Why are you here?"

"Oh, come, *amita*, surely you can guess."

It was exactly as she had feared. Warily Elena moved to the side of the bed nearest to the door. With one bound Cristobal imprisoned her on the mattress, his weight making the bed sway like a boat.

"No," she cried, thrusting him away.

"I haven't touched you yet."

"Get out. You're drunk."

"Not that drunk, Elena *mia*. Even with a few jugs of wine down me you'll never find a better man."

"Please, Cristobal, go back to your room. We agreed."

"And now I disagree. Damn you—tomorrow I might be no more than slaughtered meat. Would you deny a dying man the ultimate pleasure?"

"That's a clever argument, but not good enough. Get out."

"Then would you deny me the pleasure I was born to receive?"

His voice had dropped, his speech turning unusually poetic.

When Elena tried to slip from the bed Cristobal quickly imprisoned her under the covers. He tried to kiss her. Elena fought him, shouting for help until he clamped his hand suffocatingly over her mouth.

"Stop it! You're spoiling everything. Lie still. I won't hurt you. See, Elena *mia*, what a splendid man you're getting." Proudly Cristobal raised up on his knees, the silver moonlight bathing his heavily muscled body. "A candle then," he cried, "so you can fully appreciate me."

He jumped from the bed to light a candle from the flickering votive flame before the statue of Our Lady. Elena wished the niche had not been beside the door; there was no way she could slip past him.

She shut her eyes as he turned toward her. Then she gasped in pain as his hand stung across her face.

"Open your eyes. You won't die of shock."

Her vision blurred by tears, she opened her eyes, blinking away the moisture. He stood proudly beside the bed, naked from head to toe. Muscular and brown skinned, he had a broad, deep chest and wide shoulders, yet the perfection of his bronze flesh was marred by several deep puckered gashes that showed black in the half-light.

"Legacies of the bulls," he said, aware she had seen the scars. "Still, unlike some poor bastards, all the essentials are there."

Deliberately, he lowered the candle, drawing her gaze to his manhood, darkly frightening as it jutted erect from a bush of coal black hair.

"Now do you see what you want?" he asked thickly, his free hand stealing to his brow to wipe away gathering sweat. He wavered, threatening to drop the candle, which he hastily set down on the bedside chest.

"Cristobal, you're a fine man, but I don't want you to make love to me," she said soothingly, thinking perhaps a calm approach would work. In his drunken state, raging and screaming might only encourage him to subdue her to prove his masculinity.

"You'll soon change your mind," he promised, kneeling on the edge of the bed and almost falling off. His growing clumsiness made him laugh. Cristobal sprawled across her legs, giving her an unobstructed view of his body. He purposely sought to arouse her, unable to accept the idea that there was a woman born who did not want him.

"You've had too much to drink."

An overpowering haze of cheap wine hung about him. Sweat was trickling off his brow and his eyes were dazed. If only she could keep him talking long enough, he might fall asleep. "Go back to your own room and—"

"It's not going to work, *chica*. Don't try your damned English logic here. I'm not some naughty boy to be reasoned with. I'm going to have you. Tomorrow I might die, and I intend to go to my grave happy." His speech was slurring badly. Sliding further down the bed, Cristobal rested his head on her legs.

"If you're waiting for me to change my mind, you've got a long wait," she snapped when he showed no sign of moving.

"That's all right, *amita*, I've got all night."

"Get off me. Go back to your own bed."

"Enough foolish talk. We're going to . . . to do it, Elena . . . whether you want to or not."

"If you rape me you'll never see me again."

"What?" His dark brows drew together. "I'm not going to rape you. I'm giving you . . . a gift the women in Toledo would fight for. Didn't know that, eh, *chica*? Knives . . . knives've been drawn over me. . . ."

Her heart skipped a beat; he was so close to succumbing.

"Fighting over you? Oh, come now, what lies are these?"

Sheer rage flickered across his face. Then it subsided. He laughed. "Don't think I'm worth it, eh? You will . . . once you've had me. Like . . . like a bad habit . . . not easy to—"

"Here, lie on the pillow. You'll feel better," Elena suggested when he ran his hand over his face. As he slid in place beside her, she stiffened.

"Much better," he murmured contentedly. Now Cristobal considered himself accepted.

Elena prayed she had not misjudged his state of inebriation. His voice had become slower, thicker, and his eyes had grown heavy. Even more encouraging— his towering erection had softened. Cristobal seemed to have temporarily abandoned his original intention in favor of boasting about his prowess.

"Tomorrow, after I've killed . . . become champion . . . women always want me. Tired . . . tired before night's out . . ."

He was quiet. For a few minutes he did not stir. Aware of her fluttering heart, which seemed to have lodged in her throat, Elena tried to ease from under his arm. At the unexpected movement his eyes snapped open and he grasped her shoulder, forcing her to stay where she was. A few minutes later he was snoring. Waiting just a little longer to make sure that this time he did not wake when she struggled from under him, Elena slid from the bed.

When she stepped on the rushes, her legs were shaking. Had Cristobal not drunk so much wine, she would have been no match for him, yet, had he not drunk so much wine, he might not have tried to force himself on her. The balance was too precarious to maintain.

Chapter
Twenty-one

"Enough talk of marriage, Dolores. It's too soon. Leonora's barely cold."

"How much longer do you intend to mourn, Don Luis?" Dolores challenged, her black eyes flashing in anger. "Two months, three, maybe a year?"

"Have sense," Luis dismissed impatiently. "We both know a decent mourning period has to be observed."

Though Dolores snorted in anger at his reminder, she remained quiet. He was right; a mourning period was customary. To deviate from the usual might cause suspicion. She had no wish to invite any speculation about Leonora's sudden death. At the same time her intuition told her Luis would try to weasel out of their agreement if given half the chance. Since Leonora's death he had been a different man, sullen, short-tempered, lacking tenderness—surely to God he hadn't loved the Fragoso woman!

"But we will be married soon. Remember, Luis, you swore on—"

"Are we to argue all day?" he snarled, pulling away from her demanding hands as she sought to keep him beside her. "You wanted to watch the tournament—if we don't leave soon we'll miss the rest of it.''

Eyes narrowed, Doloers watched as he pulled a short velvet cloak about his broad shoulders. Of late Luis had taken to going out alone, looking for excuses to absent himself. Another woman was behind this change; she felt it in her bones. When she had him followed, her spies reported he merely walked beside the Tajo before going to a cheap *taverna* to drink wine. But she was not fooled by his seeming innocence. Maybe he knew he was being followed. A man like Luis was clever, yet not quite clever enough.

"Come, *querido*, let us be friends," she cajoled, slipping her hand beneath his arm, squeezing the hard muscles encased in ruby velvet. "Life's too short to quarrel.''

Luis smiled and patted her cheek. "That's what I keep telling you, Dolores,'' he said.

The noise in the main plaza was deafening. The rollicking crowd had dressed in their grandest clothes for the occasion. The tournament was half over, the individual feats of strength and a mock tourney having already taken place. Courtiers in fine armor had demonstrated their skill to the noisy approval of the crowd. Now the spectators eagerly awaited the conclusion of the sporting event. This second half promised to be even more exciting than the first, for this was when the bull-fights would take place.

Tumblers and jugglers in parti-colored costumes cavorted about the broad square to loud applause and a scattering of coins. On the fringe of the crowd, gypsy girls told fortunes, or danced seductively to the music of tambour and flute. During the lull between events, many spectators seized the opportunity to seek refreshment. Vendors selling wine and fried pies, sweetmeats and fruit thrust their way through the crowd, their raucous cries barely audible above the chatter.

Elena glanced toward the wooden stands to her left, and her heart lurched. What had made her look up at that exact moment? Luis and Dolores were just taking their seats. Jealousy speared her heart as she saw how beautiful Dolores looked in silver and white velvet, her black hair hidden beneath a silver headdress; a black lace mantilla was draped over the headdress and fell softly about her smooth shoulders.

And Luis? Forcing herself to endure the ultimate punishment, Elena turned to look at him. How handsome he looked, richly clad in ruby velvet and black damascene, his garments flashing as the sun sparked fire from random jewels sewn to the fabric. Luis looked like a prince! Royal Philip, wearing somber black velvet in contrast to his blond hair and beard, paled before this vision of a man. Her heart lurched, and she clasped her sweating hands together, unable to take her eyes off him. Had Luis been ugly, she wondered, would she have wanted him so intensely? His beauty was an added torment to suffer. And she did suffer, every bittersweet memory of their love piercing her heart.

All around her, people craned forward on the hastily constructed stands, eager for the first glimpse of Cristobal as he rode into the square. Dazzling in gold brocade, a gold cap with a long curving plume atop his black hair, the champion burst into the square to a glorious fanfare of trumpets. The cheering throng forgot that he was Don Luis's *estanciero*, that his mother was a base gypsy, remembering only that he was their idol—a fearless killer of bulls.

Elena sat very straight, knowing Cristobal would be watching for her. Her cornflower blue gown would be

easily spotted amidst the predominantly white, black
and red of the spectators in this wealthier section of the
stands. Cristobal's pace slowed, and his white horse
skittered sideways as he reined in. He had seen her.
Grinning, Cristobal stood in the stirrups, raising his cap
in greeting. Elena smiled in reply, her mind straying
to last night's near-disastrous encounter. This morning,
his sanity returned, Cristobal had made profuse apologies, swearing it would not happen again. But she could
not forget how close she had come to being raped. Each
time he tried to bend her to his will, he merely increased
the distance between them.

People turned in their seats to stare open-mouthed
at her, aware this was the foreign beauty their hero had
saved from the Inquisition. Embarrassed by the unusual
attention, Elena fixed her gaze on the finely dressed
riders entering the square.

Amidst a second fanfare of trumpets, a dozen more
bullfighters mounted on fast, light horses had entered
the plaza. The procession wound slowly about the perimeter of the square while the crowd went wild. The
parade at an end, the champions made their final preparations for battle.

Elena closed her eyes, allowing her head to sink on
her chest. Foolishly, she had glanced a second time at
Dolores Mendoza only to encounter Luis's piercing blue
eyes. Unable to look away, their gazes had locked above
the heads of the crowd. He had not smiled, his mouth
grim. Deliberately she'd forced herself to break the
contact, unable to bear the sight of Dolores nuzzling
his shoulder.

The roar of the crowd and the bellows of pain from
wounded animals told her the bloody fight was underway. Hooves thundered past as the riders skillfully
maneuvered their light-bodied horses to avoid the bulls'

piercing horns. Excited men shouted in triumph as they thrust their lances, swiftly dispatching the blundering animals. One bull charged the riders, bellowing its fear. The voice of the crowd suddenly changed, their cries revealing someone was down.

Elena craned forward, hardly able to see above the standing throng. A man lay on the ground, his leg doubled beneath him; nearby his pitiful mount thrashed in agony, blood gushing from its belly. The injured rider was not Cristobal, for his clothing was dark.

The huge, angry bull stood at bay, snorting and pawing the ground, preparing for another charge. A cheer went up from the crowd. His gold brocade doublet glittering in the sun, Cristobal was making a swift pass around the edge of the plaza. Leaning out of the saddle, he quickly sighted the bull, judging its distance. The crowd roared in delight as he began his final run. He drew close to the snorting black bull. Using great dexterity and skill, he maneuvered his horse dangerously near those deadly curving horns before he delivered the well-placed thrust that had made him famous. Swiftly, Cristobal skewered his lance through the back of the neck, close to the head, driving down into the bull's heart. Now the crowd became ecstatic, their cheers deafening as the bull sank slowly to its knees. Blood spurted from the wound as the massive head gradually dropped lower, lower, until, with a final groan, the animal lay still.

Elena held her brow, which pounded with the noise of the crowd. "Cristobal! Cristobal!" they shouted, their voices a thundering wave echoing around the plaza. Nausea she had long held in check threatened to erupt. Even with her eyes closed, she could see those poor bleeding creatures, could still hear the screams of the dying horse barely masked by the crowd's rapturous cheers.

Stumbling to her feet, Elena pushed between the
excited spectators, fighting her way down through the
stands as she went in search of a wine vendor. Her
mouth was parched and her throat burned. How many
more bulls must be slaughtered before the crowd was
satisfied? she wondered, leaning against the cool stone
wall of the building. Belatedly, she realized she had
no cup to carry the wine, so instead she bought an
orange from an old woman. The tart fruit quenched a
little of the burning in her throat.

A loud roar from the crowd told her the second event
was underway. The dead animals would have been
dragged out so it could begin again. She crouched
against the building, suddenly overcome with fatigue.
Was it the sight of blood which made her faint, or was
it more the hateful sight of Luis with his paramour?

"Get up!"

The sharp command registered slowly on her dazed
brain. Given short chance to comply, Elena was clasped
by the hand and yanked to her feet. To her shock, she
found Luis standing before her, his splendid velvet
doublet winking with diamonds and silver thread. She
blinked in disbelief, afraid he was an hallucination.

"Yes, it's I. You're not seeing a ghost."

"What do you want?"

"We have to talk. Come."

"No."

Luis's grip tightened painfully, and Elena gasped in
surprise.

"Don't make a scene," he ground out through gritted
teeth. "There are far too many things that have gone
unsaid. I can endure it no longer."

"You've known where I was."

"Aye, and think you I'd come into the gypsy's house

to speak to you? I've given you this time in his arms. Now it's over.''

"No. I won't go with you. There's nothing more to say between us.''

Losing patience, Luis yanked her closer. She could smell musk rose wafting from his clothing, the scent poignantly sweet. Oh, what memories, what pain that perfume evoked.

"Don't make me force you,'' he growled, glancing about at the milling crowd who spared them not even so much as a glance.

"What will your lovely Dolores think if you desert her now?''

"Dolores can go to hell!''

Without further ado, Luis propelled her around the back of the stands and down an alley. Elena wanted to struggle, to scream abduction, but she fell strangely silent. This could not be happening. This was not Luis beside her, dragging her heaven knows where, angrily demanding they talk.

Suddenly he halted their mad flight in a narrow, deserted street. Luis swept her in his arms, locking her tight against his chest. Elena quivered in shock and delight as his mouth closed over hers.

"Dear God,'' he whispered when at last their lips parted, "I've been waiting a lifetime to do that.''

She stared up at him, her eyes bright with tears.

"No, Luis, please, I've not the strength,'' she pleaded, trying to stop her tears from falling. "Let me go.''

Angrily he thrust her away. "I'm sorry to have made you miss your lover's next triumph. No doubt he'll be glad to relay the details of the bloody business if you ask. Just do as I say and you won't be hurt.''

And she did. Walking beside him in a daze, Elena

could hardly believe her meek acceptance of his orders. Had she no pride? No will to stand against him? But she already knew the answers to those questions before she asked them.

They walked briskly away from the main plaza, the crowd's roars faint in the background. Luis hurried her past tall white houses crowding the narrow cobbled streets, past mysterious grilled courtyards abloom with ferns and perfumed shrubs. They finally emerged in a small plaza. The sun shone warm on their backs. Elena knew they were near the Tajo for she could smell the river.

"Why have you brought me here?"

"There's a *taverna* nearby. We won't be recognized there."

The *taverna*, though shabby, was clean. Two peasant women, who must surely be Toledo's only inhabitants not at the bullfight, came outside to serve them. Luis ordered wine. Then the women returned with an earthenware jug frosty with moisture, and he carried the wine and their cups to a table beneath an orange tree. From here they had an unobstructed view of the winding Tajo, where narrow merchant crafts lay at anchor.

"How much longer, Elena?" Luis demanded after he had poured the wine. "Are we to keep up this charade indefinitely?"

Time and distance had returned her courage. Now Elena no longer felt unable to stand up to him. Gulping a mouthful of chilled wine to further fortify herself, she said, "What makes you think it's a charade?"

His face tensed. Grasping her hand as it lay on the stone table, he said, "On my part it's a charade—now, *querida*, you owe me as much honesty."

His admission stunned her. Then, a painful memory

returning, she lifted her head and snapped, "Surely you're still not pretending you take no pleasure in that woman's bed? By all that's holy, Luis, I'd thought by now you'd have abandoned that pathetic ruse. I don't believe you—then, or now."

Luis leaned back against the orange tree, regarding her grimly. "What must I do to convince you?" he asked at length.

"Short of leaving her, there's little. Now even that may not be enough."

"Why do you always make life so difficult?" he growled, downing a cup of wine. "Am I to believe you're bedding the gypsy to spite me?"

"You can believe what you will. I'm leaving."

Elena stood. In a flash he thrust her back on the bench. "No—you're staying until this is resolved. Tell me—do you love him?"

How she wanted to lie. Her mouth opened to utter the words to wound him, yet something held her back. Was it the memory of his kisses, of the sweetness of the love they had shared not very long ago?

"I've never loved Cristobal."

"Then why?"

"You left me little choice."

"Leave him."

"And go where?"

"I'll find you lodging in the city."

"Provide my passage home to England and I'll accept."

He winced at her statement. Elena steeled herself not to react. Once and for all she must free herself from the tempting, lulling safety of his lies. More likely, Dolores Mendoza's arms had begun to pall. Enough time had elapsed that now he thought it prudent to renew his attack. And she had almost succumbed. Fool! Why had she told him she didn't love Cristobal?

Looking down at the table, she could not help noticing his hands aglitter with rings. Elena swallowed, fighting a wave of pain. She felt weak as she recalled the pleasure of his caress, the arousal of his touch. Then another thought abruptly stilled the magic. Perhaps last night those elegant, lean-fingered hands had intimately caressed Dolores. More likely it had been this morning, for they were late to the tournament. Anger swiftly replaced her pleasure as she reproached herself for weakness.

"What, Don Luis, finally at a loss for words?" she taunted, desperate to wound him in payment for her vulnerability.

"I dare not leave Dolores until you're safely out of Toledo—mayhap out of Spain. The Inquisition has a long arm."

"That explanation doesn't surprise me. I expected no less. Listen, my darling, you need not give her up on my account."

"Don't," he warned, his voice deepening in anger.

More taunts formed on her lips, but Elena was wiser than to speak them. At last she whispered, "Let me go back to the tournament. This is becoming a point-less discussion."

"No, damn it, Elena, I love you. I always have—always will. Must you constantly torment me out of injured pride? You say I betrayed our love, using that to justify living with the gypsy. Believe me when I say that my only thought was to save your life. Though I never intended it, I know you were hurt. Now, in turn, you've hurt me. You couldn't have chosen a crueler revenge than to become that gypsy bastard's mistress. So now we've delivered our mortal blows, have left terrible wounds all round. How much longer must it go on, Elena? Are we never to love again?''

The pleading note in his voice made her gasp. A weakening flood of emotion possessed her. Luis gazed at her, his blue eyes soft, his face vulnerable. All the pain she had dealt him was so apparent that she wondered at the cruelty that drove her to inflict it. Had he been her mortal enemy, she could not have found more wounding a punishment. His hand lay on the table beside her own. Longing to touch him, she held back, aware if she gave in now she was lost.

Clearing her throat, Elena said in a shaky voice, ''Our love has been destroyed.''

''No. Even infidelity can't destroy true love. Only our pride was hurt. I still want you—every night, every day. Come back to me. Oh, Elena, *luz de mi vida*, don't turn away from me now.''

Their fingers brushed, and the touch ignited a thousand sparks. She looked up at him, finding her image reflected in his metallic blue eyes, a small woebegone figure, her face as pale as parchment. Luis turned over her hand to gently place his lips against her wrist, his lingering kiss melting the last of her resistance.

''Yes,'' she whispered, licking tears from her lips. How she ached to be in his arms, that need becoming a physical ache. ''Oh, Luis, I still love you. Please, listen to me,'' she began as he stood.

''It can wait,'' he murmured softly, enfolding her tenderly against his splendid red doublet. Weakly, Elena leaned against him, letting Luis take her weight. Happiness, that forgotten emotion, soared in her heart. Not in her wildest dreams had she expected today to end like this.

''I've never loved anyone as I love you,'' Luis whispered against her ear, his breath warmly caressing. They stood motionless beneath the orange trees, willing time to stand still. Finally shouts off the nearby river broke the spell. "Come inside where we can be alone," he invited huskily, his lips lingering on her cheek.

Elena understood his meaning. Usually these *tavernas* had rooms to rent by the hour. In the past she would have died with shame at the thought of keeping such a tryst. But that was many heartaches ago.

"How long can you stay?" she asked, stroking his face, shuddering at the hot, smooth feel of his flesh beneath her fingertips.

"No longer than you dare—we both have jealous partners." He laughed, holding her close. "Today we'll love for a little while—pray God we'll soon be free to be together always."

When they entered the small *taverna*, the establishment's owner grinned and pointed upstairs, already anticipating Luis's question. She registered no surprise at having such grandly dressed guests, merely smiled knowingly as they mounted the stairs.

Elena paid scant attention to the poor room beyond noticing it was surprisingly clean. Perhaps this was why Luis brought her here, yet how would he know the upper rooms were clean? Sparks of jealousy were kindled by the probable answer, before she prudently thrust away her suspicion. This afternoon was stolen from the future; there was no time to waste in jealousy.

Turning to Luis, she held out her arms. The joy of their loving embrace put all suspicion and doubt to flight. He held her close, his mouth firm, tender, passionate. Luis was all things to her. He always had been.

They lay in each other's arms on the narrow bed, the lumpy mattress readily accommodating the shape of their bodies. Their finery had been quickly discarded and lay heaped on the rickety table. In the weak light filtering through the branches of a Jacaranda tree outside the window, they admired each other's bodies.

Possessively Luis swept his hands across her silken back, caressing her hips, her thighs. His hot mouth sought her nipples, budding now with passion; he nuzzled her, his tongue so hotly arousing that it made her shudder in delight. "I'd begun to think we'd never love again," he whispered, his voice hoarse with passion. "God be praised—I was wrong."

"Wicked man! Surely it was not for this you prayed," she whispered, smiling in amusement at his heartfelt words.

"Most assuredly, Elena *mia*, most assuredly."

His tantalizing caresses made her throb with passion. An occasional clatter of pans or burst of laughter echoing upstairs were the only sounds to disturb them. Here they were alone in a world of their own making.

Luis kissed Elena tenderly, moving his mouth in a hot, tantalizing trail over her breasts, her belly, to the quivering core of her being. "This kiss is for the pain I caused you . . . this for the waiting . . . this for the loneliness," he murmured as his mouth slowly retraced its path to her lips.

"Luis, there's something I must tell you first—no, don't stop me. I want you to know."

Though he nodded for her to continue, his face tensed.

"Are you going to tell me he's a better lover?"

His bitter humor chilled her heart. Elena shook her head, aware of his pain. "Nay, sweetheart, never that."

"What then?"

"I'm trying to tell you I wouldn't know if he were."

"You speak in riddles."

"No, I speak only the truth. He and I have never been lovers."

Luis gasped, unable to keep his surprise to himself.

"But, I thought . . . after your time together in the cell."

"He told you, then."

"You don't think he'd let such a glorious chance to boast pass him by."

"I never wanted Cristobal for my lover. I still love you too much."

A dawning smile lifted the corners of his sensual mouth. His arms tightened about her pliant body. "Oh, *querida mia*," he murmured and could say no more.

Elena kissed him fiercely, stroking his smooth, muscled back, holding him so close they could barely draw breath.

"I want only one lover at a time, my darling. As long as you live there'll be no other."

Mouths welded together, bodies pressed close, they trembled in passion. Stirring embraces and soft kisses had brought them to a point where they ceased to find satisfaction in gentle lovemaking. Their separation had been too long, their pain too deep.

"Oh, Elena," Luis murmured, barely able to control his passion. He seemed to have been deprived of her for an eternity.

Instinctively, Elena moved beneath him, trembling and ready. She spread herself wide, eager to receive him, holding her breath until that glorious invasion was complete. Luis filled her with heat, with striving, throbbing passion. Gasping, she wondered how much longer she could endure such delight. Murmuring endearments in Spanish so emotional she could no longer translate them, Luis moved slowly, rhythmically. Ruled by passion, Elena rained torrents of kisses on him, clutching his springy gold hair, desperately trying to blend body and soul with the man she loved.

Rapidly soaring to the heights of pleasure, Luis swept

her beyond anything she had ever experienced before, their passion heightened by mutual pain. Never had she felt such intense love for him, nor had his body induced such wonderful arousal. Shuddering, gasping, Elena climbed to the pinnacle of desire, delaying the plunge, eager to savor all the wonder of lovemaking before she allowed it to end in that longed-for explosion of pleasure and grief. Then Luis quickened his pace, no longer allowing her to tarry, sweeping her joyously along those paths of ecstacy until together they glimpsed paradise.

Dolores sat at the table, impatiently drumming her fingers. A late spring shower drenched Toledo's narrow streets, sluicing red-tiled rooftops and ochre walls. She waited. Luis was over an hour late. Naturally, he would claim he sought shelter from the storm. Last week it had been an old seafaring friend who had taken so much of his time; the week before that, uncharacteristic piety drove him to worship daily in the cathedral. Sometimes he didn't deign to offer an explanation for his absence. In a few minutes she would learn the truth. Even now her spies were entering the courtyard to present their report.

"Well, what did you learn?" she burst out impatiently when Gonsalves and his companion entered the room.

Gonsalves bowed, his one good eye focused on Dolores. Her anger was so apparent that he swiftly reconsidered his demand for more money.

"Greetings, Doña Dolores. We have much to report."

Nudging his companion, Gonsalves stepped forward to the dark oak table. Obediently, his taller companion retrieved a scroll of parchment from beneath his shabby cloak, spreading it out amidst the wine cups and bowls of fruit.

Dolores's eyes narrowed and her breath quickened as she read the daily entries. At first, nothing unusual. Then Luis either grew careless or ceased to care if he was being observed. Twice a day here, three times there. Two days with nothing unusual—ah, those were the days he had paced the house like a caged beast. Obviously his woman had been unable to meet him.

Eyes flashing, she looked up at the two sallow-skinned men who were awaiting her comments. "You've done well. Is there one particular whore, or has the bastard a collection to amuse him?"

Gonsalves smiled slyly. "Only one, *doña*."

Half rising from her chair, Dolores gripped his arm. "Well, idiot, tell me her name."

"'It is the bullfighter's woman."

"The bullfighter's woman? You don't mean . . . not Don Cristobal's whore?" she croaked, hoping she was wrong. After all, in Toledo there were many bull-fighters."

"Yes, the foreign woman he rescued. It is she."

Dolores whirled, sending crystal goblets crashing to the floor in a splintering heap. So! He had deceived her from the beginning! Rescue Cristobal indeed! She should have known he had no love for that gypsy bastard. At the time it struck her as strange—why, she remembered questioning him about his unusual concern. Damn him for his treachery! Oh, how easy she had been, how foolishly trusting.

Hands clenched, Dolores rounded on the two spies. "Does he know he was being followed?"

Gonsalves drew himself up to maximum height, highly offended by her question. "Of course not, Doña Dolores. We excel at our craft. Is that not why you hired us?"

"Yes, very well. Go now. You've done a thorough

job. Continue to watch him and report his activities to me.''

The men bowed and backed to the door. Downstairs a door banged shut, and she snapped to attention.

"It is he. Come, this way. He mustn't see you."

Dolores thrust the two men toward a small door leading to the servants entrance. When Luis entered the room, she had resumed her seat at the table and had already masked her rage.

"You're very wet—and late."

"Haven't you looked outside," he snapped, reaching for the wine decanter. "What happened here?" he asked when he saw the shattered crystal trodden into the carpet.

"An accident," she dismissed quickly. "Now, Luis, tell me where you've been today?"

Luis glanced up. "Out," was all he said before he crossed to the window. By now Elena would be safely indoors. He hoped she had managed to slip past Cristobal unnoticed, but what matter if she had not? She owed the gypsy nothing.

"Visiting your woman at the *taverna* by the bridge?"

His hand clenched around the goblet in shock. Blood throbbed to his face, then receded. He should have known Dolores would have him followed. And of late he had grown careless.

"What if I did?"

"What if you did?" she screeched, thrusting back her chair so angrily, it toppled with a crash. "You're bound to marry me, *chico*, or has that slipped your mind? After we're wed there'll be no room for whores."

"Every man must be allowed his whores. It's part of life," Luis remarked in an amused voice as he turned about. "Most wives learn to accept that fact."

''Not this wife!''

Dolores came to him, her face dark with rage. Gripping his arm beneath the wet velvet, she dug her long nails viciously into his flesh.

Angrily Luis shook her off.

''Not one day passes that you aren't accusing or questioning. For the love of God, give me room to breathe!''

''I don't object to you having room to breathe, it's room to bed other women I find fault with. And don't try to pacify me by suggesting this is some gypsy *puta*! I know who she is!''

Their eyes met. Luis refused to flinch in the face of her unexpected knowledge. ''So you know who she is. That makes life easier for me. I've no further reason to lie.''

Amazed by his sheer audacity, Dolores was temporarily at a loss for words. Then a torrent of abuse spilled forth as she swung at him, barely grazing his face with her nails before he seized her and swung her about.

''Enough! Remember, Dolores, you don't own me. I'll do as I please.''

''You've deceived me from the start. All those lies about Cristobal, your beloved brother. It was the woman you wanted free so you could bed her. Damn you, Luis, damn you . . .''

Struggling to free herself, Dolores kicked him. Luis grabbed her by the neck and propelled her to her chair. He thrust her down and leaned over her.

''I've loved Elena for years. I'd have done anything to set her free. Admit it, Dolores, you've not been hurt. You enjoyed every minute we spent together.''

''Not hurt! You swore to marry me.''

''Only a fool would consider that vow binding.''

"You swore it on holy relics."

The reminder momentarily sobered him. Yet Luis doubted a place awaited him in heaven. What matter one more sin?

"At the time I was already married to another—the idea was ludicrous. I never expected Leonora to die so . . . suddenly . . ." His voice faded as he looked closely at Dolores. A smug smile played about her mouth. Dear God! Why had he been such a blind fool? Leonora had not died a natural death! Dolores would stop at nothing to get her way—not even murder!

"Always expect the unexpected, Luis. Leonora is dead. And we will be married. Never again are you to see this Englishwoman, do you hear me? Don't dare defy me, or you'll be sorry."

"You killed Leonora."

"I never left Toledo. Don't talk such nonsense."

"Oh, not with your own hand, you're too clever for that. You paid one of your spies to do the deed. What a fool I've been! I should've known you were behind it. Everything happened too smoothly."

"I always make it my business to plan the future," Dolores reminded, self-satisfaction replacing her anger. "Now that we both know the truth, we'll begin again. You made a bargain with me—your promise of marriage for my aid. If you want your woman to live, you'd better keep to your bargain."

"We've discussed marriage every day since Leonora's death. Until a decent mourning period has passed, I'll discuss it no further."

Dolores grabbed his sleeve, her eyes narrowing menacingly.

"Don't try to deceive me. There are many who would find your marriage proposal strange when you already had a wife. People might suspect *you* poisoned

Leonora—"

"So that's how it was done! I knew there was some other reason besides that lame excuse of too much sun. Dear God, what a fool I was to meekly accept—"

"You had no choice, Don Luis, once fate took a hand. I'm warning you, if you continue to see that English whore, you'll pay dearly."

"Will you have me poisoned as well?"

"You'll be the prime suspect in Leonora's murder. I'll see to that."

"And you dare call your feelings love?"

"Love, passion, perhaps even obsession, but never selflessness, Luis. You know me better than that. You left me once. You won't do it again."

"You forget—I, too, never left Toledo."

Dolores laughed scornfully. "You've money enough to pay for such deeds. In return for leniency, a dozen poor wretches in the dungeons would gladly swear you paid them to murder her."

Luis regarded her beautiful face with mounting disgust. How could he have played so easily into her hands? Yet, if she loved him as she swore, could she so easily consign him to death?

"Until I decide otherwise, I'll sleep in my own room."

"As you wish. One more thing, Luis, that move won't make deception easier. I've had you followed. I'll continue to do so. You'd better do as you're told this time."

Anger flared in his face, and he swung away from her when she came to embrace him.

"Even if you lock me in a cell, you can't make me love you, Dolores," he snarled, his angry reminder more wounding than he realized.

Dolores sat at the table, watching the door shudder

on its hinge after Luis had stalked from the room. Tears, so rarely shed, welled in her dark eyes. Never had Luis spoken a truer word. The only reason he was still with her was because he was ordered to remain in Toledo to protect Cristobal and that woman. And signed papers releasing them both from scrutiny lay on the table.

Folding the crisp documents into a smaller square, Dolores placed them in a secret compartment of her desk. Luis could wait for the safe conduct until he had proved himself trustworthy.

Chapter Twenty-two

Elena slipped through a side door into the deserted street. It was siesta time and the houses were shuttered. The blazing sun shone directly overhead, slanting between the tall buildings enclosing this narrow street. Luis waited for her at a *taverna* at the edge of the old Jewish quarter, not their usual meeting place, but a far more accessible one. There was no time to meet beside the river, for after siesta they both must attend the bullfight.

On this hot June afternoon Cristobal's dream would finally become flesh; he was to fight the bull unmounted. Such an uproar had met his unprecedented proposal, all Toledo appeared to be involved in the wrangle. After much discussion, the contest had finally been approved, and fortunes had been wagered on the outcome of such a novel event. Cristobal's ego was further bolstered when he learned he was the popular choice to win.

Pausing in a shadowed doorway, Elena glanced behind her. She had the uneasy feeling she was being followed, but saw nothing but a scrawny feline stirring in the quiet street. Quickly, she crossed into a narrow alley giving access to the *taverna*'s side entrance. Luis's discovery that Dolores had him followed was probably responsible for her suspicion. Dolores knew whom he met, so there seemed little point in continuing the surveillance. Though Luis had dismissed the discovery as being of little significance, Elena was afraid for him.

There he was, waiting for her in the shadowed doorway. His doublet was midnight blue velvet; a falling silver lace band circled the neck.

"Oh, Luis, I'm always afraid you won't come," Elena whispered as he enfolded her eagerly in his arms.

"I've never let you down," he reminded, holding her slightly away from him. Finding her lovely face wreathed in joy, he smiled tenderly. "And I promise I never shall. Come inside, we've such little time today."

"Luis, is it wise to keep meeting? You could be in grave danger."

"You're also in danger as long as you stay in Toledo. It appears the Inquisition loves us so well, they'd ever keep us in their sight. I've appealed to Philip for permission to travel."

"Does *she* know?"

He shook his head. Stroking the soft bloom of Elena's cheek, he marveled again at her complexion, so perfect it might have been painted by a master's brush. "You're still the loveliest woman in the world," he declared earnestly.

"Oh, Luis, please be serious. Tell me, am I to travel to England?"

"Eventually."

"But I can't leave without you. Oh, don't make me go."

"Hopefully we can be together soon. You must be brave, *querida*, you may have to travel by yourself. Surely you aren't afraid I'll be unfaithful while you're gone?"

She shook her head and nuzzled his cheek. "Wherever I go, whatever I do, I promise you my heart and soul until my dying day."

Luis grasped her arms, his fingers biting deep. Blue eyes misting with emotion, his heart rocked with the depth of his love for her.

"Come," he said gruffly, not trusting himself with words. "We've so little time."

They turned and went inside the *taverna*.

A tall shadow moved from the purple depths of the courtyard wall. Stumbling over discarded chairlegs and bales of rope, Cristobal grew clumsy in his rage. His hand stole to the curved dagger at his waist. How he longed to sink that gleaming blade to the hilt in his rival's heart. The cold blade felt good in his hand. Cristobal weighed the dagger, considering how best to kill his hated rival. Don Luis! Once again he had crossed his path with hatred and guile. Not content with stealing his inheritance, now the great man had to have his woman, too. Surely that was the reason he had sought out Elena, eager to prove once again he could take anything Cristobal laid claim to.

Elena was his! True, they had never slept together, but she was his nonetheless. Those shared days in the Inquisition's cell had cemented the bond. Now she lived in his house, and all Toledo knew her as his mistress. What sad irony that was not in fact true. Yet lately, Cristobal had begun to believe the lie himself, considering it merely a matter of time before she turned to him. Never once had he dreamed she lay panting in another man's arms, yielding all, when she would not even let him embrace her without pulling away.

Cristobal walked rapidly away from the *taverna*, conscious of the elapsing time. Today he faced the most dangerous event of his career. In a few short hours he would lay his life on the line as he confronted *el toro* on foot. For years this day had lain glorious in his dreams, been practiced for, longed for. How like Luis to unwittingly rob him of his glory. Now the wonderful event he had lived and breathed for most of his thirty years was eclipsed by the anger raging in his heart.

Despite Luis, before sunset he would reign triumphant. The mobs would carry him on their shoulders through the town. All Toledo would know him as the bravest of men.

And tomorrow he would kill Don Luis.

It was far too late to return to Cristobal's house. Instead, Elena hurried to the main plaza where the highly acclaimed bullfight was to take place. Thick crowds streamed toward the plaza, jamming the narrow streets as men and women burst with excitement over the spectacle they were about to witness. This would be Cristobal Santos's greatest triumph!

Elena wore a plain green and white gown, a white rose pinned in her hair, which she had coiled beneath a net. Not anxious to draw attention to herself, today she dressed more like a peasant girl than a grand lady. Now she could slip in and out of the stands without causing a stir. The crowd jostled her, and she gripped her black lace mantilla, afraid it would be pulled from her head. The press of people swept her along with them, making it impossible to reach her seat. Eager for a glimpse of their hero, a mob of eager Toledans jammed the narrow entrance through which the contestants would emerge.

One of the men working the bulls recognized her and beckoned her behind the barrier safeguarding the tents where the contestants dressed and rested between events.

Elena paused at the entrance to Cristobal's gaudy red and white tent, for he knelt praying before a statue of the Virgin. Crossing himself, he finally rose, his silver and gold doublet scintillating in the light. As he turned, Elena stepped forward to greet him. The hard expression on his face shocked her. Usually Cristobal swept her in his arms, greeting her like a long-lost relative.

"So you're here at last."

"I'm sorry I'm late . . . the crowds . . ." She faltered, growing alarmed when he angrily unlooped the fastening and allowed the tent flap to fall in place.

"It couldn't be that you were too busy amusing Don Luis to get here sooner?"

Elena gasped in shock, her hand flying to her mouth. "Don Luis," she repeated, not knowing what to say.

"You are mine!" Cristobal cried, seizing her wrist to pull her close. His face was like granite, his black eyes glittering with rage. In this murky light his hawk-like features looked darkly menacing. "You're never to see him again, never to shame me like this again!"

Eyes wide in terror as the murky light flashed on cold steel, Elena held her breath. Cristobal had placed a gleaming dagger against her throat. She cried out in fright and pain, for he gripped her so tightly, she was afraid to draw breath lest the blade slice her flesh.

"What does he mean to you?"

"I love him."

Cristobal cursed, speared with pain by her swift answer.

"If you see him again I'll slit your throat," he threatened after a long silence.

Wide-eyed, Elena stared up at him, terrified he intended to carry out his threat. His hand shook so that the gleaming blade trembled against her vulnerable flesh.

"I swear before God—I will kill him!" His voice was so deadly earnest, she trembled with dread. "Now go."

Elena was thrust into the fabric wall of the tent. When she regained her balance, she fled.

Cristobal watched her race down the alley between the tents, her green gown billowing as she ran. His mouth set in an unyielding line. Women were all alike. Only this time he had thought *she* was different.

He shook his head, trying to clear his thoughts. In a few minutes he would face the biggest challenge of his career. Yet, so angry did he feel, so explosive, he almost dreaded the confrontation. He needed to be calm, to be able to weigh all the options presented by the bull. The rage burning in his heart made that impossible. Today he would face the bull in anger, beast to beast.

Cristobal motioned to Paco, sending him after Elena. She must not be allowed to warn Don Luis. From now on Elena went nowhere or saw no one without his permission.

The fanfare began, trumpets blaring. He could sense the crowd's excitement as they awaited the spectacle. He had already seen his bull, a big black devil with horns branching like an oak tree. Taking the red velvet cape handed to him by one of his men, Cristobal slipped his gleaming damascened sword into its jeweled scabbard and went forth to meet his fate.

They had passed the cheering crowds who rained him with flowers. Now they walked behind the stands, silently, grimly, each man occupied with his own thoughts. No one had asked Cristobal what was wrong, assuming his surliness was due to tension. No one doubted their champion would slay the bull. Though in recent times this dangerous spectacle was unheard of, who but Cristobal Santos, the greatest of them all, had courage enough to attempt it?

Cristobal stopped. A woman wrapped in a gypsy shawl, her tattered gown grimy above her dirty feet, stood beckoning to him. Dark hair falling untidily about her face, gold earrings glinting in the light—the sight of her tugged a chord of memory. But he did not know her. Perhaps she was one of those gypsy fortune-tellers eager to reveal his fate.

"Hey, gypsy, come here. Tell me, what's to be the outcome of today's contest?" he called, assuming his usual bravado, though it was a hollow act.

The woman moved, but did not step from the shadows. She stretched out her hand to him. Now they stood so close, he could see tears gleaming in her eyes. And what eyes—black as midnight, old, hard eyes very like his own. Fear coiled in his belly; sweat beaded his upper lip. They stood, gazes locked, time falling away. Suddenly he knew who she was.

"*Madre*," he croaked, his tongue too big for his mouth. When next he looked up, she was gone. "Where's the gypsy?" he demanded angrily, looking about.

"What gypsy? There's no one here."

"I was just speaking to her—she can't have disappeared."

The others shook their heads, baffled by his questions. They had never left his side.

"Come, *chico*, there's no gypsy. A trick of light," soothed his friend, Pablo, who took his arm, urging him forward as the trumpets blared their final fanfare.

Cristobal swallowed, his face pale. The rapid beating of his heart caused the fine gold and silver doublet to shudder. Suddenly he possessed a heightened awareness of his surroundings, the hum of the crowd, the yellow dust powdering his boots, the warm breeze smelling of animals, garlic, wine, sweat . . . and his own fear!

He alone had seen the gypsy. Though in life he had never known her, in death their souls reached out to each other. She was his mother. The peasants at Carmenilla said she appeared to foretell death.

Suddenly growing angry with himself for his superstition, Cristobal attempted to reason. This was not Carmenilla—but he was a de los Santos. Reason or not, a chill swept over him. Before the setting of the sun, he knew he would die. In the heat of late afternoon, before these cheering thousands, his fate would be met on the horns of a great snorting beast reared on pasture washed by the mighty Guadalquivir. . . .

"Come," he said gruffly to his men, "I am ready."

They smiled; they patted him on the back; they joked and boasted about the wine they would drink to toast his victory. Cristobal ignored them as he stepped toward his horse, mounted and rode into the plaza.

What an unholy Trinity had sealed his fate—Elena, Don Luis and an Andalusian devil. Even now the bull glared its fury at him, eyeing him with the inborn knowledge of the victor.

Arrogantly, Cristobal rode around the plaza, sitting ramrod-straight, daring to look fate square in the eye. Could he hope to cheat death? In his heart he already knew the answer.

Elena watched Cristobal come into the plaza, aware of Paco and Jose sitting on either side of her. Twice she had tried to leave on one flimsy pretext or another; they stood when she stood, patting their knives, silently reminding her why they were there. She had not seen Luis in the crowd, for this afternoon he was seated with the royal household. How could she warn him the bullfighter intended to kill him?

"Please be seated, Doña Elena. The fight is about

to begin,'' Paco said politely, his hand on her arm. ''Don Cristobal does not want you to be hurt.''

The menace behind his calm voice made her reconsider trying to run from him. Elena looked down into the plaza where five horsemen rode slowly around the edge of the cheering crowd, exchanging pleasantries, accepting flowers, crucifixes and other tributes. As he passed her, Cristobal glanced up, nodded to his men and rode on, his dark face impassive.

Finally the grand parade was over. The riders fanned out to the edge of the plaza. Cristobal had warned them to keep their distance, leaving him plenty of room to maneuver the bull. After playing the crowd for a few more minutes, he tucked into his cap band a spray of carnations thrown to him by an admirer, then signalled his men he was ready for the bull.

The big black animal galloped snorting into the arena, the sheer force of its presence captivating the crowd, which gasped in awe. Their hero stepped boldly forth. Sunlight flashed blinding light from Cristobal's gold and silver spangled doublet. Its attention caught by the flash, the bull stopped to watch the man walking casually toward him. A few paces behind Cristobal walked a slender youth carrying the gleaming sword with which Cristobal intended to dispatch the bull.

Cristobal accepted the sword, allowing the youth to flee to safety. More used to seeing the lance used as a weapon, the crowd leaned forward, not wanting to miss one minute of this novel spectacle. Haughtily, Cristobal made a wide circle around the bull, who watched him curiously. The animal turned as he passed behind it. Taunting now, Cristobal held out his cloak, letting it flutter in the breeze; then, turning his back on the bull, he bowed to the crowd. Uproarious applause greeting this daring move, Cristobal made a second pass

around the bull. Warily, his mounted companions edged
closer, their knees tensely gripping their horse's sides
as they prepared to head off the bull if necessary.

Cristobal continued to strut and preen, still taunting
the bull, who seemed frozen in his tracks. How the
crowd loved his showmanship. They shouted deliriously—"Cristobal! Cristobal!" The champion
bowed, acknowledging their applause. Then the crowd's
screaming adulation suddenly changed to a murmured
warning of impending danger. The bull had lowered
its head. Cristobal did not flinch, merely stood there
taunting the animal, urging him to come to him. The
bull charged. Only at the last moment did he step aside,
allowing the bull to thunder harmlessly past. The crowd
went wild. Again and again he repeated this daring
maneuver, his confidence growing by leaps and bounds.
A delirium of clapping, shouting and stamping greeted
each pass. The spectators were beside themselves with
excitement.

So much for omens and peasants' fancies! Out here
he was king. He had never performed better. Cristobal
stood straighter. He had been a fool to ever doubt
himself. Even this splendid beast stood in awe of him.
Time and again he moved aside at the last instant, lithe
as a dancer. Anger only served to make him bolder.

Then, like a black cloud, memories rushed back.
Damn Luis! Damn Elena! Cristobal could feel the heat
of anger rushing through his veins. Today he would
triumph, then tomorrow, instead of a bull, he would
kill an enemy even more deserving. The mighty Don
Luis would be made to pay dearly for stealing his
woman.

The bull stood pawing the ground, baffled by this
slender, sparkling force that continued to elude him.
The riders had moved close, and Cristobal angrily

waved them back. Walking deliberately toward the bull, ignoring its snorting anger, its lowered head, Cristobal glared at the thundering beast. As the bull roared toward him, he flung his cloak and it landed on the bull's horns. Tossing the crimson fabric aloft, the bull bellowed in fury. Cristobal bowed and smiled; his fans cheered.

Insufferably arrogant, afire with rage, Cristobal was determined to show Don Luis who was the best man. Not a son of the nobility, but he, Cristobal Santos, son of a gypsy whore. Today he would even defy fate!

Now Cristobal was so close he could see the gleam in the bull's eyes—evil, hypnotic and black like his own. He paused, weighing the sword in his hand. The beast was cowed. Now was the time to step up to him, to deliver the thrust that would make today famous. Cocksure, moving almost in a dream, he raised his sword. Then his world blew apart.

With a sudden movement, quicker than anyone had ever seen a bull move, the great black head lowered, then raised—only now the man was impaled on the burning agony of those horns. Cristobal screamed as the horns sank deep in his chest and abdomen. Now there was swift, soaring flight before the ground came up to meet him. Over and over he rolled, every limb in torment.

Pandemonium broke out in the plaza. His men galloped forth, some trying to divert the angry bull from its wounded victim as it prepared to charge again, others trying to pull Cristobal to safety.

Head pounding, vision blurred, Cristobal tried to stand. He could not. Blood gushed like a river through his slashed finery. Around him were familiar voices, a great weeping and wailing from the crowd, all blending in a kaleidescope of color and sound. Then suddenly, as if his sight had been miraculously restored, he saw the gypsy woman. She waited for him by the wooden barrier, holding out her hand. And he knew now he had never had a hope of cheating fate.

They carried the wounded champion to a house on the plaza, laying him on a soft bed in a cool, airy room. An army of physicians came and went, some to bleed him—much to his men's anger—others to give potions for the pain. And none offered hope.

Elena waited in the shadows, still watched by Paco and Jose, shocked by the sight of Cristobal lying broken, bleeding and crazed by pain. The last few hours had been an unreal nightmare from which she longed to wake. When they sent for the priest, she knew the end was near.

It was dark now. The shutters had been closed.

Cristobal held out his hand to Elena, and Paco pushed her forward.

"Eh, *chica*, you're finally free," he croaked, wincing at the pain caused by the effort of speech. "If I didn't know better I'd swear you were a witch—you've saved your lover after all."

His black eyes were glazed from the painkilling posset they had given him. Tears trickled down her cheeks as she clasped his chill hand. She wept not for the braggart bullfighter who had tried to force her to his will, but for the man who had comforted her in the cold cells of the Inquisition. It was for her lost friend she grieved; his death she would mourn.

"Tears," Cristobal mocked, feeling them splash on his hand. " 'Tis not that thief, Don Luis, who knocks at death's door. You've no need for tears."

"He never stole me from you—I was never yours. We both know that," she whispered brokenly.

Cristobal tried to grin at her, the expression more of a grimace. Blood flecked his lips as he said in a harsh whisper, "Go home, Elena *mia*, you never belonged here."

For just a moment the Cristobal who had befriended her in her hour of need returned, and she laid her head against his shoulder and wept.

Finally, gentle hands moved her, and she looked up to see a dark-robed priest preparing to administer Extreme Unction. Dutifully, she got to her feet and moved from the bed. Though his lips moved in prayer, Cristobal's eyes were closed. He did not open them again.

Toledo's cathedral bells tolled to mark the passing of the hero. A drum solemnly kept time with the steps of the mourners as weeping citizens, six deep, joined the funeral procession. The coffin was borne along the narrow streets of the old quarter with its towers and ornate Moorish arches, past the *tavernas*, the streets Cristobal had known in life. Finally, he was laid before the high altar in the cathedral where a solemn requiem Mass was sung for the fallen bullfighter. Banks of fragrant white carnations and roses smothered the red-carpeted steps, the coffin itself blanketed in scarlet carnations as a final tribute to Toledo's greatest bullfighter.

All the city assumed she was Cristobal. Santos's mistress so, for appearance's sake, Elena attended the funeral Mass. Swathed in a black mantilla, her face hidden, she was a small, solemn figure following the coffin out of the cathedral when the Mass was over. Blinking, she stepped into the bright sunlight, ashamed for the masquerade she upheld. Down the shadowed street they walked to the waiting hearse that would carry Cristobal home to the graveyard of the de los Santos family in the churchyard of *Nuestra Señora de Carmenilla*.

A litter awaited her. Elena climbed inside the curtained vehicle, finding the dim interior close and hot. To her surprise, she found another woman seated there, silent and heavily veiled. Only when the horses moved forward, beginning the solemn journey, did the woman finally speak.

"Good day, Doña Elena."

Elena found herself looking into the unveiled face of Dolores Mendoza. "Good day," said Elena stiffly, trying to hide the hositility she felt for this woman. "To what do I owe this honor?"

Dolores chuckled, though the sound was humorless. "I'll come straight to the point."

"Please do."

The litter lurched, and they were virtually thrown in each other's laps. Carefully rearranging their skirts, the two women eyed each other with intense dislike.

"Leave Luis alone," the Spanish woman demanded. "He's mine."

"He's not a prize to squabble over."

"Is he not? I intend to marry him. If you value your life you'll forget you ever met him."

"We're in love."

"Oh, come, Doña Elena, that's a foolish answer. If you won't cooperate for your own safety, then do so for his."

"What do you mean?"

"If he continues to bed you it'll cost him his life," Dolores vowed, her eyes dark slits in her olive-skinned face. "One word from me and your handsome lover will be arrested."

"On what charge—heresy?"

"Murder!"

Elena gasped, her hand at her mouth. "And who is to be the victim? Or haven't you decided yet?"

Dolores smiled slyly. "I've few illusions about your opinion of me, *doña*. Luis will be charged with his wife's murder."

"Leonora died from the heat of the sun."

"Perhaps you believe that, but when I tell my side of the story, most people will not."

"You know he had nothing to do with her death! Luis was in Toledo at the time. How dare you suggest such a thing and still profess to love him?"

"My love has never been selfless. If I can't have him, no one shall. Luis dealt treacherously with me over your release—I'm merely repaying the favor."

For a few minutes Elena was silent while she reviewed Dolores's threats. Unlike Luis, she did not doubt Dolores would carry out what she threatened. One look at that malicious face told her as much.

"Luis is in love with me—he'd accept no excuses."

"If you're gone from the city he'll have no other choice," snarled Dolores impatiently.

"You forget I've been denied permission to travel."

Dolores reached inside her cloak. "Here's a paper that grants you freedom to leave Toledo. It's yours in exchange for your promise to leave Spain."

"And if I refuse?"

"The Inquisition has many cells. I don't think you're that much of a fool, Doña Elena."

They continued their journey in silence. Elena knew Luis would continue to defy Dolores, possibly condemning himself to death. The power to save him lay within her reach. Yet to save him meant to leave him. How desirable England had seemed once, the thing she craved most. No, that was not really true. She had been resigned to settle for second best. England and all that was familiar had been a consolation after she had lost her love. And now she knew what she must do to save his life. Dolores was not to know Luis had petitioned Philip to send him to England also. As yet, the Inquisition's long arm did not reach England's shores. There they would both be safe.

"We're almost there, Doña Elena. Be quick—make up your mind before we reach Carmenilla or your fate's sealed," Dolores demanded cruelly as the animals began to labor uphill.

Clinging to the sides of the litter to prevent herself from falling in Elena's lap, Dolores waited, gleefully aware of the painful battle taking place behind that beautiful face. If she guessed correctly, the English-woman would agree to her proposal, if only to save Luis. Damn the man, was he really worth such self-sacrifice? she wondered as she saw tears gleaming in the other woman's eyes. He was unfaithful; he had always been unfaithful. Dolores knew that even if she won this emotional war, she had many battles left to fight. Toledo abounded in lovely women. Clearing her throat, she tapped the other woman's arm, reminding her that her time was almost up.

"Well, we're about to stop. I can see the church door."

Her breath catching in her throat, Elena hesitated, longing to resist this woman's threats, yet too afraid for Luis to risk it.

"Give me the papers," Elean said at last, her voice husky with unshed tears. "I'll go home to England. Luis's life is far too precious to gamble, though I realize we don't share those sentiments."

"Damn you, *santina*—do you think I threaten his life with ease?" snarled Dolores, her hand raised to slap Elena.

Elena smiled faintly. Little saint, Dolores had called her. Would that she were such. "Give me the paper.

At least allow me time enough to say good-bye. If Luis knew we'd made this bargain—''

''He's be at my throat. Very well, only make the parting swift. I'm no saint. I still might scratch out your eyes if you anger me.''

The rolled parchment exchanged hands. After glancing over it to make sure it was as Dolores said, Elena folded the document and put it in her chatelaine. The litter stopped.

''May we never be unfortunate enough to meet again,'' she said to Dolores as she parted the silk curtains and allowed a servant to help her out.

That night at Carmenilla Elena slept in Luis's arms, barely able to keep back her tears, knowing she must tell him she was leaving. Her heart had ached as he had lightheartedly discussed plans for their future. She prayed Philip would soon send him to the English court. There Dolores would have no power over either of them. But how long must she wait?

''Luis, sweetheart,'' she began tentatively, stroking his face. His eyes were closed, but he smiled at her tender touch. ''There's something I have to tell you. I've been keeping it from you all day.''

He tensed, his hand staying her soft caress. ''That is?''

''I have the papers allowing me to travel to England,'' she blurted, unable to think of a better way to tell him.

''Elena!'' There was both joy and pain in his voice. ''Where did you get them?''

''From Dolores Mendoza.''

So that was why Dolores had arranged to ride with Elena from Toledo! When Luis first discovered they were unlikely traveling companions, they were already disembarking at Carmenilla. He had been unable to single Elena out publicly before the mourners lest he destroy the myth of her relationship to the deceased. "Show me."

Elena got up from the bed and took out the parchment from her chatelaine while Luis lit a candle. Smoothing out the document on the covers, he read its contents with a bitter smile.

"How clever. Have you read this?"

Elean shook her head. She had merely glanced at the wording to make sure it was a safe conduct pass. The document bore Arturo Mendoza's signature.

"You're to be aboard ship within the week. And not just any vessel—you sail on *Nuestra Señora de Carmenilla.*"

"I don't understand."

"I own that vessel—it sails the day after tomorrow."

Apalled, Elena stared at him. She thought the time to say good-bye for which she had asked had been granted, never guessing Dolores had set so short a limit. Even their parting had been maneuvered to suit her purpose.

"Damn her! I've a good mind to ride to Toledo tonight and—"

"No, Luis!" cried Elena, terrified he would carry out his threat. "If you anger them I might not be allowed to travel at all."

"Are you that eager to leave me?" he asked half in jest, his eyes hard.

"Nay, you know I'm not. Have you petitioned Philip to send you to England?"

"Yes. He said he'd take it under consideration. But then I never thought we'd be parting so soon."

"Please, sweetheart, let us consider our blessings. Once I reach England—pray God Mary's forgiven me—I, too, can work for your appointment at court,"

Elena voiced hopefully, though inwardly she had little confidence. In all these months she had received not a word from the Queen. Elena had written to notify Her Majesty of Don Alvaro's death, letting Mary know she was in a foreign land without protection; still, the Queen had not yielded. Far from bargaining for Luis's appointment at court. Elena might well have to bargain for her own. But she kept these doubts to herself. Luis had to believe in her optimism, or how else could she save him?

"I can't bear to let you go," he whispered, crushing her against him, his lips hot on her neck. "Oh, *querida*, what will I do without you?"

That small nagging voice that often disrupted her well-being supplied a ready answer—return to Dolores. Forcing aside the bitter vision, Elena held him close, her mouth against his.

"I'm just going to England. Pray God you can join me there. With the aid of your master and my mistress, surely we can arrange it."

"I've always known it must come to this, but I'm so ill prepared. Oh, *querida*, the pain's too sharp."

"Neither of us will ever be prepared to part, Luis, you know that. Look forward instead to our reunion," she whispered, forcing down the chilling thought that they might never have a reunion. How would he be able to come to England with Dolores Mendoza working to keep him beside her? But she could not afford to dwell on that terrible prospect. Hope and love were all she had left.

Elena held Luis close, tenderly touching his face, willing tonight to last forever. There were so few hours till dawn. During their separation she could sleep to her heart's content; she would not squander tonight. "Luis, make love to me," she whispered, thrusting all

else from her mind. This might be all she would have
of him, and she wanted to remember it.

The skies were overcast. Nervously, Elena waited
to begin her journey to the harbor. There she would
board a barge that would take her to the merchant ship
anchored downriver.

Going against Elena's advice, Luis had demanded
more time with her on his arrival in Toledo, offering
an alternate vessel that did not sail until the end of the
month. Doloes threatened to withdraw Elena's travel
permit and have her arrested. Enraged though he was,
Luis was too wise to risk pushing Dolores further.
Lately her threats had been far too real to be put to the
test. So, reluctantly, he had arranged passage for Elena
aboard *Nuestra Señora de Carmenilla*. Luis intended
to sail part of the way with Elena, but he received a
summons to appear before the Grand Inquisitor in the
morning. This was also at Dolores's behest. The very
air was filled with her spies, his every thought and deed
relayed to her ever watchful eyes. Damn her! Luis was
sorely tempted to disregard the order, yet until Elena
was safely out of Spanish waters, he dared not.

The smells of the river enveloped him; tar, rope, and
sour wine wafted from the barge's timbers as Luis
helped Elena to her seat beneath a fringed canopy.

Though he knew it was unwise to display affection
in public, Luis embraced her in farewell, his mouth hot
against hers.

Elena squeezed her eyes shut to stop her tears,
allowing herself to bask in the fleeting pleasure of his
arms. She held him close, her senses aroused by the
smell of his skin, the touch of his hands. Then it was
time to go. Bravely she smiled, touching his mouth,
receiving his soft kiss on her fingertips.

"*Vaya con Dios*," he said gruffly, his hand on her shoulder.

"We'll be together soon," she promised without any real hope of realizing the vow. "I'll always love you, Luis."

"Oh, Elena, *mi vida*, I love you, too."

He turned from her, his face set."

When Luis had disembarked, the barge captain gave the signal to cast off. Slowly they drifted on the swell of the Tajo, banging against the jetty until the cursing sailors set a true course. Elena watched Luis waving to her from the bank, his black doublet a somber pillar against Toledo's ochre skyline.

Suddenly the sun came from behind the clouds to wash the city with gold. The narrow stone buildings with their myriad towers and minarets huddled behind stout battlements, the mighty Tajo a jewel-bright girdle within its curving banks. What a beautiful sight! Elena had failed to appreciate Toledo's beauty until she was forced to leave it. In this place she had loved and suffered with equal intensity.

With a shuddering sigh, Elena turned her back on the ancient Moorish city, casting her gaze into the distance for a glimpse of the ship that would carry her home to England. The knowledge that Luis was safe comforted her. Dear God, what a price she had paid for his safety. She had virtually handed him over to Dolores Mendoza. Last night, when Luis vowed undying love for her, she had not doubted his sincerity. Yet he had not reckoned with the power of the Inquisition. To escape the tentacles of that almighty religious body, men endured much that was not to their liking. Luis was only human. And Dolores Mendoza was very beautiful.

Chapter
Twenty-three

Luis could hardly believe his eyes. Not the Grand Inquisitor, nor even his clerics were there to greet him for his morning audience.

"Ruy Gomez! By all that's holy! You're a sight for sore eyes."

The splendidly dressed nobleman gripped his hand in greeting. Ruy Gomez, Prince of Eboli and Duke of Alba, was here on the King's business.

"Philip tells me you've petitioned him for a place at the English court. What insanity is this when your estate—and more importantly, your lady—is in Spain?"

"No longer. Elena sailed yesterday for England."

Enlightenment dawned on Ruy Gomez's dark face. "So, my friend, you would follow in hot pursuit."

"Elena's the most important thing to me in the world. Not until after she left did I realize just how important."

Ruy Gomez cleared his throat, moved by his friend's intensity. "Then I'm a bearer of glad tidings," he announced cheerfully, anxious to lighten the mood. "Philip sends his greetings, his friendship—but most important, his command. This letter appoints you to the court at Whitehall. Provisions have been made for your servants, your baggage—"

"To hell with all that. Just give me the letter."

Luis virtually snatched the document from his friend's hand, clumsy as he fumbled with the parchment, desperate to read for himself those redeeming orders that would reunite him with Elena.

"Does it satisfy?" Gomez asked at length.

"Admirably so."

"Philip has a vessel sailing later in the month."

"I intend to sail this week."

Gomez smiled, his dark eyes shining with laughter. "Ah, the impatience of lovers," he observed, clapping Luis on the shoulder. "I'll tell Philip you prefer to sail aboard your own vessel. Before you leave, we must dine together."

"Sorry, Ruy, after I've attended to some unfinished business, I'll be gone. Will you do me the honor of overseeing my *estancia* in my absence?"

"It will be an honor indeed."

"Then we shall meet again in England."

Gomez smiled ruefully, for he was not fond of that fogbound island. "Aye, unfortunately that's most probable. Already Philip makes plans to visit his wife."

When Ruy Gomez had left, Luis mounted the stair to perform one final, unpleasant task.

Dolores was not expecting him. When the servant announced his arrival, she spun from her desk where she had been completing a report.

"So, you're still in one piece. The Grand Inquisitor dealt speedily with you."

"I didn't see the Grand Inquisitor," Luis said, closing the door. "I've come to say good-bye, Dolores. I'm leaving Toledo."

She smiled and nodded. "Very well, but don't stay away too long." She came to him, arms outstretched, lips soft and inviting. "I'll miss you, Luis, more than you know. I'll give you a week with your accursed bulls, then you must return to me.''

Luis stepped away from her embrace, tensing as he formed his speech, anticipating a passionate storm of threats.

''You must give me far more than a week—I sail for England.''

''What!'' Face livid, Dolores grasped his arm, her long nails gouging his flesh through the velvet. ''You wouldn't dare! I can have you arrested before you leave the city, before you leave the building—''

''You've not the power.''

''Don't tell me I've not the power.'' Eyes slitted, nostrils flaring, she flung an ornament at him. Adeptly, Luis ducked, and it crashed against the wall. ''I can have you thrown in the dungeons, racked senseless—''

''No, Dolores. This is a royal appointment to White-hall. And Philip still rules Spain. Your denunciation would be exposed for what it is—merely a jealous woman's desperate lies. Whether you like it or not, I'm leaving Spain to be with Elena. Even you have to admit you're powerless to control my heart.''

''When I'm done there'll be naught to return to but a patch of scrub! Damn you, how dare you defy me! I'll have your bulls slaughtered. I'll have—''

He seized her arm, his grip bruising. ''The Prince of Eboli oversees my *estancia*. Challenge his power, my love, if you dare.''

Tears glistened in her dark eyes, the pain of defeat throbbing through her veins. How dare he follow that woman after all she had done to keep him here? How dare he enlist the aid of Philip and his nobles? Greater men than Luis de los Santos had been toppled . . .

''I'm leaving Toledo today. Messengers will be dispatched to Carmenilla, informing them of my plans.

And they will get through—I warn you, Dolores, don't interfere in this. You're not meddling with petty officials now.''

Luis gripped her wrists, holding her arms at her sides when she tried to strike him.

"You're powerless to do anything further to keep me here. It's over. I love Elena. I always have. For her I've risked much. I won't back down now.''

She knew he meant what he said. Dolores blinked back tears, the desire for vengeance ebbing. Could she really condemn her handsome former lover to death? Once she would not have hesitated to say yes—now she faltered. Damn him! He had made her love him, the one mistake that rendered her powerless. And she knew she could not take his life.

"Luis, I beg you, don't do this,'' she whispered, her voice choked with tears.

"Good-bye, Dolores,'' was all he said.

The door crashed behind him. Luis took the stairs two at a time. He felt unusually lighthearted, his final decision lifting the burden from his heart. If he took a swift horse, if he rode long into the night, perhaps he could reach Cadiz before Elena's ship put into port. He could hardly wait to see her face, to feel the soft yielding loveliness of her body pressed close to his.

Within the hour Luis was riding south, the warm Andalusian wind, filled with the sound of her name, whipping past his ears. If he must he would ride day and night to reach Cadiz in time. Without Elena he was nothing. Their futures belonged to each other. She had truly become his life, his soul.

Chapter
Twenty-four

A bitter wind slapped iron gray waves against the barges moored beside the Thames. Shivering in the cold, Elena pulled her cloak tighter around her throat and hastened after Luis up the river steps.

Though it was already spring, winter had not lessened its grip on the nation's capital. England's weather seemed all the more bitter for her absence. As the icy wind invaded the fastenings of her cloak, Elena found herself longing for the warmth of Spain. Despite the pain she had endured on that foreign shore, Spain promised summer sunshine while London seemed to bring nothing but winter rain.

"Be not so grim, Elena. Since Philip announced his return, the Queen's purported to be in high delight. You couldn't have chosen a better time to seek forgiveness."

"Aye, now her darling Philip's about to arrive, let us hope she's in a more forgiving mood."

"If she's still enamored of things Spanish, you have an ally. Tell her how well your Spanish husband treats you."

The nagging reminder that Her Majesty's permission was necessary for the marriage of one of her ladies-in-waiting robbed Elena of the last shreds of her peace of mind. She and Luis waited in a chill palace anteroom for her scheduled audience. Surely marriage to a Spanish *hidalgo* would carry some weight with Mary Tudor.

A gentleman in black came to the door and announced, ''Senōra Elena de los Santos. Her Majesty will grant your audience.''

Marvelling once more at the sound of that unfamiliar name, Elena stumbled to her feet.

Nervously Elena entered the Queen's chamber. The sumptuous tapestries, gilded furniture and decorated walls and ceilings dissolved before the glorious sight of a blazing fire. Elena could hardly wait to warm her numb limbs before its warmth.

''So, you are returned, Lady Elena.''

Elena gasped at the gruff greeting that came from the depth of a padded settle beside the hearth. Hastening to greet her royal mistress, Elena sank to her knees in the rushes. Slowly she raised her eyes to that bony, aging woman huddled inside wool blankets. Steeling herself not to react, Elena was appalled by Mary's unhealthy appearance. Her small eyes red-rimmed, her lined face sallow, the sorrow of these intervening months had taken a terrible toll on the Queen.

''Your Majesty, pray accept my apology for causing you pain,'' she croaked, her voice buried somewhere in her chest. ''It was never my intention to be disloyal. Can you find it in your heart to forgive me?''

There was a long silence, during which hope for the Queen's pardon slowly began to ebb. Elena swallowed, praying that the pleasure of Philip's impending visit had softened the Queen's heart.

''I received your letters,'' Mary said at last, shifting inside her cocoon. ''What a pity our good friend Don Alvaro is no longer with us.''

''Yes, Madam.''

''They announced you as Señora de los Santos. You have married without my permission?''

''We were wed by a priest aboard ship, Madam. I hoped you would not object as Luis is a good friend of—''

''Dearest Philip . . . Yes, he has spoken highly of your Luis. A friend of Philip's is a friend of mine.''

Elena gasped, hope rising. ''Then, Madam . . . you forgive me? You won't punish me for marrying Luis? Oh, Madam, I swear I love him dearly. He's everything to me.''

Mary reached out to finger Elena's waving black hair, which had escaped from beneath her pearl gray French hood.

''So young, so lovely,'' the Queen remarked almost to herself. Sighing, she pressed her hand against her brow, trying to banish the pain that began anew behind her eyes. ''You were unwise in your choice of friends, Lady Elena. Your foolishness caused me much grief. For many months I've puzzled about your disloyalty . . . No, hear me out,'' she said, her voice deepening as Elena sought to protest. ''I've decided you did not act with malice toward me. Before the month is out Philip will be here, and my heart is full of joy. Once my health is restored, there may yet be a babe. Only this time I shan't tell all and sundry and open myself up to ridicule. . . .'' Mary stopped, her chin sinking to her scrawny chest. Eyes narrowed, she continued to stare at Elena, who knelt before her, blue silken skirts spread like flower petals on the chamomile-sweetened rushes.

''Lady Elena, I've concluded you were guilty of foolishness instead of disloyalty. And, though you married without my permission, that, too, will I overlook. Never let it be said Mary Tudor has no heart.''

A glimmer of a smile lit the Queen's gray face.

''Oh, Madam,'' Elena gasped, tears of joy and relief spilling down her cheeks.

''Nay, not tears, my dear . . . unless they be for joy. We are two very fortunate women. Soon we both will have our beloveds by our sides. Mayhap your babe and mine will grow old together.''

A flush heightened Elena's cheeks. ''Babe, Madam,'' she repeated shyly, for she had told no one. Not even Luis.

''I've become expert at detecting another woman's good fortune,'' Mary remarked bitterly. ''Now go— I'm tired. You may visit your manor if you promise to hasten back to court. Philip will enjoy Don Luis's company.''

''Assuredly, Madam. Thank you for your mercy toward me. God bless you and make you fruitful.''

''Amen.''

Elena got to her feet and backed away. Mary fingered a rosary, her mouth moving soundlessly. She had already forgotten Elena's presence.

Luis paced apprehensively in the cold anteroom. At the unexpected sight of his wife's lovely face wreathed in smiles, his heart leaped, then soared.

''You're not under arrest. And you still have your head,'' he said jokingly while Elena quailed at his poor choice of humor.

''Please, Luis, don't jest about such things. This time Her Majesty has chosen to forgive me—and also to accept you as my husband. The age of miracles is not past.''

''That's not news to me,'' he said huskily, drawing her into his arms. ''I'm living witness to a miracle, for now you are mine at last. Come, let's leave this place. We shall be forced to attend our sovereigns here far sooner than we wish. Philip should arrive next week.''

The reminder of the gold-bearded Spanish prince filled Elena with dismay. Mary's hope for immortality lay in the shape of a son. Yet, after seeing her this morning, Elena was convinced that even if Philip could be persuaded to bed his aging wife, such a miracle would not be forthcoming. Luis had confided that Philip visited England merely to enlist Mary's aid in his impending invasion of France. The promise of troops and the signing of a marriage agreement between Mary's half sister Elizabeth and the Prince of Savoy were his sole reasons for returning to this despised island. Not dreams of love, nor loneliness, made him seek Mary's side. Poor Mary. It was as well she dwelt in ignorance. Aging, lonely, sick, only her dreams would sustain her in the bitter years ahead.

Elena stopped, halting Luis beside her. He smiled at her when she whispered, ''Today I wouldn't change places with the Queen herself.'' He bent his head, his face warm against hers. All the heat of his love poured forth in his kiss, making this frigid London day warm as the Spanish sun. ''Luis, sweetheart, when we reach our lodging, there's a secret I want to tell you.''

He smiled, resting his face against her shiny raven hair. ''I thought there were no secrets between us.''

''Nor will there be once I've told it to you.''

He laughed as he led her along the narrow street. From the corner inn yellow grids spilled across the cobbles as welcoming light shone through the mullioned windows. The fragrance of baking bread and roast meat mingled in the cold air.

''Can this secret wait until we've supped?'' Luis asked hopefully, his steps already veering toward the

Millers Arms.

"Even longer than that, my love," Elena whispered, snuggling against the warmth of his body as they stood in the inn's doorway. "You must promise to make love to me before I can entrust you with *this* secret."

His smile was tender, a whispered acquiescence on his lips as he opened the door. Elena placed her hand over her flat abdomen beneath her shielding cloak. And her heart leaped for joy as she hugged this precious secret to herself.